The Pillars Of Enroden

By

Erin Osetek

To my family, blood and otherwise, thank you.

CHAPTER ONE

Time To Leave

I saw the surface. The light flickering on the water, the people swimming. Someone was waving at me to come to the surface. I swam up, broke the surface, and took a breath. The air was full of summer.

"Good job. Now go do it again," my mother cheered. I looked at her, with her red, curly hair shining in the sun and dripping from the pool water. It was like looking at Christmas. Of course, like in most of my dreams lately, I transitioned into watching myself as a third party, an observer. But I didn't care. However I got to see her, at least I got one more second to look at her. The other, younger me threw my arms around my mom and laughed. Then my mom took the diving rings from my hands and threw them back in the deep end of the pool.

"Okay, Emily, now go again. I'll be right here, waiting for you." She smiled the special smile we had between us. I saw it in the wrinkles at the edges of her eyes and the way her lips curved up. I wanted to tell little me, "No, don't go. Stay and hug her again." But I didn't. I was a bystander.

The small girl in the black bathing suit covered in little rainbows turned and dove back into the pool.

Then, like what usually happens in this dream, my mom looked right into my eyes and then walked over to the willow tree in our backyard. The tree swayed in the summer breeze, the long, thin branches going from left to right. The leaves hung on like they were on an endless carnival ride. My mother stopped, put her arm out, and braced against the tree. She turned her head, then her whole body around to look at me.

"Emily, listen to me. You don't have much time. Make sure to get the stones out of the pool. It's getting dark, honey. You should go now." The way she'd spoken caught me off guard. The sound was different than I'd heard a second ago; the younger, smaller me was forgotten among the urgency in her voice. It sounded more like the way she'd spoken the last days I'd been with her, with an urgency to tell me things, knowing there was too little time to get everything in.

She turned again and started walking to the far end of our yard, behind where the willow tree had been for the last eighteen years of my life. As she walked, I saw her bathing suit shiny and wet in the sunlight, a yellow towel wrapped around her waist. Her fire engine-red hair still dripped from the pool water. Then, as always, she started to fade away.

"Wait!" I yelled. "Wait, don't go. I don't understand what you want me to do." I couldn't let her leave yet. I wanted to look at her one more time. One more glance. I wanted her to talk to me just one second longer.

But either she didn't hear me, or she wouldn't listen. She continued to fade away into the dark corner of our yard. She was gone. And she'd been right. The sun was dimming, and the blue sky was fading into midnight black. I turned from the direction she'd disappeared and looked at the dark pool now reflecting the night sky. I was alone.

I ran at the water. Taking a deep breath as I flew through the air, I jumped in. Down I went, like a rock sinking to the bottom. I opened my eyes. The underwater grit revealed a blurry mess of liquid, concrete pool lining, and dirt. If I did what she'd been asking me to, maybe she would come back. There was only one way to tell. Looking into the cloudy water, I saw something just ahead of me. It looked like the outline of three small rocks at the bottom of the other end of the pool. They were illuminated somehow.

I tried swimming closer, but the water seemed thicker than before. My arms moved slower. The light from the surface was fading, and it was dark. I felt my body's request for more oxygen. I reached the far end of the pool and felt around with my hands. It was softer than it should have been. On the right, I could just make out where I thought the outline of those rocks had been. The soft bottom seemed like mud and sand, and I felt something slide against my leg. Looking back, it was some kind of plant.

Plants don't grow in pools, I thought to myself, then I realized I was no longer in the pool in our backyard.

I couldn't swim an inch farther. Something had wrapped itself around my leg and waist; whether it was more plants or weeds, I didn't know. The harder I tried to untangle myself, the more entangled I got. As I pushed against the restraint, I felt the sand slipping between my toes. My eyes were burning, trying to see in the underwater trap. I looked in the direction of the stones and saw a small light beginning to pulse. The rhythmic beating mesmerized me for a second. I stared for too long.

The realization that I would drown dawned on me. I was again hit with my body's intense need for oxygen. Involuntarily, I opened my mouth to take a breath, and in came water, rushing into my lungs. Pulsing light was all I saw, and a rushing noise filled my ears.

Finally, I closed my eyes, knowing that again, I had failed at the last thing my mother had asked of me. And I knew that I would never see her again. In the darkness of the end of my dream, I waited, but whether it was to die or to wake up, I never knew.

It was always the same. The same dream, the same panicked waking, and the same sense of dread that filled me when I woke. Not to mention the same gross feeling of being drenched in sweat. I had to take a couple deep breaths. I tried to concentrate on the air going in and then out of my lungs, allowing my heart rate to come back to normal.

I'd read about post-traumatic stress when a loved one dies. I even talked to a counselor about my dreams after I'd confided in my godfather, Morell. My wonderful nino (the Spanish word I called him) had been my confidant for the last few months, since Mom passed. I didn't have the dreams every night, but it was enough to start losing sleep. I didn't know who else to talk to about how much I missed her, and I was starting to think there was something wrong with my brain. Dad and I didn't talk about it much.

After I'd seen the counselor, the psychologist he'd worked under prescribed me some anxiety medication. I took the meds for a little while, and the dreams stopped, but I couldn't bear not seeing my mother in dreams. I missed her too much. It was as if my dreams were a place that she still inhabited, like a special place for just us that we kept secret. But besides stopping the dreams, the medication made me feel disconnected from my normal self, and I managed to wean off of them after a couple of weeks. That was the last time I'd told anyone about the dreams. It's funny how you can miss someone so much that you're willing to have nightmares just to see them, however uncomfortable it is.

I guessed that I was having the dreams more now because it was going to be a stressful couple of days. Today, I was leaving for college. It had been a hard decision. I was leaving my dad here, alone, in the home where my mother had passed away only a year ago. But I had to go. He'd told me that I needed to go and start my life, and moving away was something that would help me do that. I still didn't know if it was the right decision, but

I'd been accepted to Syracuse University. With a partial scholarship, I couldn't turn it down.

When all my senses seemed under control again, I got out of bed and walked to my bedroom door. I saw a little bit of black hair under the crease where the door and carpet met, and when I opened it, the door swung in with a little force as a big black lab pushed to get in my room.

It never failed. Cindy was always happy to see me. She must have been waiting outside my room for a while because she was ready to go play or, more likely, to eat. She usually slept in bed with me or at the foot of my bed, but last night, I'd been doing some last-minute packing, and I'd shut my door, so she wouldn't see the suitcase. I must have fallen asleep and forgotten to open it. She looked up at me with forgiving eyes; I don't think she cared too much.

We headed down the hall, into the kitchen. It was still a little early, and I didn't hear anything through the walls toward the other side of the house. I didn't think my dad was up yet.

I opened the pantry and scanned the shelves. They were empty. I went through to check the expiration dates just yesterday and got rid of everything that was expired. My dad had a bad habit of not throwing anything in the pantry or freezer away, and some things I'd found the day before had been... well... *interesting*. There was even a carton of mint chocolate chip ice cream from two years before. Or at least, that's when it had expired. I thought about not throwing that out. I knew that Mom had probably had a scoop or two from it. I'd opened it, smelled the mint and chocolate, and let memories of my mother and I talking and eating ice cream for dinner wash over me. Still, in the end, I decided that if I didn't throw it away, no one would, so I did it.

I put a box of Honey Nut Cheerios on the counter, grabbed a bowl and spoon, and headed to the fridge to get some milk. Cindy was right there, tail wagging and ready for whatever was to come her way. I poured the cereal and "missed" the bowl a little, so some fell on the floor for my friend. She happily found each little "O" and slopped them up. She put her head back up, looking at me for more.

"You don't need any more, puppy," I laughed to her as I patted her head. She nudged my hand and licked it. Her black muzzle was starting to gray, and she moved a little slower than she used to, but her deep, brown eyes were still full of joy and mischief. I was glad she would be here with Dad when I was gone. This dog had been through so much with our family. She was as good a dog as there ever was.

I looked around our dining room. There were pictures from the last couple years. My eyes lingered on one I'd not seen in a while. The heavy dust on the other pictures set this clean one apart as being newly placed. While the picture was new to the shelf, I still recognized it. It was a photo someone had taken of my parents and my nino's family.

My nino had been in my life as long as I could remember. My mom and dad had met him and his wife (my nina) before I was born and became close family friends. My godmother and their two children had passed away in an accident when my mom was pregnant with me, and he was on his own now. Nino was tall and had a dark complexion, with a short, dark beard and mustache. His eyes were so brown, they appeared black in the picture.

This photo used to be a in my parents' bedroom next to my baby picture. The two families had been at the Grand Canyon, Mom had told me when I'd asked. It was one of the last photos of them all. Mom was pregnant with me in the picture, and everyone looked happy.

Whoever took the photo somehow missed the exact moment when everyone was looking at the camera, however, because my poor nino had been glancing off to the side when the camera snapped, and he was the only one not smiling in the right direction.

I guess dad must have moved the picture here when he was cleaning his room a few weeks back. With everything that has happened for both Nino and with Mom, I think Dad felt like Nino understood him with a unique perspective. I knew that Dad had been there for Nino when his family had died. I think Nino wanted to return the favor. Honestly, I'm sure Dad appreciated his help and advice.

My eyes moved to some of the other pictures in the room. Being an only child, I was in most of them. Some were from high school graduation, and others were from vacations in years past. The ones I loved the most were under the glass in our coffee table. My mom and I always took a picture together on the first day of school and then placed the picture in a photo frame that held spots for a total of thirteen pictures. Enough to hold photos from kindergarten through my senior year of high school.

The photo from the eleventh grade was there. It was our last one together. I made Dad take my picture on the first day of twelfth grade, but it looked strange next to all of the other ones. Instead of the two faces looking back, frozen in time and ready for what was to come, there was just one. Just me. Alone, my face stuck in a smile my mother would have spotted as fake from a mile away. It had been a hard picture to take, to say the least. But I had finished the collage that she'd started. That was all that mattered to me.

I heard the sound of water running on the other side of the wall, then the familiar *bang* of the closet sliding on its floor tracks. My dad was up now. I sat down at the counter to eat my cereal. Cindy was right next to me. There was something about sitting at the counter that I loved about our house. We had a dining room table with chairs and a couch in the living room, but the counter was still my favorite place.

I finished the cereal and drank the leftover milk, then put the bowl down for Cindy to lick up the last couple drops. I put the bowl in the sink and went to the dining room table. I still had lots of paperwork set out there. I decided to take that all in my carry-on bag instead of packing it in my suitcase. There was my dorm room assignment, class schedule, and campus guide. The list of things to bring for the dorms and a vaccination record that was required before I could get my room key. I had kept some of the campus brochures that had information on surrounding areas and dining halls, as well as some of the information from my major's department in the health and human services building.

I was going into a dual major. I was interested in nutrition and psychology and thought both together could match nicely. I wasn't one hundred percent sure that was the right major for me, but I had to pick something, and I wanted to enjoy my life's work.

I absentmindedly stretched my legs as I looked over the papers. I had gone for a run yesterday to work some of my nerves out, and I was a little sore. I hadn't planned on running ten miles, but after I got started, it hit me that I wouldn't be running my normal routes anymore. I wanted to see them on foot one last time before leaving. So, I'd phoned Dad (I always ran with my phone as I am hopelessly addicted to listening to audiobooks) to let him know I would be a little longer than the hour I'd planned and kept going.

Cindy must have heard the noise coming from Dad's room because she got up and headed down the beige-carpeted hallway. I could hear her collar jingle all the way down to my dad's room. I heard his door open. Even though the hallway was carpeted, I still heard his footsteps.

"*Whew.*" I heard someone taking a deep breath and then letting it out again. My dad always did that. He came around the corner and walked over to the table.

"Hey, kid. How's it going?" he asked as he absentmindedly ran his hand over his shiny bald head.

"Good. I was just looking at some of the stuff I need to bring with me. I hope I remembered everything," I replied. I couldn't look at him. I still felt guilty about leaving. I had to change the subject. "What time do we have to leave again? I forgot," I managed to fill the quiet space.

"We need to leave by eight-thirty. Our flight's at eleven-thirty." My dad headed into the kitchen and started getting the coffee pot ready. He opened a cupboard door and pulled down a coffee mug with Popeye on it. He loved the character and had collected Popeye figurines as long as I could remember.

"Well, then I had better get my stuff all ready to go," I said as I headed back down the hall.

I walked back into my room, with Cindy hot on my tail. Once she was in my room, she caught sight of the opened suitcases. She went over to them and sniffed, then sat promptly on my feet. It was as if she were saying, "Please stay with me. Don't leave." She looked at me with her deep, brown eyes, and I felt the knot in my throat tighten. It would be hard to say bye to her.

I looked at my suitcases. They were packed and just needed a couple more things. I threw in the last of my clothes and zipped them up. There was a box on my desk that was full of writing supplies and pictures that Dad was going to mail to me later in the week. And that was it. My whole life packed into suitcases and a box. My room looked empty.

I rolled my suitcases out into the dining room, by the front door. I went back to my room and changed my clothes. My eyes rolled over what was left. I started second-guessing myself. *Maybe I shouldn't go. Maybe I should just stay here and go to school somewhere close.*

Deep down, I knew that was not what I needed. I knew I had to go, and I knew that Dad needed me to go too. There was never going to be any moving on for either of us if nothing ever changed. I felt the anxiety creep up into my chest. I took a deep breath.

"Come on, Emily. Get it together. Move," I whispered out loud. I turned and walked out of my bedroom.

Traffic was unusually non-existent for the morning commute in San Diego. Maybe that was a good sign. After getting through security check-in, we were at our gate with enough time before boarding to let my dad get another cup of coffee and for me to start re-reading one of my favorite books.

I had decided this summer to re-read as many of my favorite books as I could. With school starting, I'd have less time and couldn't take them all with me. Yes, I had a laptop and an iPad, so I could read them digitally, but there was something about my childhood books that, for me, went further than just reading the story. The grip of the pages in my hands and the smell of the binding kept me on the edge of my seat as I read through each of them.

For our flights, I brought a bigger book: *The Chronicles of Narnia* series by C.S. Lewis. I gladly spent the travel time pushing my anxieties about college to the back of my mind by engrossing myself in the fantastical worlds where things were divided between right and wrong, love, friendship and loyalty.

By the time we made it to Syracuse, it was about six in the afternoon. We got our bags and rental car and after loading up our suitcases, then drove downtown to get some dinner. The weather was cool at night, and I managed to fish a sweatshirt out of my bags. We ate at a Denny's. Not five-star, but they had a good tomato soup and salad, so I didn't care. My dad got his standard chicken strips with blue cheese dressing to dip.

"At least you can't take them home in a to-go box and leave them in the fridge," I joked to him. My dad not only let pantry items expire regularly, but he also had a bad habit of taking home restaurant leftovers and leaving them in the refrigerator for weeks.

After dinner, we found our hotel. It was a little Holiday Inn Express by the college. The parking lot was packed, but we found a spot. We checked in and headed up to our room. The night was uneventful. I found the gym and got in a strength training workout, then went to the pool. Something about exercise and stress relief just helped me even out. My dad had found the television directory and was watching a black-and-white episode of *The Three Stooges* when I got back.

I tried not to think about the fact that the next day, I was moving into the dorms, and he was going back home without me. I showered and pulled out my book. I fell asleep reading.

The drive to the dorms the next morning was short, but it was long enough for me to appreciate the architecture of the school and the buildings around campus. The school was old, and a few buildings had enormous turrets that looked like castles. I liked that some of the buildings remained untouched and, from a distance, looked like something out of a fairy tale, while other buildings had more of a modern feel, showing glass walls and modern metal sculptures out front. As I watched the buildings go by, I felt my phone buzz. I looked down at it.

A text message met my eyes. My godfather had stopped at the house to check on Cindy. Nino lived a couple miles away from us, and whenever we went out of town, he came to check on the dog. He had been a big help over the years.

The picture he'd sent in the text message was of Cindy in our backyard, lying in the grass. I missed home already. It hadn't even been forty-eight hours, and I was already homesick. This was going to be tough. I texted him back, "Thanks," and put my phone away.

When I looked up again, we were at my new place of residence.

CHAPTER TWO

University

The parking lot was only slightly full. Thankfully, the school allowed freshmen to start moving in during morning hours, with returning students not allowed until the afternoon. Looking at the building that was going to be my home for the next several months, I was glad to be living on the ground floor. The building was five stories high and as wide as the parking lot.

The parking lot was surrounded by pine trees keeping a cooling shade over us. Past the trees and directly across from the dorm was a large grass field lined with walking paths. Beyond the field, I could make out more buildings, but what was in them, I wasn't sure. The campus was so big, it was a little intimidating. What we had already seen wasn't even half of the university's property. The campus was sectioned into different areas. They called the different areas quads, and my dorm was in quad one.

"Let's get going." Dad could tell I needed some direction. I hated the way that my face always showed exactly what I was thinking.

I went around the car to the trunk and pulled out my suitcases. Dad had already gotten some out of the backseat. There was a door off the side of the building that was propped open. We went over to it and up the seven steps that led into the brick-lined building. Somehow, I had managed to get a first-floor dorm room. It was a suite that included both a single room and a double room.

We followed the signs leading us to the girls' half of the floor. It was a co-ed dorm – something that my dad and I vehemently avoided talking about. Not even a little bit. So, when he jokingly stated, "I guess you're going to be on the girls' side, then," and laughed, I knew he must be trying to fill the empty talking space, just like I did when I was anxious. I got another pang of guilt for leaving but pushed it aside. We had moving to do.

I laughed and replied, "I guess so."

We went down the hall. It was cool in the building. The floors were slick, gray-blue tile. The walls were beige. We passed four dark brown doors before we came to Room Five. I must have stared at the door for a second too long because my dad cleared his throat. I came back from whatever place I'd been in and turned the knob.

We'd been told that all the dorm doors would be unlocked on move-in day. We had paperwork to turn in to our dorm's Resident Advisor before we were able to get our keys, so I wasn't alarmed at the unlocked door.

Inside, it smelled like the room needed air. I wasn't surprised to find more beige walls and blue-gray tile in the common room. There was a decent-sized window with blinds over it that would let light in. I flipped on the light switch. The room was about as big as a stand-alone drive-through coffee hut, maybe even smaller. To the right, there was a dark brown door that read 5B, and to the left, there was a sister door labelled 5A. That room was mine.

I was grateful for the single room. I'd heard stories about crazy roommates stealing towels and using bathroom supplies and was glad that I'd have my own space. I went to the 5A door and opened it. My eyes were met with a simple bed with a bare mattress and a dresser, along with a small desk and chair. Not bad. It would take some filling, but the room would be just fine. My room at home was small, so the size, while still a bit smaller than I was used to, would suit me well.

We put down the suitcases.

"Not bad," my dad said. "I think you will fill it up quick though." He put my duffle bag on the bed. "Start making a list of what we need to get at the store." He was good at directing me when I wasn't able to focus. I got out a pad of paper and a pen.

"I need a trash can, some bathroom stuff..." I continued making a list as he went back out to the car to get the last bag of stuff. I was about done when he came back.

We headed out to the store but stopped at the first gas station we found to get our traditional forty-four-ounce soda and bag of pretzels. I would miss this. Normally, on the weekends, we would go for a run around a lake near our house and then stop for the pretzels and soda after. Not the healthiest option, but I figured it was our thing, so why mess with it?

We made it to the store. About a half-hour away from campus, there was a mini-mall with a Wal-Mart, Target, and some clothing department stores. *That will probably come in handy*, I thought to myself. I hadn't brought a winter jacket and knew with running, I would need to get some cold-weather clothes unless I wanted to stick to the treadmill for the winter months.

Wal-Mart was crowded. I figured they must have planned this store here, knowing the campus was close. My dad and I separated. I had my list and started filling the cart with towels, a comforter, and some sheets. I got shower sandals and some bathroom stuff. Then I headed over to the snack aisle. I ran into my dad, who was putting a plastic bin in his cart. We had decided to get one to put food and other things in to keep things neat. We grabbed pretzels, Coke Zero, Triscuits, fruit snacks, popcorn, and a couple other of my favorites.

Dad steered the carts over to electronics on the way out. I hadn't brought a television and had decided not to get one the first semester because there would be so many other things I would need to do. He picked up a small flat-screen television with a built-in DVD player and put it in the cart.

"Dad, no," I protested. "I don't need one this semester. I had planned to stick to my television ban."

"Come on, how can you not watch TV all semester? You are going to need it." He began pushing his cart toward the check-out area. I took a deep breath. I was glad that I'd been working at Starbucks all summer. It gave me some extra money to help pay for some of the stuff we bought – at least what he would let me buy. Then, before I knew it, we were pushing the carts back to the tiny rental car and driving back to the dorm.

When we got back, the parking lot was almost full. More people had arrived, and the place was packed with parents hauling bags. The hall inside was filled with laughter and students greeting people. Move-in day had officially started.

It seemed like some of the people moving in knew each other. I wondered where everyone was from. Did other people come here from California? Would I run into anyone I knew? I doubted it. I was struggling in my mind. I wanted to shed my previous life and have some distance from my pain, to start fresh. But I also wanted familiarity and the reliability of the routine and people that had been my home.

We got everything inside and into my room. I looked at my watch. It was two in the afternoon. My dad's plane was supposed to leave at six, so he would be heading back to the airport soon. I still had to pick up my keys and swipe my ID card, so we headed to the administration building.

The campus was nice. I knew I liked the view when I'd been looking at it from the car, but walking through it, I appreciated the way the trees swayed in the wind and the way the August sun reflected off the shiny green. The grass was beautiful and cut through by walkways that surrounded the quad areas.

It was warm out, and the walk was nice. When we got back, I pulled out some of the Coke Zero we had bought and handed my dad one.

"Are you sure you don't need anything else?" He was looking out my window, at the parking lot.

"No. We are supposed to go to the store tonight," I said, avoiding his gaze too.

My two roommates, whom I would officially meet today, and I were supposed to sit down and figure out what we were going to get for the common room. When the campus assigned the dorms to the new students, they also sent out a list of contact information for roommates to get in touch with each other.

I had no more than gotten the mail that day when my phone had rung, and I had been introduced to one of my roommates, Hannah. She not only had already called our other roommate, Taylor, but she'd already had a detailed plan for going to the store to get everything for the first night. That worked for me. It would be a shopping and bonding experience, I guessed.

I was a little nervous to be living with two other girls, but I usually got along well with most people. I was easygoing, so I tried not to worry too much about it.

"We will get everything we need later." I knew he wanted to get on the road. He usually got nervous before traveling. He always said once he got to the airport and was at his gate, he felt better, even if sometimes he was two hours early.

We took a couple minutes to get the stuff from the store out of the bags, then I knew it was time for him to go. I'd been dreading this part all summer. I followed my dad to the parking lot, over to where the little rental car was parked. I didn't know what to say.

"Make sure you get yourself some warm clothes before winter comes. It gets colder here than San Diego." He at least had the guts to get the goodbye conversation started.

"I will, and make sure you check the dates on everything in the fridge and pantry." I laughed a little and saw him smile. A few more moments passed, neither of us wanting to say goodbye.

"Well, I'd better get going, kid," he said. "You take care of yourself, and remember I'm only a flight away." He gave me a hug.

"I will, and you too. Thanks for everything. I'll be home soon. Take care of Cindy for me." I felt the familiar lump in my throat coming up. I bit the inside of my cheek. I couldn't cry. If I cried, then I knew it would make it that much harder for him to leave.

"I love you, kid," he said. He gave me one last mini-hug and then got into his car. He rolled the window down.

"Love you too, Dad," I whispered back. He smiled and backed out of the parking spot. He looked over and waved before he drove through the lot and out onto the road. I watched him drive away. The second I saw the car go out of sight, even with all the students and families rushing about around me, I felt alone. I missed my mom. I missed home. I wished things were different, that she would have been able to travel back home with him and keep him company.

I took a deep breath. Wishing wouldn't make things change. They were how they were. I made myself turn around and head back into the dorm.

CHAPTER THREE

Meeting Roommates

"I will be okay," I said to myself when I got back into my room. I shut the door to the common room from the hallway and looked at the chaos that was my new home. I noticed that Dad had set the television up on the dresser. He'd even put the DVD *Shrek* next to it. I was so grateful for it. I popped the DVD in and let the movie play in the background while I unpacked. I needed to go for a run. I looked at my running shoes but decided there was just too much to do right now.

I took a deep breath and began taking my jeans out of the suitcase and putting them into the dresser. Beside the dresser was the smallest closet that I'd ever seen. It looked like someone had simply put an indentation into the wall long enough for a hanger bar. There was no door, but space was space, so I started hanging up some of my shirts.

I started moving the furniture to get everything where I wanted. After a while, I opened some Oreos and sat on my bed. It was about five-thirty when I heard my phone buzz again. It was my dad. He'd boarded his flight to Texas, where he'd have a layover, then fly into San Diego early tomorrow morning. An overnight trip, but he wanted to get back home and back into a routine. He was going to work Monday and wanted Sunday to rest.

I sent him back a text saying, "Have a good flight. Thanks for everything."

I had just put the phone back on my bed when I heard the door to the common room open. Light from the hallway spilled into the room.

"Are those all shoes?" I heard a female voice say.

"Yup, I brought them all the way from Texas," another voice said as the suitcase rolled in.

The two girls walked in following the suitcase and immediately looked to the left and saw me sitting in my room. My stomach flip-flopped, and my sweet Oreo snack threatened to sour with the anxiety I felt.

I think we all had the same feeling. Their expressions were both surprised and excited, which I decided must mirror my own.

"Hi, guys. I'm Emily," I greeted them while brushing Oreo crumbs from my hands. I got up from the bed, and as I did, the Oreos fell onto the floor, upside-down. We laughed. At least the tension was broken now. Leave it to me.

"Hi," the girl on the right answered. "I'm Hannah." She was shorter than me and had blonde hair. She was the girl I'd spoken with on the phone earlier in the summer. She confidently extended her hand. "Don't worry about the mess. I've got a little vacuum that will get that quick."

"Hey, I'm Taylor," chimed in the girl on the left. She was taller than Hannah and had black hair and a tan complexion. She was the girl who had pushed in the big suitcase of what were apparently shoes.

"So, those are all shoes," I marveled, looking at the rolling tote. It was huge.

"Hey, Tay, everything is out of the car," came another voice as the door opened again. I saw a woman and a man come into the room, both holding too many bags for their arms to carry.

"These are my parents."

"I'm Mike, and this is my wife, Lauren," Taylor's dad said. Her mom was in their room, getting her stuff unpacked.

"Hi, girls," Taylor's mom poked her head out into the common room. Taylor smiled and shook her head.

I went outside and helped Hannah bring in her bags from her car, while Taylor and her parents unpacked her bags and started getting her side of their room arranged.

Somehow, Hannah had managed to get a parking permit. They were supposed to be only for returning students, but her brother had gone to school here a few years back, so he had been able to get her one, she'd explained.

It will be nice to have a car. I stopped myself. *That's assuming we even get along and that she wants to drive me anywhere,* I reminded myself.

When everyone was done for the moment, we all stood in the common room. Taylor's parents were supposed to start the drive back tonight, so they had to get going. She went out to the parking lot to say goodbye. I was glad for her to have both parents who would be able to share the drive home together. I envisioned my dad sitting on the plane next to a stranger and going home to the empty house.

"Have you met our Resident Advisor yet?" I heard at a distance. And then I heard a "Hey, Earth to Emily." It was Hannah. She was waving her hand next to my face, trying to get my attention. Apparently, I had zoned out.

Resident Advisor. Oh, yeah. I shook my head, trying to come back to the moment.

"No. When I went to get my stuff at the administration building, he wasn't there. They said that I'd meet him at the dorm meeting this weekend," I told Hannah.

Taylor came back into the room from the hallway carrying three brown paper bags. She handed each of us one.

"Hey, guys, my mom brought these for us." She looked a little embarrassed as she handed them out. It was cute. Inside was a mini-can of Sprite, an apple, and a Hostess chocolate cake. At the bottom of the bag, there was one more thing. A mini scratch-off ticket. I smiled. It was so thoughtful.

"Thanks!" I said and meant it.

"I love these. Thanks," Hannah smiled as she pulled the Hostess cake out.

"Oh, gosh, the scratch-offs. She's been obsessed with these things since last year, when she won two grand off a ticket that she got in a Christmas stocking. It's crazy." Taylor picked up the ticket and smiled then looked at us. We all laughed. I got the feeling that we were going to get along just fine.

The three of us sat and ate our mom-made snacks for a little while. We talked, and I learned that Taylor had driven here all the way from Texas. She was going to need supplies, so to save on shipping, they had decided to drive. They took the week to drive out. Her dad liked history, and they had stopped in a couple places for pictures.

She said she was a Fashion Design major and talked some about her love of art and painting. As she was unpacking, she pulled out a photo framed with a wooden rim.

It was a picture of a pool with a bear in it, and in the background, I saw her parents and brother inside, behind a sliding glass door. It looked like the picture had been taken from inside a window.

"And if fashion design doesn't work out, I'll probably do something with animals. Apparently, weird animal experiences are my other hobby."

She told us about her family's cabin in the Colorado mountains that they visited in the summertime. Apparently, last year, they had been about to go into the pool when a bear had foiled their afternoon plans.

"How about you, Hannah?" Taylor asked, looking at her.

"Well, I live about an hour away, so I'm not as far from home as you both are, but Syracuse has a good pre-med program. I want to be a doctor. I saw one of my brothers get his arm badly broken in a hockey game once, and the doctor that helped him let me watch as he re-set the bone." She took in a breath. "That was cool, but also, my grandmother taught us about holistic healing and had an herb garden she was proud of, so between the two, I thought, why not?"

She opened her mini-can of Sprite. The crack of the can and following fizz surge almost made a mess of the floor.

"My family has been up in Oswego for years. I love it there. Only thing is the snow can get intense in the winter, and you start to miss the sunshine."

She paused to take a sip of some of the soda that had settled on the top of the can.

"But summer is a different story altogether. In the summer, the leaves get big and fat, and when the afternoon sun hits them, they glisten like on a tropical island. So, you have to take the good with the bad, I guess. What about you, Emily?"

Both she and Taylor looked at me expectantly.

"So, what made you leave sunny California to live near the snow capital of the U.S.?" Hannah asked.

I always go back and forth with how to answer this question. When I left home, family friends kept wanting to know why I was going so far away. I knew it would come up quite a bit when I got here. But people from back home always thought that anywhere in New York was just like New York City. It was easy to answer their questions with things like, "I've always wanted to try the East coast." Or I'd talk about how I couldn't wait to see more open spaces in the countryside (which was true). Or I always fell back on the fact that I'd never seen the leaves change in the fall, and I'd talk about that, deflecting the question for however long they would listen.

The two girls were still looking at me, waiting for me to start talking. I was taking too long to answer. I thought I'd take a chance at the truth.

"Well, I wanted to go away to school, and Syracuse had a nutrition program. I got interested in nutrition and psychology when I took some basic courses with my mom. We had to take nutrition courses and counseling courses before she could participate in a drug trial. I liked the subject, so I thought, why not do nutrition and psychology and pair them together?"

Now the truth was out there. At least something as close to the truth as I was willing to say to people I just met. Saying things like that always made me feel like the air in the room got as thick as sap.

The girls were still looking at me, and I started to see that look in their faces. That, "Oh, I'm so sorry," look that happens when the words *"drug trial"* begin to make sense in their minds. The panic that Taylor had after giving out those precious mom-made snacks was written on her face. So, I went on and pushed the conversation forward without going back to fill them in. Moving on was always something that was complicated to talk about, and having just met my new roommates, I didn't want to be "Debbie Downer".

"Over the summer, I worked at a coffee shop. Look what they gave me as a going-away present." I walked to the edge of my room door and reached in. I gripped the side of a rollable end table I'd manage to snag from the basement when I'd taken down my trash a while ago and swung it into the doorway.

"Is that what I think it is?" Taylor exclaimed.

Hannah stared, and the curves of her mouth turned up into a smile. "Wow," was all she could mutter.

"Yup, nothing like an espresso machine complete with milk steamer and espresso pod distributor to make anyone's morning." I had to laugh. I loved coffee. I had great memories with my parents and my grandmothers drinking coffee around the table and talking. The machine was one of the only things that I'd shipped out before school. It was kind of silly to send it all the way out, but it was nice to have something familiar when I was so far away from home. And I figured that we would all need our share of coffee over the next months as school got underway.

Thankfully, the coffee machine did the trick, and the conversation was on to other topics.

"Speaking of things we need for our room," Hannah began, "we have to get to the store. It's late already, but I think Wal-Mart is open twenty-four hours." She turned to get her bag and pulled out her keys. "I'll go get the car, and you guys can meet me out front," she announced as she walked out the door of the common room.

It took about half an hour to get to Wal-Mart. The roads in Syracuse were smaller than in San Diego but moved right along. We got on a highway with a big, green sign that read 690. We stopped in some construction traffic. Hannah was talking about how long the construction had been going on. Apparently, in the summertime, road construction was big in central New York because the weather allowed for more work to get done. After a few minutes sitting in traffic, we began moving again and made it to the fully lit parking lot.

We walked in to Wal-Mart. Hannah split her list into three parts and handed us each a piece. The place was about as busy as when I'd been here a couple hours earlier. We all set off in different directions. Taylor was in charge of getting a rug and some wall hangings for the common room, I had a list of cleaning supplies, and I think Hannah said she was going to get some batteries and dishes for us to share, along with some extension cords.

We met up by the pharmacy. Hannah was standing next to the first-aid kit section, a box of band-aids in the baby seat section of the cart. We walked through some of the food aisles, deciding on coffee and snacks. I can't remember who, but someone suggested some cleaning wipes, and I ran back to the cleaning supplies to get them. We grabbed a few extra bags of Oreos and Cheez-its to share since we all liked similar treats.

It wasn't long before we were through getting what we needed at the store and headed back to campus. With the late-night hour, the traffic had eased, and we made it back in half the time it took us to get there. Hannah parked her car in front of the dorm, and we unloaded the gray, plastic grocery bags. As Taylor and I brought the bags inside the dorm, Hannah drove her car around back to the parking lot. We managed to get all the bags and ourselves down the hallway to our room in a couple minutes. Hannah made it inside right as we were opening our door. I decided that so far, meeting my new roommates and going to the store together was going well.

While we were unpacking, we decided to meet for lunch the next day, after our orientation classes. We all had different majors and would be going different places in the morning, but orientation was only for the first part of the day. That left us the rest of Sunday to unpack and get ready for the first day of classes on Monday.

CHAPTER FOUR

Orientation

I couldn't sleep. It was nothing unfamiliar. Ever since Mom died, I couldn't sleep well. Between crazy dreams and wondering how school would be, over the past month, I had managed to re-read books and watch almost every infomercial nighttime television had to offer.

For some reason, when I woke up from a dream and my mind started moving, the infomercials were the most helpful. Thankfully, I hadn't bought too much. Usually, I was able to pry myself away from whatever was the new fad kitchen utensil of the night for a run by around four in the morning on bad nights.

When I couldn't take staring at my television any longer, I decided a shower might do me some good. I didn't want to make too much noise. I still wasn't sure how the common room would carry noise between our thin walls, and I didn't want to wake Taylor or Hannah. I tip-toed out of our room and down the deserted hallway, to the bathroom.

The hot water felt good on my skin. While I still didn't feel totally awake, by the time I headed back to my room, I felt better. When I got back, I flipped the coffee maker switch to "on" as I walked into my room. Just a few minutes and I could count on a cup of coffee to wake me up. As soon as it was ready, I quietly made a cup.

I heard someone behind me say, "That smells like rainbows." Startled, I jumped and turned around.

Taylor was sticking her head out of her and Hannah's door.

"Leave it on before you go, California," she joked and pulled her head back inside their room.

I placed the lid on my cup and grabbed my bag.

On my way to my building, I walked past a huge line at an outdoor coffee cart. I whispered a silent "thank you" to the coffee powers that be for the proximity, should I ever need it, then tightened my grip on my own cup of liquid gold and kept moving. If I were ever out of coffee (as if THAT would ever happen!), I'd be able to get a boost here right on my way to class.

My class. Where am I going again? I thought as I pulled my campus map out of my backpack's side mesh pocket. *That's right. The Shale building.*

I found the structure on the shiny freshman handbook insert map from my orientation packet. I was close to it and going in the right direction, it seemed.

The Shale building was the main hub for health and human services, which included nutrition students. When I got there, I headed inside the half-modernized and half-architecturally ancient building. In the main floor area, there was a huge projection screen that had a welcoming message for new students flashing across it. The floors were gray, speckled tiles, and in the center of the floor were several wooden tables and benches. Some were filled with students.

I heard the buzz of movement echoing down the halls. It smelled like rubber shoes and coffee mixed with cinnamon buns. I think the basement of the building had a small eatery for students. Turing a corner, a small sign confirmed my thought. A symbol of what looked like a cup and an apple with a down arrow met my gaze. Below the food signal sign was another sign that had numbers and more arrows, apparently pointing to the classrooms.

Around the walls behind the center study area, there were doors leading into lecture rooms as well as a hallway that appeared to lead to another portion of the building. There were stairs to my left that headed up to the upper floors of the building. Most of the doors that I saw were propped open. I spotted a nutrition student orientation sign and followed the arrows pointing along the now beige-tiled hallway, as I was sure some of my fellow classmates were doing the same.

I'd made sure to get there a little early and hoped to get a good seat. I was supposed to meet my advisor and some of my teachers for my major courses. I wanted to make a good impression. Slowly, the seats filled. There was a low hum of conversation in the room as people who knew each other happily chirped "hello", and I heard some others introduce themselves.

At eight a.m., a quick, rhythmic clicking sound started on the stage at the front of the large auditorium, and the room began to quiet. At the front of the lecture hall, a woman walked onto the podium.

"Good morning, everyone," said the woman at the microphone. "My name is Dr. Bensing, and I am the Dean of the College of Health and Human Services. This year, it is our goal for you to learn about not only nutrition and health but about your fellow students and human beings. You will be taking your core courses and a few electives over the next four years, but you will also have the opportunity to partake in various volunteer programs."

She went on, but my ears began to pop like I was going up on an airplane. The sound of her voice became muffled, and the noise in the room fell away.

I heard the sound of doors opening. Someone must have opened the two massive, red doors at the front of the room. I started to panic a bit when I realized that the only sound I could hear was footsteps. It was the only noise in the room. The loud stamping of a heel walking down ceramic floors filled my ears like drums. Looking at Dr. Bensing, I saw her mouth moving but couldn't hear what she was saying. The pressure in the room changed, intensified.

What is going on? I thought to myself. I looked at the students to my left and right using my peripheral vision. Nothing seemed strange with their facial expressions. They simply sat there like they could hear Dr. Bensing plain as day. The hair on my arms began to prickle, and I realized I had goosebumps going up both of my arms and legs. I turned my head to the center aisle, toward the noise of the footsteps.

I felt like the air was standing still. As my head turned, I saw a woman walk down the center of the aisle. She was pale and short, with large, violet eyes and a covered head with hair that had escaped in dark tendrils from her royal blue, hooded cloak.

As she walked, her footsteps echoed in the hall. Then, when she passed me, she turned her head. She looked straight into my eyes. Her eyes were so bright. My stomach churned, and I wanted to run... or to vomit. She never stopped.

Then the moment passed. She simply turned her head back and kept walking through the room and out the propped-open door at the side of the stage.

It was then that I realized I could hear Dr. Bensing again.

"Habitat House, Dove House, The Rainbow Room, and Harding Elementary are some of the many areas where we will be hosting programs for students to connect with the community and share the knowledge they are learning." She went on. I felt my adrenaline welling within me, pumping through my veins, my flight-or-fight response awake and ready to be summoned. I took a breath, then another one. I needed to calm down.

It was probably lack of sleep. And stress. The fact that I'd just sweat through my shirt and felt the drops of perspiration falling down my spine and cold chills was probably unnoticeable to anyone else, and I needed to forget it. Lack of sleep and stress. That had to be it. I was going to land myself in the crazy bin if I let these things happen during the day. I needed to focus on what the instructors were saying not on my sometimes-crippling overactive imagination.

The day went on, but compared to the first part of orientation, the rest was uneventful. I was glad for it because by the time lunch came around, my head was starting to ache. I was tired, I realized.

When my mid-day break came, I made sure to be by the dining hall at one for lunch. I was glad my two new roommates and I had decided to meet and talk about the morning. I needed a distraction and felt a little like throwing in the towel. I hoped that listening to how both Taylor and Hannah's orientation went would take my mind off the same anxieties that I'd tried to leave back in San Diego. Self-doubt had started to creep into my mind.

As I looked around, I saw Taylor sitting on a bench to the right of the dining hall. We were in the center of campus. The pathways around the large, grassy fields were filled with students walking in the sunshine. Everyone was baring skin. One girl even walked by me with a dress so short, I suspected it was a shirt she'd decided to pair with a little belt. I'd heard winter stories of the cold from up north, and I figured she was trying to get some vitamin D and store some warmth from the end of summer.

I sat next to Taylor. She was looking in the direction of a group of guys playing a game of football down near the far end of the quad. The lawn was beautiful; it was so green. There were a couple trees here and there, all occupied by people sitting on blankets underneath them, laptops open and headphones on. Some sat in the sunlight with friends, and some looked even to be resting with their heads on their bags. It looked like a scene from an advertisement or a brochure.

The group of guys were running back and forth. Shirts, I noticed, must have been optional because only about half of the group had them on. Wow, I was going to have to get used to people dressing differently in college. It was as if being away from home gave everyone a license to dress however they felt. I kind of liked it. I would be able to do my own thing – which usually meant comfortable jeans and a sweatshirt when it was cold or running shorts and a shirt when it was nice – and no one would even care.

"Look at that," Taylor said without breaking her gaze from the group of guys as I sat down.

"What?" I said.

"That one has to be at least an eight," she whispered. She nodded her head in the direction of the far-left guy. He was one of the shirtless. He had a tan and dark hair, and his skin almost glistened in the sunlight.

"I'm so glad I broke up with my boyfriend before going away to school," she said, still watching him. "We're going to meet so many guys here. I already heard from one of the girls in my major that the fashion design department throws a party at the end of the semester every year. Apparently, it's the party of the year. I hope these guys are there." She hadn't broken her gaze the whole time she'd been talking to me.

"Hey, look at your shoe," I said. Of all the things I'd seen that morning, this took the cake. There was a little squirrel under the bench, sitting right behind her leg, resting a foot on her shoe. As I called attention to it, the animal must have sensed that I'd seen it. It turned its head and looked at me, cocked its head, and then looked over at Taylor's shoe again.

"Oh, yeah, I'm like an animal magnet sometimes. They just find me. It's kind of strange, but my brother gets a kick out of it, and it's kind of entertaining, so I don't mind." She looked at the squirrel and moved her foot.

"Move off, si-" she said but then was cut off.

Right between the two of us flew a football, hitting the bench hard. The squirrel, of course, took off, and we were both still as petrified trees. *What just happened?*

Taylor stood up. "Hey, what the hell?" she yelled in the direction she'd just been drooling. Apparently, her ratings of some of the guys were going down a couple notches because she looked mad.

Rolling her eyes, she picked up the ball from the ground and looked into her hand. She looked back at me with a small smirk on her face, then turned back to the guys and calmly threw the ball in their direction. A perfect spiral throw. The ball flew through the air, and one of the guys on the lawn caught it. It was the guy she'd been drooling over a second ago. She turned back to the bench and sat down.

As Taylor pretended to look for the squirrel, I noticed that she had half a gaze watching one of the guys, who was now on his way over. It was the guy who'd caught the ball. I watched as he jogged over. Taylor pretended to put something in her purse and zipped it shut as he got to where we were sitting.

"Hey, that's a nice throw you've got there," he marveled as he walked up to us. He looked between Taylor and me, expecting one of us to say something. There was a stiff silence. I hated to admit it to myself, but I was entertained. This play was funny. I tried to wipe off the little upturn of a smile I felt on the left side of my face. I had to almost bite my cheek.

"I would say the same for you, but I think you should pay more attention to where you're throwing the ball," Taylor sassed sarcastically back. She looked him right in the eyes and didn't move from her spot. She just sat there. "You could have hurt someone."

The guy smiled. I think he felt like she was challenging him. I almost agreed with him. "Where'd you learn to throw like that?" he asked.

"Wouldn't you like to know?" she replied. "Now, if you don't mind, we were in the middle of something before we almost got creamed by the ball." She gave him a final look and then turned to me.

The guy still stared down at her, smiling. He wasn't bothered or put off by her sarcasm at all. He looked at me and winked.

"Hey, if your friend ever wants to play a round of catch, tell her she can meet me in Logger Hall on the West side of campus. Just ask for Seth. I'm the RA in the building." He paused. Then, looking at me intently, he said, "And your name is..."

"Emily," I managed to say. I wasn't used to guys being this comfortable talking to people they didn't know. I hadn't had a boyfriend or any experiences with guys, so I was a little intimidated by his forwardness. And, of course, Taylor was right; he was attractive.

"Well, bye, Emily. And bye, Emily's friend," he teased, looking at Taylor the whole time. Without waiting for a reply, he turned on his heels and jogged back over to the game of football that was now going on without him. But before he re-joined the game, he turned and in a humorous tone, yelled, "Actually, I think I should be more of a nine and a half," and then turned back and didn't look over again.

I looked back at Taylor, my mouth open and not a word in my throat.

"Shut your mouth, or you'll catch a fly," Taylor said sarcastically, still staring in his direction. Obviously, she had been caught as off guard by the last comment as I had.

"You could have been nicer, you know," I joked. "He was just trying to apologize."

She cut me off. "I don't think I heard him apologize at all. I think he had some nerve coming over here. And a nine and a half – please." She had a little grin on her face. I had to laugh. She knew exactly what she was doing. But remembering the smile he gave and the way he exuded confidence, I think she might have met her match.

"Hey, there's Hannah." I spotted her as she approached us.

Hannah walked over and put down her bag. She had taken her books and writing pads to take notes in case there was an assignment. Taylor said she'd tried to talk her out of taking everything since it was just orientation, but she'd insisted.

"Hey, guys," she said. "I'm starved. Let's get food... now."

Hannah didn't wait for us to get up; she simply turned and headed toward the door of the dining hall. She held the door open for us.

As we walked through, she said, "Did I miss something?"

CHAPTER FIVE

The Dorms

"Oh, you know, it's only the first day and Taylor's already got the guys falling on her," I said before I could stop myself. Usually, my sarcasm could stay under wraps and I could just keep my laughing to myself, but this time, it slipped out. I held my breath. I probably just blew any chance I'd had with these guys to be friends.

Then, surprisingly, the other two laughed. I did too, but it was probably more of a tension releaser for me. Thankfully, the joke had been well-received. It looked like so far, we would be able to be friends.

"I was a bit harsh, wasn't I?" Taylor said. "Maybe he was a nine. Maybe. Oh, well," she said behind me.

We walked into the dining hall, joking and filling in Hannah on the football incident. The smells of delicious foods filled my nose, and my focus started to wean. Swiping our ID cards, we gained access to the food and dining area of the hall. My eyes tried to take everything in.

This was the first time I'd been inside the dining hall. I'd heard about the "freshman fifteen" and the weight students typically gained when they went away to college. I'd heard that Syracuse had a good food service department, but I hadn't been inside to check it out for myself yet.

I'm not sure what I'd expected, or if I'd had any expectations at all. But walking into the great dining room, I was almost blown away. Not only were the smells of baking bread and meats getting stronger, but the sounds of voices, plates, and laughs were all around me.

Right as we got through into the serving area, I had to stop and take it all in. There was an entire half of the room dedicated to different foods. A hot bar with a chef on the end, slicing a rump of roast beef. A salad bar that doubled as a home for fruit and soups, as well as vegetables. There was a line of students in what looked like a sandwich area. Off to the far end, past the salad bar and the roast beef, I even saw a dessert space, where I spotted small, round, brown objects underneath lights. And on the wall next to it, small spigots dispensed what looked like ice cream.

"Wow," I said. I stopped, and Taylor ran right into me.

"Hey, there. Watch it," she said lightly as she put her hand on my arm. But as she looked around, I heard her echo my "wow".

"Didn't you guys read the brochure? I mean, they described all the parts of the dining hall. This is only one of them. The larger one is down on the East end of campus," Hannah said as she headed to the dish area. There were large stacks of dishes and trays, along with plastic cups. Next to the dishes, there were Styrofoam containers for students who wanted to get "to-go" food and take it to their classes or back to the dorms.

We went different ways. Hannah headed toward the sandwich area, and Taylor went to fill her cup at the soda station. I picked up a plate and grabbed a fork out of the little cup next to the plate dispenser. I walked past the sandwich line and the chef with the roast beef. My mouth was watering. I was going to have to come back here at dinnertime. Looking down the serving line, there were other choices besides the roast beef. I saw potatoes, greens, beans, and what looked like hot apples and rolls.

When I got to the salad bar, the choices impressed me. There were four different choices for the salad base: lettuce, spinach, arugula mix, and, of course, the new power food: kale. I wasn't impressed with kale yet, but I'd had it a couple times and didn't think it was too bad... if I put enough stuff on it. I went with the arugula mix.

Moving down, I had choices from lots of different veggies to croutons and nuts. Filling my plate, I swung to the opposite side of the bar and was met with a line of fruits and puddings. I made what looked almost like a volcano out of the produce and added a dollop of cottage cheese at the top. Then I grabbed a small roll on the walk back to where I'd spotted Taylor and Hannah. I stopped and filled my clear, plastic cup with Coke Zero before heading to the table and sitting down.

"They have some good stuff here," I said.

Taylor had a bowl of some kind of orange soup that smelled like squash and had a grilled cheese sandwich on her plate next to it. I made a mental note to get that next time I was here. I was drooling on the inside by this point. Hannah had gotten some chips and what looked like a turkey club. She opened the sandwich and placed a thin layer of the chips on the meat, then replaced the bread of the sandwich.

"What?" she said, and Taylor laughed.

"'What' is right! What are you doing?"

"Oh, it's the best way to eat them. It gives it just a little bit of salt and a crunch. You have to try it." She bit into the meal.

"How did your orientations go?" I asked them as I started in on my lunch. I hadn't realized how hungry I was.

"It was good. At least mine was," Taylor said. "One of our teachers talked about a summer abroad program in Italy and an art scholarship that sounded neat." She blew off some steam from her soup bowl.

"That's better than ours. We found out there's a lot of classes that are only offered at certain times in the year." Hannah paused. "I'm going to have to make sure not to miss any of them, or it will put me behind from graduating.

It sounds like a good group of courses, but it will be intense."

"How was yours, Emily?" Taylor asked.

"It was fine. We are all supposed to get to know each other, and there's supposed to be some programs for us to volunteer for-" I got cut off.

"You have to do that. It's great for the resume. I was thinking of doing some also." Hannah sounded excited.

"Oh, did you guys have a prank pulled on you?" Taylor looked between Hannah and myself.

We both looked back at her.

"Well, I heard that every year, the graduating class pulls a prank on the freshmen during orientation. I think they did that to our lecture this morning. We were sitting in the big auditorium and then everything got quiet. Then this weird lady with no sense for a summertime outfit came in, walked through the hall and out. The whole place was so quiet, you could hear a pin drop. She was giving creepy looks too." Taylor put her spoon back in the almost empty soup bowl.

My enthusiasm for my lunch vanished. My stomach turned over.

"Joke or not, it was kind of creepy," she said, letting her spoon fall back into the bowl. She didn't seem as bothered by the encounter as I had been that morning. But a class prank would explain the whole thing.

"Yeah, that happened in ours too," Hannah said. "I hate things like that. It's such a waste of time," she went on. "I wonder if they do the same prank each year or if it's different. I mean, when I saw her, I just thought she was a student that was lost at first, but then when I couldn't hear what the teacher was saying, I got kind of annoyed." She'd left the crust of her sandwich on the plate and absentmindedly moved the remaining chips around with some of it. "I didn't even think that it could have been a class prank," Hannah finished, looking up at me.

"Anything happen in your orientation?" Hannah and Taylor both looked at me.

"Yeah, the same thing," I said. "I guess the joke was on us, then. Maybe they single people out or something. I felt like she looked right at me. But how could they play a joke like that on the first day? It's not like they would send out a letter to all the other students except us." I laughed. The whole thing was ridiculous, but it made me feel a bit better knowing that it had happened to the other two. I wasn't totally crazy.

"Anyway, we will have to ask John about it later," Hannah said.

"Who's John?" Taylor asked.

"John's our Resident Advisor. He's in charge of the dorms," Hannah explained. "We have a meeting tonight before classes start tomorrow. I guess they just want to go over the rules or something. The meeting's mandatory." Hannah got up and went to the soda station. She came back with three to-go soda cups complete with lids and straws. We poured what was left into our cups.

We were done with lunch, and looking at my watch, it was almost three in the afternoon. I still had to get to the bookstore to get a book I couldn't find online and a couple extra notepads for class. I picked up my tray, and the other two got up as well. I said bye to my new friends and headed in the direction of the bookstore.

Lunch was nice, but I couldn't get the odd sense of foreboding off my mind. I'd almost forgotten about the strange lady going through our class that morning. But with the other two bringing it up, I couldn't ignore it. At least it wasn't just my course.

I didn't see any way for the senior class to play a prank on incoming freshmen so early in the semester. I mean, class hadn't even started yet. I was just going to have to let it go, convince myself that Taylor was right about it being a prank, and not let myself worry anymore. I let my mind wander to the surroundings as I walked toward the bookstore. It was about four in the afternoon. The sun was out, and the day's warmth was comforting. Hannah was right; the summer was beautiful here in New York.

By the time I was done at the store, the sun wasn't as high in the sky as it had been. I felt the heat of the day slowly ebbing away.

The nights here get cool quick, I thought to myself and made a mental note to grab a sweatshirt the next time I had to go out in the afternoon. I hated to be cold.

That evening, when we were getting ready to go to the meeting in the dorm hall's common room, Hannah poked her head in my room.

"Are you planning on signing up for night hosting?" she asked.

"What's that?" I replied.

"It's just a student position that the dorms have for during nighttime, when no one's in John's office to see who comes in and out. You would sign people in and out. Three to five people work the table together every night. It's supposed to be easy money, and it would be good for when you have homework." She stopped talking and waited for my reply.

I got up from my chair and headed into the common room. "I don't know. I'm not the best at staying awake all night," I said. Taylor was sitting on the little makeshift couch that the dorm provided for the common room.

"Just say 'yes'. It's easier," she was smiling. "I think we have a class together too, and we could do our homework for it while we work," Hannah kept on.

I considered it. It would be nice to get some homework out of the way, and I knew I could always use a little extra study time.

"Sure. Why not?" I answered. Hannah nodded.

We headed down the hall a few minutes later. The gray tile floor of the hallway stopped and turned into blue carpet when we got to the common area. The chairs were an old pleather and as plain and beige as they could be. They looked like they were more comfortable than they were. An old television sat on a stand next to the wall. A couple guys from the other side of the hall were trying to get the knobs to turn and didn't seem to be having any luck. I heard static coming from the television speakers.

"Fucking thing is broken," one of them whispered as he turned a knob. I heard a light click. He must have been pulling on it a little because he almost fell back in his chair. The other guys burst out laughing, and looking out of the corner of my eye, I saw him laughing too. I smiled. One of the guys turned his head. He had brown hair and an olive skin tone. He looked over to where I was and smiled.

I felt like a deer in headlights. His eyes were blue – not sky-blue, but blue crayon-blue. As I looked at them, I noticed a familiar green ring within the blue, right around the iris. It was familiar because I had the same color eyes.

Snap out of it, Emily, I thought to myself as I realized I had a dumb expression on my face.

Then reality hit me, slamming into me like a Mack truck, and the anxiety kicked in. I involuntarily smiled and averted my eyes at the same time. It would take me a bit to get used to not only living with two other girls, but being so close to the guys in the dorms as well. I noticed the room was a little warm as I walked over to where Hannah and Taylor were getting our seats.

I hadn't seen this group of guys moving in, so that meant that they had to be upper classmen. They must live in our dorm; otherwise, they wouldn't be at our meeting with the resident advisor. I found myself wondering what the guys' names were. Especially the one that I had made eye contact with. I snuck a glance in his direction as I joined Hannah and Taylor. He was talking with his friends and didn't seem to notice.

We headed to the back of the room, where a couple chairs remained unoccupied. There was a hum of conversation, an excitement for the start of the semester. The day had been full not only with orientation but with the rest of campus moving in. We were all looking between ourselves, realizing these people around us were going to be living with us for the next year.

"Hey, I'm John. Time to be quiet." The talking died down as a tall man walked into the room from the office along the opposite wall from where we had been sitting. The front entrance to the dorm was to the left of his office. John passed out papers to the students sitting at the front. He then went back to his office and came back out with a packet of pens wrapped with rubber bands.

"These forms will explain the rules to you. The first form lists the rules. No hot plates, no alcohol in your dorm rooms, no drugs – standard stuff. The second form is a signature sheet I need from every resident of this dorm, saying you received the first form."

He paused and looked over the room.

"Okay, guys, here's the deal. I'm in my office Monday through Friday in the evenings from six to ten. Then the night hosts will take over for me, and I will be in my room down the hall." He put his arm up, pointing down to the guys' side of the floor. "Don't wake me up in the middle of the night because your boyfriend just broke up with you. Don't wake me up if you locked yourself out of your room," he went on.

I got a little chilly and realized I had goosebumps going up my arm and on my legs, under my jeans. I had the feeling someone was watching me. I looked at Taylor's arm to my right resting on her chair and noticed she had goosebumps on her arm also. Looking to my left, Hannah was sitting similarly and had the same. I nudged Taylor, mostly because I was afraid Hannah might punch me for interrupting her concentration. I nodded in the direction of her arm and then showed her mine. Her eyebrows went up.

I nodded my head in Hannah's direction, and she looked at her arm and then back at me. She leaned over.

"Maybe they just turned on the A/C or something," Taylor whispered.

"At the risk of you thinking I'm totally crazy, I kind of feel like I'm being watched," I told her.

Hannah looked daggers at us both. "What are you two doing?" she hissed under her breath.

"Hey, look at your arm. Are you cold?" Taylor asked her.

Hannah looked down at her arm. "No," she said, a little confused. "Why? What does it matter?"

I turned, and out of the corner of my eye, I saw something over the reflection in the glass window. Or, well, something saw me. Or us. I didn't know. Looking back and meeting my gaze was the pair of violet eyes belonging to the same woman I'd seen walk through orientation. Taylor must have seen my expression change. Through the reflection, I saw her turn her head to look where I was staring.

"Is that?" she said. Then I saw Hannah's head turn.

The lady standing outside the window stared at the three of us, then she turned and walked away. I watched her go, but after a few seconds, I couldn't see her any longer. My eyes refocused on the reflection and the three of us.

"Ladies, something boring you?" I heard John's voice almost out of a fog. "Ladies?" We turned our heads.

John was looking at us. The guy sitting to Taylor's right had a stack of papers he was trying to give her. It seemed they had made it all the way around the room and finally to us, but she'd been looking in the other direction, so she hadn't seen him. Apparently, he was making a commotion to get her attention.

Taylor looked at him and gave him a smile. He stuttered. She was pretty, and he looked intimidated. I had to smile. Yes, she knew exactly what she was doing.

"Sorry, got it," Hannah said. She didn't look at us this time. From the expression on her face, she was mad that we'd drawn his attention. A couple people laughed. I sank down in my chair an inch or two. I didn't dare look in the direction of the group of guys I'd seen earlier.

"So, if you guys have any questions, my hours are on the office door and on my door down the hall. We should all get along fine as long as no one is stupid and everyone takes care of their own shit... okay?" With that, John ended the meeting. He turned and headed back into the office, then came back out two seconds later.

"Oh, and for anyone who is interested in night hosting, the papers are in my office." He went back in.

Hannah got up and went over to the office. I looked back at Taylor.

"Was that the same lady you saw this morning?"

"Yeah, that was her. She obviously needs to change her clothes. It must be some joke." She stopped. Hannah was coming back with papers in her hands.

"Here's the night hosting forms." Hannah handed each of us a form.

"Did you see the lady from this morning?" I asked her.

"Yeah, it was pretty rude to interrupt the meeting. That's why I don't like jokes like that. They're distracting, and we probably missed something important." Hannah sat down to begin writing on her application. "But at least now orientation day is over, so we probably won't see her again," she added when she was done.

I hoped she was right.

Hannah got up and took her application into John's office, then went back down the hall in the direction of our room.

Taylor and I finished our applications and went into John's office to hand them in. As we placed them in the box of applications, Taylor decided to ask about the campus prank.

"Hey, John, I'm Taylor from room five," she said.

"Well, hi, Taylor from room five," John replied in a mocking tone. He looked up, smiled, and took a deep, purposeful breath. "No harm, no foul. What can I do for you?"

Taylor rolled her eyes. "I have a question," she said. "I was wondering about class pranks."

"What about them?" John replied. He looked interested.

"Well, do the upperclassmen ever pull pranks on incoming freshmen?" she asked.

John paused and looked at us again. After what seemed a little longer than I thought necessary, he looked back down at his computer and started typing.

"I don't think any classes play any pranks, or at least they haven't in years. The campus is strict with those kinds of things. Liability, you know." He was focused on other things. I saw a computer screen reflection from the picture on his wall. He was obviously engrossed in what looked like his latest game of solitaire.

Taylor turned and looked at me as if she expected me to say something. I didn't.

"Well, there you go. Whoever it is, it's just some creepy lady who needs something better to do with her time," I said to Taylor as we walked back to our room. As I entered our room, I looked back down the hall and saw John watching us.

Hannah was in the common room, making a plate out of her chemistry book that now held a couple Oreos and a Coke. "Well, how did it go?" she asked.

We told her about what John said about the class pranks. Either he was covering for something, or he was serious that it wasn't some joke. I hadn't decided which I'd rather it be. Both were bad when I considered them. Either we had a strange stalker, or we were the laughing stock of the campus. Both were things that I hadn't expected when I moved to the opposite side of the country. I suddenly felt tired.

I was ready for some sleep. It had been a long day, and I wanted to be ready for the first day of classes.

"I'm calling it a night," I said, getting up and walking to my bedroom door.

"I want to do some reviewing before classes tomorrow," I heard Hannah say. She went into 5B with Oreos, chemistry book, and Coke in hand. "Night," she yelled back through the wall. She'd left the door open, so the light she had on poured through their doorway.

"I'm going to paint some," Taylor announced as she got out some small bags from a plastic set of drawers she'd brought with her. She began to set up her art supplies in the middle room.

"Sounds good. Good night, guys," I called out as I went into my room, leaving my door open also. I wasn't sure what they were going to do, and I felt comfortable leaving it open. Besides, I was such a light sleeper that I'd hear if anyone came in.

I went to my desk and called my dad. The time difference meant that it was only 6:45 p.m. in California, and I guessed that he was getting ready to get some take-out Mexican food. Sunday nights, it was our tradition to not cook, since the week was about to start.

Down the street from my house was a little Mexican restaurant that only had take-out, drive-through, and an outside seating area. They made everything in the little building, even homemade tortillas. Even though I was not hungry at all, my mouth watered a little. I'd be hard-pressed to find good Mexican food here.

My dad was good. He told me he'd gotten home early that morning and that Cindy was glad to see him. He was planning on going to work the next day, so he said he went to the store and got some food for his lunches.

Dad and I talked for a couple more minutes and then it was time for me to go to sleep.

"I'm having dinner with your Nino this week," he told me. I was glad he was going to be getting out. He tended to stay home and not socialize.

But he will be alone the other days. It's your fault. I cut my thoughts off. My father was an adult, and he could take care of himself.

At least that's what he'd told me before I sent back in my acceptance letter to school. I'd almost not gone at all, but he had convinced me that I needed a change. It hadn't been a fun conversation, especially since talking about uncomfortable things wasn't either of our fortes. After a few more minutes on the phone, we said our goodbyes.

I laid down on my bed. My mind was more awake than my body. I tried to get right to sleep but couldn't stop thinking about the day. The mysterious lady, the night hosting, John, Seth, Cindy, my new roommates. The guy from the common room and how our eyes met. As I fell asleep, I felt the goosebumps on my arm prickle. I wanted to jolt awake, but the sleep pulled at me. It felt like I was tripping unexpectedly into sleep.

Suddenly, I startled and woke up to the smell of damp towels. The room was dark, and it sounded like someone was yelling down the hall. I tried to focus, but my eyes were hazy. I was nauseated. I recognized the haze now.

I was dreaming. That didn't make it any easier though, as I realized this was a new dream. The haze was the only thing I recognized.

In the dark, I saw something I could finally focus on. It looked like a small light. It was pulsing and getting brighter. I stood up and watched. My bed vanished as I stood.

The smell was terrible, almost like a mix of metal, dirt, and rainwater. My feet were freezing. I looked down and they were under dark, running water. I dragged my feet through the thick fluid, toward the light.

When I got close and could pinpoint its location, I looked back over my shoulder from where I'd come. I couldn't tell what direction I'd come from, nor where I was. There was only darkness and the light from the pulsing blue orb in front of me. It was beating like it was alive. I looked up from the glowing ball and back to my front.

I was met with a pair of violet eyes. A hooded woman with pale skin and dark hair stuck with sweat to the side of her face stared back at me. The expression on her face was fearful. Her eyes widened as she realized I was there. She looked as surprised to see me as I was to see her.

"What are you doing here?" she said in an accusatory manner. "Run," she hissed.

I didn't wait to find out what she meant. I turned away from the glowing light and her and tried to run, moving my soaking, heavy legs.

I woke up drenched in sweat. I focused on my phone that I used as a digital clock. It read three a.m.

Great. Starting college off right, I thought to myself. I yanked the blankets off and tried to take some deep breaths and relax.

Apparently, it worked because the next thing I knew, my alarm was going off and it was morning.

CHAPTER SIX

First Day of School

Taylor -

The September sky was clear and crisp in central New York. Taylor couldn't believe how beautiful the sky was. She was used to Texas's flat plains, where the sun shone red across the sky in the evening. But she loved the crisp, cool air and the blue of the sky. She knew the snow would come soon, and that would be another story, but she was ready. She had a box of snow boots and jackets that her mom would send as soon as she needed them.

Her first class was in the art building. Landscaping. She had to ride a campus bus down to the building at the far end of campus. She didn't mind, and the bus-riding saved wear and tear on her shoes. The bus was crowded.

First day of school rush, she thought to herself. *I may have to get an earlier one if I'm not on time today though.*

She decided it wouldn't be so bad getting there a little early. She didn't like to get up early and had made a point of sleeping in all summer to savor the free time. But if it was the difference between being stressed and rushed, she'd rather just suck it up.

Taylor looked at some of the other students. Some were listening to their iPhones, ear buds in and looking out the windows. Some were chatting. She noticed a girl looking at her. She dropped her gaze when Taylor smiled. She saw her looking at her shoes. She knew they were kind of eccentric. *They are four-inch heels,* she thought to herself. But that was her style, and she loved it.

She decided to call her brother on her way to class. He was a senior in high school, and school was supposed to start in another week or so back home. She wanted to wish him luck. It rang. Then, suddenly, she realized the time difference. Texas was two hours behind New York. Her eight a.m. class would be at six a.m. back home. That meant she'd just called her brother at quarter to five, which also meant she'd better hang up the phone fast, or she'd get an earful.

The bus pulled up to a building with a slanted pair of sliding doors. *They're supposed to be that way, she thought. Just for pizzazz.* The exterior walls of the building were maroon. There were metal sculptures around the front with small, silver, engraved plaques next to each one.

She got off the bus and walked through the sliding doors of a building that looked half-new and half-ancient simultaneously. The inside was much more ordinary than the outside. The same kind of metal sculptures that were outside lined the interior walls. They seemed to melt into the wall, as if they were carved into it. The ceiling was high. There were long, clear plastic lanyards filled with white lights that came down to illuminate the hallways.

It was a strange building, she thought. She found herself not only looking at the architecture and the lighting but at the other students. She always felt at home with the art department. They were her people, and she loved them for their unwillingness to conform.

The girl that had been looking at her shoes on the bus was ahead of her. She looked at her shirt from behind. A large lightning bolt covered the back. It was as if she were wearing a team jersey with jeans. Her shoes were just sneakers, nothing like Taylor's four-inch heels. The girl turned down a hallway, and Taylor watched her walk down the hall and into a room.

Looking around at all the people, she had a memory of her family and a friend at the fair. She'd wanted to go get cinnamon doughnuts from a booth, but her mom and her friend told her and her brother that they needed to do some people-watching. At the time, she didn't know what they meant, and of course, as she got older, she understood. This was probably the first time that she just wanted to sit and people-watch since then. The students going in and out of the rooms were fantastic. The styles, from clothes to hair, were so unique. Not everyone, of course, but most.

Taylor looked at her schedule. Landscaping. "Okay, room 222. That's where I'm supposed to go." She looked around herself and caught a glimpse of a room number. She was at room 170. Her room must be on the second floor. When she got to the staircase, she read the sign that showed the levels with 100, 200, and 300 on the first, second, and third floors, respectively. She started up the stairs.

The stairs were old and reminded her of her grandmother's house. They were a dark brown and emitted an audible creek even above the noise of the other students going up and down. Once she reached the top, she made her way to room 222. She walked into a class that looked more like an art studio, and she felt right at home.

At the center of the floor were tables. Each table was high and had eight high stools with students sitting in about half of them. There were six tables total, three in the front row and three in the back. She took the first table in the back row. She sat in the corner spot with her back facing the wall. She had been in a room like that back in her art class in high school and was unlucky enough to get a chair where her back was to the teacher and had faced the wall all semester. She would always remember how much her neck cramped from trying to see. She smiled. Now she was in college, in a real art class.

She put her things on the tabletop. There were about five others at her table, and they were quickly filling with incoming students.

"Hello, class. My name is Dr. Winters, and I will be your art teacher for this semester," the woman who walked into the room muttered. She'd been carrying several bags and balancing a folder with a coffee mug on top as she'd swept into the class.

"This course is Art 150 Landscape Design, and it looks like we have a full course. Sorry if any of you were hoping for a spot on the wait list. You will have to wait until next semester." The woman put her things down. Several students who'd been standing at the back started shuffling out.

When they were out, the teacher closed the door and turned to the class. She walked over to her desk and pulled out a large stack of manila envelopes. She placed them on the tabletop of the counter closest to her, then pulled another stack of papers from the bag she'd been carrying. She passed them out to the class, putting a stack of papers on each of the six tables.

"This is the syllabus," she said. "This class will help prepare you for drawing landscape and scenery and also help you learn about other artists and how they viewed the world. You will have one major assignment over the semester that will culminate in a final at the end of the course. Each student will get a different assignment, so it is okay to work together."

She picked up the stack of manila envelopes, then put them down again and looked at the class.

"However, remember that any material that is plagiarized will be immediately failed, and the students responsible will be reported to the dean."

With that, she picked up the envelopes again and started calling names. She handed out the envelopes to the people who answered when she called their names. Finally, Taylor's name was called, and she raised her hand. Dr. Winters came over and handed her the envelope. She opened it. She pulled out an unframed photo and laughed. This was some joke.

How did they pull this off? she wondered. There was no way they could have done it without her parents being in on the whole thing. The picture was familiar to her. It was an exact replica of a landscape she'd drawn while in her final year of high school. It looked like someone had taken a photo of her painting and just shoved it into her envelope. She looked around at the other students. Some had opened their envelope, like she had.

As she looked at the other students at her table, she noticed that one of the girls was staring at her. At first, she'd seen it out of the corner of her eye and figured that the girl had been looking at her shoes, kind of like the harmless girl on the bus, but this girl was looking straight at her. And the look wasn't nice. She'd been doing so for a while now. It was enough to make anyone uncomfortable.

She looked at the girl and met her eyes. She had intense, yellow-brown eyes. Her hair was slicked back to her head and black as a raven's. Her clothes were black, and she had enough white foundation on to make her look like a clown.

Or a ghost, Taylor thought. She took a deep breath. She wasn't easily unsettled, but this girl took the cake.

Breaking her gaze with the girl, she looked around the class and saw a window. There was a bird feeder in the tree outside the class. She knew what that meant, and she was right. To the right of the feeder, on the ground, she spotted a chipmunk. She watched as it climbed up the feeder and stole some of the seed. As if it sensed her watching it, the animal jumped off the feeder and up onto the window sill, quick as lightning. It sat there for a few minutes and then ran away.

Taylor decided she must be mistaken, and the photo of the landscape she was given must be different than her own project. Either that, or she'd been plagiarizing the one she painted for over a year. Surely, someone would have noticed

About twenty minutes before the class was scheduled to end, Dr. Winters gave the go-ahead for them to leave if they wanted to. Feeling relieved, Taylor put her things together and left quickly. It had been a little strange having the girl across the table from her stare at her for so long. She felt like she needed some privacy now. She'd tried the whole smile-back-and-say-hi thing, but the girl had simply given her an even meaner look and shot daggers with her eyes.

They were getting out a little early, and she would have a couple minutes to stop for coffee and something to eat before her next class. She pushed her unsettling classmate from her mind and headed for the food truck she'd seen at the bus stop area right off campus.

Hannah -

Hannah was ready for Chemistry. She already had her book, and her bag was full of all the essentials. She'd been fifteen minutes early, so she could get a seat where she felt comfortable. This was going to be her class. She would get an A.

She looked around. It was an auditorium with a large blackboard at the front. It looked like there was a whiteboard that could slide over it above on the wall. Even so, she didn't know the last time she'd seen a blackboard. She looked at the little silver eraser holder at the bottom of the board and didn't see any chalk. Maybe it was just left over from previous years. The school had been around for quite a while.

Each row of seats had a long table going from aisle to aisle, and the old, wooden chairs looked like small torture chambers, with their hard backs and short in-between space. *How old is this room?* she found herself thinking. She chose an aisle seat in the front row. She wanted to be close but hated being boxed in.

The room was cold. She figured that way, the students would stay awake. She had only fallen asleep once in class during a lecture. That one time was so embarrassing for her that it had never happened again. She remembered it like yesterday, and as if she had some strange form of PTSD. The shame she'd felt from feeling like she'd insulted her instructor fell on her like a wet blanket all over again.

The night before that, she'd been awake building her science fair diagram. She'd had it done early, of course, but after her dog played in the spring snow, he came in and shook off the wetness, soaking her project in the process. It probably would have been fine, but being a perfectionist, she was not happy until she had replaced almost all of the diorama pieces.

During her anatomy lecture, she'd nodded off. She'd dreamed of a face coming off the page of her open anatomy book, and it had startled her back to being awake. She'd yelled herself awake right in the middle of her teacher talking about the circulatory system. Everyone had stared. So embarrassing. She would not let that happen again.

She looked at her class schedule to see what the rest of the day had in store for her. Of course, she already knew the schedule by heart. She just needed the comfort of having something to read and do before the teacher got to class. She had chemistry lecture for two hours, then a two-hour lab after. *At least that's only once a week,* she thought. Then she had a break before Calculus and Biology. Tuesdays and Thursdays, she had biology lab and English, as well as Anthropology in the morning. And lab for

Anthropology on Thursdays. That was strange. She never pictured having to go to a lab class for anthropology.

It was going to be a tough year for homework, but in the end, when she could take other courses her junior and senior years, it would pay off. She wanted to go pre-med and make sure she had her pick of the best schools possible after Syracuse.

One of the students began passing out the syllabus from a stack of papers in the front of the room. She took one and passed the stack on. She went through it and saw how much of their grade was based on the exams and the final. It was hefty. As she read, she noticed an older man walk into the room. He had a worn and slumped look about him. He wore a wrinkled, brown suit. He was bald at the top of his head, with a kind of Albert Einstein hair, giving him a white crown. He wore dark, wire-rimmed glasses that were held up on his face by a long, pointed nose.

He carried a brown briefcase, which he set on top of the lecture podium at the front of the room. *That thing looks older than I am*, Hannah thought to herself. The man opened the briefcase and pulled out three rolls of paper towels. He set the bundles on the counter next to the briefcase. As he unrolled them, out came pens, a calculator, a ruler, and at the end, some chalk.

"That's interesting," she heard a murmur behind her.

"Yeah, interesting and weird," was the hushed reply from someone sitting behind and to her right.

Hannah got the impression that all of the students in the class were thinking the same thing and were just as stumped as she was about the paper towels and the strange man. Then the man began to speak with a thick accent. It was so thick, she had to pay close attention to understand what he was saying.

"I am Dr. Sharma. I will be your teacher for Chemistry." His voice rattled. He sounded even older than he looked. He spoke with a low tone that reminded Hannah of old vampire movies she watched with her brothers on Halloween.

"For those of you who like punishment, I may be your biology teacher as well." He paused again, and Hannah felt her hope of a challenging but fun semester die within her. She looked down at her schedule, still sitting on the desktop. Yes, there it was. Dr. Sharma's name was right next to her biology room and building.

Great, she thought. She took a deep breath and exhaled, resolving to pay attention and focus.

Dr. Sharma scanned the room. Hannah saw his eyes going from left to right as if he were looking for something. He was taking in the rear of the lecture room and scanning towards the front. *Oh, come on. Get on with it,* she couldn't help but think to herself. Then, a second later, his eyes rested on her. He lingered there for a second longer than she felt was appropriate, and she started to feel self-conscious. Dr. Sharma then did one of the strangest things any teacher had done to Hannah while in a classroom.

He walked toward her front row seat and sniffed the air. Like he needed a tissue but didn't go to get one. Then he did it again. Hannah shot her gaze to the right and the left and saw other students watching with confused faces. *What the hell?* She couldn't concentrate while he was staring at her. She'd met his gaze in the beginning, wanting to make a good impression, but after a few moments, she felt awkward and looked at the tabletop where her syllabus lay.

After a few seconds more, the strange teacher finished his silent assessment of both Hannah and the rest of the class with an ominous grin on his face. He finally spoke, to a class full of students who were understandably on the edge of their seats.

"You may turn to the person on the left and introduce yourself," Dr. Sharma went on. He looked at the class, but no one moved. "Go ahead." He waved his hand, and the students began doing just as they were directed.

Hannah turned and introduced herself to the girl sitting next to her, then looked at the teacher again. The class, for a moment, was full of smiles and an up-beat, hushed murmur, the strangeness of a few moments earlier beginning to abate. When she turned back to face the front, her teacher's eyes were gleaming, and she felt a feeling of uneasiness come over her. She knew that look. It was the look that a snake gave a mouse after it coerced it into a trap.

"Now turn back to that person and tell them 'goodbye'," Dr. Sharma said, making the instruction more of a statement.

Hannah stared at him. No one in the class moved. Someone's bookbag slid down a tableside somewhere in the room, and it echoed, the room was so silent.

"Most likely," he said with slow precision, "the person that you bid goodbye to will be taking this class again next year... or changing majors. Most people underestimate chemistry. Let's hope you do not."

With that, the man began to review the table of elements and the syllabus. Hannah settled in for the long haul. It was going to be a rough course.

Emily -

It was morning again. I was on my way to Economics. I wasn't too excited about it, but I figured that it would be unlikely that I'd like every class I took, so I tried to relax. I'd found some of an old syllabus from a couple years back for the same class, and at least some of the topics sounded interesting. I just hoped the teacher was good.

I stopped and got a coffee before class. After my bad night's sleep, I thought I'd try the coffee cart instead of my trusty espresso machine. I tried something called a caramel turtle. I saw the cart attendant load the cup with chocolate sauce, then fill the cup with steamed milk and coffee. Finally, she finished my drink off with some whipped cream and caramel sauce.

"Here you go, hun," she said, handing the drink over. However, before I took it, she pulled it back and placed a caramel candy on top. "Looks like you need some extra sugar today." And she handed it back over with a genuine smile. There was something about the coffee cart culture that I loved. Most people understood and genuinely wanted to help their customers get what they wanted.

They seemed to have a coffee cart right outside every building on campus. That must be a gold mine. "So strategically placed," I found myself saying under my breath, looking around.

I took a small sip of the steaming coffee. It was good. I'd made it to my building and was standing next to the directory. Suddenly, I realized that Seth was next to me, just standing there. I saw his reflection next to mine. It looked bigger than I'd thought it would. I turned my head, confused.

"Hey, Emily. How is your friend doing?" His sly smile showed how pleased he was that he'd surprised me.

"Hey, Seth. She's doing good. Where's your football?" I replied, a bit stunned at my ease of conversation with him. I tried to look back at the hulking reflection, but he'd moved to the stair railing. People moved around him, trying to go up to their classes.

"Oh, it's in my other bag." He put his hands innocently in the air. He had a small notebook with him and a pen, but that seemed to be it. He was good-looking; I'll hand Taylor that. The first day of orientation and she already had caught the eye of one of the hottest guys I'd seen so far. I'd have to ask her what the secret was.

"So, you're in the business building. A little far from nutrition, isn't it?" he said, still staring at me with a sly smile.

"Oh, I have Economics this mor-" I stopped. He was grinning openly now. I looked at him questioningly. "How did you know I was a nutrition major?"

"Ah, freshmen. So innocent." He was mocking me now, his eyes dancing brightly, but he seemed harmless enough. I laughed. I didn't want to seem paranoid.

"Economics in room 234 with Dr. Eagles, I think is his name," I finished, shaking my head, trying to make my face look less worried.

"That's upstairs, down the hall. I had Dr. Eagles a couple semesters back. He's nice. Just pay attention to his study notes, and you will be fine." With that, Seth turned and yelled, "Bye, Emily!" I watched him walk away. Before he got out of earshot, he yelled, "Make sure to tell your friend, Taylor, 'hi' for me!" Then he was gone.

"Bye!" I shouted after him, trying to wipe the confused smile from my face. I would have to get used to talking to the opposite sex so casually. It's not that I never talked to a guy before, but I guessed I just overthought the interaction. I wasn't sure what my problem was. And didn't Taylor refuse to give him her name? Maybe I'd missed something.

"Come on, Emily. Get it together," I had to tell myself.

I found the classroom on the second floor, just as Seth had told me I would. It wasn't too full yet, and I had a couple more minutes before class was supposed to start. I found a seat and decided to check my phone.

I had a text from my dad, saying all was fine at home and that he would call me later. He even sent a picture of Cindy, which was good for him, as he didn't like cell phones and lived with the oldest flip phone I'd seen in two years. The picture showed Cindy laying at the foot of my bed at home. I felt the lump in my throat. I missed that dog.

I texted back an "Aww" and then put my phone away as a man with a plaid overcoat walked into the classroom and placed a laptop on the front desk.

This must be Dr. Eagles, I thought to myself. He seemed pleasant, and as he opened the laptop, he looked over the class with a smile. He was short with a belly that could have been a disguise for a pregnancy. He took off his jacket, and I noticed his suspenders were decorated with...

Oh, my goodness, those are Legos, I thought to myself. His head was shiny due to baldness, but on the side, he had just enough hair to try for a halfway comb-over job. His cheeks were red, and his silver glasses enlarged his eyes just a bit. He smiled at the room, and I instantly liked him.

"Ladies and gentlemen, I am Dr. Eagles. This is your Economics course. I hope we will have a fun and exciting semester together," he said as he looked back to the laptop and typed something in. I heard the *ding* of the laptop whirring into motion, and as it did, he typed a little more. He grabbed a cable at the front desk and plugged it into the computer. About two seconds later, a screen popped up at the front of the class with a PowerPoint presentation.

"All of my presentations, as well as my syllabus, will be available online starting tonight. Today, we will just be going over many of the fascinating roles Economics plays in society. Yes, there's some math, and yes, there's formulas that predict things, but there's no reason that it can't be fun."

I was already starting to like this teacher. He seemed excited about his class.

The presentation took about forty-five minutes, during which Dr. Eagles made sure to go over a couple highlights from his course and projects we would be working on. Then he released us a little early because it was the first day. He'd said we were not going to be using books this semester and said to make sure to print off the lecture presentations and accompanying notes before each class.

So far, the start of school was going well. I hoped that Hannah and Taylor were having a good morning. Orientation was so strange that we all needed a little reprise, I thought.

As students left the class, I thought I saw Dr. Eagles looking in my direction, but when I looked back, he had his gaze back down at the laptop. I put my things back in my bag and finished the last drop of my coffee before getting up and heading to my next course.

CHAPTER SEVEN

Overnight Jobs

"Maybe it won't be so bad," I tried to reassure Hannah as she was telling us about her monster of a chemistry professor.

"Yeah, and if you need some extra credit, try to find out what kind of chalk he uses and bring him a box," Taylor joked. It worked, and we laughed a little.

"Funny." Hannah smiled and went on. "I asked around a little today about class pranks and jokes on new students, and no one seemed to know anything about it. So, there's a dead end there. Maybe that lady was just crazy, or maybe she is a security guard. Either way, we probably made too big a deal about it." She unpacked her bookbag, looking for something. She pulled out a pack of sticky notes from her bottomless pit of a bag and then looked up.

"Hey, you look in deep thought. Or are you just tired?" Pinpointedly, Taylor looked at me.

"Huh?" I jolted back to reality. "Oh, I'm fine. I didn't sleep well last night. I guess I was just nervous about classes or something. I think we all have full schedules, and it was the first day and all." I just tried to say whatever came into my head. If I talked about my childish nightmares, then they would think I was crazy. I mean, maybe not. They seemed nice, but still, we did just meet.

"Well, that's no fun," Taylor said. "But here's something that might cheer you up. My first class is a landscaping course, and we all sit at tables where there's like six of us."

She was moving her hands. She told a good story; I could already tell.

"There's a guy at the table I was sitting at today who is totally gorgeous. At least a nine on a scale of one to ten." She was beaming. "We have to do some landscaping of new places, and I'm going to ask to landscape him."

We all burst out laughing.

"Only thing is," Taylor went on, "I don't know if I'm going to sit there next time. There's this strange girl who kept giving me the stink eye through the whole class. I thought maybe she was with the guy, but she never seemed to even give him a second glance. She stared in my direction the whole time!" Taylor sounded exasperated. "Anyway, we got our assignment today that is supposed to take us through the semester. Our teacher handed us each an assigned envelope. Inside were different pictures of a scene that we are supposed to do research on to learn about who made it and when." She paused. "But when I got mine and opened it…"

She paused and just looked at us as if she didn't know how to finish her story,

"Well, I already knew it."

"Isn't that good?" I asked. "I mean, that way, you can be ahead in the class and already have your project done." I smiled. It sounded good to me.

"Well, yeah, I guess it would be, but the picture I got was the same as the picture I used for my final senior project back in school. I painted the picture. I'm the artist who literally dreamed it up. It was a weird dream I've had since I was little, and it's always of the same scene, so I decided to make it a project. But now I feel like I must have seen it somewhere before, because why would they have it here?"

Taylor sounded confused, like she'd already considered all the ways that this could have happened and come up with nothing. She pulled an envelope out of her bag and opened it. She turned the photo of the painting to show us.

Looking at the picture, something in my mind rang a bell. Something tugged at the edges of my memory, but I couldn't place it. I knew this scene, but I couldn't say from where or when. It was so familiar. I hadn't taken any art in high school except a clay modeling course to fill an elective credit, but we never did anything with paintings. I tried to wrack my brain for another minute.

" I think I have seen this before too. It looks familiar. I just can't place it." It was on the tip of my tongue, but I couldn't pull it out. I saw Taylor's face fall a little as I said it.

"I've seen it before," Hannah chimed in. "My grandma used to paint a lot, and she would do scenery. Or well, one specific scene in different ways," she went on. "Before she passed away, she had Alzheimer's. She didn't remember anything but this scene she kept painting. Her doctors told us to let her paint it since it seemed to calm her, which, in turn, helped her have a better quality of life. She always seemed to have clearer moments after she painted it."

Hannah's eyes seemed a little distant as the memory washed over her.

"The picture was always the same one. Sometimes, there were different colors or a few differences, but they were always the same." Hannah took a breath. "We saved one of the canvases and put it in the house. I'm sure my dad knows something about it." She looked at Taylor, who now had a defeated expression on her face.

"There's no way I copied that photo. I thought it was an original." Taylor shook her head. "For my project, the school did so many checks to make sure that no one cheated. There's just no way that I re-painted someone else's work." Taylor seemed more upset over her past work than her current dilemma. She looked back at the photo, her eyes darting over the landscape. She took a breath and put the picture back into the envelope as a shadow came across the light from our open common room door.

It was John. He poked his head in, just staring at us. Then he came right in and sat on one of the chairs, like he was right at home.

"Hey, guys. I just wanted to let you know that you three have first watch for night hosting this week. It'll be Wednesday, from ten in the evening to three in the morning." He paused. I think he expected us to complain. "You need to come to the night hosting meeting tonight." Then he got up and walked out. It was a short and simple conversation, but I felt myself wanting to laugh.

We spent some time re-arranging our room. Taylor helped us put up some of the decorations she'd ordered online before leaving for school. Soon, we were hungry but were running short on time. We headed down to the dining hall and grabbed some to-go containers.

This dining hall is great, I thought to myself. It was so nice to have a food area close to our dorm. I managed to get a good salad stuffed into the Styrofoam container and topped it with some cheesy breadsticks (one of my favorite foods in the entire world). Once the three of us were ready to go, we headed back to our room.

Later that night, Hannah looked at her watch. "Well, the evening went by, didn't it?"

Looking at my phone, I saw that it was already nine twenty-five. The meeting was in five minutes. I grabbed a pad of paper and a pen and handed them to Taylor, then went back into my room to get a sweatshirt. I wanted to make sure I didn't end up with goosebumps going up my arms again, whether from the cool air in the dorm or from someone watching us again.

As I put on my sweatshirt, I heard John banging on doors for people to come to the meeting. I don't know why I got such a kick out of his sense of humor, but I did. I also thought he would take care of business if ever we needed anything. Even though he put off that he was bored and tired of "dorm duty", as he'd called it when I'd overheard his conversations down the hall, he understood how to direct people and delegate.

We walked down the hall, to the common area. Hannah picked up some forms at the head table outside of John's office. Taylor and I followed her to some seats at the side of the room. Away from the back window this time, I noticed. I don't know if that was on purpose or subconsciously, but I didn't care. So far, we hadn't talked much about it. If it was a joke, it was a bad one, in my opinion.

I looked around at the people who had gathered. I think I was hoping to see the guy from the first meeting, but he wasn't there. I thought I recognized one of the guys from that night but couldn't quite remember.

John finally came back, bringing a group of guys with him. They went and took the back seats that we'd avoided. Hannah rolled her eyes. The guys were noisy and joking around, but they stopped talking as loudly when John finally came and sat with the group.

"Ahem," John started, trying to get everyone quiet. "This is the night hosting meeting. The signature forms are at the table right here." He picked up the pile of papers and put them back down on the table.

"Night hosting happens in groups of three to five. Your shifts vary in hours based on day of the week and time of the year. Each team of night hosts will rotate so that one group doesn't get more than others. If you want to trade shifts or give up a shift to another group, both parties must see me in person to get the go-ahead. I don't want to be stuck working a shift when I could be doing more important things."

He surveyed the room.

"The hours are pretty simple. Most of the time, you will start at ten p.m. and sit at the table, signing people in and out of the dorm hall. I will give you a new sheet at the beginning of your shift. I'll be in the office tonight and tomorrow, so Wednesday will be the first official start of the job. After ten p.m., everyone – and I don't care if it's your best friend's brother's girlfriend – *everyone* must give you their ID card. Every ID card, as I'm sure you noticed when you looked at yours, has your dorm hall printed on it. Those whose ID does not have a dorm hall or has a different one than this one must sign in. Those without college ID must present some form of photo ID and then sign in.

"This will usually go on until three a.m. Once three o'clock comes, you will slide the sign-in sheets under my office door for me to pick up in the morning." He paused.

"Does anyone have any questions?" He'd said it in a more matter-of-fact way than an actual question. Even if I did have a question, I don't think I would've asked it.

The outer doors of the entranceway swung open, and someone came in. Taking off his hat and coat, I saw that it was the guy from the other night. He looked right at me, then did something I wasn't expecting. He smiled. Involuntarily, I smiled back. Then he went and sat in front of me, so his back was what I was looking at now.

John looked annoyed at the interruption. "Nice of you to join us tonight," he said with a touch of venom in his voice.

"If anything happens during your shift and you feel like you need my help, my room is right down the hall from the entrance where the night hosting table is set."

He was being sarcastic. Everyone knew where his room was. It was hard to miss. There was a large RA sign on it with his name. I guessed he hated having to look at the sign all the time.

"Just come get me. There is also a telephone on the wall with which you can call campus police if the need arises. People don't like to sign in and out of the dorm, but you have to make them sign. It's as simple as that. Safety and..." He paused. "And covering our asses."

The room laughed.

"Seriously though," John began again, "it's a security measure to have you guys there. Every dorm on campus has this system, and it works. I won't have my dorm being the oddball, so make sure you do your job. If I catch you sleeping during your shift, you're off the job."

His face hardened for a moment as he again surveyed the room.

"Hand in the signature forms that you picked up and then you can go. I'll put the schedule up for you all later tonight or tomorrow morning."

With that, he got up and went back to his office. I watched him go, then sit in the office. I saw in through a hallway window that covered the top half of the wall next to the door. He was looking down at something. Then he got up and put something on the office door. He taped it there, so it wouldn't fall.

"Actually, I'll post the schedule now. Have fun." Then he went back in the office.

Hannah went up to the schedule. She knew already that we had the first night hosting shift because John had already told us, but she still had to check it. Taylor was talking to me about watching some re-runs of television shows. I was paying attention, but then my stomach flopped over as I realized the guy I'd been thinking about was not only looking at me but had gotten up and was walking in our general direction.

"Hey, I'm Sean," the mystery man said as he extended his hand. His voice sounded nice. I smiled and nodded, not knowing what to say. I heard Taylor giggle a little.

Why I couldn't find my words at that moment, I will never know.

"Hi. Emily," was all that I could put together. Clumsily, I grabbed his extended hand. We shook. His grip was solid. I couldn't believe I gave the "dead fish" shake from my end.

Oh, God. What a first impression, was all I could think to myself. But somehow, through my embarrassment, I felt something else. Was it warmth? And suddenly, I felt panic that my hand would get sweaty since yes, it was warming up. Thankfully, my awkwardly panicked moment was cut short.

"It looks like every Monday and Wednesday, we have night hosting for the next..." Hanna read from a paper in her hands, then stopped abruptly, looking between Sean and I. The realization that she'd interrupted came over her face, and I saw the smallest upturn of a smile on her lips right before she rolled her eyes and went back to our room.

I quickly let go of his hand. The warmth went away. I slid the underside of my hand on my pants, trying to gauge how sweaty it had gotten in the short seconds it had been in Sean's grip. I couldn't stop staring at him. I realized my mouth was open.

"That's our roommate, Hannah, and I'm Taylor," Taylor said, looking at me and then Sean. She smiled with what I was beginning to learn was her mischievous smile and then followed Hannah down the hallway.

I think she'd recognized my need for a rescue. I silently vowed to always make sure the coffee pot in our room was on and ready for her.

"So, is this your first year?" Sean asked me.

"Yes, freshman year," I said. I wasn't sure what else to say. Sean's eyes took the words from my mouth. He was attractive, and my limited experience muffled any clear thoughts.

Sean walked over to one of the chairs and sat down. The TV he'd been trying to fix the other night was next to him.

"Couldn't get the television to work the other day?" I said. *Why do I have to be so awkward?* I thought to myself. I felt my palms get sweaty again, a cold sweat this time. I sat on one of the chairs next to him.

"Oh, that old thing?" Sean replied, pointing his thumb at the metal box. "That thing's been here for ages. Last year, we pulled it up here from downstairs, and we've been trying to fix it since then. Sometimes it works. Sometimes it's just stubborn." He reached over and patted the old box as if it were a friendly pet.

"Ages?" I said. I wondered what year he was in. The TV seriously looked old. I mean, like one of the TVs my grandmother had in her house when I was small.

"Well, that's what John said. He told us the thing was here when he originally came here like ten years ago." He paused. "I don't even think it gets HD or anything." He squatted beside the brown and gray TV on the ground.

"Oh, I see. Are you guys night hosting too?" I asked him.

"Yeah, I did the gig last year, and it was nice to have the extra money, especially because it's an easy and entertaining job. You never know what's going to come through the doors." He stopped fiddling with the television and looked toward the front entrance. "Well, I'd better be going. I'm over on the other side of the floor, in room 13A, if you ever want to get coffee or something."

With that, Sean stood up. Involuntarily, so did I.

"I'll see you later, then," I said awkwardly.

What the heck is wrong with me?

Sean smiled, and my stomach dropped like I was on a roller coaster. Then he turned and walked down the hallway, toward the guys' side of the dorms.

I looked at the now-empty entrance to our dorm, then headed down to our room. I opened the door to both Taylor and Hannah waiting for me.

"Well!" Taylor said. She looked like a kid on Christmas morning. She was waiting for the scoop.

"Well, what?" I answered.

"Well, did you get his number?" She was to the point.

"Of course not! I just met him, and besides, I'm sure he's not interested. He's just a nice person that probably saw me staring at him and was just being social," I reasoned.

"Nah." She smiled. "He's into you. No guy will leave his buddies and come over and talk with a girl if he's not even the slightest bit interested," she said matter-of-factly. I was sure my cheeks were red now.

"You guys need to focus. There's no time for boys. We're at a critical part of our semester, and missing something that could be crucial for your academic success could impact your entire year," Hannah butted in.

She was right. I needed to think less about boys and more about school. It was only the first day after all.

"So, we're working Mondays and Wednesday for a couple weeks? How about weekends?" I asked, trying to change the subject.

"Not too many at first, but he only gave us like six weeks. It's not bad. At least we will get some study time and earn some extra money right off the bat," Taylor said, thankfully taking my lead. She handed me the paper that Hannah had gotten from John with the schedule on it. I put it down and then picked up my own class schedule. I still needed to remind myself where I was going in the morning.

The next day, we all actually had a class together. However that had worked out, I was grateful for it. All three of us had Anthropology together for both the longer

lecture class and the shorter lab class. When I'd gotten my schedule over the summer, I'd thought about dropping it, but when I found out that Hannah and Taylor both had it as well, I reconsidered.

Before I went to sleep, I laid my clothes out to go to the gym. I hadn't been to the college gym yet and wanted to see what equipment they had. I hadn't been for a run or workout since leaving home, and even though it had only been a couple of days, I felt like I needed to stretch my muscles some and let my mind get away. Something about working out always helped me clear my head and keep my anxiety and adrenaline in check.

"Night, guys. What time do we have to leave tomorrow?" I yelled through the rooms. I left the door to my room open into the common room, and Taylor and Hannah left theirs open as well.

"We should leave by seven-thirty," Hannah's voice came back.

"Wait, that's a half-hour early. Class isn't until eight, and it's only a five-minute walk. We don't need to leave until seven-fifty," Taylor said back.

"There's too much that gets done in the first class to even risk being late," Hannah replied. I felt a smile spread on my face. "Getting to the class, picking a seat, reading the syllabus, and making a good first impression, all of which, it seems to me, neither of you care about." As Hannah spoke, her voice got louder and faster.

"So, we'd better get to sleep, or tomorrow will be even more painful than right now." I heard her get out of bed and her feet walk across their room. Suddenly, the dim light coming from their room went out with the light click of a switch. I heard her footsteps go back to the bed and the covers be pulled over.

"Night, Mom," Taylor said sarcastically. I laughed and heard her laugh also.

"Good night!" Hannah snapped.

That night, I fell asleep without any tricks or counting sheep. I just fell asleep, and I think I even had a smile on my face.

CHAPTER EIGHT

Anthropology

Tuesday morning came. I was glad that I'd set my clothes out when I got out of bed. The cold room made me want to stay under my covers; they were a safe haven. I took a deep breath and realized that I hadn't even moved from how I'd gone to sleep the night before. It had been quite a while since I'd slept that soundly.

Ah, I might as well, I thought to myself as I got up.

I dressed and slipped on my sneakers. I opened the common room door into the hallway as quietly as possible. It was only about a half-mile to the gym. The morning was crisp, and I could see my breath as I walked. When I got to the recreation building, it seemed deserted. I hadn't passed anyone on the way.

Good, I thought. *Maybe it won't be crowded.* I opened the door and went in.

As I walked, in I smelled the familiar smell of a chlorinated pool and heard a whistle blow. Looking to the left, I could see through some clear windows into the pool. It looked like the swim team was practicing. There was a counter to my right. There was a sign-in sheet and a box beside it labeled "ID cards". I guess we were supposed to leave our cards here while we worked out. I placed my card in the mostly empty box, signed my name on the sign-in sheet, and headed over to the drinking fountain.

Normally, I avoided water fountains because they grossed me out. I always imagined the germs flowing into my water bottle as the water runs. This morning, however, I was afraid to wake up my roommates and had to rely on the fountain here.

I looked around, taking in the atmosphere. The room was like a huge gymnasium, with mirrors lining the walls on one entire side and clear windows on another wall, showing the pool next door. The back wall was black. The final wall, which was where the entrance was, had the sign-in desk and cubby boxes for people to put stuff in. I also saw two small doors that looked like entrances to locker rooms.

There was barely anyone in the gym. It was a total ghost town. There were a couple people in the weights section, two others on the treadmills, and a girl on a stationary bike, but that was it. And she wasn't dressed for working out at all. She wore a black skirt and fishnet stockings, a black top, and had either heavy white make-up or had just seen a ghost.

Maybe she's just checking it out, like I am, I thought to myself. *And if she isn't, who am I to judge? It's not like I dress that great all the time,* I went on in my head. I took a deep breath. I needed to work out and just get my mind clear.

I found an elliptical machine and jumped on. It was nice not worrying about there being enough equipment with it being so empty. I put my earpieces in and turned on my music. I set the elliptical for forty minutes and started looking around. It was easy with all the mirrors on the walls.

Some of the people in the weights section moved toward the check-in counter, and it looked like they were leaving. Scanning the reflection, I didn't see anyone besides myself and the stationary bike girl. The two who'd been on the treadmill were gone. It seemed like I was the only one there. It was nice to know if I came to the gym in the mornings, I'd be able to get in any workout I wanted.

The forty minutes went by fast. I had made a couple new music playlists before school started and hadn't listened to them yet. When the machine started the five-minute cool down, I jumped off and grabbed an equipment wipe and cleaned the sweat off. I grabbed my water bottle and headed to the stretching mats. I kept my earphones in but had my music off. I liked stretching in the quiet. I took a couple minutes to stretch my legs and then got ready to leave.

I stood up and turned to head out when I ran into stationary bike girl whom I'd seen earlier. She was standing so close, I could smell her. It smelled like she needed a shower after her workout because I had to take a step back. The sulfur-like smell emanating from her clothes made me cringe.

"Do you think I didn't see you looking at me?" she growled.

I took my earphones out of my ears. "What? Oh, I'm sorry. I didn't mean to run into you," I said. I was a little confused.

"Didn't you hear me?" she went on. "I saw you looking at me." She took a step forward. She was staring at me with a deer-in-headlights stare. Her eyes were wild. They were a strange color. They were almost purple but then looked brown, almost like mud depending on how the light hit them. Oddly enough, I found myself wondering if she had contacts.

"I'm sorry. Nice to meet you. My name is Emily." I decided to be nice. It was all I could think to do. She didn't reply, so I stepped around her and headed back toward the front desk.

The girl grabbed my arm.

My heart almost stopped. It felt like electricity shot up and down my forearm. Not only that, but the way she grabbed me hurt. She continued to hold my arm in an iron grip. Her eyes – I have no idea how – seemed to get wider.

"I have to go. Please stop," I almost shouted at her. By this time, I felt my normally sleepy temper beginning to wake. *Why isn't she letting me go?* I hated it when someone

I didn't know touched me. I felt a betrayal of my privacy and panic.

Trying to concentrate on my breathing, I grabbed her hand with my other one and tried to pry her fingers away from my sore arm. The electric shock happened in the other hand touching her, and I sucked in some air out of surprise. She noticed that and loosened her grip slightly, staring at me in surprise.

"Ladies, is there a problem?" a voice came from behind us. I turned to see a woman coming toward us with a towel in her hand. She was thin, about my height, and blonde. She looked to be middle-aged, maybe fifty. She wore a nametag on the upper right corner of her navy-blue shirt. Her pants were beige.

The girl let go of my arm. She then turned and, without a word, walked out of the gym, stopping only at the other side of the open door to glare at me once more. I just stared after her. My arm was killing me. It felt like pins and needles going up and down, as if they had been asleep. I rubbed at it with my other sore hand, trying to get circulation back. I guessed her grip was stronger than I'd thought.

"I'm sorry," I told the woman who had come to my rescue. "I'm not sure what I did to offend her. Thanks for your help." I wanted to say more but was still embarrassed.

"Not to worry. You should be getting to class though."

She paused and stared at me as if she were adding something up in her head. Calculating my existence. Another moment passed.

"All right now?" she asked with a nod, her eyes continuing to scrutinize me.

"Yes, thanks," I said and turned to go.

"Don't forget your ID card on the way out," she called after me.

I put my arm out and grabbed my ID card out of the empty basket as I walked by. Looking at the clock, I decided I should run back to the dorms. It did me good. I was a little freaked out.

When I got back, I had just enough time to grab a quick shower and change. Taylor had a coffee waiting for me when I got out of my room to walk to class. Hannah was already standing at the door with her bookbag and coffee, waiting for us.

"Thanks so much," I said as Taylor handed me my drink.

"No problem," she said.

"Come on, guys. We have to go. We want to make sure to get a good seat," Hannah called as she walked out the door and down the hall. Taylor and I stayed to make sure the lock clicked shut and then headed after her.

As we walked, we chatted about what we thought the class was going to be about.

"Hey, I think I ran into the angry girl from your art class at the gym this morning, Taylor," I said as we turned to go across the main courtyard.

She laughed. "Really? She doesn't strike me as a gym-goer."

"That's just it," I mused. "She was at the gym in her regular clothes, just sitting on the machines. I saw her in the beginning and then worked out and didn't see her." I took a breath. "But when I got done stretching, she came over to me and acted like I'd insulted her somehow. I didn't even do anything to her."

"That's weird." Hannah had slowed her pace and been listening to us. "This girl sounds like she needs help or something." She picked up her pace again, so Taylor and I had to walk faster.

"Yeah, I'm glad one of the staff members was there and broke it up. When the girl saw the lady that came to see what was going on, she kind of gave up and left." I laughed.

"Well, I'll give her the stink eye next class for you, if you want," Taylor joked. It was nice knowing that I had people around me that would help me out.

"No, just ignore her. It would only make things weird for you in class," I told her. "But thanks though," I added.

We got to our building. It was old and looked like it had ten stories to it. I knew that it had a basement and about three levels, but I guessed the elaborate windows at the top were only for decoration.

We walked through some swinging doors at the front and followed the signs to the auditorium.

It was busy, but there were still seats left when we arrived at our room. We entered the stadium classroom from the back and could see down to the front, where the narrowing of the aisles came to a head at a small stage with a podium and a projection mount. The stage was empty except for a small chair and, behind the podium, a small stepstool.

As we walked in, Hannah went over to one of the tables at the back and picked up a small stack of papers. She distributed one to both Taylor and myself, then she took the initiative and led us down an aisle. Of course, we were going to sit together.

"Hold on a minute." Taylor stopped. "No way am I sitting in the front. It's too close." Hannah looked from her to me, then to the aisle seats.

"What do you mean?" she questioned. I laughed. Taylor turned and went back about five rows and sat in the same place of that row that Hannah wanted in the front one.

"This is as close as I get." Taylor sat with finality.

Hannah stood where she was for a second and then slowly followed to where Taylor was sitting. "Fine, but if

I can't hear or if there's anyone talking back here, I'm moving." And with that, she sat down.

I looked at them. "Am I going to have to separate you two when class hasn't even started yet?" I said, and thankfully, we all laughed. It was nice being able to joke around. I knew they weren't mad at each other.

Both Hannah and Taylor complemented each other well, with one being laid-back and the other scheduled. *Where do I fit in?* I found myself wondering. I dismissed the thoughts. They wouldn't get me anywhere. Everything was going so well. We were having a good time together and got along great. It made being away from home not quite as bad. It was a little strange to feel so comfortable with people I just met though.

Hannah looked through the papers that she had picked up. I looked down at them in my lap.

"This looks like the syllabus," Hannah noted. "Here we are," she said, turning a few more pages in the packet. "Our first assignment is due pretty quick." Somehow, she'd already gotten out her date book and was filling it out. "It looks like the rough draft of our first project is due next week, then it seems to drag on a bit, with bits and pieces due over the remainder of the semester." She read with the syllabus so close to her face, I didn't know how she could even see it.

"What's the assignment?" I asked her as I opened my own copy of the syllabus.

"It looks like a family tree," she said, reading through the text.

Taylor opened her syllabus and went through it. "I thought this was supposed to be one of those easy classes where you just get your work done and get the grade. This looks way more complicated than that."

"Well, at least we can work on it during night hosting and get stuff done." I couldn't think of anything else to say, but thinking about that, I was glad I'd signed up. If I had any questions about the assignment, it would be nice to bounce ideas off my roommates.

The class hushed, then the sound of clicking heels came across the front stage. A woman with high heels, bushy blonde hair, and gold rimmed glasses walked up to the podium. She was petite but about my height. She carried herself like she was used to being in charge. She got to the microphone and began.

"Hello, everyone. My name is Mrs. Jean Trebule. I will be your teacher for this Anthropology 101 lecture class." She had a slight accent that I couldn't place.

I wondered where she was from. She spoke English well. I almost couldn't hear the accent, but I could just make it out. She looked familiar. In a second, I realized why. This was the same woman from the gym this morning. I didn't recognize her right away because she was dressed differently and her hair wasn't pulled in the same way as before. I leaned down and over to where Taylor was sitting.

"Hey, that's the lady that helped me out at the gym this morning."

Hannah turned and gave me a look that could kill. Taylor leaned over, whispered a short "uh-huh," and nodded in Hannah's direction with a little half-smile.

"This class will teach you about your heritage in a way that will strengthen your bond with your fellow human. You will learn about genetics and history and how often your history is not what it seems," Mrs. Trebule went on. "Now let me introduce you to my assistant, Elaine. She will be your course instructor for your Thursday lab class." She paused. "Elaine." She moved her arm over and motioned for someone to come out onto stage.

A young woman began walking across the stage. My stomach churned, and at the same time, I felt the room narrow. It was the young woman who had walked down the aisle during our orientation classes. We looked between ourselves.

"What the fuck?" mouthed Taylor. Even Hannah chanced a look away from the front of the auditorium to widen her eyes at us in surprise.

We watched as the young woman gave a slight wave and a forced smile to the class. She walked up to the podium and leaned to Mrs. Trebule to whisper in her ear.

At that moment, time seemed to stop, and there was silence. Mrs. Trebule turned her head and looked directly at us. I had to look somewhere else. No one else in the class was looking where she was; they all stared straight ahead. It was so quiet. I looked at Taylor and Hannah.

"What's going on?" I whispered. Both the assistant and the teacher were staring at us now.

Then, as quickly as it had started, it stopped. Both women turned to look at the rest of the class. I heard someone from behind us clear their throat with a dry cough.

"Students, you will be doing many assignments during this semester. I advise you to take note of when the due dates are. Rough drafts are not extra credit but count toward your class participation grade and must be turned in as promptly as your final drafts. The only difference is that you will turn the rough drafts in during your course lab class, to Elaine, and the final drafts in the lecture class, to me.

"Your first project will be the family tree. You must fill out a timeline for your family tree and give as much detail as possible. This will help to shape a later assignment, so make sure to follow the directions. The rough drafts are going to be due right away to get things moving."

The class gave a collective sigh. It was rare to get homework on the first day of a class. The only one I knew who probably wasn't disappointed was Hannah.

The rest of the class was uneventful but interesting. We learned about some of the theories behind human evolution. Then, after a PowerPoint with some vocabulary she wanted us to be familiar with, the class was over.

"Was it just me, or did that get a little strange in the beginning?" Taylor said when people began to leave. "I mean, she looked right at us, right? And the assistant. That's the same girl that walked through our classes during orientation. This is some joke."

"Maybe it's not a joke," Hannah said. "Maybe we are reading too much into what we are seeing." She had a point. "Anyway, we have too much work to do to spend so much time worrying whether someone's playing a joke on us." With that, Hannah decided it was time to get going. She got up and started toward the aisle. Taylor and I got up and followed.

I had a weird feeling, a mix of nerves, anxiety, and dread. I couldn't place all of it. I decided to put it out of my mind. Hannah was right; we had too much to do with school starting to worry about something that was probably nothing. It was only the second day of school, and this was just the first class.

We reached the top of the stairway. Hannah was already waiting for us. "I know what you are thinking. It's ridiculous, and you guys watch way too many scary movies. I've got class in the Shaw building in about fifteen minutes. I'll see you tonight in the common room, if you both don't get too scared before I get back." She smiled and then turned and walked away.

Taylor had to get going to a graphic design class, and I needed to get to a biology lab, so we waved bye and got moving.

The rest of the day, I couldn't shake the feeling of anxiety, no matter what I tried. I even tried to sit outside for a fifteen-minute break between one of my classes and relax. It didn't help. By the end of the day, I was exhausted.

I managed to get my dad on the phone for a couple minutes and check in to see how he and Cindy were. The second I heard him on the phone, I missed home. I had tried to write down some of my family tree myself earlier in the day when I'd had a break, but I still had a way to go and hoped that he'd be able to help me with it. I had down Mom, Dad, and me, then my aunts and uncles, and of course, my grandparents on both sides. But that was about it. Dad helped me get a bit further back and said he'd think about it, and if he remembered any more, he'd let me know. He said if that wasn't good enough for my project, then I should call my mom's sister.

"That would be my aunt, Dad," I told him jokingly.

Things weren't the same in the family since Mom's death. Some of her relatives hadn't come to visit or reached out since she'd died. It made me sad, but I'd been so busy, I hadn't thought too much about it lately. I wondered why.

At least in the conversation with my dad, I had learned something new though. On my mom's side, I had an adopted great, great, great grandmother, and he was able to trace it back to 1765 from an old family bible that Mom had in their room.

Dad had opened the front fold of the old book and out had come a leaf of paper that he'd thought was once attached. It was a list of those who had passed the bible down and listed their family members, the mother giving the book to her eldest daughter. It began with this great, great, great grandmother and her husband. He told me he would mail me the paper.

Later that night, I could barely stay awake. I literally fell into bed. I was so tired, I didn't even dream.

CHAPTER NINE

Night Hosting

Wednesday was busy. It went by in a blur for me. I skipped the gym since I was still tired from the last few days, and I wasn't ready to find out if the crazy girl was going to be there again. I made it to Economics and got there with enough time to get out my assignment calendar and start putting the day's agenda in it.

As I opened the datebook to this week, right there at the top of "Wednesday" was hand-written in blue ink, "Night Hosting, 10 to 3". Apparently, I had left my assignment calendar out, and Hannah must have put it in. I wasn't mad. I was more amused than anything and knew it was a nice gesture. I smiled. So far, my roommates had turned out to be nice.

My mind started to wander then, which was never a good idea. I started thinking about home and Dad and Mom. I started thinking about my friends from school. I thought about Sean. When I'd left Wednesday morning for class, I noticed someone had written a phone number on our whiteboard. "Text me if you want to get coffee," it had said underneath the number. I knew it was him.

Maybe Taylor was right, I thought to myself. But then I found myself thinking about how it was only the first week of school and that he was probably just a friendly person. I told myself that I was reading too much into all of it. I tried to put everything out of my mind except what I had to do that morning.

I got out my phone and looked at the new contact I'd put in. It was labelled "Sean from Dorm", and his number was underneath. I pressed the icons to go onto a couple social media websites and just watched what was going on in the computer world. I heard the door open, and our teacher, Dr. Eagles, walked in. I put my phone away.

Today, he had on a gray suit and a yellow bow-tie. As he got to the front, he slid his backpack off his shoulder, which was open, and spilled papers onto the table and over onto the floor like a waterfall.

"My, my, what a morning," he said as he bent to pick up the papers. A couple of us sitting in front got up to help him. I went to sit back in my seat, and class started.

I was sitting up close, and I could tell that the poor guy must have been in a rush this morning. He'd taken his jacket off, and I saw beads of perspiration on his forehead and sweat marks under his arms, coming through his button-down shirt. The sweet scent of cinnamon and sweat wafted over once in a while when he would walk from side to side, writing on the whiteboard.

The day was long but busy. I decided to text Sean and see if he wanted to have coffee on Friday morning before class. It was going to be early, but the way I looked at it, morning classes were starting, and if the meeting went poorly, I could just say that I needed to leave to get there early. I didn't think he would say "yes", though.

Surprisingly, he did. I heard the text message come across as I got back to my room that afternoon. Looking down, I smiled.

"Coffee sounds great. See you Friday morning outside the Shaw building," it said. I didn't text him right back. I didn't want to seem like I was watching for his message.

When I got into our common room, Hannah and Taylor's door was open, but I only saw Taylor. She'd pulled up a footstool next to the couch in the common room and had arranged paint supplies next to her. She was painting on an easel, and from the looks of it, she had real talent. It was beautiful. Her paint palette was on the floor, and she was pushing shadows into the castle walls with her thumb. I broke her concentration.

"Hey, how's it going?" she said with a smile.

"Hey. Good," I replied as I put down my bookbag. "I've got lots of homework this weekend. How was your Wednesday?"

"Oh, good. That girl in my Landscape class is a pill though. I almost blew a gasket this morning when she decided she would sit right next to me instead of across the table, like last time."

She rolled her eyes and went back to her painting. She wiped her hand on a towel lying across her lap and picked up the palette from the ground.

"I mean, isn't this the kind of thing that we were supposed to leave in high school?" She pushed her thumb onto the palette and then onto the canvas again.

"What are you working on?" I couldn't stop staring at the picture she was working on. The detail in the artwork was astonishing.

"Oh, nothing. I just like to paint when I'm stressed. And it better be good, because I always paint this castle. I'm obsessed with it." She laughed a different laugh than her happy one, like she was stressed. She looked away from the painting and up at me, almost like she was embarrassed to talk about her work. Then she looked back at her painting, surveying her progress, and went on.

"Sometimes I feel like I eat, sleep, and breathe this castle. I just love it." She moved herself back from the canvas and looked at her work. "But I never feel like the painting is done." She had a puzzling look on her face. "It's like I have it in my head, but it never comes out right. I always paint it again, to see if it changes, or if I like it better." I had the feeling she was talking to herself rather than me. I got the impression that she painted the castle out of need more than want.

"Crazy, I know. Oh, well." She took a breath. "The life of an artist," she laughed. I joined her on the couch and pulled out a book.

"Well, I think it looks great," I said, and I meant it.

The painting felt oddly familiar to me, as if I'd seen it somewhere before. It was a beautiful castle that sat on a small plot of land, which hovered over more land. A castle in the sky. The main body of it was a tower, and toward the top, there were sections that branched out. At the top was a small bridge that went out several steps and then ended, as if the tower was once part of a larger castle but had been ripped away. It looked old.

I stared at the painting, not wanting to take my eyes away from it. I looked up, and Taylor was looking at me and the painting.

"See what I mean?" She started putting the painting supplies back in a bag next to the stool on the floor.

"So, I guess we have night hosting tonight?" I said, then tore myself away from the picture. My eyes stung in protest, as if I hadn't blinked the entire time I'd been looking at it. I walked to my room to put down my bag. I felt like my eyes had been caught in a flash, and I had the outlines of the castle burned into them as I walked into my room.

"Ha, yeah. Did you get the little memo on your datebook too?" she said and gave a small laugh.

"Yes. Hannah must have left us reminders to make sure we didn't forget."

I pulled some of my folders out of my bag and set them on my desk. I came back into the common room and grabbed a Fresca soda out of the mini-fridge we had.

"How's your family tree project coming?" I asked Taylor as I cracked the tab on my soda top. The drink fizzed as the carbonation took in the new space of the open container. Bubbles escaped up onto the lid.

"Good. I made us some trees on the computer, so we could hand them in and have them look like an actual family tree." She got up and went into their room quickly, then came back with a piece of paper. She handed it to me. It was a white sheet of computer paper that had a tree trunk on the front and branches out to the sides. At the end of each branch was a line where we could put the name of the family member.

"Nice. Thanks a lot," I said. That would make filling it in easier than just listing it.

"I'll bring them tonight when we go to the J-O-B." She smiled and took the paper back into their room.

I went back in my room. I had to get some work done. I didn't want to get behind so early in the semester. I laughed to myself. *Now I'm thinking like Hannah*, I thought. I sat at my desk to get some work done.

Hannah got back later in the evening. She looked tired, but she seemed in good spirits. She said "hello" to Taylor and me, then she headed into their room. I heard a bookbag unzipping and a chair moving on the floor. She was already getting to work.

The evening turned into night quickly, and before I knew it, it was time to go down the hall for night hosting. I packed my backpack and put my laptop in. I had to carry the electric cord. Taylor grabbed some bottles of water for us from the refrigerator, and Hannah met us in the common room, carrying what looked like all of our homework combined.

We walked down the hallway to the front entrance room, and John was in his office. When he saw us, he got up and pushed back his chair.

"Right, so here's the deal. You guys are night hosting tonight. All you have to do, besides stay awake the entire time, is sign people in and out of the building. It sounds simple, and for the most part, it is. But there are always those people who want to buck the system. They think they are better than everybody else just because they walk the earth."

He paused to take a breath.

"But that's another conversation for another time. At ten p.m., all the entrance doors' sliding keypads will lock except for this front one here. Everyone must come through the front door. There's a sign on every door with dorm hours and a notice of the time when the doors lock, so there should be no surprises. Each person who walks through the door must show a dorm ID card. If they don't have one, they have to show the ID card of the person they are meeting with in the dorm."

John turned and went back to his office quick, which didn't take long because he had long legs and was tall. He came back carrying a black, three-ring binder with a sticker with the word "Log" written in black ink on the front.

"This is the sign-in log. Everyone who comes through those doors during the time you are on duty must sign in. We have cameras at the entrances of the other doors that turn on at night, so we will know if there is anyone letting people in without signing in. Don't worry about that." He looked at us expectantly. "Any questions?"

By this time, it was about ten-fifteen, and the hallways were quiet. When neither of us answered him John took a step back and looked at us.

"Ok, wonderful. I'll be down there in my room. If you guys need anything, just knock." With that, he turned and went in the direction he'd just pointed, leaving us alone next to a row of tables where we were supposed to sit.

We sat down. Hannah, in the middle, arranged the sign-in papers and log book upside-down so that it would look right to those entering the hall.

"Should we use black or blue ink?" Hannah asked.

"What does it matter?" Taylor asked.

"Well, if there were a copy made, blue ink would be the one to show up as the original copy, rather than a replica," she said matter-of-factly. Hannah looked at me expectantly.

"I guess blue, to be on the safe side," I said slowly.

"Yes, that sounds right," Hannah stated. She separated the blue pens and stowed away the black ones.

We got our laptops out and plugged them in, then got out our homework. Taylor pulled out a small stack of papers. She handed down a piece for me and for Hannah. It was the family tree that she'd created. Looking at the design, I noticed a bit more than I had at first back in the common room. Each side of the tree was different. The left side of the branches were for male, and the right side for female family members. From the base of the tree, where the family originates, the tree grew taller as the family extended and branched out as each individual family grew. I was impressed. She'd put good thought into this tree.

"How did your research go for the project in Anthropology?" Hannah asked as she looked at her paper. I saw her eyes calculating the spaces as she mentally reviewed her heritage.

"It went okay, I guess. I got all the way back on my dad's side through to the sixteen hundreds, then on my mom's side, I got back to her great, great, great grandmother back in Albany, New York. I think it was 1765, and that's where I stopped." Taylor reviewed her paper tree. She was smiling, proud of herself that she'd gotten that far. I was impressed; my tree hadn't turned out so full.

"You're putting me on!" Hannah said. She looked at her and then took the sheet from in front of Taylor. She put it side-by-side with hers. She looked back and forth, comparing the two.

"I went back way further on my dad's side, but was stuck on my mom's side with her great, great, great grandma the same year, 1765," Hannah said.

"Are you sure your tree is the same?" Hannah looked at Taylor expectantly.

"Well, even though I haven't known you long, I already know not to joke with you about homework, so no, I'm not joking," Taylor replied sarcastically and grabbed her family tree. "Of course, I'm sure. I worked on it the day we got the assignment and again last night. It's no big deal. I'm sure other people have similar trees. Why are you worrying about it?" Taylor said as she got out some other homework.

"What about you?" Hannah said as she put her paper down again in front of her. "How far back did you get?" She looked at me.

"Um," I said. "I had some trouble getting the dates and people from my dad. He couldn't remember all of it, so I've got enough for now, I'm sure. He said he'd give me my aunt's number if I needed more."

I didn't want to show them my paper. I decided I would go through it again before turning it in or showing them. I'd wait until I had it all down on the tree Taylor made for us. *There must be some kind of a mistake,* I thought as I began trying to figure out how I would have time to call my dad again and figure out what went wrong when I'd written my family history down.

I didn't want to say anything. So, I put away my paper like it didn't matter to me – even though it did – and I grabbed my math book. At least with math, I could get a black-and-white answer. It wasn't like the family tree, where it could be this or that, and there was nothing concrete to go off of. Thankfully, Hannah and Taylor picked up that I didn't want to talk about it anymore, and no one pressed me for more.

"Well, you are probably right," Hannah said to Taylor and me. "I'm sure other people have similar trees too. I mean, we all came from somewhere, right?" She paused. "Maybe that's what Mrs. Trebule was talking about when she said that the course this year was going to teach us about our past and how we were all so similar and connected."

"Yeah, you must be right. Going back that far, lots of people are going to be from the Northeast, and there are bound to be some people whose family is from the same area. And since most of us are in the same class, maybe ages will be similar as well," I said. I was stalling, hoping the subject would change soon.

I had the anxiety back in my stomach. It wasn't even the second week, and I already was dreading a class. I had gone to counseling the year before, after my mother had passed away. The lady I sat with week after week was nice, but I didn't feel any different after completing my sessions. I did learn, however, how to halt my anxiety when it hit me. She taught me how to "modify my anxious thoughts". If I didn't do that now, I could end up wasting my entire night and not getting anything done. I needed to concentrate on math homework. Something other than the family tree.

The night went on, and the hours crept by. Thankfully, there weren't many students coming and going. I was sure that would change as the year went on. Around midnight, we started to hear the wind pick up outside.

"Was it supposed to storm tonight?" Taylor asked.

"I'm not sure. I didn't look on the TV before we came out here," Hannah replied.

"Either way, it looks like it's going to now," Taylor said.

There was a streetlight outside in front of our building. I saw the wind blowing the tree branches in the shadows violently, as if wreaking vengeance on the foliage outdoors. It started to rain. Or, well, *pour* is more like it. The wind whipped branches and leaves past by the front glass door. I heard thunder through the walls of the dorm.

Occasionally, there was a flash and crack of lightning. This storm was nothing like anything I'd seen in California.

Where we were sitting, facing the windowed entrance to the building, it was like being in the front row of a theater. We all stared at it. We could see our own reflections, and through that, we saw the outdoors, wild and unbridled and furious.

Then we heard a loud crack, and everything went dark. Not just dark, but the kind of dark where you can't see your own hand in front of your face. Pitch-black. A few seconds went by and nothing happened. I felt like my breath was the loudest thing in the room. I could hear my own heartbeat.

"Hey, you okay down there?" John yelled down the hallway. "I have some flashlights here. I'll get them, and we can meet. We have to watch the stairs to make sure no one falls." I could barely tell the direction he was coming from.

I heard Hannah, who was sitting next to me, push her chair back from the table and move to stand up. Then one of the computer battery cables at my feet jerked, and I heard an intake of breath.

Involuntarily, I put out my hand as I knew she was about to fall.

"I got you," Taylor said at the same time I grabbed Hannah's hand. She must have assumed, as I had, that Hannah was in process of tripping over the cord.

Somehow, in the darkness, Hannah found my hand, and I felt her weight even out as she grabbed Taylor's hand.

"Thanks," Hannah said with a little laugh.

The air had shut off, and as we stood there, it started to get stagnant and warm. I noticed two lights in the reflection of the unmoving sliding doors entrance. The light outside was out, but it looked like two headlights sitting in front of the building, pointing in. The room was getting lighter from the reflection. I looked around.

I could just make out Hannah and Taylor, though everything was in a grayish-blue light.

"Why is that car sitting there?" Hannah said. Both she and Taylor were still staring at the window. As I looked at them, I noticed something from the corner of my eye and looked down.

My eyes passed over our shut-off laptops, which didn't make any sense to me whatsoever, and onto the table. Then I saw what was making the reflection. Where my hand and Hannah's were locked in place, bright, small beams of light were coming through. And it was getting brighter.

I leaned forward and looked at Taylor and Hannah's hands, and the same thing was happening.

"Um, that's because it's not coming from outside," I whispered. I couldn't take my eyes off our hands. Just like where Hannah's and my hands were grasped, so were

Taylor and Hannah's hands. Small tendrils of bright light came through and wrapped themselves around our palms where our flesh connected. Taylor and Hannah must have been as surprised as I was.

"Jesus," Taylor whispered. In unison, we detached ourselves from each other as if each of us were carrying the plague. I stared at my hands. The light was now gone.

"Hey, so did you guys bring some flashlights with you or what?" John yelled down the hallway.

"No, we're coming." Hannah moved around the table carefully, trying to avoid the cord that tripped her earlier. We both followed her. No one mentioned anything about what we had just seen.

We made it to John, who, by this time, was way down the hall on the boys' side of the dormitory floor and heading to the staircase. There were a few people who had opened their room doors and were looking around in the dim light of the flashlights.

"Just a power outage. Go back in your rooms. The generator will pick up in a minute," John shouted.

He was right. I heard a low hum from what sounded like the ceiling and floor at the same time. Then a couple bangs and the lights flickered. The ceiling lights came on dimly, and the air kicked in and started circulating.

We were far away from the night hosting table by this time, having followed the light from John's flashlight down the hallway, but we were facing the table when the lights started to come back on. I felt goosebumps run up my arms. Looking at the table now in the light, there was a man standing there. He was dressed in black. He was pale and thin and had black hair that looked soaked and plastered to his forehead. There was mud he had tracked in on his boots, giving the floor where he was standing a look of filth. He was just standing there, staring at the table. His shoulders were hunched. I couldn't see his facial expression from where I was.

I knew the other two had to see him; we were all facing the same way.

"Hey, can I help you?" John yelled. He took a step toward the entrance. There was something oddly protective in the step, I thought to myself. The air in the hallway must have been getting stagnant quick. I recognized the smell from the gym the other morning. The sulfuric, acidic smell.

The man turned, and I heard him gasp. The generator gave another kick, and the lights went totally out. For some reason, our flashlights flickered. It was pitch-black.

And then, before we knew it, the lights came back on. It was so bright that I had to squint. The man was gone. Next to our night hosting table, as far as we could see down the hall, was nothing except our chairs and the mud that the strange man had tracked in.

John rolled his eyes. "Well, that was an eventful end of the night for you guys. Your shift is almost over. You can go back and finish it. Take the flashlights with you, and just give them back to me tomorrow sometime." John paused. "I should go call maintenance and see if there's anything I need to do before morning, so I'll be up."

And with that, John went down the hall, to the office door. He didn't seem too happy. He had mentioned before that he didn't like to get woken up, but I got the sense that he would have our backs if anything ever happened and we needed him.

We went back to the table and sat down.

"Why didn't our laptops stay on?" Taylor asked. "I'm glad I saved what I was working on." She rebooted her computer.

"Yeah, maybe lightning hit the building, and they shut off for safety or something? A power outage, maybe? But I think the battery would kick in." Hannah picked up her laptop and turned it over. "If this thing is fried from whatever that was, I'm going to be in trouble. Laptops aren't cheap." She put the computer back on the table and started rebooting hers too.

"That was some storm," I said. "They certainly don't have weather like that in San Diego." I laughed a little, feeling the tension in the room and hoping no one would bring up what had just happened.

Apparently, the other two felt the same way. No one brought up the light, the man at the table, or the storm again that night. Finally, another hour later, our shift was up. The mood was dampened though. I went back to our room thinking about how, when my mom was alive, I would tell her whenever I got the goosebumps running up my arms. She would always listen and help me figure out why I was scared or how I was feeling. We even kept a dream journal, she and I. We would share our dreams sometimes. Sometimes we would even have similar ones.

Lying in bed, I smiled, remembering our dream journal conversations. Boy, would she get a kick out of some of the ones I'd had lately and out of some of the people I've met. I wished I could talk to her. She would know just what to say.

I hadn't kept the dream journal since she had died. It was something we did together, like our secret. I don't think she even told Dad about it. It was just for us.

Suddenly, I remembered my family tree project and how I hadn't filled out what I need to while we were at the table. With a small internal whimper, I tip-toed out of bed and quietly shut my door to our common room so as not to wake my roommates by turning on my light. I flipped the light switch, got out my family tree paper, and started filling it out.

CHAPTER TEN

Elaine

"Get up, Emily. We have to go." The pounding on the door and the incessant voice was the first thing I heard as I was startled awake, even though I wasn't fully aware of my surroundings, I obeyed and opened my eyes. The grit from the night's sleep made them itch, and my eyelids felt like sandpaper.

I read the clock on my phone after fumbling to pick it up from the side table by my bed. It took me only an instant to realize that I had five minutes before I needed to walk out the door to class.

Alarm. I had forgotten to set my phone's alarm when I'd gone to bed the previous night.

I jumped out of bed and opened the door.

"Wakey, wakey, sleepyhead," Taylor laughed, standing in the doorway. She laughed. Hannah was behind her, getting her bookbag ready. How had I not heard them at all?

"I'll be ready in just a second," I said. I went back into my room and threw off my pajamas, then threw on last night's jeans and sweatshirt. I put my hair in a ponytail and grabbed my bag. I didn't even think about looking in a mirror and wasn't sure I even wanted to.

I heard the coffee machine going in the common room, and I saw Taylor getting one last cup before we headed out. We left. Taylor handed the cup to me with a smile.

"Rough night, honey?" she said with a smirk.

"Man, I'm going to have to get used to that night hosting if we've got an early class the next day," I said. There was no trace of the tension that had resulted from the previous night's events. Hannah was already out the door and halfway down the hallway when our door shut.

"Thanks. I needed this today," I told Taylor as I sipped on the liquid gold. "That's good. I think you have a talent for making coffee."

"Well, it's easy. Just stay up until three in the morning and then get up at seven-thirty. The exhaustion makes it taste better." She laughed, and so did I.

Hannah was still a couple strides in front of us but slowed down as we caught up. It was nice walking with both of my roommates. No one talked about night hosting or mentioned anything about the night before. I even started to think that I had exaggerated it in my own head. Maybe it was just stress and lack of sleep, and my mind was playing tricks on me.

"I wonder how this morning is going to go," Hannah said. "Our lab class is with the teaching assistant, E-laine," she went on, sounding out Elaine's name slowly with a smirk.

"Yeah, I know," Taylor chimed in. "Maybe there was no prank or joke, and maybe she was just looking for something in the classes during orientation." She sounded convincing. I wanted to believe it, but something still felt off.

We walked up the steps to one of the newly renovated buildings on campus. Our larger lecture class was in a different, older building that was only half-renovated. Our lab class for Anthropology was in a different building. This building was large and pale yellow, with small, young vines crawling up the brick sides. With the new renovations, the vines hadn't yet taken over the walls, climbing up higher than the eye could see.

When we got to our room, it wasn't too full. The individual seats were arranged into rows and aisles. Hannah took one in the front, and Taylor took one right behind her. I took the third seat back. The floor was a whitish-gray, speckled tile with scuff marks on it from the table desks. The chalkboard read, "Anthropology lecture B". I knew there were several classes for the section since the main lecture class was so large. I was glad Hannah and Taylor were both in the same one as me.

A couple minutes after we sat down, Elaine walked in. She shut the door behind her, and the final click of it shutting and locking felt like a strange imprisonment to me. The sound was loud, and immediately, the class went silent. I took a breath and tried to focus.

"Ladies and gentlemen, you will have five minutes after class begins before this door is locked. I will be taking attendance, and Mrs. Trebule will be notified of your final number of absences, should you have any, and will take that into account when determining your final grade." She stopped talking and walked from the door, where she'd shut us in, to her desk at the front of the class.

"According to your syllabus, your first assignment is due today. The family tree rough draft. I trust you all have it with you. Please place your project in the box I will provide and pass to the next student who still needs to turn in their assignment."

Elaine paused and picked up a stack of papers from her desk.

"I will now be passing out an article for you to read. You will need to know the contents for our session next week. Also, please summarize the article in your own words, related to how the topic fits into your family tree project."

She paused and looked the class over. When her head turned in the direction of where we were sitting, I felt like she lingered there, but then her eyes kept moving. It took surprisingly long with the classroom being so small.

Elaine walked back to her desk and picked up a box and a stack of papers. She handed the box to the guy sitting in the front corner of the class, then walked to the opposite side and gave the stack of papers to a girl sitting there. The girl looked at the article and then passed them back.

I turned my head to follow the box. It was an aisle away from us. I didn't know why, but I was nervous about turning in the assignment, which was ridiculous, I told myself.

A few seconds later, I received the box from behind me and placed my paper in it. I handed it to Taylor in front of me just as she turned to hand me the stack of articles. I looked down at the article. "Decisions of the Past: Decisions and situations from the past that shaped man's future" was the title. Further down, the article read: "How choices made from the beginning have changed the way man is able to make decisions and live. We are all interdependent."

The article looked long. There must have been five pages, front and back.

"Now that we have taken care of some logistics, I'd like you all to look around the room. Notice that there are some skulls and bones, as well as rocks and maps and other things in jars all along the wall. By the end of this course, you will be able to understand many of the reasons for the changes humans underwent over the centuries, as well as some of the environmental changes that have taken place and are currently taking place as we speak."

She paused. I had just enough time to look at my watch. It had only been about fifteen minutes. I sighed. Since Elaine was about five minutes late to the class, that meant that only twenty minutes had gone by. *Only forty minutes left. Great.*

I usually liked school, but today seemed long already. I guessed that I was still tired from the night hosting. Taking a sip of my still-hot coffee, I tried to pay attention to Elaine.

The coffee was so good. Taylor did know how to brew a good cup. I adjusted in my seat.

"I will give you the rest of the hour to finish reading the article. Remember to have your summaries for next week, and to be ready to discuss the article as well." With that, Elaine sat back at the standard gray-brown desk at the front of the classroom and put the cardboard box containing our assignments in front of her. She started taking out the projects and marking a sheet with a pen as she went.

I looked up and saw Taylor looking out the window. I followed her gaze. There were two birds sitting on the windowsill. It was cute. One was a dark blood-red, and the other was a sunshine-yellow. I didn't know much about birds, but I was sure one of them was a robin. The other one, the yellow one, had a similar shape, but I didn't know if robins came in yellow. They seemed to be looking right back at Taylor, having a conversation that only they could understand. She was right; maybe she would make a good vet if the design thing didn't work out. Animals, it seemed, loved her.

I looked past Taylor to Hannah. She already had her head down, reading the article. She tapped her pen furiously on her knee under her desktop. I looked back at my own article. I guessed I would have to come up with some personal thoughts about it after reading it.

When class was over, Elaine dismissed us. Well, everyone but us.

"Everyone is now free to leave. I will see you in lecture next week. However, would Hannah Channing, Taylor

Benningson, and Emily Howard please stay for one more minute?" She looked at each of us individually as the rest of the class quietly filed out.

Elaine got up and went to shut the door again. I looked around, trying to imagine I was anywhere else but here. This was starting to get a little crazy. Elaine walked back to her desk and sat. She had three papers on the desktop in front of her. I recognized the papers with the stationary Taylor had made in her graphic design class. They were our three papers.

"Did you three think I wouldn't notice?" Elaine hissed. She stared at us. She spoke in a low tone but sounded vicious. "Do you think this class is a joke?"

"Wh-what are you talking about?" Hannah asked.

"Only the fact that each of your family trees originate in the same spot and flow identically down to the end with each of you. Do you expect me to believe that? Usually, students wait at least a month before trying to submit something so... so obvious." She picked up the three papers and then violently put them back on her desk. The three of us looked at each other. "Well, are you sisters?" Elaine challenged.

"No," Hannah said.

"Are you adopted siblings, then?" Elaine's stare was intense. This woman was crazy, I was sure of it. Her eyes were such a unique color of royal blue, but looking closer, they were not violet, like I'd thought before during orientation.

"No," Taylor answered her flatly.

"For now, I will leave the completion mark next to your names, but that is pending a meeting with Mrs. Trebule. I doubt that she will accept this work." She said the word "this" like she was talking about something dirty. With that, Elaine sat at the desk and began grading another stack of what looked like family trees.

"What?" Hannah whispered just loud enough for the rest of us to hear. Taylor cut her off.

"Excuse me, but I don't understand how you think something is wrong with our papers. Of course, some people will go back the same length, or some people can only get so far. We each worked on these together. I made the family tree papers, so they look similar, but that was it. We each completed them separately, talking to our families." Taylor stopped, looking back and forth between Elaine, Hannah, and me.

I don't think it did much good. Elaine looked like her mind was made up.

"You three will have a meeting with Mrs. Trebule. She will set the appointment, and you will be there. There will be no further discussion about this. Now go." She motioned to the door and went back to grading the papers again.

Hannah took a step toward the desk. She was angry. She reached to grab her paper. Her face was red, and one of her hands was clenched into a fist, the knuckles whitish. She looked ready to protest. Before she could touch the papers, however, Elaine moved them back into the assignment box and put the box on the floor. Hannah opened her mouth to say something, but before she could utter a word, Taylor grabbed the back of her shirt and tugged on it lightly.

"Not now," she mouthed. With that, she motioned her head toward the door, and we followed her out.

When we got outside, we looked at each other.

"So, yours was the same as mine and Taylor's?" Hannah said almost accusatorily. I didn't know what to say.

"Why didn't you say anything last night?" They both stared at me, waiting for me to say something.

"Yes," I was looking at the floor. "When I saw both of yours last night, I just thought maybe I had made a mistake and wanted to go through it again before turning it in. I went over my notes and still came up with the same family tree though."

"That's what you were doing after we got back last night. I saw your light go on before I fell asleep," Hannah said. Something clicked into place as if she'd filed the mystery away in her brain for another time.

"Don't worry about it," Taylor said. "We will talk to the teacher, whenever that will be, and get it straightened out. She said she would leave the marks that we did the assignment next to our names." She looked between me and Hannah, making sure that our friend wasn't about to explode. "Nothing bad has technically happened so far," she said.

Hannah's eyebrows moved at that. Her expression was still fierce, but she seemed to cling to that piece of information. Then she blurted, "She basically accused us of cheating. I've never been accused of cheating in my entire life!" As she spoke, her voice's tone went up.

"Maybe the lecture teacher – what's her name again? Mrs. Trebule? Maybe she will send us an email tonight, and we can get it straightened out sooner, rather than later," I tried to reassure her. "We didn't do anything wrong, and they can call our parents, so don't stress too much."

As there wasn't anything we could do, we kept walking, but no one spoke for another minute or two.

"You're right. That makes sense. All she would have to do is check, and she will see that our papers were correct. Okay, that's that, but it's still not good," Hannah said as she put her bag down and pulled out a notebook.

"Right. Well, I've gotta get to class," I said when I saw what time it was. I wanted to get something to eat from one of the carts outside of the building, so I was going to need a little extra time.

"Man, I'm so glad tomorrow's Friday," Taylor said with a sigh.

I had almost forgotten about that. It was nice to think about. I almost smiled, which, after that class, was saying something.

Miraculously, I managed to get through the afternoon. When I finally made it to the dining hall, I scrolled through my phone as I was eating and saw what some of my friends back home had been up to. Lunch had been good and warm. I was full. I'd finally gotten to try that squash soup, and it was just as amazing as I'd hoped it would be. I put my phone away and pulled out a notebook, intending to work on some economics homework for class the next day, but my mind started to drift away. I started thinking about Sean and our coffee date that was set for tomorrow morning.

Before I knew it, I was walking through our dorm hallway on the boys' side. I stopped in front of room thirteen. The door was closed. I pushed down on the handle. It was cold. My fingers, then my hand, and then even my arm felt the coolness spread as if I had dunked my arm in ice water. I had goosebumps going up my arm and through my body with the sudden change in temperature.

As the door opened, I saw the coattails of a brown, tweed jacket with patches on the elbows. It was dark, but I could make out the orange plaid just enough to recognize Dr. Eagles. He was standing next to none other than Sean. They were talking and neither noticed me.

"Are you sure that's wise, sir?" Dr. Eagles addressed Sean, looking at a large, beige paper on the floor. I couldn't make out the paper.

"It is the only way to be sure," Sean whispered back. He adjusted his stance as he bent down to get a better view of what they were looking at. His white shirt had what looked like a red Queen of Hearts on it. The queen seemed to stare at me for a second before his black jacket fell over her face.

"Besides, they need protection. We don't know how long we have, and every minute they are together, their abilities will awaken and strengthen. They may show themselves again, and the next time, we may not be able to get there in time."

"Yes," another voice said. "That was a close call... if they are who we've been looking for." I recognized the voice in a minute. As recognition dawned in my mind, Elaine walked over. Sean squatted down and pointed his arm at a spot on the paper I still couldn't make out from where I was standing. I moved to get a better look.

It looked like a map of the world. "You have talent," Dr. Eagles mused. "I remember that tapestry well."

"I didn't do this," Sean said, laughing. "She did." Both Dr. Eagles and Elaine looked up from the ground and at each other.

"There's no other explanation," Dr. Eagles said to Elaine. "It has to be them."

Without warning, Elaine turned and walked right up to where I stood, trying to see the painting better. I backed up, so she wouldn't run into me. I definitely didn't want her to see me. She reached for the door handle that had swung into the room as I passed through the doorway and slammed the door.

I awoke in the cafeteria to the sound of crashing dishes and applause. Someone walking near me had dropped their food tray on the ground.

"Damn," I murmured to myself under my breath. I hated that feeling between being awake and asleep. I managed to get moving before my body let it happen again.

CHAPTER ELEVEN

Coffee Date

The rest of Thursday was a blur, but in the end, I got back to the common room feeling relieved. I'd almost made it through the first week of school. I called my dad. I wanted to tell him how the week had gone and ask how Cindy was doing. It was about three in the afternoon in San Diego, and I thought maybe he would be at work, but I decided to try anyway. The phone rang a couple of times.

"Hello?" his voice answered as he cleared his throat.

"Hey, Dad," I said. I was more relieved to hear his voice. I guess I still missed home.

"Hey, kid. How's it going?" he said.

"It's going good. What are you up to?" I replied.

"Not much, just sitting here with your Nino and having a nice lunch," he said. I could tell he was having a good time; I heard a low rushing sound in the background and other people talking.

"Are you guys at Seaport Village?" I asked. The area is a nice one in San Diego. It's got a bunch of restaurants and is right next to the downtown area. It hugs the ocean and has a nice boardwalk for people to run or bike on.

One of my dad's favorite restaurants is there. The Pier, it's called. It's a pier, of course, but the restaurant takes up almost all of it. The sides are lined with clear walls, so guests can sit and eat while watching the Coronado Bridge and the giant Navy ships that sail in and out of the bay. It's especially nice when the weather is good because the ocean breeze blows through just enough that it's refreshing and not too cold. Sometimes people don't realize that the ocean breeze off of the Pacific Ocean can be cool.

Most of the restaurant is made from treated wood, and it's a bit rustic. However, it's definitely the place for good food in the area. I smiled, thinking of them sitting in the corner table, which is his favorite spot. There's also a break in the windows just big enough that he can throw some of his French fries to the seagulls. I could almost smell the saltwater just thinking about it.

"Yes, I got out of work a bit early. Nino called and said he was in the area, and here we are." He sounded like he was having a nice time, even if it was a little late there for lunch.

"Great. Tell Nino I said 'hi'," I added.

"I will." He paused. "Hey, it's Emily. Give me a second," I heard the sound of a chair push back. I guessed he was walking somewhere he could hear me better.

"Hey, how are you?" Dad said.

"I'm doing good. Glad tomorrow's Friday!" I told him, trying to sound more upbeat than I felt.

"You about made it through your first week. Good job, kid," he told me.

"Thanks, Dad. How's Cindy doing?" I missed my puppy.

"She's doing good. She misses you though. This week, she's been sleeping on your bed."

"Aww!" I couldn't help it.

"I tried to get her to sleep with me, and she would start there, but in the morning, she'd be back in your room." He gave a low laugh. "I brought her a hamburger last night and took off the lettuce and tomato. She ate it in five seconds, so I think she's going to be fine."

Cindy loved hamburgers, as any dog would. When my dad would come home late from work, he'd usually stop and get fast food for dinner. He'd always bring her home a hamburger.

"Hey, I'd better get going. You make sure to do your homework," he said.

"Okay, Dad. Thanks, and I'll talk to you later," I replied.

"Sounds good. Love you, kid," he said.

"Love you too, Dad," I replied, and he ended the call.

I took a deep breath. It was hard getting off the phone. I missed home, but somehow, I felt like I was where I was supposed to be. At least that's how I felt tonight.

The evening went on, and we still hadn't heard anything from Mrs. Trebule. I decided to put it out of my mind because I had other homework to worry about. I figured that Elaine would tell her by tomorrow or Monday, and we would find out at our next class.

I was determined not to let it ruin the end of my week and weekend, especially because tomorrow morning, I was supposed to have coffee with Sean. He'd sent me a text message that afternoon that read, "Still on for tomorrow morning?" I replied, "Yup, see you then." I didn't know much about him, so I wasn't sure what else to say.

Friday morning came quickly. I finally had a good night of sleep. I got up and went for a short jog before I left to stretch my legs. Something about the East coast, I decided, made the air in the morning fresh. I loved running in San Diego, but the air here seemed deeper. It was like I got more oxygen in every breath.

When I'd finished my run, I came back to my room to shower and change. I tried to be as quiet as possible to not wake up Hannah or Taylor. But when I was all ready to go and flipping on the coffee pot for my roommates, I noticed Taylor sticking her head out of the door.

"Have fun at coffee," Taylor whispered mockingly but with good humor. She smiled.

"Oh, it's just coffee," I replied back, laughing. I knew my face was red. My facial expressions always betrayed me like that.

"Make sure to tell me what happens," Taylor added quietly as I walked out the door. I smiled.

Walking down our hallways, I thought I heard another set of footsteps. I stopped short of the back door to listen and took a quick look behind. I heard and saw nothing out of the ordinary. *Man, I'm jumpy*, I half-scolded and half-joked to myself.

I wondered if I would run into Sean as I walked over to the Shaw building but never ended up seeing him. Why we had decided to meet there instead of walking together, I didn't know. I just went with what he had asked because, well, why not? It was just coffee after all.

The smells of cinnamon toast and bacon got stronger as I passed different buildings. My stomach growled.

"Sounds like someone needs some breakfast," I heard someone say. I stopped short and turned around. None other than Seth came walking up behind me.

"Fancy seeing you here, stranger," he said as he walked up to me.

"Hi, Seth," I told him. He was wearing a ridiculous white tank top and navy blue, long shorts. He had on flip-flops and long, white socks. Somehow, he still looked as comfortable as he had when he was playing football in the sunshine the first time I'd seen him during orientation.

"A couple of us guys are getting ready to start a flag football league for the weekends, if you guys are interested." He paused. "Make sure to let Taylor and Hannah know, would you? Especially Taylor, I know how she likes to watch me play," he finished, not looking at me but simply staring to the right.

"How did you..." I started.

"Oh, you know, people talk," he answered. He smiled.

We started walking together down the path. I pulled out my map. I knew I was going the right way but wanted something to hold. I was starting to get uncomfortable. Seth grabbed the map from me.

"Hey!" I had to stretch my body, reaching for the paper. The cold wind made gooseflesh run up the unexposed skin at my wrists and on my neck as I did so.

"Where are you headed so early?" He examined the map. I grabbed for it again, but he held it high. I was getting annoyed. Thankfully, I remembered the business building being somewhere to the right of the path we were on, so I knew we were almost there. I hadn't seen Sean yet. Suddenly, I stopped short. Seth had put his arm around my shoulders. I felt sick. Every fiber of who I was screamed for him to remove his arm. I squirmed out of it. His arm fell to his sides.

"What? I was just being friendly," he joked. Something in his voice gave off that he knew I would be uncomfortable with his arm, but he didn't care.

Without saying anything to him, I started walking again. He matched my stride and kept up beside me. I felt like running. My adrenaline pumped through my veins, waiting for me to stand my ground or run away. We turned a corner, and I saw the coffee cart at the side of the Shaw front steps. Near the cart was a bench where Sean sat. He looked up just as we turned. He stood, and I felt Seth's stride slow.

"Oh, how cute. You're meeting someone," Seth mocked as if he were talking to a baby. "My little girl is all grown up."

I couldn't figure out what I had done to get this version of Seth, but it was starting to creep me out.

We got closer, and Sean walked up to us. We stopped walking. Sean didn't meet my gaze but looked directly at Seth.

"Don't forget to let your roommates know about the flag football," Seth said, looking at Sean and not me.

"Okay, I will. Thanks. See you later," I said, wanting it to sound meaner than I'm sure it did.

Seth turned and walked away through the buildings off the path. It was muddy. He looked ridiculous in what he was wearing.

"Hey, Sean," I said distractedly as we both watched Seth leave. There were a couple seconds where he didn't respond. I wasn't sure if I'd made him upset by walking here with Seth, but then there wasn't anything to be upset about. I was just meeting him for coffee. So, I tried to dismiss the thought.

"How do you know him?" he asked, emphasizing the "*him*" as if he knew him and hated him. He had anger in his eyes, and it confused me.

"Oh, we met on the first day of orientation. He was playing football, and Taylor almost got hit with the ball he'd thrown," I said. Sean didn't say anything. He just stared after Seth, who had disappeared several moments ago. He examined our surroundings and looked everywhere except at me.

"So, let's start this over," I began. "Hi, how's it going?" I laughed. I was trying to forget about Seth. I was obviously too inexperienced with guys to make any sense out of it at all, so I tried to move along the conversation.

I was suddenly self-conscious. *It's just freaking coffee, Emily,* I thought to myself, trying to shake my insecurities.

"Hi. Thanks for meeting me." He as seemed ready to move the conversation to a new topic as I was. "So, what are you going to get?"

"I'm not sure. I think just plain coffee this morning. We had a rough day in classes yesterday," I said.

He gave me a questioning look. "What do you mean? It's the first week of school," he laughed. He smiled some when he talked. His skin tone was olive, and his hair was dark but had small streaks of blond in it as the rays of sun hit the back of his head.

"Oh, we have this anthropology project, and our teacher's assistant for the lab class didn't like how we did the rough draft, so she's notifying our teacher, and we are supposed to have a meeting about it. Hannah, one of my roommates, was pretty upset about it, but we didn't do anything wrong. We just have similar family trees." I figured that summed up most of it.

"I see," he said. "Well, you guys shouldn't have to worry about anything since you didn't do anything wrong, so try not to stress." He looked at me. I had trouble meeting his eyes. It was like they pierced into me and knew what I was thinking.

A moment later, I was taken back to my dream from the day before. Watching Sean and Dr. Eagles talking. I shook my head to try and clear the vision or dream or whatever it was.

Stupid facial expressions, I thought to myself.

"I hear you're from California," he said.

"Yeah, born and raised," I replied. "How about you? Where are you from?"

"I'm from here. Born and raised," he said and laughed at his joke. I laughed too. "So, what makes someone from California come all the way to Syracuse, New York?"

"Oh, I spent some time out in Sherburne, New York with some family and always wondered how it would be to live here, so when I got the opportunity, I took it." That was the easiest story I could come up with quickly. I'd had to come up with a quick story since some of my classes required group work, and almost everyone asked where I was from at some point.

He looked at me. I was sure he knew that only small parts of that story were true, but he didn't ask any more questions, and I was grateful for that.

We spent the next twenty minutes or so talking and learning about each other. He was an engineering major and told me about some of his classes, like Physics and Math. It sounded like he had a heavy load this semester.

I had to check my watch. I didn't want to be late. It was already quarter to eight. "I should probably get going in a minute. I've got to walk up to class," I said. We were sitting on the outdoor bench by the coffee cart. We'd sat next to each other, but I appreciated that Sean didn't mind my bookbag placed between us. After Seth's lack of boundaries this morning, I was a little on edge.

"Yeah, I'm supposed to meet with my advisor this morning, so I need to go as well," Sean replied. "But hey, Emily, can you do me a favor?" He looked at me like he was trying to decide what to say and didn't want to say it.

"Sure, what do you need?" I couldn't figure out what it could be.

"Well, make sure you guys are careful around Seth. He has a..." He paused, looking at the ground. "He has a reputation around here," he finally said.

I stared at him with my eyes wide. I knew I couldn't even hide my face.

"I don't think that will be a problem," I said and meant it. We laughed it off and talked for a couple more minutes.

As Sean stood up and put on his backpack, his back jacket moved and I saw the white shirt underneath. My eyes were met with a fierce Red Queen gaze. There she was, the Queen of Hearts staring right at me, just like in my dream from the day before.

What was that? I thought to myself. *It must be a coincidence.* I knew that was probably the case, but I was still rattled. I tried to calm myself down and noticed I was holding my coffee cup a little too tight. I took a deep breath and tried to concentrate on what he was saying to me.

"Well, I hope we can meet again," I heard him say.

"Yes, that would be great." I smiled and turned to go.

"Hey, wait a minute..." Sean caught me by the backpack strap, gently tugging it as I was turning away. He said that he wanted to meet Friday mornings and have coffee whenever we could, so we set the date for the next week right then.

When I headed to class, I was happy but still a bit rattled from looking at his shirt. *Coincidence. It has to be a coincidence,* I told myself.

Friday went as quickly as it had come. I relayed the morning's events to Taylor that evening, and she just stared in amazement at me when I described Seth's behavior and what he had been wearing. I managed to avoid talking about Sean's strange shirt and my daydream from the dining hall and just stuck to things that didn't make me sound totally crazy.

"Well, that takes him down to at least a five," she said, disgusted. "We will definitely not be playing flag football with him or his buddies, ever," was the last of the conversation.

We were on duty for the first weekend for night hosting. It was nice. I was tired in the morning but got all my homework done by the end of the evening. And a bonus of night hosting on the weekend, it seemed, was that it was much more entertaining than during the week, with some students coming in drunk from off-campus parties. Thankfully, it was entertaining and not weird and scary, like our Wednesday night experience – which, by the way, we didn't speak about. Finally, I decided that maybe all the strangeness had been in my head.

Saturday, we explored the campus and some of the places around Syracuse. We found a neat sandwich place that had salads, sandwiches, and all kinds of soups. We avoided talking about Anthropology. Well, except for making light of Hannah always checking her phone's email to see if we'd gotten anything from our teacher.

It was nice outside in the cool fall air. Even though it was the first week of September and during the day, it still got a little warm. The afternoon breezes were comfortable, if a bit cool. I wore a pair of running shorts and a sweatshirt, which was my standard weekend outfit even back home in California.

Saturday night, when we were night hosting, Hannah had to go back to our room for a book she'd left. She forgot to take her cell phone with her. When she'd just gone out of sight from where Taylor and I were sitting, her phone rang. I was going to leave it to voicemail, but Taylor decided to pick it up. The caller ID said "Nick".

"Oh, let's see who this is," Taylor said, her eyes sparkling. She pressed the green button on the screen and then, without warning, tossed the phone directly at me, laughing as she did so.

"Hey, no way," I whispered as I caught the phone. I looked down at the screen and saw the seconds were already ticking away, which meant that someone was on the line and listening.

Great.

"Hello?" I answered with a pause. *What should I say?* "Hannah's phone," I added, while making dart eyes at Taylor, who was laughing silently at the table.

"Hey, who is this?" replied a male voice.

"This is Emily, one of Hannah's roommates," I said.

"Oh, okay. Is Hannah there?" he asked, laughing.

"Yeah, she just went back to our room for a minute," I told him. I saw Hannah coming back down the hall. She looked at me with a confused expression. Taylor was still giggling beside me.

Hannah came around the table.

"Um, here she is." It sounded like a question more than a statement. I handed her the phone, trying to present her with the most apologetic face I could muster up.

"Hey, Nick. What's up?" she said, rolling her eyes at Taylor and me. I rolled up the biology handout that I'd been reviewing and whacked Taylor on the shoulder with it. Then we both laughed.

Hannah hung up the phone. "Really, guys?" she said. We all laughed. "That was my brother, okay," Hannah said, looking pointedly at Taylor. "Come on." She smiled and went back to her assignment.

CHAPTER TWELVE

A First Meeting

October brought the changing colors of the leaves. Scores of reds, yellows, ambers, and browns invaded each tree along our campus, until one day, when I was walking to class, I realized there was not one green leaf left. The autumn shades threw golden rays onto each branch in the morning and afternoon sunlight.

Watching the change in person happen for the first time, I realized that what I had always been taught about this change was wrong. The life of the leaf was not lost in the color change, but their lives were only beginning, with the most dramatic changes to lay ahead.

I found myself thinking, *If you had been only one way for as long as you can remember, then suddenly changed four or even five times, would that be the beginning of your life or the end?*

This time in the life of the trees was their real time to shine.

I had been eagerly anticipating the change of green to fall's browns, reds, and oranges. I was not disappointed. In California, the leaves were almost always green. I had occasionally seen them change on a vacation here and there but hadn't ever been anywhere through the transition into fall to see them in person. It was beautiful.

School got a little harder as the semester wore on. We never did hear from our teacher, Mrs. Trebule, and we decided after another particularly harsh lecture with Elaine that she was just trying to make an example out of us. My dad had sent out the family lineage page from my mom's — well, I guess it was *my* bible now. I left it in the envelope, unopened, since we hadn't heard from the teacher yet.

Nothing is wrong. We didn't lie, and we won't get in trouble, I kept telling myself to push the unease about the whole thing down.

With all the homework from my classes, the lectures and labs, even night hosting sometimes was not enough time to get it done. So, I started going with Taylor to the library.

Sometimes, Hannah would join us, but she'd taken to occupying the common room for her marathon study sessions. Sometimes, she'd be asleep on the common room floor when we'd get back, and Taylor would get her up and put her to bed. It was kind of cute. The three of us seemed to have made a silent pact to watch out and take care of each other.

I was, for the most part, sleeping a bit better. I did occasionally have that same dream as earlier in the semester though. It was always dark. There was always a light far off and a small orb of stone sitting on top of a low pillar. Elaine was always there, telling me to run, and there was always a mist around. I heard people talking and whispering. There was a smell too, which was kind of strange. I don't ever remember smelling during my dreams. I didn't even think that was possible. It always smelled like metal and steel, kind of like a working car garage.

After having the dreams, I was exhausted and dragged myself through the day. It made me feel crazy. I knew I was stressed with school and that I still missed home, but I was happy with my roommates and felt like I was adjusting well. So, I decided to just let the dreams take their course and thought they would go away.

One Sunday, I must have been looking particularly ragged because Hannah noticed.

"Hey, are you okay?" she asked. "I heard you talking at like three in the morning last night, but you weren't making any sense." She had been in the common room, and we left our doors open into it at night, so we could shout back and forth.

"Yeah, I just had a crazy dream," I replied.

Taylor came to the door of their room. "I hate when that happens. I've decided that this place is built over an old burial ground or something because I've been having strange dreams also." She paused. "But they are totally ridiculous. I just wanted to tell you I feel your pain." She laughed uncomfortably, then went to sit next to Hannah on the couch.

"What were your dreams about?" Hannah asked at me. She looked apprehensive. I hadn't planned on telling anyone about the dream, but they seemed generally interested and like they wanted to know, so I risked looking foolish and began talking. They sounded ridiculous when I spoke them out loud, rather than reviewing them in my head. But I told them every detail.

When I was done, neither spoke.

"That's it," Taylor announced and stood up. "If this is some joke, you two need to tell me right now."

"What?" I said. I had no clue what she was talking about.

"I've been having a similar dream," said Hannah. "Taylor and I talked about it a little over a week ago. I guess I was talking in my sleep and saying some weird stuff, so she woke me up."

"Seriously, guys, this isn't funny. Please tell me if you're joking." Taylor's facial expression was desperate, her normal cheery and carefree attitude entirely absent.

"I'm not making it up, Taylor, and I don't think Hannah is either," I said. "You heard her dream and woke her up, so you know her part is true."

We all talked about the dreams and decided that with everything we had going on, the extra homework was driving us nuts. We decided to go exploring around town again the next weekend to blow off some steam.

Eventually, our conversation turned more pleasant. Apparently, Seth had been sending Taylor emails and trying to get her to go to a party with him, which she insisted she'd been denying.

"Do you remember how creepy he was?" I told her.

"Sean hasn't mentioned him again, right?" Taylor replied. I tried to give her a nudge. I hadn't seen Seth since our run-in on the way to coffee a couple weeks back.

"I mean, maybe he was weirdly jealous or something?" She paused and looked up. "Maybe he didn't want anyone else having coffee with his Emily-shwemily," she finished in a tone that sounded like baby talk and half-laughter.

"How'd he get your email address anyway?" I asked her.

"Who knows? Must be some kind of student directory or something." She was still looking at her computer when Hannah chimed in from the other room.

"That shouldn't be accessible to all students, only those within the same major," she half-yelled, so we could hear her.

"Eh, he's not my type anyway," she said, smiling. But I thought that she might be changing her mind. The side of her mouth betrayed a small smile she was trying to hide.

Sean hadn't mentioned him again after our first date. Yes, I called it a date. Even though we hadn't talked about a relationship or anything of the sort, we had a pretty regular routine for most Friday mornings. We'd talked about past relationships a couple times. My nonexistent ones and his one girlfriend from a few years back.

Okay, neither of us is attached. What does that mean? I couldn't help thinking.

At least Taylor had fun with it, and my cluelessness with boys was a source of endless entertainment to her. Still, I insisted Sean and I were not in a relationship.

It was just a date... weekly... every week. Just he and I together.

Sean and I started meeting outside the dorm, and we walked together to get coffee rather than meeting there. It was funny because he was almost always five minutes late. I had to give him a hard time about it because he insisted every time he'd be "on time" at the next meeting.

We talked a lot about our classes. He tried to talk me into giving Elaine another chance in Anthropology.

"It sounds like she's just eccentric and really passionate." His eyes were not meeting mine, and he had a slight upturn to his smile.

"Really, so she singled the three of us out during class yesterday by giving an oral exam on the evolution process when we hadn't even covered the entire topic yet." The sarcasm in my voice wasn't hard to miss.

In our last class, Elaine had really outdone herself. She'd called the three of us to stand in our chairs and asked us questions on human taxonomy. Hannah aced the quiz, and out of the corner of my eye, I'd seen other students taking notes from her answers. Taylor just rolled her eyes and sat back down. I'd stood there looking like a deer in headlights, not sure what to do. I wanted to crawl into a hole.

Sean shook his head and laughed. "Just try to get through the class. I'm sure it will pay off in your grade." He took one look at my facial expression, and we moved on to other more pleasant topics.

I think I was starting to like him. Maybe he even liked me back, which would be a first for me. I got comfortable enough sitting on the bench that I no longer placed my backpack between us but to my right. We put our coffees between us, and there were a few times that I'd reached down to pick mine up and our hands had touched. I swear our hands lingered there for a second or two longer than they should have.

The rest of the night was filled with homework. I went to bed and left my common room door open, as did Taylor and Hannah. Taylor yelled out before we went to sleep, "Hey, no crazy dreams!" and we all laughed.

Then I fell asleep. Finally, I got some rest.

About two weeks later, on another random Sunday night, I heard the ding from my computer alerting me to a new email. A second later, I heard a similar ding come from the common room.

I opened my email and read:

Ladies,

I am under the impression that we must soon meet. Please come to my office, number 030 in the Shaw building, promptly on Monday next at nine in the evening. I apologize for the late hour, but we have classes that run until eight.

Thank you for your time.

Mrs. Trebule

Well, that was that. We had our meeting.

Four days later, at our next class, Elaine gave no indication that she had spoken with Mrs. Trebule and did nothing to put our mind at ease. Weirdly, when I casually asked some of the other students in the course what they thought about Elaine, they raved about how nice she was. Apparently, she was nice to everyone but us, although no one else seemed to notice.

The meeting drew closer, and I wasn't sure if it was because I was dreading it or because I just wanted it to be over, but the time dragged by. Eventually, Monday night finally rolled around.

We met for a late dinner before the meeting, then walked over to the Shaw building together. We zipped up our jackets and hurried out the sliding doors. The walk was only ten minutes, but I felt like it was going by faster than usual. I wished I hadn't eaten. The grilled cheese and tomato soup was amazing here, but my nerves made it sit in my stomach like rocks at the bottom of a pond.

Hannah started going through her family tree again. By this time, we all knew each other's by heart. We had gone over them and read and re-read each other's papers to see if there was something out of place. There wasn't, of course.

Each family tree always ended on the same side: the mother's great, great, great grandmother in Albany, New York. It was strange because it was only a couple hours from where we were at this school.

I kept telling myself what Taylor had assured us in the beginning. We hadn't done anything wrong. There was no reason to worry about our meeting. There was no problem. But no matter how many times I told myself this, I still felt my stomach turn when I thought about it. At least I'd remembered to bring the letter Dad had sent me with the family lineage inside it. I had shoved the still unopened envelope in my jacket pocket before we'd headed down to eat.

I hadn't told Dad about the meeting because I didn't want him to worry. He had enough on his plate with having to get used to living alone at home. Of course, if the meeting went badly, I'd have to tell him. We would get to that if we had to. If the teacher needed me to get any further, she could talk with my dad about it. I wasn't sure if she was as abrasive as Elaine or if she was more reasonable.

We got to the Shaw building. It was a beautiful old building. It was circular and old. The dome at the top was a sun-beaten white. It reminded me of the buildings from old pictures of Rome. The pillars along the side went to the top, where they met the dome in a molding of leaves and were carved to look like tree trunks. Toward the bottom, where the entrance was, the two pillars that marked the front had carved branches coming from them toward the doors, making it look like some forest archway.

"We got to draw this building in one of my art classes. Isn't it beautiful?" Taylor said.

"Wow, I hadn't noticed the carvings before," I told her as we walked into the building.

The inside of the entranceway was quiet. We followed a long hallway and took a flight of stairs down to the lower-level offices.

The upper level of the Shaw building was used as the campus's religious meeting place and had a space for several different stands and flags of worship. It was beautiful. In the early fall, when school had just started, the music department played here on Saturday nights. We went once when we were out exploring and listened to their guest director. They'd had John Williams visiting, and the orchestra had played some of his greatest hits, like the soundtracks from *E.T.*, *Jaws*, and *Star Wars*. It was fun. I wished we were here for something like that this time.

The lower levels of the building, where we were headed, however, were in stark contrast to the upper. It was much plainer. I don't think any of us had been down in this area yet. The hallway, like the upper one, circled around the building, with doors on the inside and no windows on the outside. I wondered if we were underground. I was sure we were.

We followed the pattern of numbers on each office door until we got to the one Mrs. Trebule had told us to go to in her email: Room 030.

We stopped. The door was slightly ajar, and we could hear people talking. We looked at each other. No one said a thing. We knew we had to go in. Hannah pushed the door slightly, and it swung open slowly.

Mrs. Trebule was sitting at her desk, talking with three other people. Hannah took in a breath and tried to shut the door, whispering, "Oh, sorry for interrupting. We'll—"

"No, no, it's quite all right. We were just going through some details for the upcoming fall food drive. It's no worry," Mrs. Trebule said cheerily. "We are about through now anyway. I must get to other business. I appreciate you meeting with me." She looked at the three adults who stood up from their seats at her desk.

Taylor, Hannah, and myself took a collective gasp when we each realized who had been occupying each of the seats at Mrs. Trebule's desk.

"Hello, Dr. Winters," Taylor began as her teacher came to the door smiling.

"Well, good to see you, Taylor. How are you this evening?"

"Good, thanks," she replied, her facial expression showing her confusion.

"I'll be seeing you in class, dear." And with that, Dr. Winters walked out of the office and down the hall.

Hannah and I both stared. Dr. Eagles and another older man carrying a briefcase walked together toward the three of us.

"Well, hello there, Emily. Very good work on your government resource paper last week. I'll be passing them back next class, but just know you did well." He wore his brown jacket and suspenders that had little red and white mushrooms going up and down the cloth.

I smiled. "Thank you, Dr. Eagles."

The older man had said absolutely nothing, but he did make an obnoxious sniffing noise as he walked by, almost as if trying to smell the three of us. It was awkward.

"Have a good night," I called to the two men as they walked down the hallway and out of sight.

For a few moments, we just stood where we were in the hallway at the opening of Mrs. Trebule's office, not knowing what to do. I looked at my two roommates and shrugged, unsure what else to say.

Hannah mouthed, "That was Dr Sharma." She looked back down the hallway in the direction both men had gone.

"Ladies, thank you for meeting with me. I apologize again for the meeting being so late in the evening," Mrs. Trebule said, looking at us with a look that was both calculating and, I think, surprised.

She took off her glasses and put them on her desk, then looked at us each individually. She didn't speak until she'd finished looking us over.

"Please sit down." She motioned to the three chairs on the opposite side of her desk.

Her office was... different. It was large and oval-shaped. She had several bookshelves around the room. One, in the back of her office, was just in the middle of the floor, not up against a wall or in a corner. There seemed to be no rhyme or reason to where she put anything. Her desk was in the middle of the room. The chairs for the three of us were in front of the desk. She had plants and a fish on a side table along one side of the room and then on the other, more bookshelves with lots of books, pictures, and figurines.

I could probably sit in here for an hour and still see things I hadn't noticed before, I thought to myself. There was just so much stuff.

"You are here..." She didn't finish the sentence.

I felt like she was staring into my soul when she looked at me. I had to look away. I heard her take a breath. She paused and cleared her throat.

"You are here because your family trees have been looked at by my teaching assistant, Elaine, and she has indicated that I should speak with you about them." She paused. "I have gone over them fully and done my own fact-checking, and it is remarkable. Do you know how rare it is to have family trees so similar?"

She looked at us again with that piercing gaze.

"It is almost impossible – unless you are related, that is..."

She paused, waiting for us to speak.

"Are you related?" she finally asked when no one spoke.

"No, we are not related. We just met when school started. We are roommates," Hannah said.

"I see. So, you did not know each other from before this term began?" she asked. It was the same question.

"We had a phone conference call, but that was it before school started. We are roommates, like Hannah said," Taylor added when it became apparent that Hannah was not going to say another word. "We are each from a different place, and there was no way we would have known each other before school started. You can call our parents, if you would like. We told them about the family tree project and double-checked everything," Taylor added. She was on the edge of her seat by this time.

"And have you learned anything about yourselves from this project so far?" Mrs. Trebule looked at us expectantly.

"Excuse me, but what does that have to do with our family trees?" Hannah clutched her seat. She looked like she wanted to walk out. There was a pause. Mrs. Trebule looked at us with a surprised look on her face.

"I'm sorry, ladies. I forgot to tell you that you are not in trouble and will get full points for the assignment. Like I said, I did my own fact-checking, and everything has checked out as you had it on your papers." She looked at the three of us again. Hannah gave a sigh of relief and seemed to relax slightly.

What does she mean, she did her own fact-checking? I thought to myself. Mrs. Trebule was still looking at us.

"Then why did you still want to meet with us?" Hannah asked her.

"Well, to apologize, for one thing," Mrs. Trebule said. "My assistant, Elaine, is zealous when it comes to cheaters, and you three caught her eye right from the beginning of class. I had to see what she was talking about." She paused. "Anyway, it was just a misunderstanding, I'm sure you would like to be going now as it is a school night. I know that you night host in your dorm facility, and it is not often you get a Monday evening free. But... will you three please humor me for just one more moment?" she asked nicely.

I found myself nodding involuntarily. Out of the corner of my eye, I saw Hannah and Taylor do the same.

Mrs. Trebule stood from her desk and went around to a bookshelf. She grabbed an old book and came back and sat with us. She put the book down. I couldn't read the spine the way it lay on her desk.

"You say you have never met, and yet, I see your mannerisms here and even in class mirroring each other's. You seem unique in your own ways, yes, but appear to have known each other for quite some time."

She did have a point. I felt so comfortable with these two girls. They were my friends, but I felt like they were best friends. And we had only known each other...

There was a knock at the door.

"Come in." Mrs. Trebule looked at the door. There was a soft *swish* of air that penetrated the room as none other than Elaine walked in and closed the door behind her. Elaine sat at one of the chairs to the side of the desk, not on the same side as Mrs. Trebule but not right next to us either.

"How do you think that is?" Mrs. Trebule went on, posing the question to us. No one spoke for a few uncomfortable seconds.

"Well, we live together in the dorms," Hannah said. "We spend quite a bit of time together and talk about our lives. That must be how," she finished.

"Yes, that surely is part of it. But do you think that is all of it?" She seemed to be calculating something in the silence again, looking at each of us. "Do you think your similar heritage could be something that is..." She paused. "...heightening your sense of awareness around each other?" I saw a slight upturn of a smile as she spoke. "Maybe your meeting was more than just chance, eh?"

She stopped talking and shared a slightly longer than socially acceptable and unblinking look with Elaine. I felt the tension in the room rise.

"In my fact-checking on your assignment, I discovered some interesting things about you three." She picked up the book from her desk and showed it to us. The title read *Hans Brinker and the Silver Skates*. I heard Hannah take in a sharp breath.

Mrs. Trebule put the book down. Then she opened her drawer to pull out a small, beige canvas. It looked like a map of the world, but it was undefined and different from maps I'd seen before. It was all brown, with black paint outlining the different continents.

In my peripheral vision, Taylor leaned forward in her chair. Then our teacher opened another desk drawer and pulled out a small, white, leather-bound notebook. She laid each item on her desk in front of each of us. The old book in front of Hannah, the small canvas in front of Taylor, and the notebook in front of me.

"Is that what I think it is?" Hannah spoke up. She was eyeing the book in front of her. I saw she wanted to pick it up. Her hands gripped the edge of the desk in front of her.

"First edition," Mrs. Trebule said. "And yes, you may come and see it any time you would like."

"How did you get that? My grandma and I used to read that book. Her mom gave it to her, and the volume had been in her family since like the 1800s. I don't think it's even in publication anymore," she finished, picking up the book delicately.

"I do some rare book collecting and came across this one only last week. It was a good find."

"Thanks," Hannah said, opening the book carefully on her lap.

"Taylor, do you recognize this?" Mrs. Trebule said, pushing the canvas toward her. Taylor picked up the map. She turned it and looked at it again. She put her fingers along the lines of the different continents.

"Yes, I think I do, but..." She stopped talking and looked up. "This doesn't make any sense. How did you even know about this?" She looked accusingly at Mrs. Trebule and Elaine.

"You have quite a bit of talent, Ms. Benningson. You should be proud of your work. I have recommended that you be placed in a higher art course. I hope you do not mind."

Taylor just stared at Mrs. Trebule.

"Emily, this I would like you to have." I took the small notebook from the desk. I opened it. The paper was blank inside. It looked like a journal. I smelled the familiar smell of un-written-on paper and un-disturbed leather binding on the small item. I looked at Mrs. Trebule, not understanding what she meant for me to do with it.

"I'd like you to write down things that come to mind when you are together. Your group thoughts or your dreams." She said the second pointedly and stared at me. I noticed my two friends become still as cement. I turned my head to look at them. No one spoke.

"Elaine," Mrs. Trebule said after she had moved several papers to the side of her desk. "Thank you for coming. Will you please be so kind as to watch these three for me? They are no longer in question for their work, but they have sparked my interest." She was looking at us again in that same strange way. A mix of surprise and calculating suspicion.

"But you said..." Hannah spoke out but stopped when she realized Elaine was looking at her. No one knew what to say; at least the three of us were silent. Why would Mrs. Trebule want to keep an eye on us if we weren't in any trouble? That didn't make sense.

I chanced a glance at Taylor and Hannah. Taylor looked as confused as I was, and Hannah had taken to holding onto her seat again, gripping it so hard that I was starting to feel bad for her knuckles.

"I want you three to keep an open mind," Mrs. Trebule said. She placed both the canvas and the rare book in her desk drawers and pushed the journal toward me. "I'd like to have another meeting and get into more detail. Tonight, I need to keep our meeting short." She turned to face Elaine. "Please, I tell you these things to hopefully gain some trust from you, especially since we got off to such a rocky beginning."

Again, she paused and looked at Elaine. Then, her tone slightly more urgent than a moment prior, she said, "Elaine." Both she and her teaching assistant nodded. A silent communication passed between them, meant only for them.

Elaine then got up and walked out the door without so much as a glance in our direction. Mrs. Trebule watched her go, and her gaze stayed at the door even after Elaine had closed it. A few silent and awkward seconds passed.

"As I was saying, we will need to have another meeting to discuss this further. Let me leave you with this before we part, however. You must realize that the choices you make in your lives influence your surroundings, now and in the future. Take care that you make the right ones."

"Is this a joke?" Taylor said. "Is this part of some campus prank that everyone seems to be in on?" She sounded like she expected an answer. She didn't get one. "Well, it's a pretty bad one, if you ask me."

I heard the frustration in her voice. She got up looked at both Hannah and myself, then walked out. Hannah's face was red, but she didn't say anything and followed Taylor. I didn't know what to do or say. I stood and moved to leave.

"Emily." I stopped in my tracks. " Don't forget this." Mrs. Trebule held out the small, white journal to me. "And just to answer the previous question, no, this is not a joke. The campus hasn't played a joke in years."

I turned my head to look at her. She stared at me. Goosebumps went up my arm. I turned and left to follow my two friends, who appeared just as confused and frustrated by our meeting as I was.

As I walked back through the doorway, I felt a sense of heat. It was quick and short, but it threw me for a quick second. As quick as it had been there, it was gone. Going into the hallway, it seemed cooler after the warm sensation. Again, the goosebumps went up my arms. I saw Hannah and Taylor waiting for me up ahead, and I quickened my pace to catch up to them.

"That went well," Taylor said.

"How the heck did she know all that stuff about us, and what the hell was my chemistry teacher doing here?" Hannah spit out. "And that book she had, my grandma read that book to me when I was a little girl."

"He is definitely creepy and a half." Taylor's face showed her distaste at the memory of the teacher sniffing as he passed us in the doorway. "And that map she showed us. That's my map. I made it when I was a lot younger. It's where the castle I draw belongs. I was tired of drawing the castle over and over and decided to try to draw where it came from. By the way, that was Dr. Winters, my art teacher, the one who gave me the painting for my class project. Don't tell me, Emily. Was the other guy one of your teachers?"

"Well, yes, that was my economics teacher, Dr. Eagles. I am completely done. The only thing that is nice to know is that we aren't in trouble or anything... I don't think," I added, hoping that it would make all three of us feel better.

We continued through the circular hallways, and as we got to the stairs, we stopped to grab a drink from the soda machine.

"What was that she handed you? That journal?" Hannah asked me. Absentmindedly, I touched my jacket pocket to make sure it hadn't fallen out and remembered the still unopened envelope. I took it out along with the journal. I looked at it and showed it to Hannah and Taylor.

"I guess something for us to write in," I said, more as a question than anything else.

"Great, a Burn Book for our room," Taylor said, and we all laughed.

"What's that?" Hannah eyed my other hand with the envelope.

"It's just a family lineage chart that fell out of my mom's old bible. My dad sent it to me when I talked with him about our project back in the beginning of the year."

"Why didn't you open it?" Taylor asked. In one hand, she had her soda from the machine, but with the other, she took the envelope and turned it over.

"I guess I just thought we might need to open it with Mrs. Trebule, but she didn't seem to need it." I didn't know what else to say.

"Let's open it now." Taylor looked at me and Hannah. I nodded and let her do the honors.

Taylor, putting her soda down on the fire extinguisher box jutting out from the wall, wiped her hand on her pants to dry the condensation off. She then carefully opened the envelope. She tuned it upside-down, and out slipped a colorful piece of paper. She unfolded the page.

"Well, this shit keeps getting better." She looked at me with confusion in her eyes.

"What?" I didn't understand.

Hannah moved to see the paper better, and I could see the concern in her facial expression. I went to Taylor's other side and looked down onto the paper.

There were connected lines and names all through the paper from top to bottom. But it wasn't the names written on the page that drew my attention. It was the background of the paper. The page was thin, like other bible pages, and it looked fragile. But as the light from the hallway shone through it, it was as if the page contained an internal drawing.   Immediately, I remembered where I'd seen Taylor's art project photo before.   Embossed into the fragile family lineage page of my mother's old bible was its exact replica.

"Oh," I whispered.

Hannah took the paper and looked at it carefully. "This is probably very old, Emily. You should put it away." She handed it back to me.

Taking the page, I carefully folded it back the way my dad had sent it and put the envelope back into my jacket pocket, sliding it right next to the journal. We looked at each other.

"I don't know, guys. I don't think my dad will know anything about it. I can't ask anyone else."

Taylor smiled. "At least if it's going to be weird, I'm glad to be here with you two," she whispered genuinely.

I felt the lump in my throat. The confusion of what was going on in our lives and the loss of my mother was fresh in my emotions. *If I could only ask her about this, but I can't. I can never ask her anything again.*

"Come on, let's get back. It's cold." Taylor picked up her soda, looking at me as if she were assessing my stability. "Besides, now that we know we aren't in trouble, it doesn't really matter."

That got Hannah moving. "I like the sound of that. Don't get me wrong. I'm really creeped out, but as long as our grades are going to be fine, I guess it doesn't technically matter." Hannah managed to crack a smile and turned to push open the door to the cold outside air.

We walked the few minutes back to our dorm, and even though I had the comfort of my friends, I couldn't shake the uneasy feeling in my belly or the goosebumps on my arms that had started in the office during the meeting. I couldn't stop thinking about what Mrs. Trebule had said.

Both Hannah and Taylor were trying to copy Mrs. Trebule's accent, and they had it down by the time we got to our room. I had to laugh, and the mood between us even seemed a little brighter. We couldn't help but almost roll with laughter when Taylor imitated Dr. Sharma sniffing the air and pretending to sneeze.

"Well, hey, maybe we are related. That would be cool, like we were long-lost cousins or something," Taylor said.

"It's unlikely," Hannah countered. "I ran my eyes over that paper, and me and Taylor aren't on it. We should be somewhere on the tree if we have the same ancestry. It's more believable that our teacher needs some serious mental assistance," she finished as she sat on the couch, picking up her chemistry book.

CHAPTER THIRTEEN

Hannah's House

I couldn't believe that Thanksgiving was coming up so fast. We had midterms and then finals were around the corner. We hadn't heard from Mrs. Trebule after the strange meeting two weeks back. So, we just went on.

Classes – especially Anthropology – were hard. I was glad for the night hosting job that gave us time to work on it together. Thankfully, night hosting was not as crazy as it initially seemed, and I made up for the lack of sleep when I needed to.

Hannah's mom invited both Taylor and me to stay at their home for the Thanksgiving weekend. Hannah talked about all the great food and shopping that would happen and made it sound so exciting that both Taylor and I said "yes", of course. Apparently, her mom made a mean apple pie, which was one of my favorites, so I couldn't refuse.

I was a little bummed as I felt bad for Dad being home by himself for the holiday, so I called to check in on him.

"Hey, Dad. How's it going?" I asked him.

"Hey, kid. Everything's good here. I'm going with your Nino to Jackie's house for Thanksgiving. I'm glad you're going to... what's her name again?" Dad asked.

"Hannah, Dad. Her family invited both me and Taylor, so I won't be the only guest there," I told him.

"Well, good. Hey, I think someone's at the door, so I gotta get going, but give me a call when you have your plans laid out. Text me to let me know you got there okay," he said in a hurry. His voice sounded pained and a little off.

I became alert; something in his voice said he needed to get off the phone now, but he was trying to play it off. My stomach turned over. I took a deep breath. My anxiety tended to get overwhelming sometimes, so I tried to chalk it up to him being busy and convince myself that he was telling me the truth, that there was someone at the door.

"Okay, Dad. Thanks for talking. Miss you a lot, and tell Cindy 'hi' for me," I said, sad to get off the phone with my dad so quickly. Our phone calls seemed to be getting fewer and farther between. I looked through my phone's call list and saw that the last time I'd talked with him had been almost a week ago.

He's busy, I thought to myself. *I'm making too big of a deal about it, being to protective.*

"Will do, kid. I'll talk to you tomorrow or the next day," he said and then our conversation was over. He hung up the phone without hesitation.

I looked at my phone, watching the screen show the ending of the call. My mind felt numb. That was probably the fastest he'd ever gotten off the phone with me.

Thanksgiving week came right after midterms. I was ready for a break, as were Hannah and Taylor. The week was thankfully short. After class on Tuesday, I came back to the dorm and started packing.

Hannah said her house was right next to Lake Ontario and that the wind off the lake made it a bit chilly. I looked forward to testing out my new winter jacket. I hadn't had to use it yet and loved how warm it kept me when I'd worn it around the department store. It even had a place in the sleeves where I could pull the ends over my hands to keep them warm. I called it the West-coaster's dream jacket.

Taylor finished packing up some of her stuff, and Hannah went around to bring up the car. We were planning on leaving around four-thirty and getting to her house later that night. That way, we could have Wednesday to help her mom with anything she needed, and Hannah could show us some of the town that she lived in. Then we had a full schedule, she informed us, that included Thanksgiving on Thursday and shopping on Friday. We'd travel back to school sometime Saturday, as we wanted to have Sunday to get back into the groove. We were scheduled to night host Sunday too, so we couldn't miss that.

We ended up leaving at about five. A half-hour late, which Hannah reminded us of several times while we packed the car. Taylor had wanted to get another pair of her shoes to match an outfit she'd planned on wearing for

Thanksgiving. I had to hand it to her; she dressed great. I needed to ask her for some pointers.

Taylor also remembered the picture she'd gotten and brought that along with her, as Hannah said her mom might be able to help. She still hadn't been able to find anything on her art assignment. She was getting desperate; the write-up of the picture was due quickly after the Thanksgiving break. She hoped she could get some information on it.

On the way to Hannah's house, Hannah told us how her father had bought the home when her brother was a baby and had done a lot of work to it over the years. She said he liked to start a project on the house, then right before it was done, he would start another one. She told us about their garden and how they would go way to the back of their property during the winter and cut their own Christmas tree.

I loved hearing the stories she told about her family. She had two older brothers and her parents. Apparently, her parents had adopted her oldest brother when they hadn't been able to have children of their own. Then, somehow, they had gotten pregnant with her middle brother, then her as time went on. They had stayed in that same house for her entire life.

Most of her family lived close to home, so holidays at their house were always big with lots of people. She told us about her uncles and aunts and who to expect at the dinner table on Thursday.

"Well, we need gas, so let's stop at the next station," Hannah said after a funny story about her brothers allowing a neighbor to ride a four-wheeler through their yard and the crash that happened afterwards.

We took the next exit and stopped at a small gas station right off Highway 481. Going over a bridge and through a crazy circular turn, we made it into the gas station. Looking at the scenery, I knew I'd never live back in California again. I loved the fall here. The crisp air. Many of the trees had already lost their leaves by now, but with the thinning to branches only, there was a unique view of what was behind the forest walls. It was like the land revealed secrets only once a year for a small amount of time, allowing the dwellers to see farther into the wood.

The houses we saw from the highway were mostly two stories tall and had big yards. The buildings along the road with the gas station were brick and cement, with the red of the brick contrasting with the whitish-gray of the cement. There was a grocery store on the corner across from where we were that read "The Big M". It looked small but had a full parking lot, and I heard the rumble of the grocery carts going over the pavement from where we were.

Hannah got out of the car to pay for the fuel. We each tried to give her some cash, but she wouldn't take it.

"I was going home anyway, guys," she pointed out, then went inside.

It was nice to get out of the car and stretch our legs. We were about halfway there, and even though the drive was only forty-five minutes, I'd run on the treadmill the day before for some post-test stress relief and pushed a little harder than usual. I knew I'd done okay on the test, but the run still helped rid my body of the excess adrenaline.

"Um, just for the record," Taylor whispered as we walked toward the gas station doors, "this is kind of creepy. It's totally deserted."

Looking around, I noticed that while the other side of the street was busy, the gas station was deserted except for our car and us.

"Well, this is as populated as you're going to get out this way." Hannah laughed, apparently not thinking a thing about it. "This place actually just got a new Dunkin' Donuts across the street."

"Wow, moving up in the world," Taylor said sarcastically. She had a smile on her face, but I could tell she was a little taken aback. We were in a city by the name of Fulton. Hannah said that from here, we're going to take the scenic route along the water. Whatever that meant.

We went in and got drinks and a bag of pretzels to share. Hannah went to the counter to pay, and Taylor went to the restroom. I brought our sodas and the snack back to the car. I almost dropped a soda but managed to hold onto it. Carrying multiple things instead of making two trips was something I specialized in.

I opened the driver's door and leaned into it, so I could place the sodas in the cup holders. As I did, my leg hit the side of the pump. Somehow, I managed to place the sodas carefully on the top of the trunk before kneeling down to hold my leg.

"Ouch!" I yelled, a little louder than I'd wanted to. I couldn't help it. It hurt a lot. It felt like something had stabbed my leg. Then I was embarrassed. I didn't want to be the baby of the group, so I immediately looked behind me. Hannah was coming up to the car, and Taylor wasn't out yet.

I quickly got back up and looked at my now-torn jeans.

Great, I thought.

"Dang, Emily, what did you do to your pants?" Hannah laughed.

"I guess I need to be more careful. I caught it on the gas pump when I was putting the sodas into the car, but hey, not a drop of soda spilled and pretzels are still intact."

We laughed a little. Taylor came back and got into the car.

"All right, guys, let's get going," Hannah said as she replaced the gas pump.

I made sure to stay away from anything when getting into the back seat before we left. I was ticked that my pants were torn. I'd have to figure out how to sew, so I could fix them. They were my favorite pair.

"Yikes," I heard a couple minutes later from the front seat. I looked up. I'd almost fallen asleep. I saw Hannah's eyes looking at me from the rearview mirror. "Did you do that at the gas station?" she asked. Taylor turned around in the front passenger seat and looked at me.

"What? My torn jeans?" I said.

I was confused and then I wasn't. Looking down, I realized that my jeans were now wet... with my blood.

"I guess so. I thought I just had a tear. Great. Now they are ruined," I said.

It hurt once I realized that it was cut. I could just see the cut from where the hole in the jeans were. It was right under the knee. I rolled my pants up my leg. The section under my knee was a little swollen by now, and it hurt quite a bit.

Hannah swerved the car a little.

"You can see it later. Keep your eyeballs on the road, lady," I said to her.

"My mom keeps a first aid kit in all our cars. It should be under your seat, Taylor," Hannah said. She still looked slightly through the rearview mirror but straightened her driving technique.

I looked under the seat, and there was the first aid kid. Taylor put out her hand to take it. I gave it to her.

"Take out some antiseptic and a bandage," Hannah instructed, all business-like.

Taylor turned her head and said, "So serious, doctor."

"Come on," Hannah said. "With that amount of blood, it's probably a good cut. Last thing she needs is to have to go to the doctor when she's out of state. Insurance would be a nightmare," Hannah insisted.

I hadn't thought about that.

"Okay, Doc. Will do," Taylor continued in good humor.

Taylor turned in her seat more, so she could face me, and told me to put my leg between the front seats, so she could "dress my wound" according to Hannah's instructions.

"Don't worry about the pants. My mom can get anything out of them. Between my brothers racing motocross and racecars and all the trouble we'd get into, she's practiced," Hannah reassured me.

As Taylor looked at my leg, I got a little nauseated. I had to look out the window for a minute. The roads seemed empty. The scenery was still beautiful. The scenic route, as Hannah had called it, was filled with houses that were white-paneled and had car ports. The yards were large with trees, and some had ponds. Mostly, the houses lined the right side of the road. On the left, through the trees, we were following the river that, according to Hannah, connected to Lake Ontario. The sun glittered off the surface of the water like a river of gold as we drove by.

I looked back at my leg. The cut was deep for just bumping into a gasoline pump. There must have been something sticking on it, or it wouldn't have left such a gash.

"You might need a stitch or two," Hannah said, looking at my leg now that she could see it next to her lap. "Hey, if you do, can I do it please?" Hannah pleaded. She seemed a little too excited. "We have some stuff to do it at home. Our neighbor is a nurse, so we have it just in case she needed to come over and help my brothers." Apparently, Hannah's brothers were either accident-prone or into rough sports.

"Sure. Why not?" I said. She was just too happy about it for me to say "no", and besides, I could still run where the stitches would be. So, I figured it wouldn't be too bad, other than it hurting.

"Taylor, take the gauze and put some pressure on it after you clean it up. That way, we can see if it stops. If it does, she probably won't need stitches."

Taylor laid the gauze on my leg and started to open a bandage. We hit a bump in the road, and I guess Hannah was looking at my leg again because we swerved a little. Taylor, Hannah, and I all grabbed my leg instinctively at the same time, trying to hold it in place.

It was like time stopped, and a warm feeling came over me. The pain in my leg was gone, replaced with heat localized to the spot that the cut was. I looked down, and there was a glow coming from our hands.

As quick as we hit the bump in the road, the glow and the warm feeling were gone. I pulled my leg back through the seats into the back. Nobody said a thing.

My pant leg rolled down when I moved my leg back, and I had to look at it again. I saw Taylor looking out of the corner of her eye as I rolled up my pant leg. I was sure that Hannah was looking in the mirror and not at the road.

The place where the semi-cleared, dried blood had been was now entirely cleared off. My leg was clean, and the only thing left was a small, moon-shaped bruise right where the cut had been. Our eyes found one another no matter our position in the car.

"So, that just happened." I didn't know what else to say.

Taylor cleared her throat and took a breath. "So, it seems like we have some skin condition that makes us glow when we touch. I'm sure that happens to lots of people." She looked at Hannah. "What do you say, Doc?"

Hannah didn't say a thing.

"Yeah, and that means we're long-lost cousins or something. Great." I couldn't stop the words from coming out.

Suddenly, the tension built in the car and was so thick, I could have cut through it with a knife. But then what I didn't think would happen did. We all laughed. And I knew that I could talk about this with my two friends. As strange and weird as it was, I knew we could talk about this together without judgment from each other.

"Well, when you put it that way, it's not so bad," Taylor said. "I guess there's no way there could be any joke that did that, so does that make it real?"

"The only way to be sure is to try it again." Hannah was serious. "I mean, they can't play pranks on us at home. I'm sure my family wouldn't go in on it, and they sure as heck didn't play one in the car now."

Hannah seemed to be thinking out loud. Hearing her made me feel better. I knew she was the most practical of us, and she seemed just as confused as I was.

"So, let's do it. Let's try it again," Taylor said seriously.

"Why not?" I said. At that point, I was just ready for the craziness to end.

"I think you guys are right. Let's try to figure this glow thing out tomorrow night, after dinner," Hannah said. "I'm sure my mom will have us busy tonight and tomorrow, during the day, but tomorrow night should be okay. And besides, we're about there."

We slowed down and turned onto a side road. The road curved around a bend and went under a small bridge that was covered in graffiti. The area was pretty. The trees that surrounded the sides of the road were thick and had pine needles, just like the Christmas trees Hannah mentioned. On the right side, as we followed the road, was a small creek through the trees. The brush was thick, but I could see the water in some spots. We slowed some more and made a right turn into a long, rocky driveway.

"I think we should tell Mrs. Trebule about it. You know, write it in that book she gave you, Emily. We're supposed to write stuff we learn about ourselves in there, right? I know we haven't heard from her again, but with the strangeness before and now this, why not?" Hannah went on. "Did you bring it?"

"Yes, I have it here."

I reached down and picked up my bag from the backseat floor. I opened the front pocket, and there it was. I took out the journal and grabbed a pen from an inside pocket. Opening the book, I turned to the first blank page.

"What should I write?" I asked. I had no idea how to put what had been going on into writing.

"Just make a list," Hannah suggested from the front. "That always seems to work for me." She sounded confident that a list was what would work for us.

"Write what we learned. That's what Mrs. Trebule told us to do," Taylor chimed in. Then she looked at Hannah. "You're so official." She was smiling as she made fun of her friend.

"Well, I can do both," I answered them. Taking my pen, I put a bullet point down on the page and wrote.

Our hands glow when we touch

Our hands heal cuts when we touch

Will try tomorrow

I added the third bullet to the list not as something we'd learned but as something we needed to do. Moving the pages away from my face, I looked at them. Nothing seemed to change. I don't know what I'd expected to happen. I stared at them for another few seconds. Then I read the bullets out loud to my roommates, and both Taylor and Hannah approved.

"That works," Taylor said just as Hannah made a right turn into a driveway.

"Oh, we're here, by the way." Hannah smiled. The fact that she'd missed home even being just two hours away was written all over her face.

The rocky driveway kept going even after we stopped. The house that we were met with had wooden paneling along the sides and was painted red. The deck off the back was still the color of half-stained wood. There were flowers lining the sides of the house that looked like they were ready to go into hibernation, like some of the trees. There was a pond off to the side where two ducks were swimming. They were the first ducks I'd seen. It was strange to me that they stayed during the fall, as I thought they would have gone somewhere warmer.

"Let's hold the rest of this until tomorrow, and we can figure more out then. That okay?" Hannah said. As she did, the side door to the house opened, and a woman stepped onto the three descending stairs to the doorway.

She was short and had the same blonde hair as Hannah. Her cheeks were red, as if she'd been working over the stove, and she wore a flower-covered apron over khaki pants and a blouse. She smiled and waved. I knew it was Hannah's mom the second I saw her.

We all got out of the car and started unloading. Hannah got out of her driver's seat and went up the two remaining steps and gave her mom a hug. I had to look at the ground. It seemed like a personal moment between them, and I felt like I was intruding.

"Hey, honey. I hope you had a safe drive," I heard her say to Hannah.

"It was fine, Mom. Glad to be back," Hannah said. "Hey, guys. This is my mom, Sarah Channing," she said to us.

Taylor looked up from the back of the car, where she'd been trying to unload her bags, and waved. I looked over and said "hello" as well. As I went up the steps into the house after Hannah, I looked at Mrs. Channing and smiled.

Before I knew it, I was in an embrace. It was a hug. A mom hug. The kind of hug I hadn't gotten in over a year and hadn't ever expected to get again. It took my breath away.

"Nice to meet you, Emily," she said with a genuine smile.

I returned the smile and, in a lower-than-intended voice, told her, "Nice to meet you too. Thank you for inviting us." I couldn't meet her eyes.

"Don't even think on it. It's the holidays, and there's always enough food, especially when you have a good garden." She pointed to some squash on the kitchen counter. Looking past her, into the kitchen, I decided it was the largest squash I'd ever seen.

Hannah showed us around the downstairs. The house felt like home. The kitchen had gray tile on the floor, and Hannah's parents' bedroom was right off the kitchen. The door was open, revealing a neatly made bed.

Walking through the kitchen brought us into a day room on the left, which shared the same archway as the living room on the right. I could stand in the kitchen and easily see both rooms as there was no hallway downstairs. The stairs to get to Hannah's room were also to the right, the hand railing going up the wall.

Stepping into the day room, I noticed the floors had blue carpet, and there were drapes a similar blue shade that allowed some sun to shine through. It gave the room a soft light. There were shelves lining the walls with trophies that held statues of people in racecars or with hockey sticks, and some that looked like dancers. There were family pictures and an old piano along the wall.

"You girls make yourselves at home while you are here," Mrs. Channing said. She headed to the kitchen. The house smelled like Thanksgiving already. There were hints of pie and cinnamon, along with the warm feeling of the oven having been on most of the day.

"Wow, lots of trophies," Taylor said as we walked to the wall next to the television.

"Yeah, my brothers did hockey and motocross, and I think I have some dance ones from when I was younger." She looked over and laughed, remembering older times. I saw the memories in her eyes.

We followed Hannah back into the kitchen.

"Hey, since you guys are here, can you go to the garden and get me some more squash, some carrots, and a couple potatoes?" Hannah's mom said.

"Sure. You guys want to see the yard?" Hannah turned and looked at us. It was still light out, but soon, it would be too dark to look around. I was anxious to see this garden that I'd heard so much about.

"Yeah," I said. It would feel good to go outside.

Taylor, on the other hand, needed a little convincing. "I'm not sure. Will it be muddy?" she asked.

"Not to worry. We have boots in the cold room." Mrs. Channing pointed her head in the direction of the room.

"Great, then I'm in," Taylor cheered.

We all filed out of the living room and got ready to go outside. I was wearing sneakers, so I decided to forgo the boots and headed out the door.

We walked down the driveway. Taylor loved her borrowed boots. They were black with colored polka dots. "These are so cute," she kept saying.

About a quarter-mile down the driveway, it ended at a large garage. I heard banging and a low hum coming from it. Hannah pulled open the front garage door. The white, dragon-like wing lifted with some effort. Afternoon light poured into the large area. There was wood lining one wall and a wood furnace burning on the left. The cement was under different colors of dust, from brown to silver-gray. There were a couple empty soda cans on some shelves.

On the right sat three men. One looked older. His gray-white hair rimmed his head over his ears, and I couldn't help but thinking of Doc from *Back to the Future*. The smile he gave when he saw Hannah was wide and grateful.

"Hi, girl!" he shouted to her. Hannah had told us once that "girl" was a nickname that her dad called her.

"Hi, Dad," Hannah said. "Guys, this is my dad, Dave."

"Hi, girls. So, Hannah, how's school?" he asked her.

"Good. This is Taylor and Emily," Hannah shouted to him over the hum of what looked like an air compressor.

"Nice to meet you guys. I hear you're staying for the big event Thursday," he said.

"Yes, thank you," I replied.

Dave smiled at me. In one instant, I felt like I'd met one of the nicest people in the world, which was strange because I'd only just met him, and we'd not even spoken ten words to each other. He stood up. He was tall and thin, and I decided that his wild hair and shiny head fit him perfectly. He walked over and gave Hannah a quick hug.

The two men sitting next to him looked over. One of them had a metal, hollow pipe in his hands, and the other what looked like a welding helmet. I guessed these were Hannah's brothers. They looked over.

"Hey, Hanny!" one of them shouted. The one on the right, with the welding helmet in hand, was light-skinned and had blondish-red hair. He wore a plaid, flannel shirt and jeans with yellow and black puma shoes.

That must be Jack, I thought to myself, remembering Hannah's description of her brothers.

"Hi," said the other brother next to him. He got up and came over to Hannah. She knocked fists with him. He turned and went back to where he'd been sitting. He had dark brown hair and tanner skin. He wore jeans like his brother, but there were more holes in them, and they looked like they'd never been washed. He kept his welding helmet up. Looking at him, I felt the corner of my mouth turn up. He looked over and caught me staring. He smiled. I had to look away, feeling suddenly awkward.

And that must be Nick, I realized as I nodded a "hello" to Hannah's oldest brother.

"Hey, guys," Hannah replied to them. "Guys, this is Nick and Jack, my brothers." Hannah pointed at Nick as the dark-haired brother, and Jack as the other. "Hey, I'm going to get some stuff from the garden for Mom and show Taylor and Emily our spread back there. You want me to get you anything?" she asked them.

"We're good," Nick said.

We walked around the side of the garage and into the grass. It was muddy. I was thinking about Nick. I knew Hannah's brother had been adopted, but he fit right in with the entire family. A second later, I found myself thinking about Sean. We'd been meeting for coffee almost every Friday morning. The last two Fridays, however, he'd cancelled, and I hadn't seen him in the dorms lately. I guessed school was getting busy for him. He had some crazy engineering classes from what he'd told me.

Then I stepped in a puddle and reality hit me with icy-cold water. Gooey mud came over and into my sneakers.

"Yuck!" I said.

"Should have opted for some boots," Taylor said, laughing.

"Mhm," I replied sarcastically, trying to wipe my shoe on the grass. "So, do you guys grow your own vegetables all the time?" I asked, wanting to get my mind on something other than my cold foot.

"Yeah, we've been doing this for the last ten years or so. I remember being little and helping my mom and brothers get the weeds out in the summer," she said.

We rounded the backside of the barn and went behind some pine trees. We followed a well-used, muddy path, complete with deep puddles that made me agree with Taylor and wish I'd opted for the offered rain boots too. My running sneakers were going to need a good washing after this.

"Wow, you guys have a lot of land," Taylor said.

"It's been in our family for years, and we love the open space." I could tell from her expression and tone of voice that Hannah loved her home.

As we neared the garden, I saw some large tree rods with pie tins tethered to them.

"Is that a pie tin?" I asked.

"Yeah, it helps keep the birds and other animals away from the plants, so we don't have as much food stolen," Hannah told us.

"But you guys have a fence and everything. It looks pretty good," Taylor said, pointing at the upcoming fenced-off area. Through the wire fence, I saw lots of rows of vegetables and some bushes, along with a couple trees that lined the corners. Late-blooming wildflowers lined the outside of the fences.

"You'd be surprised. Some animals get in here regardless of what we do, even with a good fence. They get just as creative about coming in as we do with keeping them out,"

Hannah said, stopping at the gate to the garden. "Last year, we had a huge rabbit problem, and my mom lost a bunch of her radishes. She was so mad."

She laughed a little and opened the gate. The garden was huge, probably the largest home garden I'd ever seen.

"We keep everything organic. The barrels back there," Hannah said, pointing to some metal barrels off toward the back side of the garden, "collect rainwater and snow during the off-seasons and summertime. We can water the plants and save water at the same time."

Hannah closed the gate behind Taylor after she came in. She then grabbed one of the hanging baskets that was propped on the side of the fence and started down one of the rows.

"And those barrels over there," she said, pointing to the opposite side from the rain barrels, "are compost that we use to fertilize during planting season and the summer."

Hannah looked at the ground, appearing to choose just the right place to pick her needed vegetables.

"Here we go." She squatted down. "The compost helps the vegetables grow strong and big, even if it smells sometimes." She made a face.

"That's neat." I couldn't help myself. I'd had a little garden at home when I was young. I remembered picking the weeds out of it with my mom and Dad and planting some corn, I think, but that was the extent of my gardening experience. The only other thing I'd seen planted at home were the roses that my mom planted every year, adding a new rose bush to her collection during each planting season. She faithfully tended them, and each year, they faithfully returned. She always joked that she had a "brown" thumb, not a "green" thumb, but as far as the roses were concerned, she was the best gardener there was.

"Aw, look, a deer!" Taylor pointed off in the distance. Both Hannah and I looked where she was pointing.

We laughed and then I watched as Hannah grabbed some carrots out of the ground and shook some dirt off. Then she moved to another section of the garden and pulled some squash and potatoes out of their respective hiding places.

"I like the flowers you guys have outside of the fences," I told her.

"They help keep away different bugs. That way, we don't have to use pesticides."

"So, um…" Taylor hesitantly began as Hannah was brushing off dirt from her knees. "Since we're out here, I know we said we'd wait until tomorrow to see if we're crazy, but at the risk of sounding like a lunatic, I'm thinking we should test out our little hand flashlights now?" She finished in more of a question than a statement, looking more at her hands.

"Well…" Hannah began, looking around. There was no one else there to see us. We seemed to be alone. "Let's do it. We can either find out if there's something going on or not."

Hannah looked between Taylor and myself and then nodded her head. She moved closer, and the three of us stood in a small circle. None of us could meet each other's eyes.

"I feel a bit silly," I confessed.

"Well, you're in good company," Hannah replied. "So, I guess I will count to three, then."

"One."

Hannah grabbed Taylors hand.

"Two."

Taylor grabbed my hand.

"Three."

I took Hannah's hand.

The warmth I felt in my hands started slowly in the palm and spread through the entire hand. Small tendrils of light began to seep through our clasped fingers. We held on this time, watching how the brilliant blue wrapped designs over our skin. I looked at both Hannah and Taylor and smiled.

"I guess we're not crazy," I laughed. My two friends were smiling also.

"Okay, we'd better let go. It's getting brighter," Hannah said. "I'll count again, and on three, we can let go."

She started the count.

When she yelled, "Three!" we released our hands. The light was so bright by this point that I had to blink away the flash blindness.

"Oh," I heard Taylor say. I turned and saw her looking around. I followed her gaze. Every flower surrounding the garden where we stood was in full bloom and turned in our direction. It was as if they were looking for sunlight. In the garden, the end of summer squash vines seemed to be full of new buds, as if they were about to produce a new fall crop. I turned to look at Hannah. She was staring in the distance. She pointed. Both Taylor and I looked where she was pointing.

Along the tree line where we'd spotted the deer was a full line of animals. There were deer, what looked like cats and a few dogs, and lower in the grass were rabbits and some other animals I couldn't place. On the lower branches of the trees, I saw birds. All were staring and watching us.

"Taylor," Hannah whispered, "this is your area, right?" She said still staring at the animals.

"Um, I think it's *our* area now," Taylor replied, not even turning her head.

"Hanny, come on. Ma needs you," came a yell. As we watched, the animals seemed to bow their heads and receded into the darkness of the trees.

"Startled back into reality, Hannah yelled, "Be right there," and we left the garden and made the walk back to the house.

When we got back to the house, we left our shoes at the door. I left my sneakers propped up so that any remaining liquid from the puddles could drain out. I took off my socks too, as they were soaked through. I followed Taylor and Hannah in the house when I was done. Walking into the kitchen, it smelled like coffee.

None of us talked about what had just happened, but the looks we gave each other conveyed the surprise and confusion we felt.

We sat down at the table. It was nice; the table was a large oval and had placemats and pretty fall decorations in the center. Some of the decorations I'd seen around the house looked handmade. The smell of fresh coffee seemed to ground me.

"So, what's been happening around here?" Hannah asked her mom as she got out some coffee mugs for us.

"Not much. We were getting ready to start a remodel of the bathroom upstairs, but then something came up with the racecar in the garage," Mrs. Channing replied.

She sat down at the end of the table. She looked like she'd been working most of the day in the kitchen.

"Thanks for getting the vegetables, honey," she told Hannah. "Oh, and your father finally finished the trailer," she added with a smile. Hannah laughed. She'd told us about her dad's habit of working on multiple home projects at a time.

"Really?" Hannah said. "He's been working on that forever." Taylor and I looked from Hannah to her mother.

They were smiling, and it was nice to see that they'd missed each other.

The house felt like a safe place. I was happy for Hannah, my friend. She had this place to grow up in and be with her family. I was glad to be included in their Thanksgiving.

We chatted for a little while longer, until the timer on the stove went off and Hannah's mom had to get back to cooking. Suddenly, Taylor let out a startled shout.

"Oh, yeah," she said, her eyes widening. She got up from the table and grabbed her backpack from the other room. She came back and sat down with it. She opened it and pushed through the papers inside.

"What about the picture we were going to check out? I brought my copy to compare," Taylor said as she got the envelope out of her bag.

"Taylor got an assignment from her class, and it looks like the painting Grandma did that we have upstairs," Hannah told her mother. "Is it all right if I get it and bring it down to compare, Mom?"

"Sure. Just be careful not to trip on any of the boxes up there," her mom replied. Hannah pushed back her chair and went upstairs. I heard her walking overhead, then start her way back down to the kitchen. Taylor took her picture out of the envelope and pushed it toward Hannah's mom as she walked over to the table.

"Well, that's the picture, all right," Mrs. Channing commented. "Where did you say it was taken?"

"I didn't. That's part of the assignment. We have to learn about the picture, who painted it, where it was, and everything in between. Only, I haven't been able to find a lick of information on this one. Actually, it's strange because I painted a similar picture – or, well, what I think is similar to this one – for my senior project in my last year of high school. I thought it was an original that I'd painted from my imagination, but I guess not." Taylor trailed off as Hannah came to the table with the painting.

Hannah sat down and placed the flipped-over picture adjacent to Taylor's picture assignment. She turned it over.

They were exactly the same.

"Hannah's grandma painted this scene a lot, especially when she was older and her Alzheimer's was getting worse. It was always the same. We figured it was somewhere she had been or somewhere she'd seen in a movie. It must be a famous place since you painted it, she painted it, and now you have it for an assignment," Mrs. Channing said. "I had just figured that my grandmother taught my mother, as I've also seen it in the old house that my mother lived in." She looked between the paintings on her table.

Then something on the stove sizzled, and we all jumped. The contents of a pot were boiling over and steaming on the flat top. Sarah was over there in a second and appeased whatever it was that was in the pot.

"All right, ladies, time to get out of the kitchen. I work best alone." She smiled and handed us all our coffee cups, then ushered us into the living room.

"Thanks, Mom," Hannah said. Taylor and I thanked her too.

"We've got to figure this picture thing out. It can't be a coincidence that I can't find any information about it. I still think it's the same as the one I painted in school last year. I know I didn't copy it from anywhere. When I turned in the project, the art director checked over everyone's projects, and she would have found something. I know it," Taylor said once we were in the living room, alone.

Hannah said, "Maybe someone will know something about it on Thanksgiving. We will have to ask after dinner."

There wasn't much we could do until then other than chat. We didn't want to talk about what had happened back in the garden for fear that someone would overhear us and think we were crazy. So, we watched some television and let the heaviness of the afternoon lift.

That night, dinner was delicious. Mrs. Channing made fried squash cakes with baked chicken and glazed carrots. There were honey rolls that she'd made from scratch and even a salad with kale and feta cheese. There was a glass pitcher of milk on the table from one of the homes down the road. And best of all, for dessert, Hannah's mom made homemade praline maple ice cream. She'd even used the maple syrup from the maple trees around their house. I was in awe.

During dinner, Hannah's brother, Nick, told me that from the months of February through April, they collected the syrup from the trees. Then he told us about the garden. It was interesting to hear him talk. He showed his excitement for the plants and methods of gardening. I couldn't help but think that I'd heard his voice before. It had a melodic rhythm to it that seemed to help me remember what he was saying.

A second later, I realized that I was lost in thought and staring at his perfect eyelashes when I heard, "Hey, Earth to Emily," coming from Hannah. I refocused my gaze, feeling my cheeks burn. I realized that I found Hannah's brother attractive.

"Oh," I said. "What were you saying?"

"Have you ever had maple syrup fresh from the tree, not from a store-bought bottle?" Nick asked.

"No, I don't think I have," I said, slightly embarrassed.

"No, me neither," Taylor said.

With that, he got up and went to the refrigerator. Hannah rolled her eyes. "He loves that stuff," Hannah said sarcastically.

"Hey, you do too," her brother said. We laughed. He came back to the table holding two spoons and handed one to both Taylor and me.

"Here, try this," he said as he delicately poured the maple syrup onto the spoons without spilling a drop.

Saying the maple syrup was good would have been an insult. It was amazing. One of the best things I'd ever tasted. I wanted to box some up and take it home.

"Wow, that is good," I said, forgetting my unexplainable shyness around him.

"That's great," Taylor said.

With a smile, he sat back at the table.

Later that evening, Hannah's parents went to bed, and her brother, Jack, went back out to check something in the garage before going to visit a friend in town. Taylor went upstairs to call her mom, and Hannah decided she wanted to look at her datebook and assignment list. That left Hannah's oldest brother, Nick, and myself sitting at the table.

We talked about everything. He offered to show me the greenhouse when the spring came. I learned that Nick loved the science behind planting, and he explained that the way the garden was planted encouraged preservation of the nutrients in the soil. He told me that they made sure to rotate their crops every few years to help things grow well. Nick told me about how he liked racing and building the racecar that his dad was working on with his brother.

I told him about California. He'd only been to the state once for a race with his brother and dad, but they didn't venture far from the track and then had to drive right home.

Talking with him was like talking with someone I'd known forever. My earlier shyness was gone. He put me at ease.

Eventually, I had to call it a night. I looked up at the clock and noticed that it was already 2:45 a.m. I couldn't believe it. The last I'd looked, it was around eleven. I said goodnight and went upstairs to Hannah's room.

"Well, well," Taylor whispered when I laid down on the blow-up mattress. "Look at Emily, taking a stab at Hannah's older brother," she said sarcastically and giggled. "I wonder what Sean would think about that."

Oh, please, shut up!" I laughed back. "He's nice to talk to. He was telling me about the garden and a bunch of other stuff."

"Right, because a guy would stay up until almost three in the morning without thinking anything of it, I'm sure. You really are clueless about boys," Taylor teased again.

"Oh, come on. He's just a nice person. It was cool to talk about how it is living up here. I like it. California seems so... dry compared to this," I told her.

"Right," she said. I could tell from her tone she was smiling. "Hey, Hannah, you awake?" Taylor said in a hushed tone.

"Of course, I am. How can anyone sleep with you two going on so?" she replied flatly. "And Emily, be nice to my brother."

"You guys are nuts," I said. Both of them laughed. Even though I knew they were nuts, I couldn't deny how much I'd enjoyed talking to Nick. Sean and I had talked and had fun and sent phone messages to each other, but the level of relaxation I had when talking to Nick was entirely different. I couldn't pinpoint it.

I did feel a little guilty though. I hadn't texted Sean back the last time he sent me a message, and I'd missed his call yesterday. I decided I needed to say "hi" to him tomorrow as soon as I could. We weren't dating or anything, but I wasn't sure how he felt, and I didn't want to ignore him. He was my friend.

This is ridiculous, I thought to myself. *I have nothing to worry about because there was nothing there. I just had a nice conversation with someone that lasted into the late night. And I do not need to feel guilty because my* FRIEND, *Sean, was simply that: a friend. Besides, I don't date.*

I took a silent, deep breath to try to calm my nerves. I couldn't tell why my nerves were in overdrive, and I was annoyed with myself for it.

"Goodnight, guys," I said, just as sarcastically as they had been talking to me.

"Goodnight, Emily," they said, mocking me.

I fell asleep quickly. It was almost three-thirty in the morning after all.

CHAPTER FOURTEEN

Journaling

The next day, we ran errands to the store and baked with Mrs. Channing. We stole a little time going to get some groceries and talked about the next time we would test out the strange light-touch thing we had going on.

"Let's just wait until we get back. I don't want anyone to institutionalize us," Hannah said. She was looking for a Lipton soup mix.

"That sounds fine. I think these days are going to go by fast anyway," I said.

"Agreed. I can't wait to go shopping on Friday," Taylor said. She'd been tracking the Black Friday ads for a week.

"Hey, did you write what happened in the book?" Hannah asked me.

"Not yet." I had forgotten all about it. The journal was still tucked in my bag, where I'd put it back in the car. "I'll make sure to do it tonight." I was looking down the list

Hannah's mom had given us and making sure we hadn't forgotten anything. I made a mental note to write in the journal before I went to sleep.

When we got back to the house, Jack and Nick were in the garage with Hannah's dad, Dave, again. We started unloading the car, and Nick came over and helped carry in some of the bags. He took one bag right out of my hand and then grabbed the other bag I had just leaned in to pick up.

"Hey!" I half-yelled and half-laughed to him. I felt a little useless with everyone else bringing in something except me.

"I got it," was all Nick replied.

I saw the smile on Taylor's face. Hannah was already inside, helping her mom put away the bags of groceries we brought.

"Thanks," I managed to get out as I followed him into the house.

"No problem," he replied. There was an awkward moment after he put the groceries down and turned to look at me. He seemed to want to say something, then the door to the cold room opened and Jack came in.

"Hey, I need your help with something," Jack said.

"Yup," Nick replied.

"See you later," I said.

"See you later," Nick said as he followed Jack out.

I went back into the kitchen.

The day was over before I felt like it had started. The guys worked in the garage that evening, and I didn't get a chance to talk to Nick before we headed upstairs. I couldn't fall asleep and was still awake when I heard Nick and Jack come up the stairs and go to their rooms, all the while talking about a fuel injection.

I suddenly remembered I had told Hannah and Taylor I would write in the journal about what had happened at the garden. I sat up in bed and reached over the side down to the floor. I could just feel the edge of my bag. I pulled it toward me and tried to be quiet as I unzipped the front pocket. I pulled the journal and a pen out. The light from outside came in the un-covered window and allowed me to see. I wouldn't have to use a flashlight. The journal pages looked silver under the moonlight. I opened to the first page and stared.

Underneath the third bullet where I'd written "*Will try tomorrow*" was a single word written in a neat, clean, hand-written script not of my own making. It read, "DON'T."

"Guys," I managed to whisper about an octave higher than my normal voice rested, panic starting in my chest. "Guys," I repeated, more urgent this time.

"What is it? It's like three in the morning, man," I heard Taylor moan from across the room.

"You have to see this." I held up the journal.

Taylor must have been looking in my direction because I saw her sit up in bed. I heard her take a deep breath and push back the covers. She got up and walked over to where

I was, picking up the journal. I could just make out her facial expressions.

"Did you write that?" Taylor asked me.

"No," I answered.

Taylor walked over to the small couch where Hannah was sleeping. "Hey, get up. We need to show you something." She shook Hannah, who protested, then woke with a start.

"What?" Hannah still didn't quite understand what was going on.

"I opened the journal to write in it and saw this." I walked over to where both Taylor and Hannah were looking at the first page of the book. I put my finger over where the mysterious entry had appeared.

In the moonlight, I saw understanding dawn on Hannah's face.

"I didn't write that, and I don't think either of you did." I didn't know what else to say.

"I definitely don't think we should try it again now. At least not until we talk with Mrs. Trebule. Are we agreed on that?" She looked from Taylor to me.

"Okay," I managed to say.

"Agreed," Taylor followed me. "Honestly, I can't decide if I need an Advil, a nap, or a straight jacket right now."

We all laughed. I felt some of the tension and a little bit of fear leave my center. At least if I was going to be committed, I would be in good company.

"Let's get some sleep, if we can. I'm sure Mom will get us up early to help," Hannah said and relaxed back into the pillows on the couch. She handed the journal back to me. I went back to the bed and replaced the book in my bag. When I zipped it shut, I felt like I was trying to lock the bag closed, so I wouldn't' have to deal with any of these weird happenings.

Somehow, I must have been able to relax because I remember hearing Taylor get back into her blankets and then I was waking up the next morning.

Thanksgiving Day was even busier than the day before. Hannah's mom got us up early to help in the kitchen. Then we watched the Macy's Thanksgiving Day parade on television and talked some. Dave, Nick, and Jack went out to the garage, as I noticed was their custom. Hannah said they had just finished racing season in September, and they planned to change the racecar they were running. They were trying to get most of it done before the weather got too cold.

I made sure to give my dad a call early and see how he was doing. My godfather was over, and he said they were just getting ready to go to breakfast. He'd said they were going together to Thanksgiving dinner as well, so I let him go and was glad he was with someone else. On a whim of bravery, I had called Sean to say "hello", but there was no answer, so I let the call go to voicemail. I wished him a happy Thanksgiving and told him I would try to call again after we got back to the dorms.

Taylor called her family, and I heard her talking with her brother and mom. Her dad seemed to be on the line as well. She'd kept the phone on speaker since she was helping in the kitchen. I had to admire her for her multitasking abilities.

I left the room to give her some privacy. I'm sure it was difficult for her family not to have her there this year on a holiday. Heck, I felt sad over my first one away from home, but I tried to look on the bright side. We were here together, and everyone was having a nice time.

I came back into the kitchen when I heard Taylor hang up with her family.

"Anything I can help with, Mrs. C.?" I asked Mrs. Channing.

"Sure." She looked around. Taylor was at the sink, cleaning some of the cooking pots, and Hannah was at the oven with the stuffing. "Can you set the table, please?" she asked me.

"Of course," I said and went to the place she'd piled the cloth napkins, silverware, and plates. I started setting up.

Dinner was amazing – hands-down one of the best Thanksgiving meals I'd ever eaten. There was turkey and stuffing and all of the amazing sides. The rolls were Hannah's grandmother's recipe. They were delicious – hot and sweet and just right. The basket they were in went around twice, and they were gone. Thankfully, this seemed to be a regular occurrence on holidays, so Mrs. Channing had another batch ready in the oven for when the first ran low.

Once the food was gone and the dishes were cleaned and put away, we got to work on the Thanksgiving shopping ads. Taylor was the leader in this project and let us know where and when we needed to be for whatever we were looking for. The whole family went out shopping. There was a Wal-Mart in both the city of Oswego and the city of Fulton, and we split up so that we could make the most of the sales. We got through the shopping madness and managed to get everything on the lists Hannah's mom gave us by texting each other. I had fun.

Friday evening, Nick and I spent another couple of hours chatting on the back porch of the house. We talked about the next year's planting season, and I agreed to come up and see it.

It was cold, but Mr. Channing made everyone hot chocolate, and Taylor brought out two cups for us. Of course, she smirked and laughed a bit when she threw the blanket out the back door as well and yelled, "It's cold, you morons."

I guessed this was a little unusual for the family because even Nick's mom had a laugh when we came back in the house. I wanted to tell her it was unusual for me as well but kept telling myself the nervousness I felt around him was all in my head.

By the time Saturday afternoon came, I couldn't believe I was tired from the mini-vacation. It had been fun though, and I enjoyed spending time with Hannah's family.

Nick came in from the garage to see us off. He teased his sister and said bye to Taylor. Then, as we were getting into the car, he told me not to forget to come back and see the greenhouse in the spring and gave me his number. I smiled and said that I wouldn't forget.

The drive back to campus was much more uneventful than the drive to Hannah's house. We didn't need to stop for gas, so we made good time back. It took us a little bit to get everything back into the dorms though, as Hannah's mom had sent us back with leftovers from Thanksgiving. The rolls she'd sent didn't make the drive, sadly. We ate them all in the hour before we got back.

We got settled in. We finished out our vacation with having to night host on Sunday evening. We had another anthropology article to read, which was nicer to do together with the charged topics that we were given.

Looking through my emails, I noticed that I had two unopened messages. One of them was from Hannah's brother, Nick. He'd told me he was going to email me a link to where they got their organic seedlings from for the garden.

The other message was from Mrs. Trebule.

Ladies,

I trust your holiday and travel went well. It is time to discuss your further assignments with my class. We must have a meeting. Monday evening, we will meet in the place we previously met at a consistent time. I trust you are familiar with the location and the direction. Do not speak of this meeting to anyone.

Regards,

Mrs. Trebule.

And we had our second meeting.

It was quiet in the dorm that night, even with everyone back from the short holiday break.

"I guess she does want to meet with us again," Taylor spoke up.

"What do you think the future assignments are going to be?" Hannah asked.

I didn't know what to say. I re-read the email again, feeling an idea come into my mind. Neither of us had spoken about our experience in the garden or the journal since we'd agreed to wait until our next meeting and discuss with Mrs. Trebule.

"I know it's late, but what would you guys think about..." I stalled in my sentence, not wanting to say it. Heck, I didn't even know how to say it.

"Let's do it," Taylor finished for me. I guess we were all thinking about it. Looking at Hannah, I saw her eyes go between Taylor and myself.

"I guess we can't learn about it if we don't try it," she finally said, resolve in her voice. "But if any more writing shows up in that book, I'm going to find a therapist."

The last half-hour of our shift was exceptionally long. No one came in, and we had finished our reading assignment and put our things away. Finally, when the hands of the wall clock met at the three and twelve, we got up and went wordlessly down the hallway. Going into our room, I put my bag slowly and deliberately onto my bed, trying to listen to the other two and decide if they were doing the same. I turned and walked back into the common room. Taylor and Hannah were already there.

"So, how do we do this?" Taylor spoke first.

Hannah turned and went to the common room window and turned the blinds' cord, making sure the slits were closed. Then she walked to the room door and pushed in the door lock.

"I guess we just do it… like before." She stood in the middle of the common room, between the small couch and chair. She held out her hands.

"I feel like a fool," Hannah whispered under her breath.

"Don't," I told her, getting to my feet.

"If you are, then we all are," Taylor said, taking her hand and extending her other to me.

I took Taylor's outstretched hand and then Hannah's.

I felt a small prickle in my palms and then warmth radiated up my arms. The atmosphere in our room felt thick. Tendrils of light began to climb up my clasped fingers from where my hands were gripped in those of my two friends. We all looked at each other. It felt almost hot in our room.

Taylor laughed. "Wow," she said breathlessly.

Hannah looked more relieved than anything else.

I watched the tendrils of light become thicker and envelop our hands. There were now three bright lights at the points of our hands touching. The light was so bright, I could not even see our hands anymore. Our room lit up in a blue hue that shadowed our faces and walls. I was mesmerized.

Bang, bang, bang.

Jolted from our fascination, we let go of each other immediately.

"Hey, I said," came John's booming voice through our door. "Did you leave the sign-in sheets for me?" He sounded mad. I hadn't heard him at all until he'd hit on the door. I felt a little confused. I couldn't remember what had happened to the sign-in sheets. We usually just slipped them under the door to the office when the shift was over.

Hannah rolled her eyes. "They are in your office, John, where they always are. I put them there after we finished," she yelled through the door.

"Fine," John yelled back. I heard his footsteps recede down the hallway.

"What the heck?" Taylor said. We all looked at each other. John never needed those papers until the next day. He never even left his room once he went to bed. At least not on any of our night hosting nights. Why was he out so late, and why did he bang on our door like that? I couldn't figure it out.

We looked at each other. I started laughing. I was so nervous, it just came out. Then both of my friends started laughing with me.

"Do I write that in the journal?" I had to ask.

The three of us laughed harder. When we finally had better control of our nerves, we decided it was late, and with school starting back the next day, we needed to sleep. Leaving our common room doors open, the three of us went to bed.

CHAPTER FIFTEEN

The Second Meeting

Monday felt like it came quicker than usual, which, after a vacation, is saying something. I managed to grab some of the leftover apple pie that Hannah's mom made. It hit the spot after a busy day. I tried all day to keep my mind busy and not think about the upcoming meeting with Mrs. Trebule, but it didn't do much good.

I kept coming back to three things. First, whenever the three of us touched in any way, something strange happened. Second, our family trees were nearly identical all the way down one section, from our mother's great, great, great grandmother. And third, even though we'd never met before school started and were from different parts of the country, I felt like these two girls were my sisters. I felt like I'd known them for years.

The three of us ate a late dinner after going to the library. We stopped at an on-campus sandwich cafe. It was a letdown after enjoying the last bit of leftovers from Thanksgiving. I wasn't sure what I was going to miss more:

the croissants or the stuffing. Hannah's mother made the best stuffing I had ever tasted in my entire life. It was a mixture of sweet maple breakfast sausage and sautéed celery and onion, along with fresh bread crumbs and seasonings. It was so good. I couldn't help thinking of it as I ate my cold sub for dinner.

"I wish I had some cranberry sauce," Taylor said. We laughed, realizing that we were all thinking the same thing.

The three of us headed back to the dorms and tried to avoid talking about the upcoming meeting. It was nice having a night without night hosting, even if we had the dreaded meeting with Mrs. Trebule.

We turned the corner to head to our room when we spotted someone leaning against our door. It was Seth waiting there, his dark bag slung sloppily on the floor. His white t-shirt sparkled against the dull hallway walls, and his ripped jeans and boots made his legs look athletic and relaxed all at the same time.

"What the eff," Taylor whispered to me. Then, "Yeah, he might be a creep, but he sure is hot."

Hannah stopped a couple feet from our door. Taylor and I were behind her.

"Ladies. How are you this evening?" Seth looked at us. I had a strange nervous feeling. Even though I thought he was attractive, I was not attracted to him.

"Hi, Seth. How are you?" Taylor almost hissed. She wasn't letting him get to her that easily. "Are you a stalker now?"

"Nah, I just wanted to invite you to the end of semester party off-campus. I hear it's the place to be." He grinned.

Taylor rolled her eyes then turned to look at Hannah and myself. She took her time turning back around to face Seth.

"I'll take that as a 'yes', then." He stood up and stepped closer to Taylor. He bent down and whispered something in her ear that I couldn't make out.

"Hey, guys, everything okay?" John walked up to us. I was relieved.

Seth looked at John like he'd just seen his arch enemy. He hissed, "Fancy seeing you here," with such a distasteful tone that I was surprised John didn't punch him outright.

John looked at us all and then at Seth. "These guys have night hosting tonight, Seth. Why don't you visit another time? Or, well, don't visit another time," John said, talking *at* Seth rather than to him. The vein on the side of John's head pulsed as he restrained his attitude. I kind of wished he would hit Seth. I hadn't liked him much since our last meeting, and my feelings hadn't changed.

"Well, isn't that just convenient," Seth replied, slowly staring at John.

I heard the door of the dorm open, and around the corner came Sean. He carried a soda in one hand and a Styrofoam container in the other.

"Yes," Seth said, looking at Sean and then back at John. "Yes, it is. Isn't it?"

With that, Seth turned and walked in the opposite direction and around the corner. I heard the side door to the dorm open and close just after he disappeared.

"Hey, guys. How's it going? And why was Seth here?" Sean asked, looking at us and then sharing a glance with John. I would have missed it if I hadn't gotten to know Sean over the past weeks.

"Oh, nothing. It's fine. Thanks for getting rid of him though," Taylor said.

"Hey, Emily, I brought you some of the peanut butter bars from the cafeteria. I can't meet for coffee for the next couple Fridays, so it's a peace offering." He smiled, and I couldn't be mad, especially because he had brought me chocolate and peanut butter.

"Thanks a lot. Not to worry. I know where you live," I said, trying to be nonchalant about the whole thing. I felt my cheeks turning red. Taylor gave me a side glance.

"Okay, well, I was just wondering if you wanted to cover the night hosting shift tonight? We need a couple extra shifts covered." John was still there and was looking at us expectantly.

The guys down the hall had a bad habit of leaving their posts early. About a week and a half ago, there was a theft on the top floor of the building, and the guys hadn't signed people in. Needless to say, that was their last shift.

"Sorry, John. We can't do it this time. Maybe next?" Hannah said.

"Why not? Come on, don't leave me hanging on this. You three are our best team. You do what you're supposed to and don't complain or come get me all night long," John argued.

"Sorry. We've got a big project we're working on and have to go to the library," Hannah said again. It was a good thing she had chimed in when she did because I'd forgotten Mrs. Trebule's warning of telling anyone about our meeting.

"Come on, man. I'll see if our group can do it," Sean said. He turned to me and said, "See ya later," then walked back down the hallway with John. I watched them go into the front room office.

We had about fifteen minutes before we had to leave for our meeting. Hannah, Taylor, and I were in the common room.

"Okay, we need a plan for this meeting," Hannah said. She ripped off a piece of paper from her notebook. "So, as far as I can see, this is what our main objectives should be." Hannah wrote a few lines on the paper and turned it around for us to view what she had written.

1. Light when our hands touch

2. Are we related?

3. Cut on leg

4. Journal

"I mean, this is what it comes down to, right?" Hannah said, looking at her paper. I saw the frustration she felt in trying to make sense of the whole thing. Neither of us said anything. I looked at the clock.

"It's time to go," I stated. The other two followed my gaze, and we all stared at the time piece for a second before we got up to leave.

The wind was blowing, and the night was downright cold. I wished it would snow. I thought, *If it's going to be this cold, then why not have snow to play in?*

As if she had read my mind, Taylor said, "I wish it would snow!"

"Me too," I said.

We got to the Shaw building quickly, as the cold made us walk with a purpose. It took me a couple seconds after we got into the building to feel my fingers. I'd kept them tucked into the bottom of my jacket sleeves, but it hadn't done much good.

We headed down the stairs, then around the circular hallway with the lined doors. We stopped when we came to the right one. At the bottom of the doorway, next to the frame along the wall, was a small, cardboard box labeled "Assignments". It was about half-full. I wondered what class that was for. Mrs. Trebule seemed to always be busy with courses and grading. I guessed that was why the meeting had taken so long to arrange.

The door was slightly ajar.

"Okay, here we go. And if we don't have a legitimate explanation for this entire thing by the end of this meeting,

I'm having myself committed tomorrow," Hannah whispered as she gently pushed the door open.

The office was empty. We hadn't been expecting that. We looked around and didn't see anyone.

"What the heck?" Taylor said as she stepped forward into the room.

"What?" I followed her into the office. She walked toward Mrs. Trebule's desk.

"Are you guys seeing the same thing? It's not just me, right?" Taylor went on holding up a picture that had been sitting atop the desk.

"You three are... observant," a voice from behind us calmly interrupted. We turned around, and as the door was about to hit the wall, in walked Mrs. Trebule and Elaine. They looked flustered, and mud and dirt lined the bottom of Elaine's hooded cloak.

I guessed I was staring because a minute later, I felt their eyes on me. Mrs. Trebule spoke first.

"Well, sorry we are late, dears, but it couldn't be helped. And Emily, it's not polite to stare." She crossed to where Taylor stood, looking at the picture on her desk.

Elaine continued to look at us with a cold and calculating look. Her eyes went slowly from Hannah to Taylor and then to me. It was like she was taking inventory of who we were and what we were doing any time she looked at us.

"Have you three thought about anything we talked about at our last meeting? Surely, you have some questions for me?" Mrs. Trebule chatted as she sat down at her desk. She looked up at us expectantly.

"Well..." Taylor spoke up first. I don't think Hannah or myself could have found our voices at that moment. "I thought this a few minutes ago. We were walking here, and we realized that it had only been a couple of months that we've known each other, and yet, we feel like we've known each other forever."

"I feel like I've known these two my entire life," Hannah cut in. They both looked at me.

"I feel the same way." I smiled. It had made the time away from home bearable, knowing that these two new friends of mine had the same thoughts as I did and felt as close to me as I did to them. Even though it was bitter cold outside, and I was still chilled from our walk over, I felt like a small internal candle had been lit as I realized that I had gained two lifelong friends. I didn't feel as alone.

There was silence.

"All right, here it is," Hannah said, then took a long breath. "The first weekend into school, when we had that big storm late into the night, our power went out in the dorms. We were night hosting that night."

"Hannah." I thought it was too soon to say this part. She was jumping in with both feet and her hands outstretched.

"No. If this is some crazy prank, we end it now. We can't keep going like this and wondering how crazy we are."

She gave both Taylor and me a look that would stop a wild horse in its tracks. I shut my mouth.

"Keep going, then," Taylor whispered.

"The power went out. We were going to meet our RA down the hall to get some flashlights when I tripped over the computer cord, and when I slipped, Taylor and Emily both caught my hands." She paused to take a breath.

I looked up from the spot on the floor I'd been trying to concentrate on, so I wouldn't run out of the room in fear or embarrassment. I noticed the blank expressions on Mrs. Trebule and Elaine's faces. Even though their expressions were unreadable, I noticed that neither one moved in that second. No movement, no breathing. It was like a pause in time.

Hannah started talking again. She was whispering. I knew this was hard for her, telling a teacher something so unlikely, impractical, and unreal.

"A light started coming from our hands. At least that's what it looked like. We thought it was from a car driving by outside, and I almost convinced myself that was the case. But then, on our way to my house over Thanksgiving break, Emily cut her leg at the gas station. We were helping her with it, and our hands touched again, and another light came. Only this time, it wasn't just the light. The cut on Emily's leg *healed*."

Hannah stopped talking and looked between Taylor and me. No one spoke.

"We actually tried to hold our hands together back at my house over break. The same thing and more happened. When we let go, the flowers had changed and animals were watching us." She had a confused look on her face, like she didn't believe what she was talking about.

"We all saw it," Taylor spoke up.

I couldn't believe the conversation I was in. I was committing myself no matter what came of our meeting. I tried pinching my arm to see if this was another dream.

"It's crazy, I know. It sounds crazy. Or, well, it did. Now it sounds insane. But that's exactly what happened," Taylor said. At the end of her sentence, the octave of her voice went up as her nerves got the better of her. "And that picture on your desk here..." Taylor pointed to the framed still. "It's the same one that I painted in high school, that I thought I'd made up! And the same one that Hannah's grandmother painted."

As she spoke, Taylor reached into her bag and pulled out the picture she had been given from her art class. She placed it on Mrs. Trebule's desk, so it was side-by-side with the teacher's picture.

Mrs. Trebule then did something odd. I saw her small Adam's apple bob as she swallowed and took a breath. She seemed like she was going to say something and looked up at Elaine, who stood by her side. She let out her breath and then reached to her side drawer. She pulled out the bottom drawer, revealing files.

Then she pushed the files back and pushed down into the bottom of the drawer. The bottom of the drawer gave way and revealed a secret compartment. She pulled something out of it and placed a roll of cloth parchment onto her desk. Then, out of another drawer, she pulled an old polaroid camera.

"I knew it. Here's where we find out we were on TV or something," I said. I couldn't help it. I felt like a trapped mouse. My heart was beating in my throat. What was about to happen? I just hoped we weren't in trouble. If my dad found out about this, he would be disappointed, I was sure.

"What the heck is the camera for?" Hannah said. I saw her temple pulsing. Taylor was still pushing down on the photo she'd placed on Mrs. Trebule's desk. The tips of her fingers were turning white, she was pressing so hard.

Elaine stood. "You know nothing," she whispered. "Stay there and let her take the photo, please. You will understand soon enough." Her tone through her lowered voice, while short, was softer than she usually spoke to us.

So, we stood there. Mrs. Trebule put the camera up to her face and pushed down the shutter button. I heard a click, and the following flash blinded me for a couple seconds. It must have been an old camera. But as my vision came into view, I heard and saw the resulting photo come out of the bottom of the device as smoothly as from a vending machine.

Mrs. Trebule took the photo out of the camera and waved it in the air for exposure, then placed it on her desk.

"Sit, please," Mrs. Trebule commanded to the three of us. "Thank you for obliging me," Mrs. Trebule said, softer than before.

She looked over at Elaine. Her eyebrows were raised. She had that look of surprised wonder on her face that I'd seen earlier.

"I never thought I would live to see this day." Mrs. Trebule turned her head to look at us. What she was talking about, I had no idea. She had this glassy-eyed look, as if she were about to cry.

"Finally, we found you," Elaine said as Mrs. Trebule opened the drawer back up and put away the camera. Instead of shutting the drawer right away, she pulled out something else. It looked like a small knife. She closed the drawer.

Mrs. Trebule then took the knife over to the rolled-up piece of parchment and slit the wax seal that held it in its rolled-up form. She put down the knife, then unrolled the cloth and placed the polaroid next to it. She and Elaine, who was leaning over her shoulder, simply stared. Their expressions were unreadable and still. Then, almost in unison, they looked up at us and then back down at the contents of the desk.

"I didn't want to believe it. We have been looking for so long," Elaine said in almost a whisper.

"What are you guys talking about?" Hannah demanded in a harsh tone. She had obviously had enough of being in the dark about the entire situation, and she realized that both Elaine and Mrs. Trebule knew something that the three of us did not.

Mrs. Trebule turned around the polaroid that she'd taken, then the cloth, and pushed both toward where we sat, so we could see them. No one said a word. I looked at Mrs. Trebule and Elaine. I felt like I was going to throw up. The hair on my arms stood straight up. I knew Hannah and Taylor had to be feeling the same way.

On the cloth was an old painting. The painting depicted three women who resembled the three of us – Taylor, Hannah, and myself. Each woman in the picture had distinct features. Hannah's nose, Taylor's height, and my eyes. Only they looked slightly different. Their clothes and bags were strange. They looked older and more weathered.

"Is that-" Taylor started and stopped. She put her finger on the cloth, pointing to a place on the painting behind where the women were.

"Yes, it is," Mrs. Trebule answered.

As she did so, my eyes focused behind the three women in the picture. The background of the painting on the cloth was the same as the picture Taylor was supposed to be working on for her art class. The same as the one on Hannah's wall, painted by her grandmother, and the same one that had been sitting just moments before on Mrs. Trebule's desk.

"What the heck is going on?" Taylor said. She sounded both defeated and panicked at the same time.

"Please, listen to what we have to say." She paused, and before Mrs. Trebule continued, she looked again at Elaine. The look that passed between them lasted two or three seconds. Then she began again.

"A long time ago, these three women came here from another world because of a prophecy that foretold of three young women like yourselves. Three women who, if conditions were right, had the potential to help save our world. That prophecy said that when our world needed it most, three descendants of our great leaders would come to help us defeat the great lord of the dead, Saharon. The three women you see here had to flee in secrecy from even their closest friends and journey through Saharon's own land to get here. All to ensure that those who could save our world would return." Mrs. Trebule stopped and looked at us. She looked at Elaine and then nodded and turned back to us.

"These women are your ancestors. They began their lives and grew up to become who they were in a world that is and has been unknown to you. Our world, one in which you three are descended from, is Enroden. I am sorry everything has been so secretive, but it was the only way to keep you three safe. The Evil One, Saharon, would have hunted you and your family if they had suspected your heritage."

Mrs. Trebule and Elaine looked at us without speaking. It felt like a thousand years before anyone spoke again.

"What?" Hannah whispered.

"Here, read the caption at the bottom of the scroll," Mrs. Trebule instructed as she pointed to the words painted at the bottom of the cloth.

Hannah read to us aloud:

What was once a whole has to part, reuniting when times are dark.

The roots have set, the stones have moved. Return they must, or love will lose.

As time grows dark, evil will follow. Haste they must make, or worlds shall become hollow.

When new creatures become heathen, look for the stars to move like the wind.

Only then you will know the chosen ones have returned to fight the final battle of Enroden.

Hannah finished and looked up. She turned her head and looked back at Taylor and me with a defeated expression on her face.

Taylor picked up the polaroid and placed it directly below the cloth. She noticed how similar everything was. "What does this even mean. That we are related?" Taylor asked.

"Yes, you are," Elaine said to us with a slight upturn of her mouth and a nod of her head. "But even more so, this means you must learn who you are and decide if you are willing to help fulfill the prophecy and save the world that, while remaining unknown to you, lies dear in the hearts of many real people and creatures. But not only that. When your ancestors went through the underworld and got to your world, the thin veil that separates Enroden, your world right here, and the world of the dead, where Saharon is the ruler, was torn."

"Which means that not only your world is in trouble but ours as well," Hannah added in the silence after Elaine finished.

Mrs. Trebule nodded. "Precisely. Now what we are showing and telling you, you must never speak with anyone about, ever," Mrs. Trebule began. "Not your parents, not your boyfriends, not anyone. You must keep this secret, or you will be in grave danger, and our world as well as yours will be at risk." Mrs. Trebule and Elaine stared at us solemnly.

I didn't know what to say. So, I nodded, and out of the corner of my eye, I saw Taylor nod, then Hannah after a few more seconds.

Mrs. Trebule looked over our heads at the door. Then she looked at Elaine and nodded.

"Okay," she said as she picked up the cloth and then set it down again, almost like she was re-thinking her words. "The picture you've been given, Taylor, and the picture at your house, Hannah, it is not a coincidence that they are the same as the picture on this cloth here. They are all, in a way, identical, in that they were each made by the three of these women. Each woman kept the painting and, using one technique or another, passed it down through her family."

"I don't understand. What is so important about the painting being passed down?" Taylor asked.

"Those paintings are the gateway between Enroden and your world here."

"How is that even possible? You're saying that these pictures – the one in my house that I watched my grandmother paint over and over – are gateways? That's not real. That can't happen." Hannah sounded like she was about to flip her lid.

"Those pictures are going to save our lives," Elaine cut in. She glared at Hannah, her newfound kindness toward us suddenly gone. "Those pictures are the only hope we have of saving our people, our worlds," Elaine said in a softer tone.

Mrs. Trebule picked up her arm and placed it on the side of Elaine's hand.

"When your ancestors left our world, they had to travel through the veil between the worlds. The magic that they used for that is dangerous and beyond the three of you at this time. These pictures were the only way they found for you to safely travel back to our world. They took a great risk in painting them and bringing them with them." Mrs. Trebule stopped.

"What do you mean?" I asked her.

"We are not alone in this world here. As your ancestors crossed the veil, Evil became aware of the plan and somehow crossed too. Thankfully, we also were aware and could follow, but by the time we did, we were unsure of the ancestral line and no trace had been left for us to find out who you were. There were signs we looked for and magic we tried to use, but in your world, sometimes magic works a bit different. We have noticed you three over the years and were hopeful. But we could not draw attention out of fear that Saharon would catch on.

"As far as the pictures, we suspect the idea was that they would be passed down through generations, which meant that the pictures would outlive your ancestors. Hannah it appears that they were passed through memories. Your grandmother painted it from a memory that was passed down from her mother and so on. Taylor, the same memory must have surfaced in your mind, and being the artist you are, you did what came naturally to you: you painted it. Emily, we are not sure if your family retained theirs. Were you familiar with the picture before seeing it here at school?" She looked at me, expecting an answer.

I reached into my jacket pocket and pulled out the now open envelope. I opened it and let the light paper fall into my hand. Unfolding the creases with new care that border lined on a feeling of dread, I turned the family lineage page over and placed it on Mrs. Trebule's desk.

Mrs. Trebule looked between me and the paper on her desk. Elaine took in a breath.

"I had thought I recognized the picture when Taylor showed us earlier this semester, but I couldn't place it. Then my dad sent me this when we were assigned the family tree project. I had it with me when we met last time but didn't need it, so I showed Hannah and Taylor, then put it away. I guess I recognized the picture from this. My mom and I didn't really talk a lot about the family bible, where my dad found it, so I don't have a lot to go on, but it must mean something. Sorry," I finished.

"Don't apologize," Mrs. Trebule whispered. "This is the third piece. The hidden document, the memory and the intuition that helped us know you three are the true heirs to your ancestors' responsibilities." She turned her head and addressed the rest of the room. "This picture here has the ability to take the three of you, myself, and Elaine to Enroden. It is a portal of sorts, if you will. Elaine and I were sent here to search for you and to protect this portal in the hopes that we would find you and help you return to Enroden."

Mrs. Trebule paused. No one spoke.

Just then, Taylor's cell phone started to ring. She pulled it out of her pocket and looked at the screen.

"Please, dear, leave that to voicemail," Mrs. Trebule instructed her. Taylor looked at her with a quizzical expression.

"It's just my brother. Let me answer it, and I'll tell him I'll call him back," she said.

"Actually, it may not be anything resembling your brother," Mrs. Trebule cut her off just as Elaine reached for her phone, took it, and silenced it.

"Hey!" Taylor fumed.

"Now that we have found you, we have to protect you. If you are together, then that means that the prophecy has started coming true. That also means that Evil will be near and try to find you, just as Elaine and myself have been. You have to be vigilant. Protect yourselves, even from those who appear to be family and friends. The Evil One has searchers and creatures that are good at hiding right under our noses. They can creep into your mind and control your thoughts if you let them. You have to be careful."

Mrs. Trebule looked at us each in turn. There was another long pause. Elaine handed the phone back to Taylor. She must have seen the fear in our eyes because she then added, "Don't fret. We have our defenses and spies as well. You will be protected."

"What is Enroden?" I cut in. I wasn't sure if she meant this "other world" was like a city or a town or an island off the coast. It didn't make any sense. This wasn't a science fiction novel. It was the real world.

This time, Elaine spoke up. "In time, we will explain. You must understand that your ancestors set in motion a prophecy. This prophecy." Elaine pointed back to the cloth on the desk. "Understand me when I tell you, you three are not just roommates."

Elaine paused again. The room was so quiet, a pin could drop and sound like the liberty bell.

"You three are destined to become three of the greatest sorceresses in our world and yours. You come from a bloodline of great sorceresses who have sacrificed and risked everything for the survival of not only our world but yours as well. They foretold that one day, you three would return, and when you did, we would finally be safe and free to live our lives without fear."

"So, you want us to believe that first of all, there's another world, and second of all, we are descendants of sorceresses?" Hannah challenged. Her face turned a darker shade of red. She seemed to be trying not to shout. "Very funny, okay? You can come out now. Joke's on us," Hannah mocked as she walked around Mrs. Trebule's office. Hannah looked at Taylor and me. "Come on, guys, this is nuts. There's no way that this is real. It's just some sick joke." Her earlier cooperation with the conversation had apparently been exhausted.

"What about the light that happens when we touch?" Taylor said. "We have to listen to what they have to say. If it's some joke, then we will all have a good laugh later." She looked at Hannah and me.

"Come on, this isn't funny," Hannah said with less force this time. "Let's go, you guys." She was through with the conversation and was about to turn and head out the door. As she did, Taylor looked at me, and I nodded.

Taylor grabbed my hand, and I grabbed Hannah's. The room then burst into light. The light was stronger this time, brighter even than when we had been in the garden. We held our hands together for a few seconds. Hannah tried to pull her hand away at first, then gave in and looked at them, silenced by her understanding that there was no way this could be a joke.

We let go of each other.

"I knew it. I just knew you were the ones."

Mrs. Trebule was up and around the desk in a second.

"Now listen fast to me. We only have a little time." She spoke in a hushed tone. "Enroden is another world that is much different from this one, although in some ways, it can be much the same." Mrs. Trebule took a deep breath. "You three have to make the choice to join us and help save our world. But know that if the world of Enroden falls, eventually, your world will fall as well. There are already signs and whispers of Saharon's workings here."

"Your ancestors were able to delay Saharon for a time," Elaine said as Mrs. Trebule went back around her desk and sat down. "They even believed, at one point, that he was defeated. But he was not. He remained hidden in the years following the last battle in our world, growing his armies and winding into our world unnoticed. Now we know that unless Saharon is defeated indefinitely, we will all perish."

"It is more urgent now than ever that we get you to Enroden so that you can fix the tear and stop the destruction of both of our worlds," Mrs. Trebule said, staring at the parchment.

There was a pause.

"Look, I understand that you are saying there's a prophecy and that there's other worlds in danger, but I don't understand how we are supposed to help any of that. What does all of this mean?" I had to ask. None of this made any sense to me. No one had ever told me of any sorceresses or other worlds growing up. My knowledge of that was limited to my love of reading fantasy novels and an occasionally crazy dream after I ate too much chips and salsa.

"What we are trying to tell you is that you three must travel back to Enroden with us. We must fight to defend our world," Elaine answered.

"What?" said Hannah. There was silence. Hannah looked stunned at the realization that this was her new reality.

"We don't have a choice, do we?" I asked after no one said anything else. "This Enroden place, the place where you say we actually come from, needs us to go there and do what?

None of us knows anything about the world, or what's in it, or this Evil One, Saharon, or even-" I had to laugh- "sorceresses, or whatever you want to call them." I laughed nervously.

Mrs. Trebule took a deep breath. She reached onto her cluttered desk and turned the cloth with the three ancestors over. There was a mural of different creatures over the back, one creature above another, all bordering the edges of the cloth, boxing in lines from the old cloth's aging and stretching through the center.

"These creatures," Mrs. Trebule said, pointing to the mural, "are all real. What we are telling you is real. Behind these creatures, the lines on this cloth are faded, yes, but they continue to represent a map of the world of Enroden."

"This map, with its different countries and oceans, is all real. This place is real. These creatures are real. Your past, as well as your future destiny, is real. But in a short time, in your absence, all of us will cease to exist," Elaine stated.

She moved behind Mrs. Trebule to look at the map. She had a distant look on her face, as if she were remembering another time. She looked up at the three of us. Then she moved back around the desk and over to the office door.

"Our time is short. We will tell you what we can, but some of it must wait for when we are not pressed," Mrs. Trebule said to us. "This map is significant. Each creature's head is in correlation to where they originate from. This map is old, and many of the alliances that had been in place at the time of its creation have changed. I must also tell you that you three have gifts that you will need to learn about and explore. And I am afraid there is little time for you to do so.

"Your ancestors had unique gifts that made their power greater than others of their time. They were leaders in our world. They were not only powerful, but they held a great responsibility to our people, our communities, and the world of Enroden itself.

"You three are not only connected to the three ancestors, but you are also connected to the lands, the creatures that inhabit them, and part of the world itself. That means, as Enroden dies, you three will eventually perish with it."

Mrs. Trebule finally took a breath.

"Elaine – or Ellah, as is her correct name – and myself have been looking for you three for over two hundred and fifty years. That translates to roughly over a thousand years in the world of Enroden." Mrs. Trebule paused. "Tonight is not the time to get into everything we must, but I will tell you this. Without your help, we will all die – all of us in this room, all of the people and creatures of Enroden, and everyone you hold dear to you here in this world and who we hold dear to us in ours.

"Ellah, go ahead and make sure the path is clear. I will send the girls back to their dormitories shortly," she instructed. Ellah got up and went out the door. Before she left, she looked at the three of us and smiled. It made her seem gentler. Then she turned and left.

"Make sure you three keep this meeting and the things we've spoken of a secret. There's a reason you three have come together, and the Evil One, Saharon, will be trying to find you, just as Ellah and I have been. We need to have another meeting again soon, so Ellah and I can teach you about your heritage."

Mrs. Trebule smiled at the three of us. I looked over at Taylor and then to Hannah. They still looked as I'm sure I did: a bit dazed.

"Also, I have a request. Please do not try to join your hands again. After seeing how bright your power has gotten a moment ago, I'm sure Saharon will be able to detect it.

"The Journal…" Hannah spoke up.

"Yes, that was me. I apologize for not forewarning you about my ability to read what you write on the pages, but I am not sure you would have believed me if I had." She looked between the three of us. "Every time you three join hands, your power will be strengthened. There is a chance that when you use your power even as individuals, Saharon will be able to detect it. For now, please, try not to join your hands again." She seemed almost sad to tell us this. Then she went on.

"I must make arrangements this week and will be out of my office, but if you need anything, Ellah will be close. Remember, you must act as if nothing has changed. I'm sorry to give this information to you and then have to leave. Just try to stay calm and level-headed until I return, and we can discuss everything then," Mrs. Trebule said as she got up and surveyed us with her gaze.

She walked to the door. We got up from our chairs and followed her. Taylor grabbed her picture from her class and put it in her bag. We walked to the door and went into the hallway.

"I hope to see you within the week," Mrs. Trebule added and then she shut the door to her office.

We were alone in the hallway. No one spoke. Taylor didn't even break the tension with her good humor. We walked back to the dorms. No one talked during the walk back. It was cold, and I felt like my face was going to freeze. I didn't remember it being so cold on the walk over. How long had we been in the office with Mrs. Trebule? It couldn't have been that long.

We had to go around to the front to get into our dorm, so we went in and waved to the on-shift night hosts. It was Sean and his group. Apparently, they had filled in for John. I looked at him and saw concern in his eyes when he saw me. I smiled a bit. I couldn't imagine what my face looked like after the evening we'd had. Sean partly got up from the table, as if he was going to stand.

"Looks like you need that peanut butter chocolate bar. How's it going?" he asked us.

"We're doing good. Nothing new," Taylor said. Hannah was still silent. I didn't think she wanted to talk to anyone at that moment.

"That sounds good right about now," I lied. I just wanted to go back to our room. The thought of eating anything made my stomach revolt. Taylor and Hannah went over to one of the other guys' computers, where they were watching some videos.

"It's cold out there. What were you guys doing out so late?" Sean asked me.

"Oh, you know, just taking a stroll in the hot sun," I said, involuntarily tucking my fingers back into my winter coat.

Taylor and Hannah looked up from the computer screen at me. Both were as ready as I was to head back to our room.

"I'm beat. I've got to get ready for tomorrow. I'll see you then," I said as I walked down the hall, leaving Sean with his night hosting friends.

The three of us headed to our room. Once we were all in the common room, Hannah shut the door and then came and sat down next to me.

"Well, that was unexpected," Taylor started.

"I don't know what to believe anymore," Hannah followed. She sounded defeated.

"I guess we just wait until this meeting again next week?" Taylor asked.

"I think so. Do we just go about our normal business now with school and everything?" That seemed strange to me. How were we supposed to go back to normal after finding out this crazy stuff?

"Of course, we do. Our finals are coming up in like three weeks, and we all have a ton of homework," Hannah said. She sounded like she'd made up her mind, and I couldn't deny that it was comforting to me. A decision had been made; no more open-endedness.

"We will just have to pretend none of this happened and do what we already were doing. Go to school, go to class, and maybe the whole thing will just blow over," she continued.

Hannah looked at Taylor and me. She bent down and picked up a book from beside the chair. She came back and sat down, reading it, as if to make her point. She was right. We still had finals coming up, and we had to keep going to school, or our grades would suffer.

"It doesn't matter what Mrs. Trebule said. She doesn't want to do anything about it," Taylor added.

I looked over to her, then to Hannah, and nodded. It was decided, then. We would just pretend the whole crazy thing never happened. At least for now. Or we would do as Mrs. Trebule said and "act normally"

CHAPTER SIXTEEN

A Party

The week turned into two weeks and a weekend. We heard nothing from Mrs. Trebule or Elaine about our meeting. If anything, Mrs. Trebule was eerily silent. She'd had Elaine fill in for her in the lecture class and had taken a leave of absence. At least Elaine's – or Ellah's – initial sharpness to us seemed to have abated. But the amount of work we received was growing like a weed in a grassy field.

In a way, I was grateful for the work the teachers piled on before finals prep. At the same time, however, with the approaching weekend, I was glad Friday night was finally here. Tonight, Taylor walked around our dorm room with a smile that said "personal triumph".

She had finally talked Hannah into going out to a college party. Her first one. We had suggested she take a break after Thursday, when she came back into the dorm room after a particularly hard study session in her Chemistry lab. She'd gotten acid all over one of her lab coats, and Dr. Sharma had yelled at her for making a mess. The teacher seemed to be making some kind of example out of Hannah. He called on her during most classes to recite equations or explain the day's lecture that they had learned the previous class. If she made any mistakes, he would point them out and them assign her more individual work than the rest of the class. It sounded to me like this Dr. Sharma was plain crazy, but Hannah kept saying how accomplished he was and that he would be a good addition to her resume for med school.

The party was a little controversial for us, and we'd debated even going in the first place. It was the same one Seth had invited us to a few weeks back. The party was off-campus, at the apartments down the road from our dorm. It was about a half-mile walk. Taylor had been there before, so Hannah and I followed her when it was time to leave. Even though she was not the least interested in Seth (she told us that, anyway), she was dressed to the nines and looked like a million bucks.

I asked her for help with my hair when we got ready. I hated my hair. I felt like taming it was probably similar to disciplining an independent child. But whatever she'd done to it, the beast stayed put as we walked to the apartment complex.

Taylor also helped me with my outfit. I was ever a jeans-lover, so that was nonnegotiable. I was not wearing a dress, but she let me borrow a top from her massive collection, and between me and my mirror, I thought I looked good. Too bad it was so cold. As we walked, I decided I was never taking my jacket off again.

Eventually, we got to the party and squeezed into the door of a crowded room. It was blessedly warm in there with all the bodies. In a few minutes though, I started fantasizing about being back outdoors. It was just packed. It looked like everyone else in the art department building must have gotten the same invitation Taylor had.

I figured that everyone on campus probably needed a break, just like we did. Between the cold, studying, and homework, there wasn't much time to relax. We were about a week out from finals, and everyone seemed about done with the semester.

Looking around, there were red arrows taped to the walls. We followed them into the apartment hallway and over to the open apartment door, then down the hall. Arrows went up and down the hallway. Other apartments in the building must have been participating. I thought it was a neat idea.

Taylor looked right at home. She navigated her way through the crowd. I admired her confidence. Whenever I bumped into someone accidentally, I always felt like I needed to apologize. I had to stifle the reflex several times as we went through the crowded entrance. We went up to the open apartment door. There was someone there taking coats. We gave the girl our coats, and she gave us each a small paper raffle ticket. That got a nod from Hannah.

"Organized for a college party, isn't it?" she mused. She made no secret that she'd not wanted to come out tonight, but we were grateful that she'd decided to go anyway. She needed the break, and she knew it.

Hannah followed Taylor farther down the hallway and through another open apartment door. This apartment was a little less crowded. The music was loud and had a kind of garage punk style to it. Whoever was in charge of this section seemed to be into black lighting, but there were less people over this way, and it was a little calmer than the first area of the party we'd been through.

"Hey, isn't that Seth?" Taylor said. "Wait, don't look. He's looking over at us now," she followed in a rushed but hushed tone.

Of course, I looked right when she'd told me not to. And just as I looked, he made eye contact with me. My stomach flopped over in anxiety. But he smiled, smooth as silk, and started walking over.

"Too late," I whispered to Taylor apologetically under my breath.

"Great. Now here he comes," Taylor replied, trying to keep her mouth still since he was coming closer by the second.

"Hi, ladies. Glad you could make the party," Seth said, looking at us with alert and piercing eyes. The whites of his eyes had a slight pink tint, so I guessed he was flying high right about now.

"Well, hello, Seth Hallbut," Hannah said. This must have touched a nerve as Seth involuntarily straightened and look right at her. "You see, I can look things up as well. I hear you've been here at the school for a couple years," Hannah went on. "I heard several things about you."

She stopped. It looked like she was challenging him to a duel. Just when I thought he was going to take the bait, however, he shuddered and turned his head to Taylor. He extended his hand.

It was gloved in black leather. He smiled in an attempt to apologize and took Taylor's hand. He had the tall, dark, and handsome thing down, but something about his apology smile stopped short before it reached his eyes. I felt my stomach flop over again. Surely, Taylor wouldn't fall for this insincere gesture.

Hannah rolled her eyes and turned to go to another part of the room, where there was a sofa chair. Somewhere, she'd picked up a can of Coke, and she clutched the can as she walked away. She sat down in the chair and flipped open the tab on the top with a loud pop I was surprised I heard over all the party noise. She didn't take any crap from anyone. It was one of the things I liked about her. I stared at her. Taylor was even surprised, which was evident from her facial expression. Seth just watched her without saying a word.

"Wow, you guys are pretty good to your host," Seth said, looking at Taylor and me.

"Sorry about that," Taylor began. "She's been a little stressed with finals coming up."

Taylor smiled. She seemed to be less hostile to him than she had intended to be earlier, when we'd talked about possibly running into him.

"Thanks for throwing the party. We needed a night out. Especially some of us," she said, hinting in Hannah's direction. Taylor smiled at him again. I felt like the third wheel.

"I'm going to see where Hannah got that Coke. Are you good here?" I looked at Taylor. She nodded and turned back to Seth.

I went into what looked like the kitchen, walking over the sticky floor to a large tin container of ice. I dug around, my hand freezing in the cold water, until I saw a red can and then pulled. Out came my Coke.

I grabbed the towel on the counter to dry my hands and was met with a damp coldness. I dropped the towel back where I found it and, carrying my wet can of Coke, brushed my hands on my jeans to dry them. I had seen a couple people I thought I recognized in the hallway, so I headed out there.

I saw the girls I knew from one of my classes and went over to chat. We talked small talk for a few minutes, mostly about how one teacher or another dealt with finals and test prep. Then we parted ways when a group of drunk guys grabbed one of the girls from the group and another went with them. It was fine with me. I'd started feeling strange. I thought at first it was that I needed some food. I'd been doing homework before we'd left and hadn't eaten much. I guzzled some of the Coke, thinking it would help.

I looked around and went back to the apartment where I'd left Taylor and Hannah. Walking over to where Hannah was still sitting, I saw Taylor flirting with Seth. I actually felt a little annoyed with her. He was a creep. Couldn't she just shoot him down and move on?

From where I was, it looked like Seth was trying to talk her into going somewhere. They walked to the doorway and lingered there for a bit.

"What's up? Enjoying the party?" I asked Hannah, half-serious, half-poking fun at her.

"Funny. I shouldn't have let you guys talk me into this. I hate parties." Hannah looked at me and smiled. "But I guess we all need a night out sometimes." She took a deep breath. "How's she doing over there with that weirdo?" Hannah asked me as we watched the exchanges between Taylor and Seth.

Taylor laughed a little too loud, and as quick as a bird, made eye contact with me.

"I think she wants us to go over there," I said.

"How do you know?" Hannah asked.

"She hasn't looked at us until now, and she obviously knew right where we were, so I'm thinking she needs a rescue." I tossed my empty Coke can in the small trash bin next to Hannah's chair. Hannah put her book away and stood up. Together, we walked over to where the two stood.

"Well, you two are welcome to come as well. My friend's apartment's only a couple of blocks away. The party is a little calmer there. We could talk and have a good time," Seth said as we approached. There was something in his tone that put me off. His normally smooth way of talking seemed a little broken up, almost like he was struggling to stay calm or like he was frustrated for some reason.

"Well, that's fresh," Hannah blurted out. I laughed.

"Hey, Taylor, I've got more homework, and we've got to night host tomorrow night, so we should get going," I said to her, which was mostly true.

"Yeah, I know," Taylor replied. "Well, I'll see you later, Seth. Thanks for the party."

"Ladies, don't go yet. Homework can wait, I promise," Seth called to us as we left. He didn't move from his spot, however, and we walked away with Taylor in tow.

"What's the deal?" I asked Taylor as we went and got our coats.

"I don't know. That got creepy fast. He seems harmless enough, but I just got this weird feeling and wanted to leave. If I've learned anything from the dating game, it's to trust your instincts," she said, putting on her coat.

I understood that. I had wanted to leave for a little bit myself. I just felt a bit off, and Hannah, well, I don't think she was too disappointed in our leaving either.

"I hear ya. I feel like crap," I said, trying to make her feel like no one was mad that we were leaving. I started to feel sick then. I tried taking some deep breaths, and the feeling ebbed a little.

We left the apartment complex and walked toward our dorm. It only took a couple of minutes to get to the apartment complex on our way to the party, but it seemed to take forever now that we were on our way home.

We had almost made it to the dormitory when I had to stop. I thought I was going to hurl. I turned to look at

Hannah, who was walking slightly behind Taylor and me, to let her know I needed a little break.

I saw something behind her. A car drove by, its lights illuminating the darkness and giving light to the shadows. The shadows fell over something that had a tall outline and seemed to be walking in our direction. The thing I saw behind Hannah had the dark shadow of a person when I squinted at it. It looked like Seth. I turned my gaze back to Hannah and tried to get her attention.

"Hey," I whispered, and Hannah looked at me. "Hey, is that Seth? Is he following us?" I looked back to Taylor, who was waiting for us. She turned and came back to where Hannah and I were standing. She must have heard me because I saw her gaze go from focusing on us to looking behind us.

"I can't tell. It looks like an old man, and I can't see his face," Taylor said quietly.

"Sorry. I feel bad. I must have gotten a stomach bug or something," I said, trying to laugh but just grimacing instead. I did feel bad. It was as if the Coke I had downed at the party wanted to explode in my stomach.

I looked again at whoever it was that was behind us. It started to move again, slowly at first, then faster. Now it was running, what looked like two swinging poles at its sides and a long jacket billowing out behind.

"Oh, man." Hannah had noticed it too. "We've gotta go."

And with that, she took Taylor by the side of her shirt, being careful, it seemed, not to touch her. She looked at me and tilted her head. I got up and we ran.

We moved down a side street and behind a garbage bin that smelled like old, used cat litter. I couldn't see what we were running through, but I was glad of it because as we hid behind the bin, I felt something wet soak into my sneakers. Oddly, I wondered how Taylor was doing in her ballet flats. I was sure her feet had to be soaked as well.

Whoever it was went running past us. We waited for a couple minutes more and then got up.

"That was a little too real," Taylor said.

"Yeah, now what?" I said, not sure what to do at that point.

"I don't know. Let's just get back to our room," Hannah said and turned in the direction of our dorm. We ended up retracing our steps a bit and then got back to the dorm without running into anything. I had never been so happy to see one of those blue emergency lights that lined our campus pathways at night. We went into the dorms and got to our room without saying anything else.

"I think we should email Elaine, or whoever is in charge. You know what I mean," Hannah said.

We'd decided to use Elaine's name as we'd originally known it to keep with Mrs. Trebule's warning of not letting anyone know what was going on.

"What just happened fits in with all the other crazy stuff that's happened this semester. Why not let them know? She might know something." She looked at us. I nodded. Taylor just sat on the couch, staring at the floor.

"Super glad I didn't go out with him now, and even more glad I didn't give him my number," Taylor said, looking up at us. She laughed a bit, trying to ease the tension.

The rest of the night was uneventfully short. It had been about one in the morning when we had left the party, and we were tired. We slept that night in our room and left our doors open. Hannah designated herself to be the one who would email Elaine about our little adventure. She did so, then I saw her turn out the gray common room light.

I heard her get into bed and then I drifted into sleep myself.

CHAPTER SEVENTEEN

The Last Night

Hannah was prepared. She had her laptop, flash cards, biology and chemistry books, and a full, twenty-four-ounce cup of highlighters in every color. She exhaled as she put them down onto the night hosting table.

Taylor was already set up and trying to figure out how to write her paper on the picture she had been given. She had started calling it the "fake picture" for fun. She had sent Elaine an email the night before and asked her how to write her paper, as the picture was supposedly not a picture. The teaching assistant's advice was to simply write about the author as if it were herself, which, according to Taylor, was about as helpful as another sunny day in the middle of a drought.

"And I'd know about droughts. I'm from Texas," Taylor finished.

I was trying to study for my math final. Thankfully, we had a good teacher, and she had given us the option to have one small index card with us during the exam. We could write on both sides of the card. I had brought my pencil sharpener with me so that I could ensure the finest point of my pencil to get the smallest writing possible. I was determined to fill the card with whatever I was going to need.

My stomach was not in the best shape. Ever since we went to that party a couple nights back, I hadn't felt right. I figured I had either a stomach virus, or that the upcoming finals week was making my anxiety rear an ugly side. Either way, it was starting to wear me out. I was determined to take advantage of the night hosting time, however, and got myself to work.

It was snowing outside. We could see ourselves in the reflection of the front windows as the darkness outside began to take over the outdoors. In the darkness, I could still make out the snow falling through the glass. It was pretty. It dulled the street lights lining the paths to the entrance.

The news had talked about this snowfall being a "Nor'easter" and said that we should expect at least a foot before the weather system moved through. I was excited. I'd experienced snow occasionally but nothing like what the news said a "Nor'easter" was going to be. It sounded like a big deal.

No visitors came in to the dorm tonight. It was quiet. There were a few people that scanned their badges to get in, but they already lived here and brought no guests.

I decided to take a break from the miniature test card I was making. My hand was cramping because I was trying to write so small, and my eyes were getting tired from squinting.

I put my pencil down and straightened out my legs. I picked up my water bottle, which had a new drink in it that I was addicted to, thanks to Taylor. It was water with cucumber and lemon. Taylor said she wanted to try to make some flavored waters and had done so the past week. She let me try some, and I loved it.

I watched the snow fall for a minute and noticed how much better I could see our reflection. I saw how much longer my hair had gotten over the semester. I had to smile when I saw Hannah's reflection. She was highlighting like a madwoman. She must have felt that someone was watching her because she looked up. I waved at the window reflection. She gave a slight smile, shook her head, and went back to work. Taylor looked up then and met my eyes. I put my arms up to stretch. She seemed to look at the reflection as I had.

"Look how dark it is out," Taylor said to us. She said it as a statement, not expecting an answer.

"Yeah, the snow must be coming down to block out everything else," I replied. I could barely make out the lights outside now. All I could see of them were faint, gray points in the darkness.

A wave of nausea hit then. I took a deep breath and reached for my water. It was cold, and drinking iced water helped sometimes. I felt some sweat come onto my forehead. I got hot then.

I must have a fever, I thought to myself. I looked over to Hannah and Taylor. They were looking at me, their facial expressions showing concern.

"I might have to go lay down. I feel like crap." I tried to laugh a little. I got up, and as I did, I knocked over my water. Hannah reached over and caught it before it fell too far, but some water had already spilled out.

"Sorry-" I started but was cut off by the sound of the doors opening and a cold blast of wind hitting me. My index card went flying.

Elaine burst into the entrance of our building, covered in white flakes that fell to the floor, making a slippery mess.

"We have to leave," she said to us. We stared at her. "We have to leave *now*," she said again, more urgently than before.

"What?" Hannah managed to get out.

"What's going on?" Taylor followed. "We can't just leave the night hosting table. John will kill us," she said when it was clear that Elaine wanted us to follow her.

"The dorm will be fine. Trust me, John will understand. We will make sure you don't get in trouble, but we have to leave now. Please. Mrs. Trebule is expecting us," Our guide said in a voice that was a mixture of urgency and calm. "Make sure you follow close behind me. Leave your things here."

She reached into the bag she'd been carrying on her shoulder. She pulled out three cloaks that were wrapped tightly into balls. She threw them onto the table at us.

"Put these on. They will keep you warm while we're outside. Make sure to keep the hoods up." She paused.

"Now we have to go. I will go in front, and make sure you guys follow right behind me. Take each other's hands."

"But what about the light?" Taylor worried. Her eyes were wide. "Won't that show other people who we are?"

"We will have to deal with the light and..." She paused. "Anything that sees it as we go," she finished in a quick, low tone. As she spoke, I heard the wind picking up outside.

She walked away from the table, and we followed her. First Taylor, then myself, and then Hannah. We held hands like she told us to. It was a little awkward, and I felt like a kindergartner walking in a school line, but at the same time, something in me felt at home when I was holding my two friends' hands. We headed to the stairway in the back.

"The alarm will sound," Hannah said.

"No, it won't," Elaine replied, and as she pushed the door open, no alarm was heard.

Outside, the snow was deep, and the wind was loud. It was dark, and we could just make out Elaine in front of us. The light that made the gray world look like a snowy television screen came from our palms. The pathways weren't even visible anymore. The school must have been waiting for the snowstorm to pass before doing any plowing. Suddenly, Elaine stopped before we were even away from the protective cover of the trees next to the dorm.

"*Glotono Azul,*" she whispered so low, I barely heard her. A small blue light appeared hotly in her palm. It looked like electricity. She looked at us with a mischievous smile on her face.

"Damn," Taylor said as Elaine made a throwing motion and threw the light into the empty snow covered parking lot and street. The little electric light flew from her fingers in the intended direction. She turned back to us.

"We have to wait a minute. If we're lucky, we can confuse anyone following us. At least we have a fifty-fifty chance of that."

The light faded, growing dim as it moved away from us down the street. We left our shelter and started in the direction of the Shaw building. Elaine moved quicker and more surefooted than we did and quickly got ahead of us. I could just make out her outline when I noticed she wasn't moving anymore.

I felt lightheaded. I guessed the movement of the snow was throwing off my equilibrium. Then, like in my dreams, the darkness of the night enveloped me. I saw a hand with fingernails half the length of the fingers. They were sharp. The hand was a pasty-white leather, and the tips of the nails were slick with dark liquid. Then it was gone, and I saw the snow again.

My hands, clasped in the hands of my two friends, were slick with sweat. I felt cold. We were standing still behind Elaine. When she moved, we moved. And that is how our travels went for another few minutes.

When she sped up, we had to almost run to keep up with her. Our cloaks were long, and while they didn't get in the way, they didn't help either. The snow started to look like glitter as the light from our hands turned from blue to gray.

If I hadn't been so scared, I'd have liked to look at it for a while.

I could just see some of the lights from another side of campus. I noticed that they were starting to go out. Every second, as we went by, I saw one less light.

The wind and snow blew around us. Elaine stopped again and put up her hand. We stopped too. She looked at us, then inserted herself between Taylor and Hannah and grabbed their hands so that we formed a small circle. The light in our palms got brighter, and I had to squint my eyes. The light dimmed, and I noticed a ring forming around us. Elaine let go and stepped back. The ring stayed.

"Now we must run. They know you are here. They will be searching for you." With that, she turned and ran. We followed.

We saw the Shaw building. Suddenly, Taylor tripped and was pulled back. We all stopped. I had hold of Taylor, and Hannah had hold of me. Taylor knelt on the ground but put one leg back up and then was standing. We kept running. Every bush felt like a death trap as we ran. I heard something growl.

That can't be right, I thought.

Then, as if to answer my thought, Hannah yelled, "Shit! What the hell is that?"

I was so surprised to hear the word "shit" come out of her mouth, it took me away from my momentary panic. I think I would have even laughed had I not been so scared.

Just then, a large, black, standing wolf ran up alongside us. It reached for us. The ring around us seemed to act like a fire line, however, because it cut the monster down. I heard his body thud against the snow in a wet defeat. We kept going.

Finally, we made it to the building and through the doors. The loud wind and snow were silenced by the closing doors. Elaine turned around and faced the doors. She waved a hand at the entrance. The light around us dimmed and moved into a line against the doors. Flowing away from where we stood, it rippled in the night as it moved away from us. Then it faded and was gone.

Elaine turned and motioned for us to follow her. I was still gasping for breath from the excursion. I was in good shape for running, but that was hard. We had stopped holding hands, but I could tell that Taylor and Hannah felt the same. We just looked at each other. I noticed Taylor's robe was torn.

"What happened back there? What was that?" Hannah said.

"That was a Rakshasin," Elaine told us. "They are controlled by Saharon and report to him with their findings. Remember, they have been searching just as Mrs. Trebule and I have been."

I looked at our little party. Taylor looked more out of breath than the rest of us. I guessed her fall may have hurt a little.

"Your robe got torn. Did you catch it on something?" I asked Taylor.

"No, I don't think so. It felt like something grabbed my arm. It stings."

Looking at the torn sleeve of her robe, I saw some of the flesh of her arm. She had a good-sized scratch going down part of her forearm. How she had managed that, other than being grabbed, I had no idea. There was a little blood coming down her arm, soaking into her shirt.

"This just got real, didn't it?" she said with a nervous laugh.

"Yeah, right?" I replied. Hannah just looked at us. We turned and followed Elaine to the basement stairs.

We made our way down into the lower section of the Shaw building. The offices blurred by us as we rushed after Elaine to Mrs. Trebule's room. The door was already open when the four of us arrived.

Elaine stopped us before we went bursting in. She turned and put a finger to her lips and whispered, "Shh." She went into the office. We looked at each other as we waited for the all-clear from Elaine to go in.

For a few seconds, I didn't hear anything coming from the room. Then she reappeared into hallway and motioned for us to go into the office. Mrs. Trebule stood in the corner of her office, by a bookshelf. She had several books open on her desk, but her attention was to the book in her hand. She quickly paged through it, looking for something. She looked up.

"Well, it's about time. What took so long?" she said, looking at Elaine.

"We were spotted on the way here. Luckily, we were faster than they were, but I had to throw them off with a mirror," Elaine told her.

"That's unfortunate," Mrs. Trebule said. I was confused.

"Isn't that good?" I asked.

"No, it is not," Mrs. Trebule said. "Now they know we are protecting someone, and it will draw them closer. Their urge to search will be greater." Mrs. Trebule turned to look at all three of us.

""We had a run-in with a Rakshasin," Elaine told her. "They must know you are here. Otherwise, they wouldn't have risked exposure."

"What do we do now?" Hannah asked Elaine and Mrs. Trebule.

"You three must make your decisions now. I'm sorry that we do not have more time to explain, but as things stand, your lives are in danger, as are ours. Without us, you three are as good as caught. Without you three, our world and yours will perish," Mrs. Trebule said, and the room was silent for a few seconds.

Then Hannah spoke up. "Wait. You want us to go with you right now?" she said. "What about school? What about our families and the holidays?" Hannah went on.

She said exactly what I was thinking. I couldn't be away from home on Christmas, let alone miss any of my finals. I had good grades, but the tests at the end of the semester were weighted so that a zero would kill my grade point average. This was crazy.

"We can plan a time after we figure stuff out, maybe this summer or something, but we can't go now," I said. I knew my dad would be sad alone by himself on Christmas. I couldn't be gone during that time.

"We have made arrangements, should you choose to go. We thought this might happen. You three are to be studying abroad for the next semester, and your families have already been informed. Your other teachers have been notified that you may need to leave early, and you have been excused from your finals with your grades remaining consistent. You should not worry about school," Elaine replied to me.

"Your families were proud when they were notified that you were selected by this new program," Mrs. Trebule told us. "Be sure, there is no middle ground here. You must be certain of your choice to go with us. There will be no going back anytime soon. You must decide right now."

I wanted to call my dad and ask him what I should do. I didn't want to be gone. I couldn't think about leaving him there by himself more than I already did by going away to school.

"This can't be real," I said, thinking to myself out loud. But although my brain told me it wasn't real, I knew it was.

"You have to decide now," Mrs. Trebule said again. "The ways between worlds are few. There are two that we know of. One of those ways is here in this picture. We can get to Enroden, but to be honest with you, we know of few ways to return," Mrs. Trebule added softly. "The decision is a hard one, but you must know and decide for yourselves."

I needed to sit down. None of this made sense. I looked at Hannah and Taylor. The looks on their faces said everything I felt: confusion, denial, and disbelief.

Mrs. Trebule pulled the cloth out of her desk drawer again. Then she pulled out two bundles. She unrolled them, handed one to Ella, and took one for herself. They were dark, maroon, hooded cloaks, not unlike the ones we were wearing. There were gold embroidered leaves at the cuffs and on the hood.

She went back around her desk and opened another drawer. She pulled out three side bags. I had the odd thought about how much she kept in her desk. Surely, she couldn't put anything else in there. It must be full to the brim. She handed the side bags to Hannah and told her to pass them to me, and I passed the final one to Taylor.

"Ladies, have you made your choice?" She looked at us.

"I don't see what choice we have," Hannah told her. "If we don't go, apparently, everything is going to fall to pieces."

"I will go," I heard myself say. I didn't know how I said it or why, but I said it nonetheless. Taylor and Hannah looked at me.

"Fine. I'm in too," Hannah said.

"Me too," Taylor finished.

Mrs. Trebule took the picture down from her shelf. She placed it in the middle of the desk.

"Ellah, my dear, it is time." Mrs. Trebule looked at Ellah, who still stood by the closed door, leaning on it. Ellah straightened herself and turned to look at the door. She looked back at us once, touched the doorknob, and then turned back to us and walked toward the desk. She put her finger on the painting, as did Mrs. Trebule. The painting grew to half the size of the desktop. A rushing noise came from where Ellah and Mrs. Trebule's fingers were pressing. The painting seemed to move within its borders.

"Take each other's hands," Mrs. Trebule said. Ellah then took Taylor's and Mrs. Trebule's hands, and Mrs. Trebule moved around the desk to take Hannah's hand. I was between Hannah and Taylor.

The light began slowly at first, then pulsed brighter as the seconds passed. It was bright and sharp, stronger than all the other times we had touched.

Bang!

The sound brought me out of the mesmerizing moment of light. The door to the office shook. Ellah broke the circle. Mrs. Trebule didn't miss a beat, however, and took up Taylor's hand as Ellah left it.

"Go!" Ellah yelled. "You must leave now! I will follow when I can."

She turned and braced her hands against the office door. The whole room shook. I didn't know where to look. It was like an earthquake, rumbling and shaking with loud noises.

Ellah was still at the door, but she was being pushed back. I saw the crack in the door opening wider. Then a pale hand – *the same from my hallucination,* I thought to myself – gripped through the doorway. Fingernails scraped the door next to where Ellah's face was as she put her weight into keeping the door closed. My vision started to swim, and I felt like I was going to faint.

"Whoa," Taylor said, and her grip on my hand strengthened.

"What's going on?" Hannah yelled.

"We have to leave now." Mrs. Trebule put her hand, with Taylor's still in hers, onto the painting. She looked at Hannah and me, and we did the same.

The light in the room became so intense that I saw nothing else. It filled my eyes like a glass full to the brim. Then, in the white of the brightness, all I saw were dark outlines of Taylor, Hannah, and Mrs. Trebule. Then the light became so bright, I had to shut my eyes. The noise was almost unbearable.

An instant later, the noise stopped, and the world around us was quiet.

CHAPTER EIGHTEEN

Evil Begins Again

"You mean to tell me you had her in your grasp, and you were unable to finish the task?" Saharon looked at his Rakshasin.

The tall, dark creature looked down at his hands and then back at his master. His breath came in quick wisps after traveling through the void.

"That is accurate," he replied between breaths. He opened and closed his hands, and each time, his long, poison-encrusted fingernails cut into his flesh. He relished the pain.

"You have failed me," the evil master said, his voice slithering and snakelike.

He put out his hand and took the hand of the minion before him. He looked into his servant's eyes and saw that the creature knew what was to happen to him, yet felt indifferent to it.

"And yet..." Saharon paused as he read the images of what had transpired during the chase at the university. "And yet, there may be some progress made after all," he said as he watched Taylor fall to her knees in the snow, when she'd almost been caught.

He gazed at a frozen memory of her torn sleeve.

"Hm," he muttered.

Filing away the information, Saharon thought about his servant. The creature had helped quite a bit, and he had been directing the search parties for quite some time now. Still, an example had to be made. No one could think to survive if they did not complete the tasks he set before them.

"It is no matter though. The job was not completed."

The master put his hand back onto the forehead of the creature and looked into his eyes. There was a hint of fear there. It gave him pleasure to see.

"Be done now, my servant," he whispered to him.

He stepped back to look at the troll again. He hated getting dirty, but he knew it couldn't be helped. He allowed the force of his power to rise within him. The Rakshasin then lifted his arms to shoulder-height, his muscles rippling with sweat as he tried to resist the inevitable.

His hands turned at an unnatural angle toward his own flesh, and with pleasure, Saharon heard the bones and ligaments snap as the now writhing beast screamed in pain. Then, an instant later, the creature pierced his own chest with his fingernails, bringing them swiftly down so that the sharp ends entered his coarse skin easily. Both of his hands were embedded now in his own chest. The screaming became more intense.

Saharon kept his eyes locked with the Rakshasin.

"I had thought better of you," he said disappointedly. He tilted his head, and the hands in the troll's chest jerked.

The servant fell to the floor. He had killed himself. In his left hand was his heart, which began to still, continuing to beat slowly as the blood left its home.

Saharon turned and went to wipe off the blood from the troll. The thing had made progress, yes. Now he knew that these three he had been watching for some time were the ones he was looking for. And he knew the face of one of them now. She had turned when she was caught, when her arm was grasped.

He went over to the troll, now lying on the ground in death. He bent down, trying to avoid the stick of the crimson mess enveloping his floor.

He felt which hand had been the one to grip her. The power from her blood left its mark and its scent. He lifted the hand and put the fingers in his mouth to taste the blood. Yes, there was power there. He could taste it.

He would be ready at the next encounter. He would know this witch. He would control her. Eventually, he would control all three of the chosen ones. Then he would have the world of Enroden, and his abilities would move beyond being stagnant in this world. The tear in the veil was small, but with time and with the help of the three chosen ones, it could be fully opened. Then he would be able to cross, to enter and own other worlds.

Some of the fault for his discovery lay with the ones who were allied with the king. They would have to atone for that with the crown. If they hadn't exposed themselves, he may have not noticed the shift in the energy at the school. He had felt it once before, but the draugr he'd sent to investigate had never returned.

He needed a new servant, to increase his ranks of creatures, and to find the three before they knew the vast span of their abilities.

He was in deep thought when he was interrupted by one of his slaves.

"Massster," it hissed. "Massster, you must come outside and look at the sssky."

The being lingered in the doorway, waiting for him. He knew what would await his gaze if he looked to the sky. However, he walked to the opening anyway.

The balcony where he stood was high on the cliffside. Sometimes he lingered on the view over the treacherous landscape and found a sad beauty in it. There was a time he may have found something other than the bleakness in the view, but that time was passed. This was a time for relishing in pain and sadness and death. He looked up into the night, already knowing what he would see before it met his eyes.

The stars streaked across the sky. One after the other, they flew as if on a mission to arrive at some unknown destination. They lit the sky like fireflies. The sight, while expected, gave him the feeling of betrayal. This world was his. Not anyone else's. The sickening sensation of failure mixed with anticipation of what was to come enveloped him.

This cannot be happening, he thought to himself. He knew what this meant, and he knew that he was still one step behind the searchers.

The prophecy was coming to fruition.

Maybe this was just what he needed for him to grasp the prophesized ones. It would be easier. They would be more in his grasp now that they were in Enroden. He had eyes and ears everywhere, and when they used their powers, he would know. They would turn up soon, he knew.

They would turn up in his dungeon, for him alone to have. To kill, to drink in their life's blood, their power.

He took the axe from his weapons belt around his waist and swung at the slave still in the doorway, killing him instantly. The life force from the slave rushed into him, and he felt its power as it absorbed throughout his body. He screamed with the new strength and with the knowledge that he would soon have the energy from the three chosen ones. Then not only would all other worlds become his, but they would become his alone.

He screamed again, giving the sound power and strength, and heard it echo into the vast canyon before him.

CHAPTER NINETEEN

Enroden and Edelsvein

The blinding white was fading. I heard wind and knew I was standing on something.

What just happened? I thought to myself.

I could just make out the outline of what I thought were shoes around me, and as my eyes began adjusting to light, I felt someone squeeze my hand. I squeezed their hand back. Looking up, the shapes became the familiar faces of my two friends and the teacher that accompanied us.

I was with both Taylor and Hannah, as well as Mrs. Trebule, but we were no longer in the oddly-arranged office within the basement of the Shaw building. Now it appeared we were standing in something like sand.

"What just happened?" I asked, this time out loud. My breaths came heavily. I felt Taylor let go of my hand and Hannah do the same.

"Welcome to Enroden," Mrs. Trebule said. She looked around and took in a long breath. "It has been too long," she said to no one in particular. She stared into what appeared to be an ocean.

Looking past our teacher, I noticed that it was, in fact, sand that we stood in. It was a beach but not one that I had been to before. The water was a greenish-blue that reminded me of the Pacific Ocean, but the tips of the choppy waves glittered like the sea was alive and breathing.

As I followed the beach line farther down the shore, I saw trees and the edge of a forest. The trees were different sizes but had similar leaves – thin needles in thick bunches. They looked almost like pine trees.

Looking up, the sky was a deep blue that faded into a purple night on the horizon, like it was night and day at the same time. On the purple edges, I saw shooting stars that faded as they grew into the lighter blue areas directly over us. It was heavenly.

There was a sun overhead, but when I turned to look over the ocean, I saw a moon as well, shining through the sky in direct competition with the starry sunlight.

I couldn't get over how beautiful the sky was. The shooting stars drew my eyes to them. They grew brighter and brighter, until I could follow them across even the light blue sections of sky overhead.

No one spoke. Then Mrs. Trebule broke the silence. "Do you still think this is a joke?" she asked us.

I turned to look at her, then I looked at Taylor and Hannah.

"Where are we?" I asked her.

"Enroden," Mrs. Trebule replied.

Hannah walked a few feet ahead of us, along the waterline, taking everything in. "There's no way this could be a joke. This has to be real, which also means that everything you told us…" Hannah paused. "It's all true," she finished.

Again, no one spoke. We just looked at each other, the realization of how terrifying all the information was dawning on our faces.

I felt like I had been here before, like this was déjà vu that was entirely wrong.

Taylor put down her pack and opened it. She pulled out her photo. Somehow, she had managed to shove it in before we had left. The scene from the photo was eerily familiar to where we stood now.

"Where is Elaine? Or, well, Ellah," I asked, correcting myself. I guessed that we could probably use her real name now. "What happened right before we left?" I finished. I remembered the door cracking and Ellah leaving the circle but wasn't sure what was going on.

The words hadn't been out of my mouth for more than three seconds when I heard a loud crack, like a lightning bolt splitting a solid rock. I saw a flash out of the corner of my eye, farther down the shoreline. Then I saw a person running toward us. Mrs. Trebule took a deep breath.

"There she is," she called back to us as she left us on the beach and ran toward her friend. The three of us looked at each other, then followed her quickly.

Ellah looked a little disheveled, but overall, she looked fine. She had some blood running down the side of her face but still smiled when we greeted her.

"That was close," she said to Mrs. Trebule as she hugged her.

"What happened?" Taylor asked.

Ellah looked at her, then at Hannah and myself. She smiled. "Well, we were being chased. I put up as many protection spells as I could, but they weren't strong enough."

She stopped to take some deep breaths.

"When we were leaving, we were followed by more than the Rakshasin. A draugr also followed us, but he must have remained out of sight because he managed to know where we were and somehow got into the building. He made it down to the office," Ellah said, looking at Mrs. Trebule as if the three of us didn't even exist. "I was able to hold it off long enough for the portal to disappear and then I followed in its wake. Which reminds me, you will need to send a message back to have someone fix your office. I don't think they will leave it tidy when they figure out what just happened."

Ellah laughed, and the two hugged again. Watching them, I suddenly felt like the world was swimming before my eyes.

"I need to sit down for a bit. I'm not feeling well." I felt as if I were going to be sick.

Mrs. Trebule and Ellah turned to me with serious faces. I knelt a bit to steady myself. The cool sand felt good on my fingers.

"What do you mean?" Mrs. Trebule said almost sternly.

"It's nothing. I'm just not feeling well. I ate something bad a couple days ago, I think." I wasn't sure what the big deal was.

"We have to get out of the open. Now," Ellah said, looking around, her eyes wide orbs of white and violet. She took Taylor's hand, and Mrs. Trebule hauled me onto my feet. Then she looked at Hannah and had her get my other side. We hobbled up into the tree line off of the sandy shore.

Ellah whispered something into her palms and blew. The wind picked up, and I saw the sand where our footprints were indented rearrange itself.

The evidence from our arrival now gone, Ellah motioned for the rest of us to hide behind some of the bushes around the trees. Mere seconds later, from around the corner of the shoreline, three large creatures ran by. They were so fast. They were strange-looking. I hadn't ever seen anything like them before. They almost looked like bald rats. They had slits going down their sides and left a trail of viscous fluids as they ran by. Their arms looked sharp, and their legs were large and muscular.

"Fomori," Ellah announced. She turned to look at me. She sounded as much in awe at seeing a fomori as she was terrified. "You must trust your instincts. You will discover that within you is the ability to sense when danger is advancing. You have not been sick these past days. Your body has been trying to warn you."

I looked at Taylor and Hannah. We were at a loss for words.

"When you feel ill," Mrs. Trebule began, "it may be that you are in danger. It is a protective mechanism that served your ancestors well. If you are to succeed, you must trust yourselves. This is no game, and the stakes are high."

Mrs. Trebule stopped talking for a minute. She looked at the sky, as if she were waiting for something.

"For now," Mrs. Trebule began again, "Ellah will take you into hiding. You are to travel as quickly as possible and without being seen. You will have help along the way."

Ellah turned to look at her. "Are they coming?" she asked.

"Yes," Mrs. Trebule replied. "You saw the stars going across the sky, no?" she asked us.

"Yes. They were beautiful," Taylor replied.

I looked again to the sky, expecting to see the stars crossing the sky. But while the immense open space was still beautiful, the stars were gone.

"That was the sign that was prophesied about. That was to let those in our world know you had arrived in Enroden. Your world calls them meteor showers. Here, that kind of event is a rarity and means the fulfillment of a prophecy. This event lets us and those in our cause know that you are here, and that our hope of freedom from Saharon is possible.

"If Saharon saw this same sky, he will know something has come to pass. We can only hope that you have remained hidden to him before this. That he does not know your identities is advantageous to us. But be wary. If he did see the stars, he will know about you, and he will be more interested in having you and therefore be more dangerous." Mrs. Trebule paused, letting her words sink in.

Suddenly, I heard another loud crack like before. Far off in the distance, a small crowd was visible. They looked like people. They ran from the shoreline, up in our direction. As they got closer, two broke away from the main group and headed in our direction while the others turned and entered the tree line.

"There they are," Ellah said.

"You know the path," Mrs. Trebule said, turning to Ellah.

"Yes, it has been set for years. We will take the brush and back route. Hopefully, the loyal continue to maintain their posts. They will help if they can," Ellah replied. "If they saw the sky, they will be ready. When we get there, we can get into Edelsvein through the underground tunnels.

"You must travel to the city of Edelsvein, where you can learn about your past and your ancestors. You have to learn about your gifts and abilities if you are to defeat Saharon," Ellah said, looking at us individually.

"Your journey is not an easy one, and I am afraid our time together here falls short of how I hoped it would be," Mrs. Trebule told us, then stopped talking as she watched the two approach across the sand. "I must leave you now. Ellah will take you where you need to go. I must contact those in our alliance to ensure that your families are safe and continue the arrangements that were left unfinished, as we left so quickly."

"Wait a minute," Hannah cut in. "There's others back home who know about all of this?" She looked as if her eyes were on fire.

Mrs. Trebule turned and smiled. The two newcomers were close now.

A feeling of recognition kicked in as two men joined our group. My stomach turned in anxiety and surprise.

John, our resident advisor, stood next to Ellah, and next to John stood Sean.

"What the hell are you doing here?" Taylor said and semi-laughed as she said it.

"Surprise," John said. "Don't think you guys are going to get all the fun now." He turned to look at Mrs. Trebule. "We notified the alliance before we left. We were right outside when they tried to intercept your departure. We managed to delay them, but eventually, they broke through. They had a fomori with them."

"So, the tear in the veil is big enough to allow not only the Rakshasin and the draugr but fomori as well," Mrs. Trebule answered, her face a puzzle of expressions. She took a breath and looked between John and Sean. "You did well."

Both John and Sean nodded. They were being formal.

"So, this whole time, you knew," I whispered almost involuntarily to Sean. I couldn't believe it. I felt like my friend had lied to me. The whole semester, all the meetings for coffee, was just so he could spy on me. It hurt. I couldn't believe that I'd thought he liked me.

"I couldn't be sure. We have been looking for a long time, hoping that our trust in the prophecy would come to fruition, but we had no way of knowing who you would be when you finally came," he said apologetically. "I'm sorry I didn't say anything."

"Aw, how cute. But do I need to remind you guys that we're kind of out in the open here? We need to get going," John said as he surveyed the terrain.

"You are right. There are others who know about our cause in your world. However, not all of them had the best of intentions," Mrs. Trebule said gently. "The task of bringing you three here has been none too little or too short. There will be time to discuss that, but now is not it. I must go."

I was in disbelief. The whole thing felt like a crazy dream. I was in a different world from my own. I was one of apparently the last three great sorceresses and part of a prophecy to save this strange world that was foreign to me. Then the realization that there were people around me back home who knew all of this and didn't tell me washed over me again. That hurt the most. I wasn't sure whom I could trust.

Then I thought about what Mrs. Trebule had said. Our families, the danger everyone was in back home and here.

"Wait, our families – why do they need protecting?" I said, thinking of my dad back home.

"You said that you have to make sure the alliance is still with us, and you also said that we didn't have to fear for the safety of our families," Taylor said. The three of us looked at Mrs. Trebule and Ellah now.

"Yes, that is exactly what I said. There are already things in place to help keep your families safe. You must know, however, that as our world suffers, yours suffers. There is already evidence of evil's influence on your world. On its people, on its land, and in the oceans. Soon, there will be no denying its presence. Many cannot see Saharon for who he is, but they will notice the changes nonetheless.

"So, yes, I said that, and yes, there are protectors for your families, but make haste in your travels because they will not last forever. And if you fail, there will be no ebb to the flow of evil that will eventually penetrate your world," Mrs. Trebule finished.

A few seconds later, Mrs. Trebule sighed and changed the subject. "I am so happy I was able to see you finally return to our world," Mrs. Trebule said. Then she turned to Ellah, John, and Sean. John handed Mrs. Trebule a small satchel that had been at his waist belt.

"Thank you for your help, my dear, and for yours, my friends. I hope to see you all in Edelsvein soon. Protect them with everything you have." With that, Mrs. Trebule embraced her friends and even had tears in her eyes.

"Travel safe," I heard Ellah say as she watched Mrs. Trebule walk toward the ocean, down the sand. Then she turned to look at us, nodded to John and Sean, and headed toward the deeper part of the forest. She vanished in a few seconds. As I watched her go, I heard another loud crack, and when I turned to see what it was, Mrs. Trebule was gone.

Taylor, Hannah, and I looked at each other. John and Sean stayed with us.

"All right. Now we have to go," John reminded us. "Bring up the rear, Sean," he instructed as he headed in the same direction that Ellah had.

"I guess we should follow her?" I suggested.

"I guess we should," Taylor said. Still, neither of us moved. We just kept standing there, still and unmoving.

Then Hannah spoke up. "Let's go," she said. And she simply put one foot out and started walking. I watched both Hannah and Taylor disappear as Ellah and John had. Still, I wasn't sure if I could move.

"We've got to go, Emily," Sean said to me kindly.

And I knew the choice wasn't my own any longer. This was bigger than myself and my fears. So, I did the same thing my two friends had. I put out one foot and began to follow it. One foot in front of the other. One step at a time.

Ellah led us through the thick trees and brush and out into a field. At the edge of the forest, we had to stop and rest. John and Sean went ahead to scout the field and make sure there weren't any traps laid for us. It had been several hours, I guessed, and difficult navigation through the trees. We all were a little tired.

Ellah stayed with us until they returned. When they got back, they carried brown balls the size of coconuts. They cracked them open and began to drink. I could see the clear fluid drip down the side of Sean's face as he drank. John handed one of the balls to Ellah, and Sean handed one to me and then one to both Hannah and Taylor.

"What are these?" Hannah asked.

"They are like coconuts. They are a plant that has water within it. You can drink. It is safe," he said. We all rested for a few more minutes. Then Ellah stood, and we were ready to move again.

Ellah eyed the field before we entered it. There was tall grass with small spots of red among the green. Flowers were everywhere. I looked down at my feet. One of the red flowers was there. It looked small and had square petals. I hadn't ever seen this kind of flower before. I put my hand down to touch it, and the petals closed around my finger. When I pulled my hand back, they opened again, and the plant was again in full bloom.

Ellah stepped out of the end of the forest, onto a small footpath that disappeared into the field of high grass. She motioned for us to follow. The path was small, and if I had been looking on my own, I probably would have missed it. But I saw the wear and tear along it, plain as day up close.

John and Sean, who had gone ahead, returned about a half-hour after we started moving again. They were each carrying large bundles that looked like heavy blankets. We stopped, and Ellah went over to see what they'd brought back.

"Is this?" she asked, sounding surprised.

"Yes. After all this time, they were still there," John said. He put his pack on the ground and started to unroll it. As he did, a beautiful sword was revealed. There were emeralds and sapphires and rubies in the hilt. There was a sheath next to it. John picked it up and gave it to Ellah. She took it, then buckled the sword onto her belt and sheathed it. Then he unrolled the pack a bit more, and another sword came out. This one, he buckled on his own belt. I looked over at Sean.

He had unrolled his pack and put on his sword. He fastened a purple cloak around his neck. Both he and John looked official.

"Wow, you guys look good," Taylor admired.

"Oh, don't be fresh, Taylor," Hannah called over from where she was sitting and laughed. We all laughed a little. It was good for us.

"Enroden is more beautiful than I remembered it. The fields and trees are alive, and the flowers are the sweetest-smelling you will ever find." Ellah looked happy for a few seconds. "It is good to be home," Ellah said, breathing in the air around her.

"How long have you been gone?" I asked Ellah.

"It was over two hundred years in your world and over a thousand in this one," Ellah said. She sounded introspective and sad. "But it seems the test of time leaves its mark on not only creatures and land here, but it has left me stunted. I return here having aged less than my surroundings. The land is different..." She trailed off.

I suddenly felt pity for her. It must have been hard for her to leave her family, friends, and home for so long. It made me think of my own home and leaving my dad.

"What was the name that Mrs. Trebule said earlier? The place she is supposed to meet us?" I asked, wanting to both fill the thick silence and change the subject. Taylor and Hannah had caught up to us now.

John had gone to stand watch, and Sean was getting something out of his side bag he was carrying. It looked like a leaf. He put it into his mouth. I looked at him, puzzled.

"I think she said it was Edelsvein, or something close to it," Hannah replied, bringing me back to our conversation.

"You are correct. Edelsvein is our home. The city is alive and bustling. You three will be safe for a time there and will have a chance to learn about yourselves," Ellah told us. She whistled. Sean went over to John, and they met Ella's gaze. In an unspoken consent, both went ahead. Ellah started walking again.

"What do we need to learn? I mean, we've been ourselves our whole lives," Taylor said.

"You need to learn about your heritage, about our world, and, of course, train with your abilities," Ellah said as she increased the pace of her brisk walk.

"Train? I don't do training," Taylor said.

"You will do fine. It's in your blood," Ellah stated as if it were the most normal thing in the world, as if she wasn't talking to a young woman who just learned she had magical abilities.

We spent some time taking in our surroundings as we walked. The grass from the mountain we were ascending was thinning, and rocks dotted the small footpath. The flowers were scarce here, and as we walked onward up the hillside, I noticed the tops of some of the trees from the forest. We had crossed through the low valley and were heading up.

"Ellah?" asked Hannah.

"Yes?" she replied.

"Why did Mrs. Trebule choose this place to go when we got here, this Elven city?"

"Well, I guess now is as good a time as any for you to start learning." Ellah took a breath and began.

CHAPTER TWENTY

War and History

"Edelsvein gets its name from the great Elven king of the past war. The king was named after the last battle. During the battle, Saharon was nearly at the gates of the great city, which, at the time, went by the name Providentia. The lands and all the dwellers of our world, including creatures that are so vast and great that you could talk for days and not name them all, were assembled to decide how to prevent evil from running rampant through our land. No one could understand how Saharon had walked through the veil between the dead and undead and come into the light of our sun." Ellah paused. A moment passed where she seemed to share a glance with Sean. Their eyes seemed to argue about some unsaid thing. Then after a moment, she began again.

"The people of our world signed a treaty to help defeat evil. Everyone realized that we had to work together regardless of beliefs, heritage, wealth, and location. The idea was borne from one of the king of Providentia's sons, Prince

Sigrun. But while the intent for peace was there, the ability and means to do so were still a mystery to them.

"Even with the treaty in place, they were left wanting, however. While the king was good and his people loved him, he was also old and vulnerable to influence. He eventually became a pawn for Saharon. Somehow, the king, King Turk Edelsvein, had allowed one of Saharon's minions into his court as his advisor. The advisor filled the king's mind with lies and fears of the unknown. Eventually, the king, while not in his right mind, entrusted the fate of his city and, in truth, the world of Enroden to this being. Saharon moved fast, as he knew the power that lay within the city, and he knew that whoever controlled the city had the ability to control our world.

"King Turk Edelsvein had three sons. Saharon knew that he had to demolish the bloodline of King Turk Edelsvein for the people to believe that there was no other option for a king. The invasive right hand to the king manipulated the minds of two of the sons, Prince Jahem and Prince Aleon, and they battled to the death in a duel.

"The third son, Sigrun, the youngest of the three, was wise for his young years. He saw through the farce of the king's assistant. This Prince Sigrun convinced the council of elders that the king was not in his right mind, and with the help of your ancestors, a treaty was proposed. With the whole of our world cooperating together for a common purpose, Saharon was pushed back, and eventually, King Turk Edelsvein saw his advisor for who he truly was. There was a war, and Saharon was beaten back into the underworld."

John slowed down and began walking with us. Ellah fell silent her expression unreadable. Sean, who had joined us in the back of our group, picked up the story after a few seconds of silence.

"After a time, it became known that the king was ill. The last years of his life leading up to the war had been difficult for him, as the possession had drawn on his energy stores. Soon, the king was on his death bed. The city and the land mourned. During this time, King Turk Edelsvein named his only remaining son, Prince Sigrun Edelsvein, as his successor.

"The city Edelsvein is named after this king. King Sigrun was wise, and the people knew how much he loved Enroden. The story of how he enlisted the help of your ancestors was told all over the kingdoms of our world, and the people welcomed him as their new king. The city of Providencia was given a new name and became the great city of Edelsvein. It was used as an international port for the entirety of Enroden, receiving trade and resources for distribution all over the lands." Sean stopped telling the story, as if he were done.

We walked for a short time before one of us spoke.

"I don't understand," Taylor said. "If Saharon was beaten back, then why do you need us to come here and help?" She talked with caution, almost as if she wanted to know the answer but didn't at the same time.

Ellah took a breath before answering her. "You see, Saharon got so far to begin with because evil prays on every tendril of our beings. There had been increasing deaths in the city, a sickness among my people that took the lives of many, especially the women and children. The same was happening throughout the land, among other races and creatures. The inhabitants of our world had desperation running rampant in their blood. Saharon pounced on this, spreading his influence like wildfire through the channels of fear and hostility that sadness brought.

"It is in a similar way that we fear Saharon has again come to visit us. We have had word of sickness and war among the races. The treaty has been forgotten, and while the remaining council did meet recently, many fear they have lost touch with the needs of the surrounding lands and their inhabitants," Ellah went on.

"After the fall of Saharon, things got better for a time. Our families grew again, and the city prospered. But soon, reports from outlying lands began to reach us through our trade routes. Missing livestock, ransacked villages, missing family members and children. People began to be afraid again." She paused. "We had to be sure it was Saharon before we spread more fear among our world, so a convoy set out. A party traveled to the ends of our world. They faced terrible danger and, after many months, arrived at the entrance to the underworld. The veil was intact as far as they could tell. However, they found fires lining the large void between the worlds all the way to the entrance where the veil lies and the void narrows."

"Apparently, it looked as if someone had been trying to break open the gates of hell," John cut in.

"After a time, we realized that what had been hailed as Saharon's final defeat was simply only the beginning of our worries. We knew then that we needed the help of the Great One," Ellah continued. "Long ago, when we realized what was happening, your ancestors began to travel around our world. They tried to encourage the races to hold up parts of the treaties they had agreed to, and they were successful at first. But when things got worse, they knew even they needed help. They tried to find the Great One of our world to ask for advice and guidance.

"Their time was running short. The fear and trepidation from the first war were rekindling quickly, and many refused to work with the Elves after they were unable to halt the sicknesses in their communities. They believed that the Elven community was hiding a cure because they were less susceptible to illnesses and fewer Elves died. The lands began to separate, then, with different creatures lacking trust in each other, and our world began to change." Ellah stopped walking and scanned the horizon here. "We need to go this way."

Ellah took a right heading up the side of what appeared to be a small hill. The path became more complicated than before as the hillside became a mountain side and the path was littered with rocks. The three of us were listening raptly, hanging onto the words our guides told us.

"During all of this, in the land of Pharmancia, one of the provinces of our world, a boy was born and given up for adoption. The child did have parents, but they were killed soon after his birth, and he had no one to take him in. Your ancestors were called to his bedside by a gypsy woman who had noticed his gifts. The child had power. Afraid of the boy, this woman named him Fovos. Your ancestors took

Fovos from his caregiver and wanted to raise him in the educational arts of his powers and magical abilities.

"But as he grew, his thirst for power intensified, and some of his darker and more morbid obsessions came to light. Your ancestors had grown to care for the boy and wanted him to be raised with the woman whom they had taken him from in his early childhood. He was to cease his magical education and was schooled in the arts of medicine and healing.

"But his gift of power still left him wanting. Fovos grew and sought magical lore, then began creating a following. He felt that the ancestors had corralled their powers and wanted themselves to be the only ones who could use them. He preyed on insecurity and jealousy and the fears of those he encountered. His following grew. Eventually, he deceived many, and inhabitants of our world began to believe this boy, now in manhood, could be the savior of Edelsvein. That he would be able to deceive Saharon and rid our world of the evil he had wrought.

"When they heard of his great following and that many wanted to elect him to a position of power and influence, your ancestors asked for a meeting with him. They had not seen him in many years. Still, they had hoped to see at least a shadow of the boy they once knew. They met and recognized Fovos for who he was. Evil. The boy was evil. Somehow, they knew it and understood it after the meeting. Instead of exposing him for who he was, however, they brought him before the Hoyt."

"Who are the Hoyt?" Taylor asked.

"The Hoyt are soul readers and protectors of our city. They can tell if you are being truthful."

She paused as we headed up a steep slope of rocks. She let us rest for a minute to catch our breath once it leveled out some.

"Fovos was brought before the Hoyt. However, not before he had instructed his following to be wary of your ancestors, the Elven people, and even the ancient truth beings. As the man went through his examination with the Hoyt, he began a rebellion by killing his examiner. Feeling provoked, their leaders attacked many who followed Fovos and began slaying those within the city walls, and blood ran among the streets.

"A new war began. However, it was short. Fovos was not seen from again after his examination, and there was no body found other than his examiner's. The fighting and unrest created a rift that still stands today among our people and the and creatures of our world. The treaty is no more. The one good thing that came from the man being examined by the Hoyt is that your ancestors and the king understood that there are still ways evil can enter our world. And they tried to stay one step ahead of it. With Fovos out of the picture, they campaigned for peace. The three found The Great One, and this is where the prophecy for you three came into being."

"So, this Great One, this is who gave the prophecy?" Hannah interrupted.

"Yes. Few have seen him, and even fewer have visited and returned to tell about it," Ellah finished as we all stopped.

"What we do know is that he helped your ancestors get to your world, and that was the last time he was seen," Sean cut in. He sat down on a rock on the opposite side of the path, directly across from me. I looked at the ground. I didn't want to talk with him.

The clouds barred our view of the top of the path, but it looked like we still had quite a way to travel. The sun had stayed in the same place as this morning but looked dimmer than earlier, and the moon, also in the same place, looked brighter. *It must be getting toward the end of the day*, I thought to myself. I had the strange thought about a flat earth, where the moon and sun stayed stagnant.

"Was Saharon doing with this Fovos?" I asked Ellah.

"Saharon used this man as a tool to separate our world. The people and creatures would not unite. They would not work together or help each other. Mistrust and hatred of your neighbor was rampant. There was mistrust in trade, the border walls closed, and segregation spread to all continents in our world. Immigration halted. We were no longer allowed to travel freely from country to country. Many began to believe that their races fared better in the war than others because they were better or more pure than others. You see, Saharon used our own differences to create an imbalance within our world, and that imbalance, when it was tipped in his favor, created a space in the heart of our world for hate to grow," Ellah explained.

"You see, it is said that in the beginning of our world, the Great One provided three stones that, together, kept the balance of our world and the fates of the underworld separated. The stones belonged in the Book of Life. This book told of the creation of our world and others and many other secrets that have become legend over the years. The stones are not only powerful, but they are the key needed to open the book itself.

"According to the legend, the Great One entrusted the secret of where the book was, as well as where the stones were, to your ancestors. They needed the stones to tear open the veil and get through into the underworld and then into your world. But doing so meant that the stones had to be separated from the book. This is all legend, but it is the closest belief we have to what happened and how they were able to escape. In any case, they never spoke of it to anyone, and it was never confirmed that they actually had either the stones or the book, but Saharon does not care. He believes that you three are the key to finding them."

"In truth, you must find them, because if he finds them first, he will be unstoppable. He will tear the veil all the way open and, with the book as well, understand how to control and master our world," John added as we went up another rise in the path. There was silence for a few minutes.

"So, we have to find these three stones and a book and then close a veil in the underworld in order to save the world of Enroden?" Hannah spoke up. "Where do we start looking? It's a whole world that we have to look through." Hannah spoke more to herself than to us, I thought.

"Before you can start looking, we have to teach you about yourselves. How to protect yourselves, how to utilize your gifts, what your gifts are. You have no knowledge of our world. You have to learn to beat Saharon. And this is why we must go to Edelsvein.

"Now we must be quiet here and speak of none of this should we meet anyone along the way. We are getting close to the city. We are only a few hours away, and the road here looks to be a bit more traveled than the one we were just on," she said as she inspected the ground. "John, can you check the road ahead?"

He headed out in front of us.

"Make sure to hide your faces, and do not speak or let anyone know who you are. Your identity, as long as it is hidden, is your safest strategy for the moment. Remember, it is not always clear who is working for Saharon and who is on the side of good. Do you understand?" Ellah looked at us, and we nodded.

Climbing the mountain was hard. The path was small, and we had to go single-file. We wound our way up regardless, going through small openings in large rocks and through mud. The path was eroding toward the top. It was cold. I was grateful for the warm cloak that we had been given. There was frost over the grass and ice on the path. We could see our breath as we walked.

No one spoke. I tried to keep my eyes forward, watching where Ellah put her feet on the path, especially when the path was close to the edge, but sometimes I had to look out over the view.

We were about to go into the cloud cover again when I got a small, clear view of the path down and back over the valley. For that instant, I glimpsed all that we had traveled. It was beautiful. I should have been paying more attention to where I was going.

I bumped into Ellah and fell. As I fell, I rolled onto the side and over the edge of the path. I grabbed a root sticking out from the ground. Ellah was too far away to catch me, but somehow, Sean's hand reached down and caught my other hand. Before I knew what was happening, he hauled me back up onto the trail.

Looking at him, he didn't even seem taxed by the effort. It was as if he simply had picked up a stick and put it back down. I was so surprised at the whole thing that I didn't know what to say. I just stood there.

"Thanks," I said to Sean, realizing how close I'd come to taking a flying lesson off the edge of a mountain.

"No problem," he replied.

"Wow, Emily, that would have been some fall," Taylor said as she looked over the edge. I didn't follow her gaze. I'd already seen it. Ellah shook her head, turned, and began to walk ahead again. She started her story again as she walked.

"Saharon has many powers and many creatures that work for him. He may be able to see you or sense you when you are together. It is important that you do not join hands unless we tell you to. The change in energy may draw attention from those looking for us."

We started moving again. As we ascended, we seemed to be walking into the clouds. The thickness of them intensified until I could barely see an inch in front of me. I could just see the ground at my feet and Ellah in front of me.

I knew Taylor and Hannah were behind me. John had stayed ahead of us, and I hadn't seen him in a little while. I heard Sean's footsteps behind us, falling slightly heavier than ours. We followed that way for what seemed like miles and hours. I could have sworn we were almost at the top before I tripped. But I guessed now that the sky and clouds had made it seem so. There were almost no trees up here. The ones we passed looked long dead, their branches gnarled and whitish-gray.

After what seemed like a long time, I noticed I was breathing hard still, but the terrain was less steep. Then, soon after, the terrain leveled off, and we broke out of the clouds. The view was like something from an airplane. I felt like I was at the top of the world. It was hard to see the valley below with so many clouds, but I could just see part of where we had come up the slope. Then I followed Ellah's gaze.

"That's gonna hurt tomorrow," Taylor said as she saw how high we had climbed. We all admired the view.

The other side of the mountain was beautiful and mostly clear. I saw the rolling hillside, which I was thankful was downhill as I didn't think I could stand any more travel going up. Then I noticed there was a glittering at the edge. As I looked, I saw the dark blue line at the edge of my view. I realized I was looking at an ocean.

The glitter must have been the sun on the water, I thought. Then I looked closer.

"That is the city of Edelsvein," Sean said, coming up beside me, his shoulder brushing against mine. Ellah came over too, still looking in the direction of the city.

"We should be there soon. I had planned that we should make it there tonight." She paused and looked at Sean and me, then turned and walked back to Hannah and Taylor.

"It's getting late. We may need to camp here for the night," John announced as he came up to the group. He put down his pack and sat down on a gray rock close by.

Ellah followed his lead. I realized that she must be as tired as we were. She pulled her pack to her and opened it. After a moment, she took out a small bundle that, with some unfolding, turned into a blanket. She draped it around her shoulders. Even though we had on cloaks, it was still cold.

"No fires tonight. I'm sorry. It's just not safe yet," John told us. Ellah nodded.

She turned to us and said, "There should be one of these in each of your packs. They will keep you warm. They are from the wool of a sheer from the land of Animalden." She paused. "Don't be dismayed by their appearance. It will be useful. Make sure to always keep them with you in your bags."

I opened my pack, and so did Hannah and Taylor. I pulled out a gray blanket that was so light, I hadn't even known I was carrying it with me. Ellah was right. This could come in handy if it kept us warm. I wrapped it around my shoulders, and the wind that had bitten through my robe and clothes, making me cold, was gone. I felt like a caterpillar wrapped in a cocoon. The lure of sleep began to creep into my eyes.

Sitting down against more rocks, Hannah, Taylor, and I must have looked pitiful. But I felt so warm that I was almost happy. I looked over to Ellah. She was staring at us, smiling. Ellah, Sean, and John decided to take turns for watch through the night. Ellah was up first, and John had already laid down and appeared to be sleeping, waiting for his turn.

"What is that right there?" Hannah pointed to the largest outline on the edge of the horizon we were facing.

"That is the castle within the city," Ellah said.

"No, that, to the right of it. It looks like it's on the outskirts of the city." She pointed again and moved her arm to show the direction.

"That is one of the oldest protections of our city. Remember I told you of the last battle? After the battle, when other creatures were not to be trusted, sickness was again creeping on us, and the treaty was broken. The great wall was erected to help isolate the city. Of course, your ancestors rallied against it, but the king had no choice but to do as his people demanded.

"At the entrance and exit points to the city are those I spoke of earlier, the Hoyt. They can look into the soul of the person entering the city and are supposed to ensure that those entering the city have no evil intentions. It was a compromise that your ancestors and the king had with the people. This way, the city could stay open to travelers and continue to hear about surrounding areas." Ellah looked down at her feet. "I need to take my watch. You need to rest." Ellah stood up and walked a few feet farther away.

"Well, this is nice. I guess we should get some sleep," I said to Taylor and Hannah.

"Yeah," Taylor said in a half-yawn, half-laugh.

"Mhm," Hannah mumbled as she nodded off.

Then, before I even knew I was asleep, I was starting to wake up. I heard Taylor and Hannah breathing in the cool night air, rhythmic and calm. When I opened my eyes, I saw John's outline on the ground across from us. My body was tired, but my mind was wakeful and ready. I wished I had a cup of coffee. *Something familiar would be great right now.* I wondered if they even had coffee here. Was the food the same? The feeling that I was in over my head crept into my soul and intensified.

I tried to relax.

"Hey, I see you're up," whispered someone. Turning my head toward the voice, I saw Sean. He did a shallow wave of his hand and nodded his head to signal me to follow him.

I managed to get to my feet without waking anyone. I moved in the direction Sean had tilted his head. He was waiting for me just at the edge of our little circle of sleep. It was colder, and I wrapped my cloak around myself.

The sky was a deep ocean blue. It held few stars, but the ones it did were bright. I still saw a slight shadow of the sun in the moon's nighttime luminescence. I had no idea if it was night or early morning. Sean walked with me over to where Ellah had kept her watch. We sat in silence for a few minutes. I wasn't willing to begin a conversation with him. I was still mad that he'd lied to me the entire semester.

"You know, I am sorry I couldn't tell you about anything back at school," he whispered.

I didn't answer. I wasn't sure what to think. I was confused because I had thought he might have feelings for me, and now I felt like he had only been spending time with me to keep tabs on me. Our friendship, or whatever it was, wasn't genuine. I also realized that I must have feelings for him. *Great,* I thought to myself.

"I know. I get it," I told him. He smiled slightly and handed me a cup with steam rising out of it. The cup felt fragile. It looked like a leather pouch and felt pliable. Taking a drink of it, I tasted hints of honey and tea, but the liquid was black in the light we had.

"You should try to get some more sleep," Sean said after another couple of minutes. "The captain plans to get us going in a few hours, and I don't think we're going to be stopping for another night on the road."

Draining the small pouch cup, I stood and handed it back to him.

"Thanks. That was good," I said and started walking back to my sleeping spot.

"You're welcome," he replied. I felt his eyes watching me go back to the camp. I didn't turn around or say anything else. I didn't know what to think about him anymore. I was grateful for the tiredness and my heavy eyes when I laid back down.

Morning came quickly.

"We have to move now," Ellah said as I woke to Hannah shaking my shoulders. "The day is begun, and we cannot waste time getting you to Edelsvein."

She had already packed her blanket in her bag and was ready to go. Sean was waiting for us with Ellah. I didn't see John but assumed he was up ahead, making sure it was safe. Packing my things quickly and joining our group, we followed Ellah down the path.

At least, I thought, *this time, we are traveling downhill instead of up.*

It seemed to go a little faster. However, my legs screamed in protest. We made it to the bottom in much less time than it took getting to the top. No one talked much on the way down. I noticed the sky's changes as we walked. The moon was dimmer than during the night, and the sun was back to its previous glory.

Once we got to the bottom, we went through another low valley. It was filled with large, moss-covered trees that had small white leaves on the branches. There were large blue and orange flowers dotting the landscape as well. They grew in clusters between the sunlit areas in the shade of the trees. I found that a little odd.

As we moved on, however, and rose from the strange valley, the trees grew less moss and I saw the bark protecting each tree from the elements. They had grayish trunks with lined patterns from something I was sure was some kind of animal or bug. I heard what I thought were birds, although I hadn't seen many animals over the last day or so. I was about to ask Ellah about that when suddenly, our group came to a stop.

"Wait here," Ellah said, pointing to a spot next to what looked like a willow tree beside the small rise in the earth. We did as she asked and waited. The three of us looked at each other and at our surroundings, and Sean stood to the side, keeping an eye out over the landscape. We were too tired to talk.

Ellah and John went around the small rise to the right of the tree. I watched the huge tree after they'd passed from my vision. The willow looked old. In the slight breeze, I heard the leaves rustle. It sounded almost like the beginning of a rainstorm. The leaves were different shades of green, and when the wind blew, the changes that ensued when the leaves moved made the tree look like it was beneath a shimmering pool of water.

Before long, Ellah was back and motioning with her hand for us to follow her. She waited for us to catch up to where she was. In an instant, she pulled Hannah's arm to the ground. Like sheep, we followed her instantly. I felt my heart begin to race.

"What is it?" I looked around, feeling like a deer in headlights.

"We have to get into the city undetected and can't go in through the front gates. It is a precaution, just in case the gates are being watched. Even though the Hoyt can prevent some from getting into the city, if we are spotted, Evil will know where you are and possibly catch a glimpse of you. Remember what I said about your anonymity."

Ellah moved aside a brush branch, revealing a wooden door which, when pulled open, led to an underground staircase.

"This is a way into the city. You must follow us." She turned and disappeared underground.

CHAPTER TWENTY-ONE

Getting into the City

Descending into the hole that Ellah had opened on the side of the hill, we each climbed down a ladder one by one. When Sean closed the hatch of the opening, the dark was intense. I couldn't even see my hand in front of my face.

"*Sphera lux*," Ellah said. As she did so, a small orb of faint light appeared above her palm. "You three can say this too, and you will be able to see your way easier. When you are done with it, whisper, "*Se fin*," and it will go out." She demonstrated. "We have a small bit of travel to do yet."

She moved to our opposite side, grabbed two unlit torches from the wall, and whispered, "*Fuerte*." I could hear her breath as she blew on the end of the wood. An instant later, the torches began to look like embers, and small tendrils of flame licked the tips. She handed one to John and the other to Sean.

"But you said Saharon could detect our magic?" Hannah brought up.

"Here, you will be doing your own individual magic, and while you three have definite strength together, Saharon should not notice this small change in energy. When you join together and combine your powers, that becomes a different story."

We all looked at each other.

"Why not?" Taylor said, looking at us with humor. She was the first to try the spell. *"Sphera lux,"* her voice whispered. In her palm, the blue light came. "Wow, this is neat," she said excitedly. She looked at us with her eyes wide and a smile across her face as the blue orb gleamed in the darkness.

"Sphera lux," Hannah said, a little louder than I think she intended to. She jumped when her hand began to emit small, yellow light from the center.

"Okay." I cleared my throat. I suddenly felt like I had laryngitis. My mouth was full of paste and bone-dry. I had to detach my tongue from the roof of my mouth. *"Sphera lux,"* I whispered.

My hand began to feel warm. The light began at my fingertips and travelled under my skin like veins and into my palm. Then the light rose from my hand like a mist and formed into a small ball of dark, blood-red light.

I looked up and to each of our hands. The lights within our palms were beautiful. I smiled at my two friends. They smiled back.

"Wonderful. Now are you ready? We have to keep moving." Ellah turned and looked at John. "Can you let them know we've arrived?" John nodded and headed off into the darkness. She looked over at Sean. "Stay close. I haven't been in these tunnels in years. I don't trust my direction." Sean also nodded.

As we made our way through, the tunnel opened up. The deeper into the cavern we moved, the higher and wider the cave seemed. The ceilings were so high, the shadows covered the ceiling, and we could not see it.

With our lit palms, we could make out the ground, which was dirt and roots. Occasionally, we passed by a door or under what appeared to be a fixed doorway without a door. Ellah never hesitated though. On we went, farther in and farther back.

Sean moved with us, his eyes always scanning through, around, and behind us. He held the torch Ellah gave him easily as he walked. I slowed a little to walk alongside him.

"Have you ever been down here?" I asked him.

"Yes, a long time ago, in another life," he whispered back. He didn't follow that with any explanation, and I got the feeling he didn't want to talk about it. I let the issue go. I felt myself forgiving him, not being mad any longer.

"Maybe, if they serve coffee here, we could get together sometime," I said. Out of the corner of my eye, I saw his expression soften.

"I'd like that, but we do have to keep moving now," he said. We walked together for a few more minutes.

Up ahead, I began to make out something in the darkness. It seemed like light in the distance. I was grateful, as I was beginning to wonder how far underground we had come. The closer we came to the light, the more I realized that what I had been looking at was more of a reflection of the light that the six of us were carrying. There was a wide opening in the tunnel as we came up to an area of darkness. The light was about eye-level. We got closer.

John stood there waiting for us, holding his lit torch. But while I could see his light, I also noticed that the reflected light on the walls around us was almost gone. The cavern we were now in was so big that the walls and ceilings fell away from us. It was almost as if we were outside.

In front of us, on either side, making it appear as a gateway, were two great, big statues. They were so big that I had to crane my neck to look up at them. One on the right and its twin on the left. I wasn't sure what kind of creature they were. They looked human, but they were sitting catlike and had blank expressions on their faces.

Their heads had a human-like quality to them but with sharper features, and their ears were pointed. Their hair, which was molded into the statue on the top of their heads, moved from their brows down their backs, to a pointed place midway to the ground, like an upside-down triangle. Looking at their feet, the front two were hooves and the back two paws. I had never seen anything like them.

Looking back up, toward where the end of the hairline was, the statues had two places opposite each other where large wings were sprouted and poised as if ready for take-off. I kept my gaze moving upward, trying to take in everything about them, and when I got to their blank faces once again, I noticed their eyes. Both had their heads bowed down as if they were watching whoever passed beneath them, but their eyes were blank.

Their eyes were silver, shining orbs and looked seamless with the statue, as if the silver had been made within the molding rock of their creation. I saw the warped reflection from our palms and the torches there, reflecting off the surface. I felt pulled, in that moment, to go and see the statue closer.

"Wow, what is this?" Hannah asked. "It looks like an entrance of some kind."

"You are correct," Ellah answered. "This is the Porta Verum, or the Truth Gateway of Edelsvein. Long ago, each leader in this world gave a piece of themselves to the Elves of Edelsvein. This was so that the city could become a place of peace and all could claim a hand in their dealings. The leaders of the races came here to partake in their creation. The place was secret and only known among those who signed the treaty or needed it for passage during emergencies. Those who helped create it were sworn to secrecy. A spell was placed on all who signed the treaty. Should they tell anyone about the entrance, they would meet their end."

Ellah paused, looking up at the statues. She seemed a little uneasy. It was one of the first times I noticed that she might be a little nervous.

"As one walks through the gateway, the secrets of their souls are laid bare before the gatekeepers. There are no secrets from them. But that story is also for another time.

We simply must keep going. Perhaps when we get to the castle, you can learn about it in your studies," Ellah finished.

I looked through to the other side of the Porta Verum and noticed a small heap of what looked like an old satchel bag. It was completely still. Everything in our surroundings was.

"As you pass through the gateway, the statues will decide if they will let you enter the city. They may ask you questions or simply let you pass. Those few who have come through have told different accounts of their experiences." Ellah noticed the confusion on our faces. "I will go first, and you can watch."

With that, Ellah gave us a smile and turned and walked through the gateway. Watching her, I could swear that she almost hesitated before she took her first step. I felt my heartbeat quicken as she approached the center of the Porta Verum, but she simply walked right through. When she got to the other side, she turned back around and waved. It was one of the most anticlimactic things I've ever witnessed.

"Come on! We have to hurry," she shouted. The gateway was long and probably measured about a hundred yards to get through.

John went next. He stepped forward and walked right through. Hannah, Taylor, and I took another minute to decide. Something about those eyes looking down at us made me nervous.

After a few seconds of silence, I looked at Sean and heard myself say, "I'll go."

Hannah and Taylor looked at me and nodded. Sean smiled, and I wanted to take his hand, but I caught myself. I turned and walked forward, taking one step at a time. The path was soft and got deeper in sandy dirt as I went through. I had to keep one hand upturned so that my red-lighted palm could help me see in the darkness. I tried to concentrate on putting one foot in front of the other.

"*Why do you wish to pass?*" came booming out of the statues. I stopped and looked at them. Their frozen faces remained so. There had been no change. I had to laugh at myself and decided it was my nerves. But when I tried to move forward, "*Do not do that,*" boomed through my mind. Then nothing happened. Silence again.

After a few more seconds, they spoke again. "*Why do you wish to pass?*" came the request again.

"I wish to enter Edelsvein," I said. I couldn't think of anything else. The reflection in the eyes of the two gatekeepers seemed to take on their own glow, and I thought I noticed a turn in one of their heads, as if it was trying to get a better look at me.

"*Why?*" I heard again. This time, the voice seemed concentrated to one side. The voice sounded female, light and wisp-like.

I didn't know how to answer. I figured saying, "So-and-so told me to," wouldn't cut it for these guys.

"*Why do you wish to enter?*" I heard again, the sound seeming to come from the other side now. The voice seemed more urgent, as if it was hungry for something.

Looking toward the left side of the gateway, I saw the heap that had caught my glance earlier. The wind was blowing, and the heap seemed to move and flap. There was something eerie about it. Without thinking, I took a step forward. Instantly, I felt pain in my head. I saw a flash.

"Why do you wish to enter Edelsvein?" I was asked again. The words were so loud, I couldn't make out which side they were coming from this time.

"Evil has returned!" I shouted, looking left and then right. "Evil has returned, and we have come to help stop it," I said, more confidently than before. I didn't know what else to say.

Suddenly, I felt warm and like the skin on my chest was being rubbed with sandpaper. Then I felt wind picking up. I looked to the side and noticed the heap of cloth I'd seen before was flapping back and forth more furiously than before. There was no bag there. It was a jacket, and there was something half-under and half-over it. With a start, I realized that it was a body, a dead person. I couldn't get the images of the half-decomposed body out of my head. I felt my fight or flight instinct tell my body it was time to run.

Before I could shout, the sensation in my chest was gone. I felt the beginning of panic start to creep into my mind. What if they didn't let me pass? Would that be me lying there forever in the sand, in some magical gateway to an old city in another world?

"We know of evil, and return, it has," I heard. I wanted to sprint. *"You may pass,"* I heard, and suddenly, I was aware of Ellah watching me. I saw her nod slightly.

So, I took a step, and nothing happened. I took another step. And a second later, I ran to the other side of the Porta Verum. I was through. I turned to see Taylor and Hannah. Taylor had decided to go next. As she approached the center, I held my breath. But nothing happened, and she walked right through. The same happened with Hannah and Sean.

"How was it?" I asked as Taylor came up to us.

"Ellah, I think your gateway's broken," Taylor said. "I didn't feel a thing or hear anything."

"What?" I asked.

"Yeah, I just started walking and went right through, just like you did," Taylor went on. "I thought maybe they would talk or something, but I guess not."

Hannah walked up to us.

"Hey, some trip you took, Emily," she said.

"Yeah, you went and stopped and moved and stopped again," Taylor followed. "I don't know about you guys, but that was the easiest test I've ever taken." She had a relieved look on her face. She looked at me and her expression seemed to go from lighthearted to serious.

"What?" Hannah said.

"Nothing" I said. I couldn't understand why my trip was different than my two friends'. I felt like someone was watching me. I looked up to Ellah meeting my eyes for just a second.

"Did you see the guy lying on the ground?" Taylor asked us. I was grateful for the distraction. "He looked dead a few times over."

"There's no telling how long the man had been there," Ellah said. "Time is something that has always remained unclear in the gateway. If you died in the same spot a hundred years ago, your body would be preserved there forever."

Ellah looked at us and then she started walking. I looked back at the huge gate with the statues that had been there for thousands of years. I had a feeling that I would see the gate again, but I hoped I wouldn't.

We walked for what seemed like another couple of hours. Then our path narrowed and, after a short while, stopped. My eyes adjusted to the darkness, and I saw dirt and cave. I wondered how far underground we were. I wondered how many years of digging this tunnel had taken. Meeting our eyes at what appeared to be the end of our road was an old staircase. We climbed it. It was steep.

At the top, the stairs ended at a small landing. Ellah looked up and brushed aside some roots from the ceiling. Behind them was a wooden door.

"You must extinguish your lights here." She looked back at us waited a moment and then turned the handle and pulled. Down came the door, swinging down and open. There was no sign of John. He'd been at the Porta Verum but had gone ahead once Sean had come through.

Ellah pulled herself up and through the opening, then extended her hand and pulled each of us up with her.

We were in a small room. The floor was dirt and wood. There was a small table pushed to the side. Wooden walls had been built up around where we were, so I couldn't tell what kind of place we'd come into. I heard cheers coming from the other side of the walls. Along the walls was another door. I had to laugh to myself silently. I felt like Alice from *Alice in Wonderland*, trying to pick a door, but in our case, there was no sweet candy or drink to help us change shape and decide what direction to go. I realized then how hungry I was.

Ellah bent down into the hold we had just ascended from and pulled the door shut. She then kicked dirt from the floor over it and placed the table back over the passageway. She seemed to know what she was doing. She turned to look at us.

"We are in the city now. Make sure to stay close to me. Do not draw attention to yourselves, and keep your hoods up. It is growing into evening, and it will be cool out, so the cloaked hoods will not look out of place. We will be walking through a small shop and out into the street. Do not speak to anyone. Just follow me," she said, looking at us each in turn. "You know where we are going, Sean?"

He nodded as he put the now extinguished torch he'd been carrying in a corner. There was a second one there. I assumed it was John's from when he came through ahead of us. Ellah turned and walked to the door. She took the handle and pushed it open.

We entered a shop of sorts. It looked like an antiques shop. There were clocks, benches, and what looked like tools along the walls. There were framed maps and paintings and stringed instruments. I caught a glimpse of a man standing behind a glass case but couldn't see what was in it.

As we walked through the store, I saw other people looking around. They looked like us, although I wasn't sure what I'd expected people to look like in a new world. I tried to look up, but it was hard as we kept moving, and I was trying to keep my eyes down to not draw attention or make eye contact with anyone. My robe pulled suddenly.

"Oops. Sorry, Em," I heard Taylor behind me. She'd stepped on the back of my cloak.

"Please be careful," Ellah whispered back to us. She opened another door at the far end of the shop. We filed out. We walked down an uneven street that was lined with stones. I tried to look up every once in a while as we moved through the narrow streets. Out of the corner of my eye, I saw Taylor's cloak behind me. There were shops on both sides of us, and we were surrounded by groups of people going about their business. Oddly, I wondered what time it was.

We walked so quickly, it was hard to process the bits of things that I saw. We passed one store's glass front that had a sign which read "Port" and had a variety of things in the window. There were bags, jewelry, and books. Then we were past it. I saw lampposts and some fires in bins but never saw a car or stoplight. The technology we knew back home seemed non-existent here. I felt like we had been thrown back hundreds of years.

We passed what looked and smelled like a small horse stable. I heard the horses' hooves and whinnies as we quickly walked by. One of the horses was being brought out of the stable and neighed and reared up as we walked past. The stable boy in the pen put up his hands, and the horse quieted down. Still, we kept walking, turning here and there as if we were going through some kind of maze. *Or evading a big, scary monster*, I thought.

We suddenly stopped walking. I was so startled that I bumped into Hannah. She grabbed me and steadied me before I could fall. I was so clumsy.

"Sorry," I whispered.

I noticed we were at a pub or inn. There was a sign outside that was loosely swaying in the wind. I could just hear the creaking of it. On it was a carved a picture of a mug and a bed. Under the sign, I read the words, "Hide Away".

Ellah turned to us and instructed us to wait for her while she went inside.

"Emily, how do you feel?" she asked me before she went in.

"Fine," I answered.

"Make sure you pay attention to how you feel. If you feel sick, like when we were on the beach, hide." As she said this, she made quick eye contact with Sean. He nodded. "Make sure you don't talk to anyone. Keep to yourselves and stay here. Keep your heads down and your hoods up. I will be right back."

With that, Ellah turned and went through the heavy, black wooden door.

Sean leaned against a wall and seemed to pay no attention to us or anyone around us. He'd brought out a small book from his side belt and looked at it. He seemed to be looking through it. In his other hand was what looked like a small black pencil, which I wouldn't have noticed if he hadn't been trying to mark something in the book while I was looking at him. The three of us stood there, looking at each other, not knowing what to do or say.

"Well, I guess I missed my biology class," Hannah said, breaking the silence. We laughed, but her laughter felt a little short. I knew she was still trying to come to terms with everything. We all were.

"Man, this is like something out of the movies," Taylor said after some time.

"Definitely," Hannah replied.

"Did you see what they had in some of the stores? There were things I'd never seen before. One store had a bunch of glass balls in it. I couldn't make out what the sign said. It was a symbol or something. Part of it was in some other language, I think," Taylor went on.

"I saw a bookstore, I think," Hannah broke in.

"I hope we can come back here. I'd like to see what other stuff is around."

"Did you guys notice anyone with a cell phone, or electric lights, or anything like back home?" I asked. They shook their heads.

"No cars or streetlights either," Hannah pointed out.

"I guess we're not at home anymore," Hannah replied to me after a brief pause.

I was looking through the heavily crowded street when I heard what sounded like an argument to my right.

"And how do you think I am supposed to sell this? You idiot! When I'm through with you, there won't be anything left to clean the storehouse." We all turned to look in that direction. There was a man yelling at a young man just up the street from where we were standing. They were in front of what looked like a bakery, with carts outside holding lined sheets on rows from bottom to top.

The man held what looked like a large loaf of bread. As he continued to yell at the boy, he started to push him and then hit him hard. The boy went flying back and landed on his back. He stayed still for a second and then propped up on his elbows. The man walked over to him, bent over, and picked up the boy by his shirt. He lifted him off the ground so high that his legs dangled in the air.

Before I thought about what I was doing, I walked over and stepped in next to where the man was. I put my hand on the boy, and the man, seeming astonished, lowered him to the ground.

"Is this necessary?" I asked. In a moment, Sean, Hannah, and Taylor were beside me. "Sir, he's just a small boy. I'm sure he can make more of what you need to sell."

The man's eyes filled with more anger than I had seen before. His face was furious. Taylor stepped in, took the boy's hands, and led him to the side of the street. The man stared after her. As soon as she let go of his hand, the boy ran from Taylor and was gone.

"You have no place in my business, stranger. That boy lost me a half-day's profit, and he will have to pay it back to me." He looked around, trying to find the boy in the crowd that was beginning to gather. "But since you have such an interest in my business, why don't you take his payment upon yourself? As you have taken the boy, I will look to you for what he owes me."

The man took Taylor's hand, yanking her to the other side of us, and raised it into the air, showing those who had stopped to watch. Hannah and I stared, not sure what to say or do. I felt a strange anger rise in me, watching the man take my friend.

"So much for keeping our heads down," I heard Hannah whisper. The man then reached out his hand to grab me as well.

Sean moved in front of me. "Sir, I would advise against that," he warned.

"Is there a problem here?" I heard from behind. Then I saw Ellah walk past us, up next to the man. She walked with confidence, her hooded cloak still on, but back enough that the hood lay at her shoulders, bearing her face and head. She looked the man straight in the eye.

The man's eyes were wide then. He opened his mouth to speak, then shut it. Then he looked at the three of us and back and forth between Ellah and Sean. Then he took a breath and looked at the ground. It seemed he was trying to figure out what to say. He brought his face back up and looked at Ellah again.

"These three took my servant boy while I was trying to punish him for losing my profit from tomorrow's baking. The law dictates they, in turn, became responsible for his debt to me. They must pay," he insisted to Ellah forcefully through angry teeth.

Ellah turned to look back at us. The crowd had become a little thicker around where we were standing. Ellah took a deep breath. She pulled out a small bag from inside her pocket. From the bag, she took out several silver and gold coins. She then turned back to the man.

"I assume that this will cover their debt to you." She handed the man what looked like half-dollar coins. He looked surprised. His eyes widened, and the corner of his mouth turned up in a greedy smile.

"Well, yes, of course, but they should still be punished for interfering with my servant. He is my property and now lost to me." As he said this, he looked at us with a hungry gaze. He took a step toward Ellah. Sean moved an inch closer. His body tensed.

"That is a generous offer, sir. I'd hate to retract it," he advised, his hand brushing against his sidearm.

"You wouldn't dare flout the law," the man spit back. "What would the council say about that?" He looked smug.

Ellah simply shrugged, put her hand back into the small bag, and then put another coin in the man's hand.

"This is for your servant boy. Tell him to come to the castle when he returns, and I will put him to work for me there. He is no longer in your charge," Ellah said, turning to look at us, annoyance written all over her face. We started to walk away, leaving the man standing there with coins in his hand. I heard him rubbing them together as we walked away. The clinking of metal sounded like chalk against a board.

The crowd dispersed as we followed Ellah to where we had previously been waiting for her. She opened the door to Hide Away and went in, motioning with her head for us to follow.

I turned to look back as I walked through the door after Taylor and Hannah. The man was still standing where we had left him, just staring after us.

Questions ran through my mind. *What had the angry man in the street seen in Sean and Ellah that made him stare like that? Why did he negotiate? What would we have done if Sean hadn't been there?*

Sean bumped into me as he entered the room last. I made a startled noise, and Ellah turned and gave me a stern look. The door shut loudly, but I didn't think many of the people around us heard. It was loud enough in the large hall we entered to drowned out any noise.

The room was full of people and tables. The smell of beer was overpowering. The conversations were deafening. No one even seemed to notice as we walked through the room, over to the bar. We followed Ellah. Sean was still behind me, scanning the room.

She leaned over the bar and spoke to the person behind it. It was a small woman who seemed a little overwhelmed, as the bar was full. But she still greeted Ellah with a smile and shook Ellah's hand. Then she pointed to the back corner.

Ellah nodded her head, turned, and walked in the direction that the small woman had pointed. My gaze followed our path. There was a table, and I saw the back of someone sitting at it, alone. That was right where we seemed to be heading. Navigating the room took a little longer than I thought it would. There was even a bar fight that crossed violently in front of us. Those in the crowd cheered and laughed as tables were overturned. I heard glass smash in the background.

As we approached the man, he turned his head. He seemed to know we were there before we were. He stood. I thought he was about to leave. He turned and looked at us. When he stood, I couldn't help but be surprised by how short he was. His legs couldn't have been longer than my arms. His head came to about my shoulders, and he had long, sand-colored hair that could have passed for strawberry blond in the dim light of the bar. He wore a leather jacket and pants and had a belt over his pants that contained a small sword, sheathed from the side.

The man looked at Ellah and then at the three of us. Finally, his eyes rested on Sean. He nodded and started walking back the way we had just come. Instead of going out the door when we got near, we went around the bar and down a hallway that was hidden behind it. We passed doors and heard people all the way down the hall. At the end, the man stopped and looked up a flight a stairs. He looked left and opened the door that was next to him, checking the stairs a second time before walking in. Ellah followed him into the dark room and beckoned for us to follow.

I could just make out the silhouette of the man walking around the edge of the room, then I heard someone moving something heavy. Before I knew it, I heard a loud *whooshing* sound, and torches started at the center of the room, their flames lighting the dark brown wood, turning the color a dirty shade of gold.

As my eyes adjusted to the light, I saw a large table in the center of the room. On the table were three piles. Next to the table was John. We went over to them, and the man gave Ellah one of the torches.

"Here, put these on now." He pushed the piles at each of us. It looked like another set of clothing and cloaks. I was confused. We looked to Ellah for what to do.

"This is Gregor. He is here for us. He will help us get to the castle." She turned as the door slowly swung open. I held my breath. A small woman came through. It was the woman from the bar. She was carrying a tray with mugs and a small loaf of bread. She placed the tray on the table.

"And this is Gregor's wife, Marta," Ellah said with a smile. The small woman was even shorter than Gregor. She had dark hair, unlike her husband's lighter sandy locks. She wore a long housecoat and apron.

"Oh, Gregor, did you ever think you would live to see this day?" She turned to her husband. Some of the hardness left his eyes as he looked at his smiling wife.

"Aye, Marta, now we must be goin'. Get along to the bar, and make sure no one has followed us," he told her. The small woman smiled at us and her husband. I felt myself instantly liking her. She seemed soft and, I thought, probably straightforward.

She looked back one last time as she walked out the door. As the door shut and clicked closed, I heard her yell, "Now, you know that's not the way to the pot, Rhonnie. Get out of here!" Then I heard her footsteps as she walked back down the hall.

"What kind of cloth is this?" Taylor was looking at the robe.

We had changed into some of the clothes, and Hannah and I had put our robes on, but Taylor was holding it in front of her. Feeling my own robe, my fingers moved over the strange, silky texture. They were light, but pulling a little to test the fabric, I felt how strong the material was. The robes we had changed into had longer sleeves, down to our fingers, and went almost all the way to the ground.

"I mean, they are so light but so warm. What is it?" She looked from Ellah to Gregor.

"These cloaks were sewn from the hair of horses from Animalden, the island of the animals. Once a year, they trade with us at the docks. Their hair is the best for making cloaks. It will keep you protected from the hot sun but warm in the night."

Gregor went to the wall and pressed his hand down. The shelf to this right moved out slightly. He swung the shelf back to reveal a small hole in the wall. He brought back a small box and placed it on the table. John brought a chain out from under his clothes. On one end was a small key. He looked at us and then he looked at Ellah.

"You need to join hands for this." Ellah looked at me then my two friends. "Do it now," she said.

I hesitated but put out my hands anyway. My ability to trust was being tested. I felt Taylor, then Hannah's grasps as they found my hands as shakily as I'd found theirs. The light from the torches at the table seemed to dim, but the room still got brighter. Ellah placed the strange key in the keyhole of the box, and the lid clicked open. Three small bracelets were tucked into blue velvet inside. The bracelets looked old. The metal was braided, and in the middle of each was a round, glowing stone.

"You may release your hands now," Ellah said after the box was opened. "These bracelets were left for you from your ancestors. They wore them, and now, you may wear them. The braided metal represents the three of you and your connection to each other. The stone represents your individual and unique powers," Ellah said as she took out the bracelets.

She placed one on each of our wrists. When they had been in the box, the center stones were a clear, gray color, but as Ellah placed them on our arms, they turned color. One by one, we each saw our stones change. Taylor's was aquamarine, clear and shiny like the ocean water. Hannah's turned a brilliant emerald color, and my stone changed over and over again, finally settling on a white, glittery opal. My arm was warm. It was a strange sensation.

I hadn't noticed, but Marta, Gregor's wife, had come back into our room. I looked to the left and saw them holding hands, watching us.

"Okay, now we must be going." Ellah turned to Gregor. "My friend, will you help us get to the castle? We are expected, and it is no longer safe here." She grasped Gregor's hand.

"You are right. Of course, we will help. To the end of our world, we will help," Gregor said. He went over to John. They exchanged some words and then John nodded. I kept looking at my bracelet. The clasp where it had come on had fused, so the ring of metal was uninterrupted.

"What do you need?" Marta spoke up.

"An escort, for now," Ellah said. Marta nodded. Gregor came back and gave his wife a hug. He took her hand and kissed it.

"I will be back soon, my sweet," he said to her.

They turned to us. "Hail the Pillars of Enroden. May you protect us, guide us, and save us from what is to come," Marta said as she knelt on the floor. Gregor followed and, surprisingly, so did Ellah, John, and Sean, all in turn, repeating what Marta had said.

The three of us looked at each other. I didn't know what to say. It was one of the strangest experiences in my life. Having people I barely knew take a knee to honor me... I hadn't done anything to deserve that. The expression on both Taylor and Hannah's faces read how I felt: confused.

What are the Pillars of Enroden? I thought.

I was grateful the moment passed as quickly as it came upon us. We were all standing up a second later.

Gregor walked Marta out of the room and closed the door. He walked back to the center and moved the table aside, then moved the floor mat underneath the table. Like the floor entrance in the city, when we came up out of the tunnels, there was another opening. Gregor pressed on the opening, and I heard a loud click.

The floor under the table gave way and moved aside to reveal a ladder going down into the ground. He looked up at us and pulled a small bundle from his side belt. He unwrapped it and handed each of us a small knife that was sheathed in leather.

"Just in case," he told us. "You don't yet know how to use your powers, and while most who know of this entrance are with us, evil has a way of infiltrating even the tightest of security."

With that, we each took one of the knives and watched as he headed down the ladder. John went after Gregor. Then Taylor, myself, Sean, Hannah, and finally, Ellah.

"I will follow after you," Ellah said, looking at us. When we were all through and had our bearings and the torches were lit again, Ellah turned to us. "We must go," she said.

I wondered where this tunnel would wind up. Would there be another experience like with the Porta Verum? What was waiting for us down in this tunnel?

I had to turn off my thoughts as we moved through the underground. At least we were all in this together, whatever it was.

CHAPTER TWENTY-TWO

Castle Brion

"What?" Taylor whispered in the darkness as we walked. "I didn't hear you," she said and stopped.

"I didn't say anything," I said to her as I looked back.

"Oh, I thought I heard something," she said as we started moving again.

The dark tunnel was similar to the hold we had been in earlier in the day. The same dirty ground and roots were along the side of the tunnel. The difference was that there were more turns, and the space was smaller. Less room for movement. If we met anyone coming in the opposite direction, I doubted there would even be enough space for both parties to pass each other at the same time. I had no sense of direction; we had made so many turns and took so many forks in the road that I almost felt dizzy. I had to bite back my claustrophobic feelings.

Sean was walking behind me. Occasionally, I felt his shoulder brush against my back. It steadied my nerves, and I was grateful for it.

"What?" Taylor said again. She sounded annoyed this time. We stopped. Ellah looked at her pointedly.

"No one said anything, dear." Then Ellah paused. "Roll up your sleeve." She motioned for Taylor to do just that.

As she rolled up her sleeve, I saw the glowing light from her bracelet. The blue was sparkling.

"Your ancestor, Christina, heard the thoughts of others, so it is no surprise that you have the ability as well." She paused. We all looked at one another. "Now is not the time to discuss this. We have to get to a safe place. I will explain more when we get there. Just know that as you spend more time here in Enroden, especially in the city of Edelsvein your powers will begin to strengthen and you will recognize them in a way you never have before."

She turned and left us to wonder about what she had said.

"Okay," Taylor said, sounding confused. She rolled her sleeve back down her arm.

We started down the tunnel again.

It was strange. In that moment of confusion, from being in a world where everything was new and scary and beautiful all at the same time, at the forefront of my mind, Nick popped into my thoughts. I wondered what he was doing. He had wanted to plan a get-together after school was out and before I flew back home to California. I hoped he didn't think I was standing him up. He was so nice. I found myself wondering what he would think about this place.

My mind was wandering. I took a breath and refocused my attention on following Gregor and John.

Despite my efforts, my mind wandered to my dad and Cindy. I thought about my mom and how much I missed her. What would she think about all of this? Would she certify me as crazy? Probably not. We had our dream journals and told each other about our crazy dreams. She never called me crazy then, so I'm sure she wouldn't now.

In an instant, I was looking at my parents' bedroom. The light beige carpet, the dark brown hutch with the television in the center, and photo albums along the shelving at the sides. I was sitting next to the bed. Their closet had sliding doors, and I had one shoulder to that and one to the bedside. The comforter over the bed was dark evergreen with an occasional small purple flower. I was sitting with my mom. I could tell that it was near the end of her time with us.

She was not talking but pointing to something, trying to get my attention. She pointed at the ground, her finger bony and protruding through her thin skin from all the weight she'd lost. It seemed like she wanted me to pick something up. She was moving her mouth, but no sound came out except for short whispers, as if she'd used up her strength and it was all she had left.

"Get it," finally I made out. "Okay, Mom." I nodded and turned my head in the direction of where her finger pointed for the millionth time, trying to come to terms with the fact that the medications she was on made her say and do things that made no sense. One of our hospice nurses had even told me when Mom had done this another time, "It's not your momma anymore, hun. Just pay no mind," and she'd given her a bath and left. I hadn't seen that woman again. I was glad.

My vision cleared. My emotions at that moment were another story. It was like all the feelings I'd bottled up inside myself were at the gates of my throat. I made a small noise and put my hand out to the wall. We stopped. My arm radiated a bit. I looked at my bracelet. It was black and no longer opal-colored. I took some deep breaths. Ellah came up to me. Hannah and Taylor turned to look. Sean put his hand on my back. He must have thought I was about to fall. I tried to take deep breaths.

"A vision?" Ellah said shortly.

"Memory. I'm fine," was all I could say. I didn't want to cry in front of these people now. We were all stressed.

I noticed it was getting hot in the tunnel now that we'd stopped.

"Fine?" Ellah questioned, looking at my eyes. I looked back and then avoided her gaze. It was too much for me at the moment. "We need to keep going," she added to our group as a whole.

The best thing I could do when things like that happened was to forget them. My Nino had told me that in times like this, my brain was just holding out hope that her death would change, and I needed to not dwell on my memories of her. Even with my deep breaths, however, my anxiety started to creep up.

After what seemed like a long time following Gregor, we came to the end of one of the tunnels. It just simply ended. No big door, no guards, no shiny torches. The only thing marking the end of the tunnel was what looked like a large tarp. Gregor pulled on it, and dust flew everywhere. We all coughed. There was barely enough room for the seven of us.

When the dust settled, I could just make out the form of an old ladder braced against the wall. It went up, but I couldn't see where it ended because of the darkness. Not only did it go up, but the hole it went into was small. We would have to climb one at a time and put our side bags in front of us, against the ladder, if we hoped to fit up through it.

Gregor looked at the rest of us and then at Ellah. He started climbing. His small size was perfect for the task. We all followed. We went up for what felt like ten minutes. I was glad that the tunnel was close because if I could see how far up we were, I might be too scared to keep going.

I heard a sudden snap and then felt a tug. Hannah had broken a rung on the ladder and grabbed Taylor just in time. I grabbed Hannah to steady her. We held on for a second until she got her footing again and then we kept climbing. Thankfully, we didn't make the light this time. I guessed that one of us was holding onto cloth or something instead of skin-to-skin contact. I wasn't even sure if that was how it worked.

When I didn't think I could climb any farther, the ladder ended, and I crawled off the wooden rungs onto a dirt floor. The others behind me followed. We all coughed some; the dust was heavy in the air.

"We're almost there. We have a short distance and then the door will be upon us," Gregor said to Ellah. She nodded. I couldn't figure out what they were talking about. I was just so glad to be off the ladder that I didn't care much. Then, before I caught my breath, we were moving again.

We went out of the room and into more tunnels. My eyes were gritty from all the dust. I decided that a person could probably die in here if they didn't know where they were going. There was no way they would make it out alive. The number of tunnels and forks in the road would have an unsuspecting person traveling for days before they would even know they had gone in a circle.

"There must be enough tunneling down here to move the city underground," I wondered to Sean.

"There is. This area used to be shared with the dwarves. They lived right under Edelsvein," Sean said.

Sooner than I thought, we were at another end of a tunnel. There were two doors here, one to the left and one to the right. Both appeared identical, except for the doorknobs.

Gregor pressed his hand into the one of the knobs, and it began to glow. The door opened. He went in first, and each of us followed. Ellah came last, waiting for everyone else this time. Then, right after she came through the door, the door dissolved, and a wall replaced it. The doorway was entirely gone.

"What the heck?" I whispered to myself.

We were all trying to catch our breath. Ellah looked at us.

"That doorway has been in place for thousands of years. When your ancestors foretold of your coming, they made sure to have a secure place for you to return. The door was to let you in, in case of Evil already having infiltrated the city. This way, you could get here undetected. We are certain Saharon knows of your presence in Enroden, and without knowing who you are, he has no way of knowing how to find you," Ellah told us. "This door was a vanishing door. It was created to serve only you. As its purpose is now fulfilled, it has vanished, never to be used again."

Once I stopped staring at the wall, I noticed other things in the room.

"Hey, look!" Taylor said behind me.

I turned to see a huge tapestry. The picture on it was similar to the one from the scroll in Mrs. Trebule's office. The three ancestors stood together, their hands clasped, looking serious and prestigious. Hannah walked closer to it. Then she turned and looked to the left. There were books lining the wall, shelved all the way to the ceiling. She walked over to the shelves and started looking at some of the volumes.

To the left side of the tapestry was a large staircase. It was beautiful, white marble with black and gold trim on the banister. There was a carpet going up the stairs and leading down a hallway at the top. I looked up to the ceiling. It was so high up. At the top, there were paintings of clouds and what looked like fairies. I smiled, then my smile froze on my face as I noticed that one of the fairies was moving. As I watched, I saw its wings close in to its body, and it turned, starting into a dive bomb heading straight for us.

"Watch out!" I yelled. Everyone looked up. Taylor and Hannah ran to where I was, and we all dropped to the floor together. Well, the three of us did, anyway. Ellah, John, Sean, and Gregor stayed standing, amused expressions on their faces.

I heard the wings flap and felt the wind pressure as whatever it was that had flown at us halted right above where the three of us were crouching.

"Hello, *ladiesss*," the thing hissed, lingering on the S. I looked up. "I trust your journey went well."

Its voice was light but sounded soft and deeper than I would have expected. I noticed that it held its hand out when it spoke. Well, it actually looked like a female up close. Her clothing was a sheer pink and beige and almost translucent over her white skin. She had a blue tint to her hands and face. Her hair was gold with what looked like crystals in her braids. We stared for probably longer than was acceptable.

" I am Queen Amori of the Strata. I am here to take you to the king," she said airily. I noticed that she never moved her lips when she talked. She held out her hand. "Do not be afraid. I will not harm you. My kind has been protecting this entrance to Castle Brion for centuries. It was our obligation of thanks to your ancestors. Now that you have come, that obligation is at its end."

"Queen Amori, we must see King Sigrun. We have no time to waste. Saharon knows they are in Enroden. It is only a matter of time before he realizes where they are," Ellah told the fairy-like woman.

"I understand," Queen Amori replied, looking back at Ellah. "Your guides have done... well," the fairy woman stated, looking us all up and down.

She turned and began walking to the stairway, then began climbing the stairs. Her wings had a living quality. They swayed with her as she walked and reminded me of a dragonfly's.

We followed her. The castle was beautiful. We passed marble statues, wall paintings, and armored knight statues. We went by rooms and other staircases. There were great, lit candles that looked like torches but were so elegant. I had never seen anywhere so majestic.

Queen Amori stopped right outside a large set of double doors.

"The king is out at the moment. He is seeing to business in the fields of our lands. He will return on the morrow, and you may stay here for this night." With that, the winged woman turned and flew back down the great hallway, toward where we had first met her.

"I must leave as well," Gregor spoke up. "I will meet you tomorrow, when you see King Sigrun. Until then, stay safe." He smiled and bowed his head, then walked back in the same direction that Queen Amori had traveled.

Ellah took a deep breath.

"Ah, fairy queens. Why she couldn't have told us the king was out before we'd walked all the way down here, who knows?" Ellah said sarcastically. She turned to John and Sean. "Thank you both. You can rest now, even if it's only for a short while."

Both John and Sean looked at us and smiled. "It has been a privilege," John warmly announced. He turned and left.

Sean gave me a small smile before he turned and walked away. He silently mouthed "coffee" to me. I knew we were okay.

The four of us walked along the hallway. I admired the portraits on the walls. A few minutes later, we came to a beautiful set of oak doors. They were enormous. Their shiny brown wood reflected the light from the torch-lined walls, and the handles were a golden brass that had been shaped into large leaves. The doors were carved with roots and foliage. With the reflecting light shining on its surface, I could almost mistake the doors for being alive.

Ellah pushed open one of the doors with a round handle. She made it look effortless. As the door swung back, we caught our first glimpse of what was inside.

The first thing to meet us as we walked in was a large, marble statue of someone who looked a lot like Ellah. The person, frozen in time, had on a cloak, but I could still make out her slight form. Her hood was down, revealing long hair that was pinned back, showing her pointed ears.

At the top of her head was a crown of leaves. It was in contrasting color to the white statue, silver and glittering all over. The woman had a long, slender arm extended, as if she were reaching for something. Over her shoulder was a quiver of arrows and a bow that was slung back.

Ellah went in, and we followed. She stopped at the statue and stared.

"This woman is my ancestor, Praelia. She was one of the first elves to help create Castle Brion. She was one of our fiercest leaders, who helped create the first alliance."

We all stared at the figure. The woman was beautiful, even etched in stone. I noticed something else different about the statue. Around its neck was a talisman. It was glowing slightly and looked as if it was lightly vibrating.

Ellah then reached out and put up her arm.

"*Cito*," she whispered, as if she were talking to the statue. The talisman then lifted and unclasped from around the statue's neck and floated to Ellah's outstretched hand. She then placed the necklace on and turned to look at us.

"When I left for your world, I left my talisman here. This is part of who I am. It was passed from my family down to me, and I am the only one left to wear it. I was unsure of whether I would return to my world and had no one to leave it to, so I left it here.

"In your world, its energy would have attracted Saharon's searchers, and our identities would have been uncovered. This connects me to my world. To the earth, the sky, and life itself. To those who have gone before me." She bowed her head, as if saying a silent prayer.

When she dropped the necklace to hang around her neck, I noticed that the center of it was a diamond-like stone that was wrapped in silver and molded to look similar to the leaves around the crown on the statue. It was beautiful. The glow coming from it vibrated, as if in a rhythm. I couldn't help but stare at it.

As if she could read my mind, Ellah spoke again. "The glow you see is the rhythm of my heart. The connection between our people and our talismans are so great that, should the talisman be destroyed, our powers and longevity will be destroyed with them. Once the talisman is given by a family member, when they pass on, it is endowed to the next in line, or a family member can choose to give it to someone."

Hannah spoke up. "That means that you were given this one from someone who is no longer here?" We looked at her. I didn't know what to say.

"Yes, but for me, it is a bit more complicated." She paused. Suddenly, I smelled something delicious. "Ah, but we will leave that for another time. Now it is time for food," Ellah said, seeming relieved that the subject was changing.

We walked farther back into the room. There were canopy beds around a large, wooden table. On the table was one of the most beautiful displays of food I'd ever seen. Somehow, Ellah had already seated herself and was putting some of it on her plate. I hadn't realized how hungry I was until I saw the food. Then I was famished.

As I got closer, I noticed how colorful all the food was. I had no idea what some of the foods in the display were. Some of them, I wasn't even sure how to eat.

"What are you waiting for?" Ellah exclaimed. "Eat!" she almost shouted. She smiled, and it was genuine.

She had a silver plate in front of her, and it was full of every color I had seen. It looked like fruits and pastries and breads. There were what seemed to be grapes and apples and melon slices, as well as a rice mixture with what I thought were vegetables.

I tried one of the grape-like things. It was fantastic. It was just like a grape but tasted so much stronger. I took a plate from the pile of dishes and handed it back to Taylor, and she handed it to Hannah. We did that until we each had a plate.

Taylor put some of the rice like mixture on her plate. She tasted it, and I could tell from her facial expression that it was good. She smiled.

"This stuff is great. What is it?" she asked.

"That is oryza. It's like what you would call rice with milk, honey, and fruit," Ellah said as she grabbed a roll. I noticed that the things I had thought were vegetables were actually chopped pieces of fruits.

"That is a sugar cookie," Ellah laughed. She was obviously getting a kick out of our curiosity. We laughed. The tension from our travels lessened some with the good food and the thought of upcoming rest.

"Many of the foods here are similar. However, we do have some specialties, and you will notice how much better the food tastes here, as we have different agricultural practices than in your world. Also, you will not find any meat in our castle. We avoid killing creatures for food and find that we are sustained well on a plant-based diet," Ellah said matter-of-factly. She went back to her dish of food.

We ate for a little while longer. I couldn't remember the last time I'd had a good meal. I thought about Thanksgiving, and Nick popped into my mind again. I bet he would enjoy hearing about an entire new world and how they grew their crops. I thought about sitting on the porch over Thanksgiving with him. I would be lying if I'd told myself I didn't find him attractive. He had been so nice, and we had talked for such a long time, I felt like we were already friends. But he was Hannah's brother, so I'm sure part of our "friendship" was that he was just being nice to his sister's friend.

We finished eating, and Ellah took us into the next room. There was a large, marble fireplace. In the floor of the room were three depressions. In the front of the depressions were gold spouts and a lever. On the side of each was a basket filled with small, white blocks.

"We've traveled a long way. You must bathe and rest before tomorrow. I must leave you for the night. I will be back tomorrow, before you go to meet the king." She walked back toward the entrance of the room, and we followed her. She stopped before she went out of the room. "You can relax and rest here. You will be safe. There will be a lot to discuss tomorrow, and you will need your strength."

With that, she unlatched the door and let it close. I could hear her footsteps as she walked back down the hall, leaving us for the night. Her earlier gayety was gone, taken over by exhaustion.

"This room is amazing," Taylor said as she walked around. We were in the bedroom now. The canopies were dark purple. There were dozens of pillows on the beds, and the comforters were plush and lined with gold threads. Whoever had made them would have made a fortune back home.

I sat on the end of my bed. I wanted to sleep. I knew that Ellah had told us to rest, but I wanted to talk to my friends and share in this madness with them.

I looked over at Hannah. She had found a book on her table side. This room had books and desks next to the beds. In the center of the room was another desk with three chairs. There were mugs of tea and what looked like crackers on the tray, as well as a few more books. Hannah got up and walked to the table.

"*Narratio del Turris*" was printed on the front of the book she had picked up.

"What is that?" I asked Hannah. I walked to the table. The book seemed old.

"I don't know. I can't read it. It's not English. It looks like Latin."

"I speak some Spanish but never took Latin in school," I told her as she put the book onto the table again and opened it. The fragile binding creaked as she did so. "How old do you think this book is?" I asked her.

The pages seemed stiff. But at the back, a small section of paper was shoved into the book. Hannah took it out and looked at it.

There was a drawing of a small castle in the middle of the page. There was a spot of land underneath the building, then blank space and land below that. There was a small word at the bottom that someone had scribbled.

It read, "*Turris*".

"Hey, that's the same word from the front," Hannah remarked. She turned the book back over and looked at the front cover.

Taylor came into the room.

"Hey, guys, have you seen those baths in the bathroom?" She looked between Hannah and me. "They have this scented soap. It smells amazing." She looked between us again, shook her head, and then walked back to the other room.

"This whole place is so strange, but it feels good to be in one place after all that walking. And good to be above ground after those passages," I said.

"Don't forget that we get to sleep in beds tonight," Hannah said. "Let's make the best of tonight and try to get some rest, then we will see what they have to tell us tomorrow."

"I think Taylor is filling the tubs," I said when I started to smell flowers. Hannah smiled and turned to look in her direction.

We walked into the bathroom area. The walls had robes and towels, and the floor and walls were lined with what felt like marble under my feet. Taylor had filled the bathtubs, complete with bubbles, and set a robe beside each basket of soap.

"Look at the color of the water," Taylor said, smiling. She seemed to be having a great time. Looking at the water spouts, I noticed that it was a lavender color. It was pretty and smelled great. The thought of a relaxing bath and sleep was tempting.

"Guys, we don't know what tomorrow will bring, but right now, we have the chance to take a bath and get some rest, so I vote we take it." She was right.

I spent the rest of the evening doing my best to relax. The three of us talked and explored the sweet we'd been given for our room. Finally, after a couple of hours and a few cups of delicious hot tea that had mysteriously replaced the table of food that had somehow magically been cleared, I decided I should try to get some sleep. I had no idea what time it was. The bed was so comfortable, and it didn't take any time before I started nodding off.

Just as I was drifting off, I started to notice something as my eyes were heavy with sleep. A small shadow of light seems to be resting at the foot of my bed. I could just make out the rest of the room. The two other canopy beds were on the other walls of the room, and the center table was oddly already cleared off from the earlier tea. The sleep seemed to leave my eyes and I came awake. Staring at the end of my bed, I saw a small dust of light. Not a ball of light but something softer and less defined. I blinked at it, and it seemed to notice my attention. It rose to eye-level with me and then floated toward the door, lingering at its base.

I swung my legs over the side of my bed, trying to make as little noise as possible. The cold stone met my feet. I put my cloak on over my nightdress to help keep me warm. I crossed the room to where the light was resting. As if it were baiting me, it moved under the door to the outside hallway. The darkness in its wake was deep. A small orb still reflected in my vision, like someone had just taken a flash picture with my eyes open.

I turned to again look at my roommates, my eyes beginning to adjust to the darkness. They were still sleeping. I gripped the door handle and hesitated. What would Ellah say? I took a deep breath. One look out the door couldn't possibly hurt anything. I cracked the door open.

There was the small, soft light again. Waiting for me. It floated midway between the floor to the ceiling, just above my head. Again, it seemed to notice me, and as I walked through the doorway, it moved away down the hall and around a corner. Its light reflected on some of the paintings as it flew by. I followed it. My feet were grateful for the carpet over the cold tiles.

I lit my own orb once I was far enough away from our room door. "*Sphera lux*," I whispered in to my palm. The vein-like tendrils created a small light for me to see by. My bracelet became warm, and I found myself not needing my cloak.

As I approached the corner of the hallway, I slowed. There was a painting of one of the Hoyt at the end. I paused to look at it. The artist had been good. The image was a reflecting silver and captured the statue's eyes and bodily posture as if they were miniature versions of the real ones.

"Amazing, aren't they?"

I jumped. Sean had walked right up to me. I'd been so absorbed in the painting, I'd not even noticed him.

"What the hell?" I whispered, trying to calm myself down. I didn't like it when people snuck up on me, especially in a dark hallway in a huge castle. My hand still held the small ball of light, but looking around, I didn't see the light that I'd followed down here anywhere.

"I was hoping my notice would find you," Sean said. I must have looked confused because he went on. "We have the ability here in the castle to send messages. It's Elven magic, but they have allowed some to study and learn small things like work or..." He paused.

"Meeting someone for coffee," I finished for him.

"Yeah, stuff like that," he said. He turned and headed down the hallway from where we were standing. I followed him. At the end was a small table set with two mugs, a kettle at the center, and two chairs.

"Come on, let's talk," he said. Sean pulled out one of the chairs.

"What are you doing?" I asked him. "I don't think I'm even supposed to leave our room." I was suddenly nervous that Ellah would come upon our little table and begin yelling obscenities at us.

"It's going to be fine. You will be back before anyone wakes up. I just wanted to officially apologize and begin our new tradition of having coffee here." He paused. "With no secrets this time. I don't know when the next time we will get to have coffee together will be, so I wanted to do this tonight," he added when I didn't say anything back.

I lifted the cup to my mouth and took a sip. It was good. It tasted just like coffee but smoother. There was a creamy texture to it. It looked like he'd put cream in it already, and it was sweet, so I guessed some kind of sugar too.

"It's fantastic. What's in it?"

"This is kind of like coffee back where you are from. But instead of cream and sugar, I put in hazelnut milk and honey." He looked like he was proud of the surprised look on my face.

"Wow. It's good. Thank you," I said and meant it.

"So, I want to ask you about something, but don't get mad," Sean mentioned timidly.

I looked at him. What could he have to ask me? I didn't know anything about where we were or what was going on.

"What happened with the Hoyt?" he asked.

"Nothing," I replied after a second. "They just asked me why I wanted to pass."

"But when you went through, you seemed to stop and go. And at one point, you looked in pain." He looked at me with an intense stare. He was trying to get to something, but I wasn't sure what. I felt myself begin to get defensive. I gave him the question back.

"How was *your* trip through the lie detector?" I said, harsher than I'd intended to. I remembered when he went through, he'd stopped only once and then moved on, going the rest of the way undisturbed.

"Same as you," he said, not quite looking at my eyes. He took a drink of his coffee.

"Well, anyway, I'm glad it's over," I said, not willing to talk about it anymore. "I have something to ask you. What are the Pillars of Enroden?" I needed to know this. I'd been wondering about it since the group had bowed down to Taylor, Hannah, and myself the day before.

"Isn't that obvious? The pillars are you three. You three are the ones prophesied about, who are here to save our world," he said matter-of-factly.

"How are we supposed to do that? We don't know anything about this place."

How could anyone expect the three of us to know what to do in a battle or in a confrontation with some kind of magical monster, let alone if we were confronted with the lord of the underworld? I shook my head.

"I think your prophecy was wrong," I said and rose to my feet, looking at Sean. I still had the small light in my hand, which had been resting on my lap. Apparently, when I closed my palm, the light stayed there. "I'd better get back."

He stayed sitting down at the table. I turned and walked down the hallway and turned the corner. He didn't follow me. I got to our room and whispered, "*Se fin*" to distinguish my lit hand. Carefully, I opened and shut the door, walked across to my bed, and got in.

I knew I had been asleep when I woke to someone shouting at me.

"Hey, Emily! Get up. Get up! You have to see this," I heard as I tried to open my sleep-filled eyes.

From over my bed, I could see through the canopy to the table at the center of the room. There was food at the table. I saw a pyramid of fruits and a pyramid of pastries besides it. My stomach growled. I got up and headed to the table.

There were three places set, one for each of us. Hannah was already sitting at the table and looking at *Narratio del Turris* again. She turned to the back again and looked at the pages with drawings on them.

Taylor was looking next to her bed, on the small dresser that was placed there. We each, I noticed, had one next to our beds.

"Look at these. Did any of you see anyone come into our room last night? It looks like we've got all new clothes. And who put food in the middle of the room without us knowing?" she said. "This is strange."

Taylor walked to the table and sat down with both of us. I took what looked like a cheese Danish from the pile of pastries on the table and a glass of what looked like milk. The pastry was so sweet. The bread was crusted with glazed honey, and the center had a soft, sweet cheese that had been caramelized on top. There were crushed pecans and sugar dusted over the top. It was probably the best pastry I had ever eaten.

The white drink I chose did taste like milk, but it was much sweeter. I wondered what it was. But it was so good, I didn't care, and I drank it down.

"Do you think King Sigrun came back last night?" Taylor asked as she was eating. "I mean, if he doesn't come back, then what will they do?"

"I'm sure he's back. He couldn't stay away for too long. He is the king after all," I said and grabbed a piece of fruit.

"Do you think Ellah will be back soon? She said she would be here this morning. What time is it?" Hannah looked around. I hadn't realized that there was no clock in the room and had no idea what time it was or how long I'd been asleep. I didn't even know if they kept time the same way here.

We finished eating and then dressed. The clothes fit so well. I put on the traveling pants and top and draped the cloak around my shoulders, leaving the hood down. I had just finished dressing when there was a knock at the door. The two doors pushed open.

"Look who I found outside," Ellah said, smiling and walking through the doorway into our room. She seemed more rested than the night before.

"Ladies, how wonderful it is to see you here in Edelsvein," Mrs. Trebule said as she and Ellah walked into the room. "I hope you've found your accommodations satisfactory."

She smiled as she walked in. She passed the statue and put her hand on its base. She paused and dipped her head to the beautiful Elf warrior, then kept walking toward us. Ellah followed her. She looked different, less like the crazy teacher and more confident. I wasn't sure what it was.

Mrs. Trebule walked into our room and over to the center table. She grabbed a glass of colored liquid. She then walked over to Hannah's bed and sat down.

"I am glad to have arrived. My journey here was not without its challenges." She pulled off her cloak, and I saw bandages on her wrists, going up her arm.

"What happened to you?" Taylor exclaimed.

"I ran into some of the draugar while I was traveling. But I made it out, barely," she replied.

"What is a draugr?" Hannah asked. Whatever it was, it sounded like something that I didn't want to know.

"The draugar are a kind of evil warrior. They are made from the underworld, the land of the dead. Saharon uses them to search for what he needs to sustain himself. He is using them now to hunt for you three. Apparently, the tear in the veil is large enough that they can travel through just as we did. There's no telling how long this has been going on."

Mrs. Trebule stopped and looked at us, then took another drink out of her glass.

"I'm afraid he knows you are in Enroden. It was only a matter of time before he figured it out. I also think he knows that Ellah and I were the ones looking for you."

She looked at Ellah.

"He remembers us, Ellah. He sent this to my quarters before you arrived last night. We were lucky to get into Enroden when we did." She reached into a pocket of the side bag under her cloak and handed Ellah something small. Ellah stared at her hand. I got up and moved to see it. Hannah was standing next to her and was staring down at the small article. Looking over her shoulder, a small, royal blue feather was delicately resting in her palm.

"He does know, doesn't he?" Ellah said to no one in particular. Mrs. Trebule just looked at her and took a slow breath.

Hannah, Taylor, and I looked back and forth from Mrs. Trebule to Ellah.

"Today, we have much to do." Mrs. Trebule began in a lighter tone.

"First, we must go back into the city and get some supplies. Then we will be going to meet King Sigrun. I hope you are rested." She stood. She asked us to bring our side bags and leave everything else from our room there. We followed her out of our room and into the hallway.

"Make sure you three keep your heads down out here. We will not be taking any secret passages, like you did on your way in. This will be a trip to a shop and then back. There will be people all around us. Remember, anonymity is your friend now," she finished.

"There is a rumor that the Kern have access to the city," Ellah told her.

"Through the gates?" Mrs. Trebule asked.

"Yes. We are not sure how, but they've managed to get through, according to Gregor."

"Then time is that much more important. We must move and remain one step ahead of Saharon. We must be off."

CHAPTER TWENTY-THREE

Meeting the King

We followed Mrs. Trebule and Ellah into the hallway. The halls were still lined in marble and black stone, and there were tapestries over the walls depicting farms and animals. I wanted to stop and look at their intricate colors and shapes, but moving with the group made that impossible.

We made a left turn down another hallway. This hallway was lined with family portraits. Many of them were large families. I wondered who they all were. Again, I felt the pull to stop and examine them. As we went down the hallway, the families grew smaller, and the expressions on the faces of those in the portraits increased in seriousness. We even passed one or two paintings that only had one person in them. I wondered about the differences in the pictures, but then the rest of the paintings gained back their populations and looked more like the ones in the beginning.

We went down a smaller staircase then. It looked like it was a passageway to another part of the castle. I smelled cooking food and heard sounds from what I thought was a kitchen.

We got to the bottom of the stairs and then went down yet another hallway. I couldn't help but think about the panic I would experience if I ever got lost in the castle or had to escape. It seemed so complicated to get anywhere. It was the same feeling I had in the tunnels underground and throughout the city. It seemed like everything was laid out like a maze, intended to be a trap to make sure everyone stayed within the city.

In about another minute, we came to another door. Mrs. Trebule opened it, and we were met with the sounds and sights of the outside courtyard. We walked out into the bustling castle yard and a few paces before stopping. I looked up and saw where we had just come from.

It was the first time I had been seen the castle from the outside. It was magnificent. The stones were light gray, and the towers rose farther than my eyes could see. I saw balconies and windows and people lining the tops of the walls.

We huddled in a small group. Mrs. Trebule gave us some instructions.

"Ladies, follow me closely. I need not tell you that you must speak to no one and that you should keep to yourselves when we do stop. Make sure to make little eye contact with anyone. If we get separated, stay where you are, and we will find you. Do not go with anyone that claims to know you unless it is either one of us." Mrs. Trebule paused. "Do you understand?"

She looked at us. We nodded together. A second later, Mrs. Trebule started walking again. We followed her, with Ellah coming behind us.

I lost count of how many alleyways we turned down and how many shops we passed. I was impressed that the shoes I'd put on this morning fit me so well and were so comfortable. They were sheepskin inside and leather outside. Even the rocky, paved street didn't bother my feet.

Finally, after what seemed like an hour of maneuvering around the city, we stopped at a small shop. Mrs. Trebule went in first and held the door for us. We filed in after her, and Ellah closed the door behind herself. I looked up when I heard the latch of the door click closed.

It must be a supply shop, I thought to myself. Then, as my eyes adjusted to the lighting, I noticed that not only did they have supplies, but they had lots and lots of books. There was something about a bookstore that had always resonated with me, so I relaxed just a little and took in all the books around me.

Hannah walked ahead of us and looked around the shop. Once in a while, she pulled down a volume and read the spine. She flipped through it and then replaced it on the shelf.

Mrs. Trebule turned to us. "Look around. Find what interests you. Just remember to stay close and within the walls of this shop alone. I will call you to me shortly." With that, she waved her hand, dismissing us. She walked down a book aisle, and I lost sight of her after a second or two.

The store was dirty, and it looked old. The books were shelved, on desks, and even piled on the floor. It looked like the store owner needed to find a bigger shop. I walked over to where Taylor was looking at some books on a table. She was flipping through one of the books that had pages full of drawings of animals and writing. Looking closer at it, I thought the writing looked handwritten, almost like the book had been someone's journal.

"Have you ever seen a bookstore like this? I mean, this book is like these other ones here. They have hand-drawn pictures of animals and other things, as well as writing in them. There's some printed text, but most looks handwritten." She put the book down.

"No, I've never seen anything like any of this," I said to her. I walked slowly over to a low bookcase that was full to the brim with books. I could read most of the titles: *Herbology, Alchemy, The Sight, Enhancing Magical Powers,* and *Dragon Lore.*

I even thought my eyes were playing tricks on me when I came across a copy of the King James Bible. I picked it up and opened it. It looked just like our bible at home.

The expression on my face must have given away how strange I thought finding this book here was because behind me, I heard, "Dear, never underestimate the power of a good book."

I turned to see where the voice had come from. I was instantly startled. I was almost face-to-face with a tall, shaggy-haired old man. He looked a little like Albert Einstein but with better hair. The man had wrinkles in his skin, and his hair was white, but he seemed pleasant enough. He wore beige, loose-fitting pants, a red, buttoned shirt, and leather shoes.

"Or in this case," he said, "*the* good book." He laughed and then reached out and removed the book from my fingers. He had a slight half-smile on his face, and his eyes seemed to glitter, like he may be having fun.

"I'm sorry. I didn't mean to—" I stopped. I wasn't supposed to talk to anyone. Suddenly, Mrs. Trebule came over from behind a bookshelf to my left. This store was crowded with books.

"Ah, Mr. Diavan, I have been looking for you. You have quite a selection here," Mrs. Trebule said to the shop owner. The man turned his head and smiled as he met her eyes. "King Sigrun has me here on official business. He sends his regards and wishes you well."

The man looked at her. "Aye, and how is the king this morning? Word on the street is that he has been out re-enforcing the fences and the walls of the city." He looked at her with a little more intensity in his gaze this time. "One would think he was getting ready for another war," he said slowly, looking calculatedly at our group.

Mrs. Trebule walked in front of me and stood next to him. She put her arm out and touched him. "Antonio, friend. You know as well as I that we all are on borrowed time. Please tell me you've kept what we are looking for."

There was a pause in their conversation, then the tall man took a deep breath.

"Are you sure that you have the right ones?" the man questioned, looking us over. His eyes picked us apart with scrutiny. "Cunningness, it is," he said, still not moving from the spot where he was. Apparently, Mrs. Trebule had had enough, however, because she turned and motioned for us to come to her side.

"Ladies, please come here," Mrs. Trebule asked us. We walked over to where she was standing. She eyed the windows around the shop and called for Ellah.

"Ellah, would you be a dear and draw the window dresses, please?" I didn't see where Ellah was, but in a heartbeat, the shades came down over the windows. We were all alone, and the world outside was shut out.

"Please hold your hands together briefly and remember that you must let go of each other when I say," Mrs. Trebule instructed. If I wasn't mistaken, she sounded a bit annoyed. "On the count of three, please. One, two, three."

When she finished saying, "three", Taylor, Hannah, and I took hands and made a small circle. The light began to glow. I noticed some of the papers on the tables around us start to ruffle and move, as if they were in a breeze.

"That is enough," Mrs. Trebule voiced after only a second or two. We let go of each other quickly. She gave us a thankful smile and then turned to Mr. Diavan.

"Do you have what we need now, old friend?" she said with a half-smile in a forgiving tone.

"Well, I never thought I would see this day," the man began, looking at us with a bewildered look. "Yes, I have what you need." He turned to walk back to the counter at the far end of the store. Mrs. Trebule followed him.

"Ladies, please choose some books to take with you, and bring them to the counter in the next few minutes. We must get going back to the castle promptly," Mrs. Trebule called back to us.

I looked at Hannah and Taylor. Hannah already had two books in her hands. She put them up to show us. *History of Enroden*, one read, and the other had calligraphy scrawled on the front in bold capital letters. *"Protection and Reflection"* I read aloud as I scanned the cover. I wasn't sure what that meant.

Taylor walked back to the table she had been at before we met the shop owner. She picked up a book with animals on the cover. She brought it back to where we had been standing. I had no idea what to bring back. I looked at the table.

What should I pick? I thought to myself. I felt my wrist. The books on the table closest to me seemed to vibrate. I could hear them pulsing, like they were alive. A few moments went by, then one of the books opened. *The Long War* was the title of the book.

"It must be a book on the war that Ellah told us about. That might be good to learn about, if we have time. Surely, we can take the books with us, since Mrs. Trebule wanted us to pick them out." I looked at Taylor and Hannah. "I guess we should meet them up at the counter, then?"

The other two nodded. We walked through the store, back to where Mrs. Trebule was standing with Antonio.

When we walked up, Antonio was on the other side of the counter, rearranging the top display to make room.

In the center of the counter, laid before us, were three boxes. "Ladies, please come here." We stood around Mrs. Trebule and watched as she showed us what she was looking at. "These three boxes were left for you by your ancestors. They have been in the bookshop, passed down from keeper to keeper, for centuries. They have been waiting for you."

She took the first box and turned it, so the side was facing me. On the side of the box, I saw an indentation that looked like the shape of my bracelet. Mrs. Trebule moved each box so that the indentation was visible.

"As you see, each box requires you three to open them, and each one is tailored to you as individuals," she told us, handing each of us our box. "Put these in your bags, and do not take them out until I tell you," she turned to Mr. Antonio. "Thank you, friend."

"It is the least I could do. I'm glad I was the one who got to give them to you three. It has renewed my hope that our world is not lost entirely," he professed with sadness written in his expression.

We followed Mrs. Trebule to the front of the store.

"Please put the window drapes back up before you leave," I heard the old man say as we walked out. I heard the sound of cloth being draped back as we walked out the door.

We stopped a few minutes later to let Ellah catch up with us. We headed back to the castle. We seemed to take the same path as when we had left it, but I was still confused. The streets and the hallways were all a blur. I was grateful for our room when we got back.

"I will be back soon to take you to meet King Sigrun. Please gather your things and bring everything with you." She turned and left the room, Ellah following behind her.

"I wonder what the king will be like?" Taylor said.

"I don't know, but I hope he will be able to answer some of our questions, like what are we supposed to do here, and how do we save the world?" Hannah said, and we laughed some. She was sitting on the end of her bed, looking through one of the books she had brought back.

"This is interesting. This book says that there is some kind of ancient tower in this world, and if I'm reading this right, the tower is *in the air*. It doesn't say how to get to the tower, but apparently, some great, wise creature lives there. The legend says that the creature will help you on your journey if your intentions are good, and that the tower has been in existence as long as anyone can remember." She looked up from skimming the book.

"Do you think that's someplace that could help us figure out what to do?" Taylor asked.

"I mean, it sounds strange, but everything is strange now, so why not?" I had wondered the same thing. If this tower had been here for that long, then it would know what happened with our ancestors. Maybe whatever creature lived there would be able to tell us what to do next.

"Do you think there are more people like us? Do you think we're the only ones with these prophecies and powers that they are all talking about?" Taylor asked us.

"There must be others like us. Our three ancestors found each other, why can't we find others like ourselves? Maybe that is something we can ask Mrs. Trebule. If we can find others who know how to do these things, then maybe we can learn from them," Hannah said, putting down her book and moving to begin packing.

"We have a lot to figure out. Hopefully, we can learn something from the king later. I hope Ellah and Mrs. Trebule will finally have a moment to tell us things now that we are at the castle," I said.

"Yeah, because they've been so forthcoming with information this far," Taylor said, and we laughed again.

We finished packing and sat at the table for a little while. Once again, the mystery tea that had appeared the night before was there, and we drank it, thankful for the small break. We didn't talk, each of us seeming lost in our own thoughts. After what seemed like a long time, Taylor spoke up.

"Do you guys think we will get to go back home ever again?"

No one answered her. We all just looked between ourselves. It was something we'd all been thinking. Would we get to go home? Were we going to have to live here forever? What would happen to us if we were captured, or even worse? I couldn't think about that.

I wished I could tell my dad that I loved him one more time. I wished I could talk about how I was feeling and the craziness of the past few days to someone. Memories of the talks my mom and I used to have came to mind, about how we felt about music and art and the world around us. If I was ever worried about anything, she always put my mind at ease.

Then, strangely enough, I thought about Nick again. I couldn't help but feel bad that I wouldn't be emailing him back at all. Surely, he would think I didn't appreciate his kindness. Of course, that was if he even thought of me at all. Just then, as if I was being saved from my own thoughts, the two double doors opened, and in walked Mrs. Trebule and Ellah.

"Why are you three not ready?" Mrs. Trebule was looking at me. I had been slower to pack than my two friends. I felt embarrassed. I noticed how nice both Mrs. Trebule and Ellah looked. I wished I had taken another bath and cleaned up some, or at least done my hair.

I got up and got my things ready as quickly as I could, but in the middle of packing, I had to stop. I felt ridiculous. I felt my temper rising within my body, ready to break the surface.

"How do we know that any of what you are telling us it true? How do we know that we can do any of these things?" I asked, looking from Mrs. Trebule to Ellah. Neither Taylor nor Hannah broke into the spew of words coming from my mouth. "You called us the Pillars of Enroden because of some prophecy that was told by a person you've never met and no one has seen in thousands of years and expect us to fix a huge problem that we had no part in creating."

I couldn't stop myself. I went on shouting now.

"Is there any way we can ever get home? What about our families? We need some answers, now."

I stopped. I stared at Mrs. Trebule and Ellah, and so did Taylor and Hannah. We needed something to go on, something that made this whole experience make sense.

Neither of them said anything to us for a few seconds. Normally, I was uncomfortable in these kinds of silences. This time, I let it ride. We needed answers before we were just blindly thrust into a war.

That is what it would be, I realized. A war.

The silence went on for another minute, then Mrs. Trebule spoke up. "Can you please simply trust that you will know soon?" The empathy in her voice was evident. Something about it did ease my mind some. After a few more seconds, I looked between Taylor and Hannah, then back to Mrs. Trebule and nodded.

"For now, yes, but we need something to go on soon," I said.

There was another pause. I felt like I was going to lose it. I started getting my bags arranged on my bed and finished packing, then sat down again.

"Are you ready to leave?" Ellah asked. I hadn't noticed that she had moved over to where I was. She looked at us a little differently than before. When she looked at me, there was understanding in her eyes, like she knew what we were going through and that we had no choice in anything.

I looked at her face and noticed her change in clothes. She was now wearing a tight, black bodysuit that could hold whatever weapon she chose. There was weaving in patterns around the cloak that draped her shoulders. On her head was a ring of small leaves that came to a point on her forehead, which ended in what looked like a diamond that beat to a similar rhythm as the talisman around her neck.

When we were all ready to go, Ellah stood and walked with us out of our room. Queen Amori was waiting for us. I was relieved we weren't going to be dive bombed by her this time. Following her out, I noticed that Ellah was carrying a sheath of arrows and a bow. The bow was close to the weapon Queen Amori was wearing. She looked similar to the Elven statue in our room, so much so that if the color of her clothes and skin had been different, it would have been as if the statue had leapt off its marker and joined us in the walk to see the king.

Mrs. Trebule's clothing was not similar to Ellah's; however, there were some similarities in the patterns. She wore a similar headpiece but in a golden color, not a silver one like Ellah's. She also carried a sword at her belt, underneath her cloak but around her dress.

"Why would we need weapons in the castle?" Hannah asked. I looked back and forth between my friends and my two guides. Her question went unanswered.

We walked in the opposite direction we had earlier in the day. Mrs. Trebule was in the lead, then Ellah and Queen

Amori, then the three of us. The staircases we took rose in their grandeur as we moved on. The banisters were lined with more marble and gold and silver leaves pressed into the handrails. The floor was carpeted, with a deep, red velvet set into the path.

As I followed the trail of the red velvet, I noticed that at the end of this staircase, which must have been the grandest we had taken yet, were two huge, black doors. Outside the doors were two men, standing still, with long swords in front of each. Both men stood at attention. They looked ready to move in a second's notice.

As we neared them, I got the feeling that I was looking at two crouching lions, ready to pounce. I realized a second later that I knew the men. Both John and Sean were guarding the entrance to the king's throne room. They were standing strong and straight, swords out and before them.

Their attire was similar to that of what Ellah was wearing: the black, leather-like suits and the robe behind. However, neither guard wore the headdress.

As we approached them to enter the room, both men stood aside. They bowed, and the two double doors opened before us. I tried to catch Sean's eye, but he kept his composure. I guessed he was working, after all. So, I didn't think much of it.

Mrs. Trebule turned and looked at both Ellah and Queen Amori. They nodded, as if they were in silent conversation. Each walked to either side of Mrs. Trebule, and as she ascended into the great hall that lay before us, they walked beside, if not slightly behind her.

The path of the velvet, red carpet followed us into the hall. My eyes followed it back into the room, and at the end, there was a small set of stairs and a large chair. Someone was sitting in the chair. And as I got closer, I saw it was a man, and he was old.

On his head was a golden crown of leaves, each leaf imprinted with what looked like a ruby. His robe was dark purple, and his clothes underneath were a deep, forest-green. There were no weapons about his person that I could see.

When my gaze reached his eyes, however, every hair on my body stood on end. His gaze was wolf-like. He stared at us as if he could see directly into our souls, as if he were making decisions simply by looking at us, deciding strategy and eerily holding himself back. I found myself intimidated, to say the least.

Upon our approach, this man stood. Ellah and Queen Amori stopped walking, but strangely, Mrs. Trebule kept going. Both Ellah and the fairy queen then took one knee.

"A great day has arrived, and the legends have proven true. You three are among us now," said the king, looking at us. Mrs. Trebule stopped walking as she approached the king.

"My king, my husband, it has been too long," she greeted him in a voice I had not heard from her before. It was a mixture of relief and sadness that was moving simply to hear.

Then, an instant later, I realized what she had said. "My king, my husband." My heart started racing. Mrs. Jean Trebule, our Anthropology teacher, turned then and moved to stand beside the king as his queen.

"Ladies, this is King Sigrun," she announced, moving her hand in the introduction. The three of us bowed, as we had seen Ellah and Queen Amori do. The king walked down from his chair, more agilely than he looked capable of. He shook each of our hands in turn. His wolf-like gaze fell on each of us but somehow set my mind at ease.

"Truly, it is I who should bow to you," he declared and then did just that.

Then he turned and walked with Mrs. Trebule back to his chair, and I noticed another thing that I had missed prior to getting so close to the throne. There were two other chairs, one on either side of his. Mrs. Trebule turned when the king did, and they sat in unison in their respective places at the throne as if they had never done it any other way.

"I trust your accommodations here have been acceptable. After all, that room was left here for you centuries back and has been waiting to meet you as much as we all have."

He looked at us calculatingly as he sat in his chair. I didn't understand what he was talking about.

"Ah, I can see that you do not know much about your ancestors or our world, do you?" he commented with a slight smile. Then he stood. "This is a great day. The stars have shone in the sky this week. Prophecy will be fulfilled. Come, ladies, and share in my table."

He motioned with his hand to the side of the room. There was a long table, filled with food and drink, along the wall.

I turned my head to look at Mrs. Trebule. She nodded. The three of us followed the king to the table. We sat down. Servants came out and placed plates and glasses in front of us. They served us food from the table. The king motioned with his hand, and the servants left us.

"You three must understand that we must be sure you are who you say you are. We cannot afford mistakes. And although you have gotten this far, I must see you use your gifts to be sure you are the three descendants."

He paused and ate some of his food. No one spoke for a few minutes. I wasn't the least bit hungry.

"Many within our land have lost hope and feel that the prophecy we have been waiting for is simply a legend. But they fail to realize that many times, legends have a spark of truth to them." He paused to take a drink. "Although I could not blame them for losing faith, there have been no signs of your return for centuries. But many claimed to have seen the sky a few days back. That is why I was out when you initially came to meet me. I needed to investigate these claims.

"You see, the moment you arrived, the stars shone like no one had seen before, and they moved in the heavens, and the earth began to shake. I saw the sky myself and was in disbelief. There was no warning. I simply happened to look up and see. But as quickly as they appeared, they vanished. I was unsure of whether it had been real or the fantasy of an old king. So, please forgive my lack of faith," the king admitted to us in earnest.

I noticed then all the lines in his face. The king did not have a talisman as Ellah did. Nor did Mrs. Trebule, when I thought about it. At least not one that I could see. Then, as if he knew what I was thinking, the king looked directly at me.

"Ah, Emily, my dear. Alas, I will have an end to my life, as I have given my life force to another. I have been aging for quite some time now, slowly but surely. I am grateful that I can see my oldest friends once again," he said, his eyes quickly darting back to Mrs. Trebule and then up and over to Ellah and Queen Amori behind us. He had a small smile on his face.

"As you will understand, it is the duty of a king to put his kingdom first, and for me, that meant giving that life force to another. But do not be sad for me, for you three have validated my choice to do so, and I now have renewed hope for our world and others." The king took another drink and paused, looking at us again. "Now eat. We have more to discuss before your departure."

With that, there was little more conversation as we all ate.

After our meal, the king waved for servants to take away our plates, and we stayed at the table.

"You three have much to learn about our world and yourselves, and you have little time to do it. You must take the next several weeks to educate yourselves. There is a room here in the castle that was made for just this purpose so that, upon your return, you could enter it and remain safe for a short time. The room will protect you as long as our castle is standing."

The king stood and motioned for us to follow him. Mrs. Trebule still sat on her throne, and Ellah and Queen Amori were still where they had been when we went over to the table. They each came over to where we were then.

We stopped at a large tapestry along the wall. The scene in the tapestry was similar to the picture that Taylor had been trying to figure out for school, as well as to the scene that met our eyes when we first set foot in Enroden.

"Is that..." Taylor said.

"Yes, dear," replied King Sigrun. "This tapestry was placed here by your ancestors." He moved his hand, and the tapestry slid to the side. Behind it was a line along the stone wall. "This is the entrance to the room I spoke of. You will have a few weeks at most to study and then will have to begin your journey. I apologize for our time being so short, but now that you are beginning to use your powers, Saharon may be able to find you sooner. Then all hope would be lost." The king paused. "This is the opening point. You each need to place your hands next to mine."

The king put his palm up to the line along the wall. The brick was cool to the touch, and I felt a chill go up my arm. Taylor and Hannah did the same as I did.

The line along the wall turned from black to glowing red and then to white. One by one, the stones that made the section of the wall along the line fell away, folding inward. I couldn't see what was beyond the entrance. There were one or two steps that I could make out and then the light from the area blocked out what I could see. It enveloped the entranceway.

I looked into the light and knew with every fiber of my being that we had to go in, even though we had no idea where we were going. I looked at my companions. Hannah and Taylor looked as scared as I felt.

"Do not be afraid. This room was meant for you three, and it will stay protected as long as we are here. We will not leave you," Mrs. Trebule assured in a soft tone as she walked to the three of us. The king stepped aside to listen to her. "Do not be afraid of learning what you can about your gifts as it will help you on your journey. The people of this world will need you more than you can imagine, and knowing about them will help you as well." Mrs. Trebule looked at me as she said this.

"Will we ever see our world again?" I asked. I knew the answer before she said it.

She looked at us for a long moment. "There is a chance, yes, but I see no certainty in that. I feel you will be home eventually, but that is all I can say." She looked sad then.

"We have to do this," I said, looking at Taylor and Hannah. They nodded. We took each other's hands.

I was motivated by the thought that if this world perished, if we failed somehow, that our world would be next. Whether we got to see our world again didn't matter. If Saharon entered it, there would be no world left to go back to. We had to do this for our families and our friends. For everyone.

"Ladies, I must say goodbye. I will see you again. Remember, trust yourselves and your instincts."

Mrs. Trebule gave us each a hug.

"Trust yourself," she whispered in my ear when she came to me. And then she turned and walked back down the hallway, and she was gone. As I watched her go, I noticed that both Queen Amori and Ellah were gone as well. The three of us and the king were left in front of the bright doorway.

"Well, what do you think?" I asked, already knowing what we were going to do.

"I think it's time to go," Hannah stated.

"Do we count to three or something?" Taylor added with a hint of humor.

I put my hands on either side of me, and my two friends grasped them. Taylor, Hannah, and I took one step forward, closer to the blinding light of the doorway, our own bluish light mixing in with the brilliance of it.

"One," I shouted.

There was a loud rushing noise, and I felt like I was going to be blown over.

"Two."

I was breathing hard and felt like my grip strengthened on my two friends' hands. I was afraid; I couldn't deny that.

Suddenly, I heard myself yell, "Three!" and we stepped forward into the light onto the top ledge across the threshold, without knowing where we were going or for how long, only that it was the right choice.

Turning to look back at the king, my heart stopped. I almost let go of my friends' hands. Through the light, I saw movement toward the doorway. It looked like a man, running.

He came closer. I recognized him. It couldn't be. Not possible.

The man stopped at the doorway, taking a knee in front of the king. I saw him clear as day, with his black attire and robe and a small headpiece lined with leaves. The man stood next to the king.

As the doorway closed, sealing us in for however long our ancestors had deemed necessary, my last vision of the world we had left was of Nick, whom I now knew was the Prince of Enroden, the son of King Sigrun.